SHADOW RIDGE

ALSO AVAILABLE BY M. E. BROWNING

(writing as Micki Browning)

Beached

Adrift

SHADOW RIDGE

A JO WYATT MYSTERY

M. E. Browning

CROOKED
LANE

NEW YORK

Copyright © 2020 by Margaret Felice

Published in the United States by Crooked Lane Books, an imprint of The Quick Brown Fox & Company LLC.

Crooked Lane Books and its logo are trademarks of The Quick Brown Fox & Company LLC.

Library of Congress Catalog-in-Publication data available upon request.

ISBN (hardcover): 978-1-64385-535-6
ISBN (ebook): 978-1-64385-536-3

Cover design by Nicole Lecht

Printed in the United States.

www.crookedlanebooks.com

Crooked Lane Books
34 West 27th St., 10th Floor
New York, NY 10001

First Edition: October 2020

10 9 8 7 6 5 4 3 2 1

For David

Part One
TYE

1

Detective Jo Wyatt stood at the edge of the doorway of the converted garage and scanned the scene for threats. She'd have the chance to absorb the details later, but even at a glance, it was obvious the occupant of the chair in front of the flickering television wouldn't benefit from her first-aid training. The stains on the ceiling from the gun blast confirmed that.

Officer Cameron Finch stood on the other side of the sorry concrete slab that served as an entrance. "Ready?"

The only place hidden from view was the bathroom, and the chance of someone hiding there was infinitesimal, but someone always won the lottery. Today wasn't the day to test the odds. Not when she was dressed for court and without her vest.

She pushed the door open wider. Her eyes and handgun moved in tandem as she swept the room.

A mattress on the floor served as a bed. Stacks of clothes took the place of a real closet. A dorm-sized fridge with a hot plate on top of it made up the kitchen.

Jo avoided the well-worn paths in the carpet and silently approached the bathroom. Its door stood slightly ajar, creating enough space for her to peer through the crack. Never lowering her gun, she used her foot to widen the gap.

No intruder. Just a water-spotted shower stall and a stained toilet with the seat up. A stick propped open the narrow ventilation window above the shower. Too small for even the tiniest child, but an open invitation to heat-seeking raccoons.

"Bathroom's clear." She holstered her gun. The cut of her wool blazer ensured it fell forward and did its best to hide the bulge of her Glock, but an observant person could tell she was armed. One of the drawbacks of having a waist.

She picked her way across the main room, staying close to the walls to avoid trampling any evidence. A flame licked the edges of the television screen—one of those mood DVDs of a fireplace but devoid of sound. It filled the space with an eerie flicker that did little to lighten the gathering dusk.

Sidestepping a cat bowl filled with water, Jo stopped in front of the body and pulled a set of latex gloves from her trouser pocket.

"Really?" Cameron asked.

She snapped them into place, then pressed two fingers against the victim's neck in a futile search for a pulse—a completely unnecessary act that became an issue only if a defense attorney wanted to make an officer look like an idiot on the stand for not checking.

The dead man reclined in a high-backed gray chair that appeared to have built-in speakers. In the vee of his legs, a Remington 870 shotgun rested against his right thigh, the stock's butt buried in the dirty shag carpet. On the far side, a toppled bottle of whiskey and a tumbler sat on a metal TV tray next to a long-stemmed pipe.

"Who called it in?" Jo asked.

"Quinn Kirkwood. I told her to stay in her car until we figured out what was going on."

Jo retraced her steps to the threshold, seeking a respite from the stench of death.

A petite young woman stood at the edge of the driveway, pointedly looking away from the door. "Is he okay?"

So much for staying in the car. "Let's talk over here." Not giving the other woman the opportunity to resist, Jo grabbed her elbow and guided her to the illuminated porch of the main house, where the overhang would protect them from the softly falling snow.

"He's inside, isn't he?" Quinn pulled the drawstring of her sweat shirt until the hood puckered around her neck. "He's dead." It should have been a question, but wasn't. Jo's radar pinged.

"I'm sorry." Jo brushed errant flakes from a dilapidated wicker chair and moved it forward for the girl. "Is there someone I can call for you?"

She shook her head.

"How well did you know—"

"Tye. His name is—was—Tye Horton." Quinn played with the tab of her hood string, picking at the plastic that kept the ends from fraying.

Jo remained quiet, digesting the younger woman's unease. She was all angles: sharp shoulders, high cheekbones, blunt-cut dark hair, and canted eyes that looked blue in the open but faded to gray here in the shadows.

A pile of snow slid from a bowed cottonwood branch and landed with a dull plop. The silence broken, Quinn continued to fill it. "We have a couple classes together up at the college. He missed class. I came over to see why."

"Does he often cut class?"

"He didn't cut class," she said sharply. "He missed it." She pulled out her cell phone. "The project was due today. I should tell the others."

What would she tell them? She hadn't asked any questions. The pinging in Jo's head grew louder. "Did you go inside before the officer got here?" She looked at the woman's shoes. Converse high-tops. Distinctive tread.

Quinn launched out of her seat, sending it crashing into the porch rail. "I called you guys, remember?"

"It's a simple yes or no."

The smaller woman advanced, and Jo fought the impulse to shove her back. "No, Officer—"

"Detective Wyatt."

The top of Quinn's head barely reached Jo's chin. "Tye and I were classmates with a project due, *Detective*. I called him, he didn't answer. I texted him, he didn't respond. He didn't show up for the game last night, which meant something was wrong. He never missed a game."

Football. Last night Jo had pulled on her uniform and worked an overtime shift at the Sunday night game. Despite the plunging temperatures, the small college stadium had been filled to capacity.

"Did you check on him afterward?" Jo asked.

"No." Color brightened Quinn's pale cheeks. "By the time the game ended, it was too late. After he missed class today, I came straight over. Called the police. Here we are. Now, can I go?"

"Was Tye having any problems lately?"

"Problems?"

"With school? Friends?"

"I shared a class with him."

Another dodge. "You knew he wasn't at the game."

"I figured he was finishing up his end of the project. Are we done? I've got class tonight."

"I need to see your identification before you leave."

"Un-fucking-believable." Quinn jammed her hand into her jacket pocket and removed an old-fashioned leather coin purse. Pinching the top, she drew out her driver's license and practically threw it at Jo.

"I'm sure you understand. Whenever there's a death, we have to treat it as a crime until we determine otherwise."

The air left Quinn in a huff of frost. "I'm sorry. I'm just . . ." She dipped her face, but not before Jo saw the glint of tears. "I'm just going to miss him. He was nice. I don't have a lot of friends in Echo Valley."

"Were the two of you dating?"

The sharpness returned to Quinn's features. "Not my type."

"Do you know if he was in a relationship?"

"Not that I know of."

"Would you know?"

Cameron joined the women on the porch and extended his hand to Quinn. "I'm Sergeant Finch."

Jo sucked in her breath and covered it with a cough. The promotional memo hadn't been posted even a day yet.

"I'm sorry about your friend," Cameron added.

Quinn crossed her arms, whether for warmth or for comfort, Jo couldn't tell. "Your badge says Officer. Aren't sergeants supposed to have stripes or something?"

"It's official next week."

"So. Really just an officer."

Jo bit the inside of her cheek to keep from smiling. Served him right for acting like an ass.

"I wouldn't say *just*." Cameron hooked his thumb in his gun belt.

"Of course you wouldn't." Quinn drew a deep breath and let it out as if she feared it might be her last. "What happened?" she finally asked.

Jo spoke before Cameron could answer. "That's what we're here to find out." She opened her notebook.

Quinn sized up the two officers like a child trying to decide which parent to ask, and settled on Cameron. "Will you get me the laptop that's inside? It's got our school project on it."

"I'm sorry," Jo answered. "But until we process the scene, everything needs to stay put."

Quinn sought confirmation from Cameron. "Really?"

Jo shot him a look she hoped conveyed the slow torturous death he'd suffer if he contradicted her and compromised the scene.

Cameron placed his hand on Quinn's forearm. "I'm certain it won't take long, and I'll personally deliver it to you as soon as I can."

"Thanks." She shook off his hand and addressed Jo. "Am I free to go?"

Prickly thing. Jo handed Quinn's license back to her. "I'm truly sorry about your friend. May I call you later if I have any questions?"

Cameron stepped closer, all earnestness and concern. "It would be very helpful to the investigation when she realizes she forgot to ask you something."

The coin purse snapped shut. "Sure. Whatever."

"Thank you," Jo said, then added, "Be careful."

Quinn jerked. "What?"

The wind had picked up, and waves of snow blew across the walkway. Jo pointed toward the street. "The temperature drops any lower and it'll start to ice up. Be careful. The roads are going to be slick."

Quinn bobbed her head. Hunched against the cold, she climbed into her bright-yellow Mini Cooper.

Snow had collected on the bumper, and Jo noted the plate. She'd seen the car around town, its brilliant color and tiny chassis a contrast to the trucks and four-wheel-drive SUVs most locals drove.

The car crunched down the driveway. Jo returned to the task at hand, ignoring Cameron as he followed her.

Two buildings—the main residence and the converted garage—stood at the center of the property. The driveway dumped out onto an alley, and the hum of downtown carried across the crisp air. Dogs barked. Cars slowed and accelerated at the nearby stop sign, their engines straining and tires chewing into the slushed snow. A sagging chain-link fence ringed the property, pushed and pulled by a scraggly hedge.

Built in the days when a garage housed only a car and not the detritus of life, the building was barely larger than a tack room. A small walkway separated the dwellings. She followed the path around the exterior of the garage.

Eaves kept snow off the paint-glued windowsill on the far side of the outbuilding. Rambling rosebushes in need of pruning stretched skeletal fingers along the wall. Jo swept the bony branches aside, and a thorn snagged the shoulder of her blazer.

She studied the ground. Snow both helped and hindered officers. In foot pursuits, it revealed a suspect's path. But the more time separated an incident from its investigation, the more it hid tracks. Destroyed clues. This latest snow had started in the early hours of the morning, gently erasing the valley's grime and secrets and creating a clean slate. Tye could have been dead for hours. The snow told her nothing.

As she stood again at the door, not even the cold at her back could erase the smell of blood. The last of the evening's light battled its way through the dirty window, failing to brighten the dark scene in front of her.

She tried not to let the body distract her from cataloging the room. Echo Valley didn't have violent deaths often. In her twelve years on the department, she'd investigated only two homicides, one as an officer, the second as a detective. Fatal crashes, hunting accidents, Darwin Award–worthy stupidity, sure, but murder? That was the leap year of crimes and happened only once every four years or so.

Cameron joined her on the threshold, and they stood shoulder to shoulder. He had a shock of thick brown hair that begged to be touched, and eyes that said he'd let you. "Why so quiet, Jo-elle?"

The use of her nickname surprised her. Only two people had ever called her that, and Cameron hadn't used it in a long time. "I don't want to miss anything."

"What's to miss? Guy blew his brains out."

"It's rarely that simple."

"Not everything needs to be complicated." He laughed. The boyishness of it had always charmed her with its enthusiasm. Now it simply sounded dismissive. Perhaps it always had been, but she'd been too in love to notice. "Hey, you got plans tonight?" He tried to sound innocent. She *had* learned that voice.

"Other than this? I don't see as that's any of your business."

"Of course it's my business. You're still my wife." He stared into the distance as he said it. A splinter of sun pierced the dark clouds and bled across his unguarded expression.

Yearning.

Jo stood as if on ice, afraid to move lest she lose her balance.

He seemed to wake up, and after a deep breath, he surveyed the room. "The landlord is going to be looking for a new tenant. You should give him your name. It's got to be better than living with your old man."

Fissures formed beneath her, and it took her two blinks before she recovered her footing.

"I need to get my camera. I'll be right back."

She left him at the door. The December chill wormed through her wool dress slacks as she trudged the half block to her car. She drew breath after breath of the searing chill deep into her lungs to replace the hurt, the anger, the self-recriminations that burned her. She sat in the passenger seat and picked up the radio mic. She wasn't ready to face Cameron. Not yet.

To buy herself some time, she ran a local warrant check on Quinn. Something wasn't quite right about the woman. A warrant might explain things.

Dispatch confirmed Quinn's address but had nothing to add.

Jo grabbed her camera bag and crime scene kit and schlepped back to the scene, prioritizing her actions as she went. She'd need to snag another detective. Interrupt a judge's dinner to get a search warrant. Swab the victim's hands for gunshot residue. Try to confirm his identification. Hopefully, the person in the front house would return soon so Jo could start collecting background on the deceased. Take overview photos of the exterior first. Inside there'd be lights. Then evidence. Identify it. Bag it. Book it.

She reached the door before she ticked through all the tasks. Cameron was circling the chair.

Jo stopped on the threshold, stunned.

"No wonder they didn't promote you." Cameron peered into the exposed cranium. "If you can't tell this is a suicide, you got no business being a cop—let alone a detective."

"Get out."

"We're not home, sweetie. You can't order me out here."

9

"Actually, I can. Detective, remember? This is my scene, and you're contaminating it."

He laughed. "Sergeant outranks detective."

"I think it's already been established that you're not sporting stripes."

"Yet. Couple more days."

Three. Three days until he started wearing the stripes that should have been hers. Three days until he outranked her. Three. Damn. Days. "And until then, Officer Finch." With exaggerated care, she took out her notebook and started writing.

"What are you doing?"

"Making a note of the path you've taken." She paused for effect. "Try to retrace your steps. I'd hate to have to say how badly you mucked things up—you getting promoted and all."

"You're such a bitch."

"Is that how you talk to your wife?"

He picked up the overturned bottle on the TV tray. "Johnnie Walker Gold." He sniffed the premium Scotch whisky. "And here I would have pegged him for a Jack fan, at best." Cameron tipped the bottle back into place and retraced his steps.

The latex gloves did nothing to warm her fingers, and Jo shoved her hands in her pockets. Had he changed or had she? "When did you become such an ass?"

"When'd we get married?" He shouldered past her, swinging his keys around his finger. Outside the streetlamps flickered to life. "I'll leave you to it. Even you can see it's a slam dunk."

She didn't want to agree with him. "It's only a suicide when the coroner says so."

"Oh, Jo-elle."

There was that laugh again, and she hated herself for warming to him.

"You've got to learn to choose your battles."

2

Squint MacAllister was what Jo's mother would have called a tall drink of water. He'd earned the nickname as a child, but no one could remember why. Some said it was due to the slight narrowing of his eyes before he pulled the trigger when picking off the prairie dogs that undermined his family's ranch. Others suggested it was because he couldn't see past his nose. Considering no one on the department could outshoot him, Jo suspected the varmint story was closer to the truth. It wasn't until she'd made detective and heard him testify in court that she'd learned his real name was Jessup.

"What do you think?" Squint asked quietly.

On television, detectives rarely asked someone what they thought. Fictional detectives peppered their dialogue with declaratives and commands. Jo chewed on the question. Squint had been her training officer when she'd joined the department twelve years ago, and she'd learned that he liked reasoned responses when time allowed, and decisive action when it didn't. "Glossing over the fact that we haven't positively identified the victim, initial impressions suggest Tye Horton suicided."

Echo Valley had a grand total of three detectives, and two of them were in the room. The third, their supervisor, was on a beach somewhere along the Gulf Coast. Because Squint was the senior detective, he was in charge, although the swing-shift patrol sergeant checked on their progress throughout the night.

They worked systematically, processing the small dwelling. Sketches, photos, identifying evidence, more photos, collecting evidence. Squint dusted for latents. Jo vacuumed trace evidence. It was a lot like cleaning house, only with an evidence log that established them as the first link in the chain of custody.

Now they were waiting on the coroner.

Jo leaned over the body and shivered. His remaining brown hair curled over the neck of a long-sleeved T-shirt emblazoned with a pi symbol. Jeans and furry slippers completed the ensemble. All were in decent condition, other than the blood spatter and brain chunks that had rained down on them. "There's no sign of a struggle, no defensive wounds, and the angle on the shotgun blast is logical for being self-inflicted. Trying to get that angle on a person who doesn't want to die would be problematic at best."

The conventional wisdom regarding any death investigation was to treat it as a homicide until the facts proved otherwise. Some murder scenes were staged to look like suicide. Some suicides were staged to look like murder. If the investigator was lucky, the distinction was obvious. A person stabbed sixteen times in the back didn't commit suicide. But not all crime scenes gave up their secrets. Well-meaning family members covered Aunt Betty's nakedness, hid Junior's meth, destroyed the suicide note in hopes that their guilt and shame would disappear along with the message.

"But I'm concerned," she admitted.

"Talk me through it."

She had to smile. After all these years, he was still training her. "Ideally, to be considered a suicide, three basic things need to be established. We've got the gun. And the way he sat on the chair with the gun between his legs is a viable way to inflict the wound."

"But?" Squint pressed.

"Where's the note?"

"Not everyone wants to share their final thoughts."

"Okay, fair enough, but you still have to establish why a person wanted to end his own life. What's his motivation?" The room pressed in around Jo. "I mean, he's not living in the Ritz, but he had a roof over his head. His fridge is small, but he had plenty of food. Fresh stuff, too. I have lettuce more wilted than his."

"What else?"

Squint saw things. Jo recognized what was missing. The different perspectives made them a good team.

She pointed at the ceramic bowl with *meow* scrawled across it in a hard-to-read font. "Where's the cat?"

"The window's propped open. Clean ledge, toilet tank. Easy access for a cat. Could be outside."

"Too damn cold." Until tonight she'd never thought so much frigid air could come through such a small window. "And where's the food? I only saw a water dish."

"Significance?"

"No idea," Jo admitted. "It just struck me as odd." She returned to her scrutiny of the victim. Talking aloud helped clarify her thoughts. "Speaking of odd. Have you ever seen a chair like this?"

"Can't say as I have."

Excessively padded, the high, curved back of Tye's final resting place fused the comfort of a recliner with the apparent efficiency of an executive office chair. Built-in speakers were at about ear level—or would have been if Tye had still had ears. "My guess is he's an audiophile, although I find it strange that the television is muted. Come to think of it, where are the movies? Music? There's a DVD in the player, but where's its case?"

The remote had been bagged for prints, along with dozens of other small items. Black powder covered the less portable surfaces. The only things still to be collected were the supplements and meds on the bathroom counter.

Jo grabbed her clipboard, secured a new evidence sheet on it, and relocated to the bathroom. "What's even odder is the missing laptop." She separated the health supplements from the prescribed medications.

Squint wrangled the scattered evidence bags and placed them next to the door. "How do you know he had one?"

She wrote the name of a supplement on her evidence list and dropped the bottle into a brown paper bag. "He's a college student. Of course he had one."

"Assuming facts not in evidence."

"Just making sure you're still awake," she teased. "The RP was his classmate. She asked if we'd retrieve it and give it to her. Apparently, it has their team assignment on it."

"We haven't found the car yet. Could be inside."

"Along with the note, his movies, and the cat, if we're lucky."

"What did Doc Koster say?"

Jo selected a vial of insulin and rotated the bottle to read the label. She'd called Tye's doctor while Squint was throwing powder. "Mixing alcohol and insulin wreaks havoc on the human body. Tye could have easily miscalculated his sugar levels and gone into hypoglycemic shock. Which, by the way, makes the shotgun a bit of overkill."

"True."

She noted the dosage on her form and added the vial to the growing collection in the bag. The majority of the insulin had been stored in the refrigerator. "When I explained why I was calling, Dr. Koster immediately asked if I suspected suicide. Apparently, it's not uncommon for diabetics to suffer from depression. But there's not a single psych medicine here." She removed a poke-proof tube from her evidence kit and slid three unused hypodermic needles into the clear plastic vial and sealed it with a Styrofoam cork. "Without his patient notes, the doc couldn't remember if he and the victim had ever discussed depression issues. I'll follow up with him at his office tomorrow."

Jo's radio clicked. "David-three, Echo." The dispatcher's slight twang was as soothing as morning sunshine.

"David-three."

"Coroner's en route, ETA less than ten."

"Roger."

"Call dispatch, your convenience."

Jo grabbed her phone and stripped off one glove to dial. "Hey, it's me. What's up?"

"Hang on." The line clicked. A second later Dakota Kaplan picked up again. "Sorry, I wanted a nonrecorded line."

Crap, more sergeant condolences. Jo didn't know how many more sorries she could gracefully accept before cracking.

"Thought you should know the coroner sounded soused."

"Dr. Ingersleben?" The man was the living embodiment of propriety, and Jo suddenly found herself pining for the promotion pity. "Thanks for the heads-up."

"I saw the posting. You got screwed, Jo."

A dead body, a tipsy coroner, *and* pity. This night couldn't get any better. "Cameron will do a good job."

"Cut the horseshit, honey, it's me. On an unrecorded line."

Jo cradled the cell phone between her ear and neck and dug out another latex glove. "He will." If she said it enough times, maybe she'd start believing it.

"Just so you know, I'm sending him to every shit call I can on his first day."

"Remind me not to piss off a dispatcher."

"Damn straight. Sunday. Little Pine Creek. Bring your snowshoes. We've got trail to break and bodies to bury."

Headlights raked the dirty window.

Jo dragged on the glove. "Gotta go. The coroner just pulled up."

"Oh, hey, I'm screwing with you about Doc Ing." The line disconnected.

Jo stared at the screen, then shoved it in her back pocket. "I need a new best friend."

"It's been my experience that the ones worth keeping are the same ones you most want to strangle." Squint straightened the contents of his crime scene kit, making sure everything was in its place, and set it with the evidence bags by the door.

The coroner tapped a rapid staccato against the door. Squint pulled it open to admit Dr. Sidney Ingersleben. He doffed his flat tweed cap, brushed the snow from his field coat, and nodded a greeting. Give him an over-and-under shotgun with a break action and he could be coming in from a gentleman's hunt. In Scotland.

Both detectives waited, silent.

Dr. Ingersleben cleared his throat. "Someone has to die in order that the rest of us should value life more."

Thirty seconds passed before Squint spoke. "Marcus Aurelius?"

"Not all great quotes about death originate from warriors, Detective MacAllister." Ingersleben ran his fingers around the brim of his hat. "Detective Wyatt?"

Jo repeated the quote to herself. Something about the doctor's ritual calmed her, reminded her that even death had purpose. "It strikes me as Victorian. One of the Brontës?"

"Closer, but no. Any other guesses, educated or otherwise?" He glanced between the detectives. "Well, then. This stark admonishment comes from the inimitable Virginia Woolf."

"Room With a View?" Jo asked, fully aware that Forster and Woolf could never be confused.

"Detective, surely you jest."

Jo had never been outside the country. She'd been over the state line only a handful of times. But she'd read far enough beyond her borders to earn a scholarship to Western Colorado University in Gunnison. "Yes, Doctor, I do."

He cast about for a place to put his cap before setting it next to Squint's Stetson on the CSI kit. "You are incorrigible, my dear. Now shall we to it?" He pulled paper booties over the feet of his knee-high wellies and picked his way carefully to the deceased. "No doubting he's dead, I see." He looked at the ceiling. "Bit of a mess, there. Eh?" He pulled wire-rimmed spectacles from his breast pocket and put them on. Peering over the top of the lenses, he addressed the detectives. "You've got everything you need, I'm assuming?"

"Everything we could get without you present."

The coroner placed his hands on his thighs and squatted in front of the body, his face mere inches from the goop that Jo wished she'd never seen. "Shotguns are such efficient delivery systems. Shall we?"

Jo and Squint positioned themselves on either side of the body, careful not to dislodge the paper bags taped around the victim's hands to preserve trace evidence. Even knowing what to expect didn't fully prepare her for the unyielding rigidity of Tye's body as she worked her hand under his armpit. Together they leaned him forward, his body retaining the bent posture of the chair, while Dr. Ingersleben examined the back and buttocks of the victim. "A rather strapping lad, no? Can you tip him a bit further? I'll get a look at his thighs. There. Yes."

Jo turned her head away from the carnage uncomfortably close to her face. Even the Vicks VapoRub she'd smeared under her nose wasn't up to the task of masking the smell.

"All right now. I'll hold while you get your photographs."

Dr. Ingersleben exchanged places with Squint, and the body swiveled a bit toward Jo.

Squint retrieved his camera and snapped an overview photo of Tye's back, then several more close-ups.

Dead weight was technically no different from any other weight. That said, Jo was pretty sure the numbers on Tye's driver's license vastly underrepresented the mass she held in her arms.

"Still quite stiff, I see. Do we know when he was last seen?"

"No," Jo answered. "He was supposed to meet some people last night but didn't show."

"That's quite a time window." Dr. Ingersleben applied pressure to the arm, checking its resistance. "If he died before his engagement, I'd expect rigor to have started dissipating by now, but then again, it's cold in here. That will certainly impede the process."

Squint unwound the camera strap from around his neck. "I'll take the remaining photographs when the mortuary fellows place him on the gurney."

"Fair enough. They should be along anytime now. I telephoned them on my way here."

They eased Tye back into the chair. Jo rubbed warmth back into her hands.

Dr. Ingersleben extracted a handkerchief from his trouser pocket and polished his glasses. "How does a ten-thirty autopsy suit you?"

Squint nestled the camera into the foam of the Pelican case and snapped it closed. "I'll be there," he confirmed.

"Ah, that means you drew the proverbial short straw, eh?" the doctor said to Jo. "The psychological autopsy is so much harder than weighing organs and such. It's a difficult task to delve into the recesses of a man's mind."

They all looked at the crownless man in the chair.

"Metaphorically speaking, of course," he added.

3

Quinn Kirkwood opened the door of her yellow Mini Cooper and dropped her cigarette into the snow, where it sizzled until it died. Frosty night air invaded the car. She shivered and clicked her heater knob up a notch.

The lighted police sign in front of the Echo Valley station cast a dingy glare through her windshield. What the hell was taking the detective so long?

The two-story building guarded a corner lot a block east of the city's main drag and a block west of Broadmoor Avenue, where overpriced Victorians were painted in nausea-inducing pastels. Black letters identified the department, as if the boxy structure and surveillance cameras didn't make it obvious.

The distance from her car to the door was a no-man's-land of icy sidewalk. Spindly shrubs and two iron park benches flanked the covered entrance. She'd already used the emergency call box next to the locked lobby door to talk to a dispatcher. Braving the cold, Quinn sprinted across the salt-strewn path to the box and pressed the frozen receiver against her ear a second time.

"Communications, what's your emergency?"

The dispatcher spoke with a god-awful twang that suggested she was a few states north of home.

"It's Quinn again. Any update on Officer Wyatt returning to the station?"

The dispatcher clicked off to check, and Muzak flooded the line with a bad rendition of Metallica's "Fade to Black." James Hetfield should sue.

A low retaining wall surrounded frozen bushes and separated the building from the street. At the corner, a life-sized bronze police officer held a young girl in his arms. Snow had dusted the edges of his hat and settled on his shoulders. It looked like he had a bad case of dandruff.

The music switched to a bubblegum pop hit. By the second stanza, Quinn wanted to kill herself. It took two more refrains before the dispatcher came back on the line. "Detective Wyatt advised it shouldn't be much longer."

"Great," Quinn answered, but the dispatcher had already disconnected.

She retraced her steps to the car and drew her hoodie closer around her body. She couldn't put it off any longer; she'd have to get something filled with feathers. Patagonia, maybe a Marmot. Something easy to boost from the mountaineering store on Main.

She reached for the pack of cigarettes in the console and stopped. The nicotine kick had kept her up as she waited for Wyatt, but did she really want to stay awake all night?

She tilted her head back and closed her eyes. The image she'd glimpsed of Tye replayed for the gazillionth time. Her eyes shot open, and before she knew it, she was drawing warm smoke deep into her lungs. Holding it hostage. Taking everything it would give her.

Tye.

Sad sack of shit, truth be told.

She released the smoke, and it bounced against the windshield and curled back at her.

She'd miss him.

Main Street was ground zero in Echo Valley. From there, the streets either shared the same altitude or climbed into the mountains that kept the city from escaping. On warm days, it reminded her of her home in San Francisco. Hills she knew. Add a layer of ice to them, however, and they became the equivalent of a Slip 'N Slide, only colder and not nearly as much fun. Even now, headlights fishtailed as the drunks headed home.

Finally, a steady set of lights approached, and a plain dark Impala nosed into one of the parking stalls along the side of the station reserved for police cars. There were no markings on the car, but there was no doubt it belonged to a cop.

The trunk lid of the patrol car opened before the officer got out of the cab. She emerged and slung a large black bag onto her shoulder and then gathered several brown paper bags from the trunk, pinching them together at the top and clamping them in her left hand.

Quinn opened her door and started to drop the butt of her cigarette in the street but thought better of it and drowned it in the coffee dregs at the bottom of an old cup from the Burnt Bean. Raising the hood over her head, she approached. "Detective Wyatt?"

The officer slammed the trunk lid, and Quinn could have sworn she looked like she wanted to draw down on her. "Yes?"

"I was hoping for a minute of your time." Maybe ten.

"I'm really sorry about your friend, but I don't have anything more to share yet."

The detective had put on a wool hat since Quinn last saw her. Gloves, too. She looked warm, sensible. Safe. It pissed Quinn off. "He's still dead, you mean."

"I'm sorry," she repeated. "Dispatch said you wanted to see me. Is there something else about Mr. Horton that you'd like to share?"

"I need your help with something else."

"I see." The circles under the officer's eyes seemed to darken under the streetlights.

"I've been threatened," Quinn said.

"Threatened?"

"Over the internet," Quinn clarified.

"The internet." Wyatt paused. "So, not in person."

"No."

"Do you know this person?"

"Plural—people—but no. I don't know them."

"Have you had any problems at your home?"

Quinn shook her head.

"School?"

Another shake.

"Work?"

"It's not that simple," Quinn said.

"Look. I'm still on the call involving your friend."

Quinn tucked her hands under her armpits, trying to keep them warm. "Threats, Officer Wyatt."

"So you said." She sighed, still holding the bags. "What kind of threats?"

"Oh, you know. Murder. Rape. The usual."

"Threats aren't that common in Echo Valley."

"Exactly my point."

"I'll call another officer for you. You can wait in the lobby. It's warmer there." Wyatt raised the bags to eye level. Red evidence tape sealed them closed. "Let me drop these off inside, and I'll come around to let you in."

"Wait." Quinn grabbed Wyatt's arm.

All semblance of Wyatt's fatigue vanished, and she suddenly seemed like one of those tall, fierce warriors who lived on that all-woman super-hero island. The detective pointedly looked at the hand on her arm, then raised her gaze to stare down Quinn. "You may want to rethink that before I consider you a threat."

Quinn released her grip. "That's rich. That's why I'm here, remember? If I wanted another officer, I wouldn't be standing here freezing my ass off."

Wyatt sighed. In the cold, Quinn could literally see the officer's frustration—a long through-the-nose exhalation that sounded exactly like what Quinn's mother used to do. Like what her sister still did.

"What do you want from me?" Wyatt finally asked.

"Do your job," Quinn blurted.

Detective Wyatt stiffened, then held up the bags of evidence. "I am." Presenting her back to Quinn, she started for the employee door at the far end of the building.

"'The only things you're good for is as a place for my cock and making me a sandwich.'"

Wyatt spun, her eyes slitted. "Excuse me?"

"Or how 'bout this one? 'I hope you get raped. It's the only way some-one's gonna fuck you.'" Quinn spoke normally, but the words sounded overloud in the quiet neighborhood. "The death threats are always fun. They've expanded to include my family. One guy even threatened to run over my dog."

"Do you have a dog?"

"Not the point." Geez, why did cops always focus on the wrong thing?

"Why would someone target you?"

"It shouldn't matter, should it? They're threatening me, and it's getting worse."

Wyatt raised one shoulder like she was too tired to shrug them both. "The why shouldn't matter, but sometimes it makes the situation easier to understand."

That made sense. "I play video games."

"Video games." Light from the streetlamp stretched the detective's shadow to the curb. "This is a joke, right?"

"Nope."

"All this over a game?"

Gaming had been a part of Quinn's life since she could wrap her baby-fat hands around a console. Games had comforted her when she switched schools and no one wanted to befriend the new girl. The nerd geek. People who didn't play didn't get it. Games had saved her life.

"All this because I'm a *woman* who plays video games," Quinn answered. "It's not the same thing."

"Sounds to me like you need a new hobby."

"Yeah. Cuz I'm the problem." Cops. They all sucked. The only thing she'd get out of tonight was frostbite.

Quinn stomped to her car and yanked the door handle. Her hand slipped and tore her frozen nail down to the quick. Cradling the injured finger against her chest, she watched her blood splat against the snow. "I thought you were different. That you of all people would get it."

The officer had followed Quinn to the front of her car. "I'm tired. You're going to have to spell it out for me. Get what?"

"Being an outsider." Anger chased away the cold. Her chest burned with it. "I saw the way that other cop treated you. Trying to take over and be all Mr. Nice while doing his best to make you look like his fucking sec-retary." She leaned forward conspiratorially. "That's gotta make you feel special. When are you going to get *your* stripes, Sarge?"

A stoic mask of indifference settled on the detective's face. "It's two o'clock in the morning. You don't need to shout."

It wasn't the first time Quinn had seen cop face. It probably wasn't even the first time it had been directed at her, but never before had it pissed her off to the point of stupidity. "So, you'll break away from your fucking report to arrest me but can't be bothered to help me. Priceless."

"Let me get you a Band-Aid," Wyatt offered. "You're bleeding."

Sarcasm? The detective's face gave nothing away and it looked like a genuine offer, but Quinn didn't care. "Fuck you." She wrenched the car door open so forcefully it bounced back and hit her on the hip.

"Suit yourself." The detective readjusted her grip on the evidence bags. "I'm working tomorrow." She hesitated, then blew another of her dragon-frost-through-the-nose sighs before digging in her pocket and retrieving a business card. "Lose the attitude. Bring me the printouts. We'll talk."

4

"The hell we'll talk."

Quinn entered the curve a little hot, and the car fishtailed.

Stupid snow.

The road that clawed its way to her apartment wound around towering trees and was three times longer than any hilly street in San Francisco, and at the moment it was covered in snow.

Why'd she ever leave California?

Because I had to.

Habit made her glance in her rearview mirror. No headlights.

She eased off the gas so she didn't slide past the slippery slope of her driveway. She cut the corner and swore. Just once she'd like to come home and park in her own spot. It wasn't even a good spot, crammed between a dumpster and a light pole that hadn't worked a day in the year and a half she'd lived there.

The other seven parking spaces were full, and she inched her car behind the gunmetal-gray Challenger trespassing in her spot until her front bumper kissed its ass. No use calling the landlord. The property management company didn't take calls after hours. Not that they were keen to take calls any other time either.

Stan? No, Stu. Stu stood in the doorway of his apartment holding a bong. Light poured out around him, and she couldn't see his face until he flicked the lighter in his right hand and took a hit. He watched her over the flame.

She got out of her car and slammed the door. Techno-thump bullshit assaulted her ears, and she raised her voice. "You're in my spot."

He held the smoke in his lungs a long moment before releasing his breath. "You hit my car."

"You're lucky I didn't ram it right into your fucking apartment."

He held out the bong. "Here. You obviously need this."

"I need my parking spot."

He dug into his pocket and tossed her the keys. Instinctively, she snatched them out of the air before they landed on her hood. The metal banged against her injured finger. Another fucking injustice to add to the night.

"I'm not your valet."

"You want your spot? I'm too buzzed to drive. I get another DUI and my folks will kill me."

"We could only hope."

The wind bit through the thin fabric of her sweat shirt. Living on the hill gave her a great view but did nothing to stop the frosty gusts that threatened to freeze her eyelashes. Could that happen? She brought her fingers up to her face but stopped before she touched them. The way the day was going, they were already frozen and she'd snap them off.

She sighed. The road to warmth meant jockeying cars. Arguing about it would only delay the inevitable. "This is the last time."

"You said that last time."

"Next time, I empty a bottle of Jäger on your front seat, smash your car into the college gate, and call the police. Tell them I saw a drunk guy with shitty taste in clothing and an impossibly large Adam's apple run into your apartment."

"Seriously, take a hit. You're making me feel bad—and don't park in the handicapped spot this time. The last ticket sent my parents off the cliff."

She backtracked to her car and double-parked it behind an unfamiliar Jeep with Oregon plates. She hit the fob to unlock the Challenger and slid into the leather seats. The engine roared to life, and she adjusted the driver's seat closer to the steering wheel than she needed. She found a pack of gum in the center console and helped herself to a frozen stick to chase away the nicotine and dead-coffee taste that had taken up residence in her mouth.

25

She goosed the gas as she left the parking lot. Instead of making an angry statement, the spinning tires only confirmed that she didn't know shit about driving in snow.

The interior of the Challenger wrapped around her like a cocoon, and she stretched the tension from her shoulders. This was nicer than her Mini Cooper. More stable. He had a full tank. How far would that take her? Her grip on the steering wheel tightened. Would it be far enough?

But she'd made a promise.

Reluctantly, she pulled into the admin lot of the college, bypassed a row of empty spaces, and parked the Challenger in the handicapped space by the building. Cold seeped through her jeans as she trudged back to the apartment building.

Finding the apartment had been a fluke, and she'd rented it sight unseen. Even in a godforsaken outback of humanity like Echo Valley, rentals went quick, and most weren't ever advertised. She'd overheard two college students yammering on about the great apartment they should rent up on the hill. As one gal was giving the number to the other, Quinn was dialing. It might have been a mistake, but at least she could walk to class. Save on gas. Fulfill the promise she'd made to her mom. Even if it killed her.

When she got back, Stu took in the snow clinging to the lower part of her jeans. "You parked in the gimp spot, didn't you?"

"Yup. Seat's up, too. Sure hope you don't forget when you try to get in." She wound up and threw his keys back. He had to sidestep to avoid getting nailed. Nice to know she still had her pitching arm.

Quinn eased the Mini Cooper into her assigned spot, and the car's headlights settled on her neighbor. It'd be so easy to jump the parking bumper.

No, if she was going to run someone over, she should have chosen the detective. Stu annoyed her. Wyatt had royally pissed her off.

"You know, if you just went out with me, I wouldn't have to park in your spot to get you to talk to me."

"Look, Stu—"

"Stan."

"Whatever. I'm not interested."

"You gay?"

For a moment she thought about saying yes, but that was chickenshit. She had too many queer friends to lie about something like that. She slung her messenger bag across her chest and headed for the steps.

"It's okay," he called after her. "I'm a lesbian trapped in a man's body. We can work something out."

She flipped him off as she climbed the stairs. Assclown.

Her steps slowed as she neared the top of the staircase. The music still thumped its aggressive tempo from downstairs, and she tried to filter it out so she could detect other sounds. Nothing. She hugged the outside rail to get the best view of the corridor formed by the apartments on one side and a shaky railing on the other. Empty.

Footprints mashed the snow in front of the other three apartments on this level, but none of the steps pointed toward her door. A thin layer of snow dusted the window ledge. Frost crawled up the glass. Good.

She brushed her foot against the threshold and cleared a small bit of snow away from her door. About an inch from the ground, a folded business card jutted from the jamb. Still there. She'd have to find something a tad more waterproof. Wet paper might stick to the door when it opened, and that wouldn't tell her squat about anyone breaking into her apartment.

She quietly unlocked the deadbolt and stooped to retrieve the card. Tomorrow she'd swap it for Detective Wyatt's glossy business card. Apparently a card was all she was going to get from Echo Valley's finest.

She twined the keys through her knuckles until her fist looked like a low-budget Wolverine knockoff. The heat of the apartment blasted her as she entered and hit the light in the same stride. The overhead light sputtered, illuminating her small living room and kitchenette. Empty.

She crossed to the bathroom. The shower curtain remained pushed to the side. Good.

Running the wall, she took a breath and entered the bedroom. Closet door open. Window shut. No one on the other side of the bed. Clear.

She stood for a moment and let the warmth wash over her.

Normal people didn't have their mattress on the floor. Normal people didn't worry about someone hiding under their bed. Normal people weren't afraid to open their computer. Read their email. Go home. Live.

She kicked off her shoes and retraced her steps to the living room. Double-checked the dead bolt, slid the door chain into place, and crammed one of her two kitchen chairs under the doorknob. Then she settled down on the love seat that served as her couch, opened her laptop, put on her headset, and grabbed her gaming console.

Fuck normal.

5

Whoever said home is where the heart is had never dealt with a broken marriage.

Even in the dark, the lines of Jo's childhood house stood out, backlit by the gibbous moon and lingering clouds. To the casual observer, the house looked the same as it had when she'd grown up within its walls. But she saw the differences: the broken gutter, the neglected garden, the slightly askew mailbox from when her father had backed into it last winter. The house sagged, as if it still mourned the loss of Jo's mother.

Home—at least for now. At the end of this kind of night, all she wanted was ten uninterrupted hours of sleep in her king-sized bed. But that was still at the house she'd shared with Cameron. What she'd get tonight was a blow-up mattress on the floor of her old bedroom and an alarm clock jolting her awake in little more than three hours.

The tires of her Ford Explorer crunched through the icy crust of snow that had accumulated in the driveway. She'd have to allow enough time to scrape the windshield in the morning. Maybe she should have waited until the spring to leave Cameron. At least then she'd still be parking in their garage. *His* garage.

She grabbed her backpack. Keeping to the shadows, she hurried to the dark porch. Her dad had removed the bulb from the fixture. No sense giving someone a clear shot. Maybe it was better that way. Over the years, the drab two-bedroom clapboard house seemed to have shrunk. Putting a spotlight on the porch would only highlight the flaws.

Inside, she unzipped her jacket and then thought better of it. Her mother used to keep the heat a click below tropical. Every time the power bill came, her parents argued over it, but in the end, her mother's smile had always melted her father's anger.

Embers smoldered in the fireplace and spit a wan glow into the hallway. Her father slept in his battered recliner in the living room. Jo closed her eyes against the image of another man—a lifeless man—in another chair, but knew it would be a while before that memory faded. Memories of the dead never completely disappeared.

Gray strands outnumbered the brown on her father's head, but it all looked dark in the flickering light. In sleep, the creases in his face softened, and he was the father of her childhood. When he could do no wrong. Before she'd learned better.

Other than DNA, Joseph Charles Wyatt shared only two things in common with his daughter: a name and a crooked nose. The first he'd given her over her mother's protestations that a girl shouldn't be saddled with a man's name. Her mother had suggested Josephine, or Joanne. He'd held firm to Joe. Her mother had smiled at the time, and then quietly erased the final letter at the hospital.

Genetics had determined her father's nose. Jo's was another story. That had come from a drunk driver who didn't think "a little girl" like Jo could make him go to jail. Turned out he was wrong.

Her father had been the watch commander that night. He never once asked her what happened, simply told her that if anyone disrespected the uniform like that again, she'd better put him in the hospital, not jail.

She eased the tumbler from his hand. His snore turned into a snort, but he slept on.

Raising the glass to her nose, she sniffed. Bourbon. Her dad drank Old Crow only with Cameron. A moment later she found the second glass on the mantel next to the police scanner. Heaven forbid her soon-to-be ex actually walked anything to the sink.

Ever since she'd left her husband a month ago, Cameron and her father had become thick as thieves, and just as clandestine. She found their nascent camaraderie suspicious. And hurtful. It used to take an act of God to get Cameron to accompany her when she visited her father for Sunday dinner. Growing up, the meal had been a tradition as rigidly adhered to as attending church on Sunday morning. Brisket, mashed potatoes, green beans, rolls. Her mom always baked a pie. After she died, her father cooked. Following the second fire department response, self-preservation kicked in, and Jo took over the culinary responsibilities. Her father caved without an argument, and it marked the last time he tried to maintain the high standards set by his wife.

When Cameron joined the department six years ago, her father had been his sergeant. Respect was something Joseph Charles Wyatt demanded from his troops and they had to earn in return. Coming in, Cameron had three strikes against him: he wasn't a local, he rooted for the Patriots, and he was sleeping with the sergeant's daughter. Marrying her only made it a modicum better.

That was before her father retired. Things had changed since then.

She walked the glasses into the kitchen and set them in the sink. Barbecue-smeared containers from the Feed Trough littered the counter next to the nearly empty bottle of Old Crow. Her stomach growled. Food or sleep? Did one rank higher on Maslow's hierarchy of needs? She splashed a dram of the amber liquid into her dad's glass and shot it. Alcohol probably hadn't made the list, but after the day she'd had, she was fairly certain Maslow wouldn't begrudge her the nip.

Tye Horton.

She reached for the bottle again, then reconsidered.

Growing up, she'd been a willful child with a rigid sense of justice constantly at odds with her mother's. After one particularly egregious dressing down for some forgotten indiscretion, Jo had laid on the floor with her arms stretched wide, her body forming a perfect cross, and played dead. She waited for her mother to find her, hoping she'd realize how unfair she'd been to Jo and die of grief. Her mother stepped over her and told her to set the table for supper.

But that was literally child's play. What could override all instinct of self-preservation and prompt a person to take his own life for real? Diabetes? Depression? Relationship issues? She'd seen enough despair during her career to know that people often sought to escape the pain of the now, forgetting that they were erasing their tomorrows in the process.

What had compelled Tye Horton to such an end?

She didn't have a clue, but tomorrow she'd find out. Talk to the people who knew him. Landlord. Doctor. Professors. Friends.

Quinn had said they shared a couple of classes. Was Tye failing? That would certainly add stress to the life of an undergrad. The academic quarter was nearing its end. Their project was due. What if he'd shirked his share? Or did it have something to do with the missing laptop?

She should have asked Quinn more questions earlier instead of trying to keep her estranged husband from ruining the death scene. She'd had two shots at Quinn and blown them both. She scrubbed her hand across her face. The screw-up at the station was on her. With any luck, Quinn would return to the department tomorrow. After her little meltdown, though, Jo doubted Quinn ever wanted to see her again.

You of all people should understand, she'd said.

Quinn knew nothing. Jo had spent her entire life in Echo Valley. In a town that defined its locals by the depth of their roots, she was as inside as could be.

When you going to get your stripes, Sarge?

Jo plunged the glass under icy water and rinsed away the fumes.

She was pensive tonight. Death calls, though infrequent, always did that to her.

The chime from her mother's clock tolled the half hour.

She'd always been a little jealous of her parents' relationship. Not that she wasn't loved—she was—but they shared something that excluded her. Something she'd never felt with Cameron, and even now, she wondered exactly what it was.

Loyalty?

Her father claimed he'd taken only two oaths in his life. One to his wife, the other to his department. The only reason he wasn't still pounding the beat was because of the blown-out knee he'd earned chasing some mope who stole a six-pack of Coors from the gas station on the edge of town. That night they'd both ended up at the hospital.

Cancer had severed the vow he'd made to her mother. The pain of her death had crippled Jo, but it almost killed her father.

Who, she wondered, would mourn Tye Horton?

Jo scooped coffee into a filter. Eyeballed it. Added another heaping tablespoon and set the timer on the coffeemaker. In a couple of hours, she'd pull on clean clothes, shrug off her fatigue, and do her best to shed light on the darkness of Tye's final days.

6

Jo entered the detective bureau and hung her coat on the old wooden rack by the door.

Squint peered over his computer. "Any luck?"

"Does bad count?"

"Wasn't exactly what I was hoping to hear."

The police department employed a total of forty-four people: six civilians and the rest sworn. The building held a collection of administrative offices, holding cells, a property room, his and hers locker rooms, a briefing room that occasionally doubled as the emergency ops center, and an armory. Technically, it was a two-story building, but the upper level was only a fraction of the size of the lower one. Located on the second floor, the detective bureau was hardly larger than its name and not nearly as grand. Jo's desk abutted the back of Squint's. The sergeant's office had space for only a desk and a locked file cabinet, but at least it had a door. Factor in a small break room and an even tinier interview room, and every available inch was in use.

She flopped down in her chair and unlaced her boots. "I was on the landlord's porch at seven, but no one answered. My business card was still wedged in the door. No tracks in the snow."

"I'll stop by the assessor's office after the autopsy and see who owns the place."

"I peeked through the curtains. If I had to guess, I'd say an elderly lady. Lots of chintz and china, although the gun cabinet might skew the odds."

"How long have you lived in this town?"

"I said *might*." Jo peeled off her wet socks and then dug around in her bottom desk drawer until she found a dry pair. "I canvassed the whole block. Made contact with six people: the couple next door, two sorority girls who only knew Tye as the owner of the old Volvo covered in Pokémon stickers, a blind woman across the street, and a creepy guy who didn't know Tye but invited me in for breakfast anyway."

"Was it good?"

"Let's just say I'm still hungry." She folded the tops of the wet socks over the lip of the drawer to dry and pushed the drawer closed. "I need a new pair of boots. These suck."

"You can always get a pair of those green rain boots the good doc wears."

"Ever run in a pair of wellies?"

"Can't say as I have."

"I have. My mom had a pair she wore when gardening. I used to clomp around in them. Of course, I was six at the time."

"I heard you found the car."

"Thanks to the sorority girls. It's pretty distinctive once you know what to look for. Dickinson's sitting on it until I can get a search warrant." She drew on the dry socks and reveled in the warmth, flexing her toes.

"How'd you get so wet?"

"I saw something silver down the river embankment. Thought it might be the laptop."

"And?"

"It wasn't." She powered on her computer and waited for it to wake up. "You?"

"Horton's been contacted by the police twice. Two years ago, deputies nabbed him for an open container on the Fourth of July. Nine months ago we took a report from him when he reported his bike stolen. The sheriff's office listed his address on the north end of town—the same address that's on his driver's license—but he lived on Fifth when his bike was stolen."

"I don't suppose the report mentioned the name of the landlord?"

"No, but Horton thought some things inside the house may have been stolen too. Said he'd check and call back. Never did."

"Damage to the door?" Jo asked.

"Wasn't locked."

"You'd think that would be a lesson."

Squint slid the file onto Jo's desk. "Criminal history is negative. No warrants. DMV is clean. Couple of parking tickets. No pawns. Credit is middle of the road. No guns registered to him."

She flipped through the documents in the folder. A lifetime reduced to a bit of ink revealing that Tye Horton had been your average law-abiding citizen. "Who'd the shotgun come back to?"

"It's not registered."

"Of course it isn't. That'd be too easy," she said. "I'll contact the gun club. See if anyone knew him."

"Might have come out of the gun cabinet in the main house."

"Maybe. I noticed two empty slots." She tucked one leg under her while her boots dried. "I can't get in to see Dr. Koster until they break for lunch, so I'll knock out the search warrant for the Volvo and then head up to the college, see what I can find out. Try to track down Tye's professors."

"Why don't you let me pull the warrant? I've got time before the autopsy."

"Promise to let me know if you find the cat."

"You have my word."

Jo propped her elbows on the desk and rested her chin against her folded hands. "You ever have a really bad feeling about something?"

"Every time you walk through the door."

She closed the file and leaned back. "I've got a really bad feeling about this."

7

Echo Valley College perched on the east bluff and overlooked the town. Dubbed "Harvard on the Hill" by the locals, the only thing the liberal arts institution shared with an Ivy League school was its tuition rate.

"There's no way I was going forty-three through a school zone," Professor Frederick Lucas said.

Early in her career, Jo had discovered that policing a town where she'd grown up had both pros and cons. She often knew where the bodies were buried, but everyone expected her to let them get away with murder. "That's why we have court."

The college office was even smaller than the closet Lucas had occupied when he worked for the city as its one and only IT tech. He rocked back in his desk chair, and it leaned against an overflowing bookcase filled with software manuals and DVD cases. She read a few of the titles before realizing they were video games and not movies.

He waved his hand toward a second bookshelf stuffed with modems, gaming consoles, and devices in various stages of dissection that choked the shelves and spilled onto the floor around Jo's feet. "As if I have time for court."

Which is why you were speeding. "Can we get back to Mr. Horton?"

"I am getting back to Mr. Horton. You scratch my back, I'll scratch yours."

"You want to leverage your student's death to get out of a speeding ticket?"

He shrugged. "They're expensive."

"Maybe you should slow down."

He shifted his weight forward, and the front legs of his chair smacked the linoleum. He folded his hands in front of him and leaned over the cluttered desk toward Jo. "Maybe you should get your information elsewhere."

When she'd first met him, she'd noticed that Fred Lucas had the smoothest hands she'd ever seen on a man. No calluses, no freckles, not even hair dispelled the impression that those hands had never worked an honest day's labor. That had been eight years ago, and except for a couple of liver spots, they hadn't changed.

"According to the admissions office, you're his only instructor this semester," Jo said. "Your class was the last one he needed to graduate. Most people celebrate that milestone. So what happened?"

Lucas flicked his wrist and glanced at an expensive-looking watch. The pay must be good up on the hill. "I've got to administer a final in ten."

"Have you noticed Mr. Horton acting differently lately?"

He thrust a stack of papers into his canvas messenger bag and stood. "I'm late."

Jo remained seated. "Do you have such little regard for your students?"

"I am truly sorry to hear about Tye." He stepped around his desk and leaned over Jo to grab his coat from the hook on the back of the office door. "But I can't afford another point on my license."

This was a new low—even for a man who'd resigned after a shipment of desktop computers disappeared from the city inventory. Nothing had ever been proven against him, but the cloud of suspicion followed him like blowflies on roadkill. It didn't speak well for the college's human resources department.

"What was he working on?"

He shoved his arms into his wool coat. The addition of tweed did nothing to enhance his credibility.

"This isn't about me, Fred," Jo said. "Think of his family."

"We're through here, Detective." He loomed over Jo and thrust his chest forward in an obvious attempt to intimidate her. He must have forgotten about his hands.

"I can subpoena your records." Jo crossed her leg over her knee.

"I'm sure you can."

"You won't need to," Quinn said from the doorway. "We were working on a new game together. It was our capstone project. Professor Lucas was our adviser."

"Well, there you go, Detective." Lucas sidled around Jo's chair and rested his hand on the doorknob. "Now if you'll excuse me, I have to lock up."

Jo gathered her portfolio and stood, forcing Lucas to take a step back in order for her to pass and join Quinn in the hallway. Several of the other staff doors were open for office hours and students milled about, waiting to see their professors.

Lucas locked the office door behind him and pocketed the keys. Almost as an afterthought, he addressed Quinn. "Did you need something, Ms. Kirkwood?"

"Ah, it can wait."

Lucas drew on a pair of gloves. "Well then, good day, ladies." He didn't wait for an answer before sauntering off.

"How long were you at the door?" Jo asked.

"Long enough to know he didn't give you squat."

Lucas disappeared around the corner of an intersecting hallway.

"Is he always so evasive?"

"He was when Tye confronted him about stealing his game idea and trying to sell it."

Jo swung her gaze back to Quinn. "He tried to do what, now?"

Quinn readjusted the book bag hanging from her shoulder. "Sell Tye's game without telling him about it."

"Your capstone project?" Jo pressed.

"I wouldn't be worried about my grade if that were the case."

Profit had certainly motivated its fair share of murders. Did Lucas have something to do with Tye's death? Had Tye threatened to expose Lucas? This opened up a whole new line of inquiry, and she wanted some facts before having another sit-down with Lucas.

"Let's find someplace quiet to talk."

"Can't."

"Can't or won't?" Jo lowered her voice. "Look, I'm trying to do right by your friend."

Quinn's bluster fled. "Lucas is a prick," she finally said.

Jo was inclined to agree but held her tongue.

"Look, I've got an eleven o'clock final I can't miss."

Twenty minutes. Not nearly enough time to ask all the questions Quinn's revelation had sparked. Jo had a slew of things she needed to do today, but nothing that couldn't be rearranged. "What time will you be finished?"

"Maybe you should have listened to me last night."

"I believe I invited you to come back to the station."

They were at a standoff. Quinn crossed her arms. "You'll check out the emails?"

"Yes."

"Fine, but we have to meet somewhere I can get a cup of coffee that doesn't taste like it came from a vending machine."

That ruled out the station. "How about Hank's Diner?"

"I'll be at the Burnt Bean at three."

8

Jo hunched over a copper-topped table with her back to the wall and waited for Quinn. Rain drummed on the roof, and the small coffee shop smelled of spicy chai, earthy coffee, and wet wool.

The day after a major event was always busy, and Jo didn't have time to wait on a spoiled college kid.

The shop bustled with tourists and students and an eclectic mix of unfamiliar faces. Despite the overstuffed chairs and intimate conversation nooks, the space lacked warmth. People came and went, lingering only long enough to gulp their coffee.

Jo reviewed her notes again, but all she saw were questions.

The interview with Dr. Koster hadn't revealed any new medical insight. Tye Horton was a diabetic, had been for years, and was successfully managing the disease with medication. He'd last visited the doctor a month ago, and there hadn't been any mention of depression. By all accounts, he was a model patient.

According to his medical records, Tye's emergency contact was his sister, who lived in the adjacent county. Jo had arranged for a deputy to make the death notification. Some things needed to be done in person. She'd follow up with a phone call after the notification was complete. Hopefully, the siblings had stayed in contact.

The coffee shop door opened, and wind rattled Jo's notes. Officers Ryan Estes and Elijah Dickinson entered. Both wore dark-blue police uniforms, but the similarities ended there. Estes lived life like he chewed his gum: loud and full of smack. Dickinson, though taller, always seemed to fade into the background. When they both landed on day shift, patrol had taken bets on who would kill the other first. Jo put her money on

Dickinson. She'd trained him. Sure, he was quiet, but those were the ones you had to look out for.

The officers ordered coffee, then approached her table, their progress marked by the eyes of curious patrons.

Estes spun a chair around and straddled it. "I hear you're stirring things up again."

She wondered briefly what he meant, then decided she didn't care. "By all means, please join me."

Dickinson stepped around his partner and claimed another seat. "Don't mind if I do." He surveyed her notes. "That's a lot of notes for a suicide."

Jo tapped her pen against the page. "And not nearly enough if it turns into something else."

"Finch said you're chasing your tail over this." Estes cracked his omnipresent gum.

She imagined that Cameron said a lot about her when she wasn't around. She focused on the bright logo on her recyclable cup. It lacked the heft of the plain crockery of Hank's Diner. There, if someone wanted a to-go cup, they brought in their own thermos.

Dickinson leaned in, the scent of coffee on his breath. "Tough break about the sergeant's test. I was pulling for you."

Estes snapped his gum again. "No surprise about Finch, though."

Dickinson backhanded his partner on the shoulder.

"What?" Estes asked. "Everyone knew he'd get promoted."

Dickinson raised his voice to be heard over the hiss of the espresso machine. "You're being insensitive."

"I'm the most sensitive guy you've ever met." Estes turned back to Jo.

She hooked the tab of the tea bag under her finger so it wouldn't hit her face and sipped her Earl Grey. They really didn't need her for this conversation.

A woman in high heels splashed across the street at a full sprint and barely paused to open the door. A blast of arctic air followed her inside. Jo shivered and wrapped her hand around her tea, but the cup had already cooled. How any woman could run in heels defied comprehension. Add in puddles, sleet, uneven pavement, and traffic, and it should qualify as an extreme sport. Which probably explained why Merrells and UGGs were the most popular shoes in Echo Valley.

"It's nothing against Jo, I just think Cameron's the better man." Estes stopped chewing his gum long enough to take a pull of coffee.

"Using that criterion, I'd have to agree," she said.

Estes elbowed Dickinson. "See, she gets it."

"An absolute paragon of sensitivity," Dickinson said.

Jo glanced at the notes she'd made at the doctor's office, again. She was missing something. He was a diabetic. If he had consumed alcohol, wouldn't his body have started to go into hypoglycemic shock? He'd have been disoriented at best, and comatose or dead at worst. Would he have been physically able to manipulate the shotgun? Then a more obvious question presented itself. Jo tapped her pen against her notes. "Why would a man shoot himself if he could overdose on insulin?"

"What?" both men asked in unison.

She lowered her voice so the people at the next table couldn't hear her. "Is there some macho reason a guy would blast his face off rather than just overinject his medication if he wanted to suicide?"

Dickinson tapped his finger against the table while he contemplated the question.

"I know more men than women suicide with guns," Jo continued. "But if you had a relatively easy way to check out, wouldn't that be your first choice?"

"We don't know what went through the man's mind," Dickinson pointed out.

Estes's jaws worked overtime. "Last I heard, it was double-aught buck."

Jo shot him a withering glare. "Have some respect."

"Relax, he can't hear us."

"Don't you have reports or something?" Jo asked.

Estes pushed off from his chair. "As a matter of fact, I'm down four." He picked up his coffee cup and tipped it toward Dickinson. "You coming?"

"I'll catch up with you later."

"Suit yourself."

Another blast of icy air tore through the small shop in his wake. That was one more reason Jo hated this place. It didn't have a foyer to keep the people inside from freezing every time someone opened the door. She should have insisted on meeting Quinn at the diner. At least at

Hank's a person could hear themselves think, have a cup of coffee that didn't cost a day's salary, and know who was sitting in the adjacent booth. Plus, no one ran a short-order line like Hank, and even at three thirty in the afternoon he'd serve her breakfast to make up for the one she'd skipped earlier.

"Don't mind him." Dickinson took a long pull on his coffee. "He forgets to engage his brain before his mouth. You think there was something more going on with your call?"

"I owe it to the man to find out."

He rolled the edge of his cup along the table. She recognized the stalling tactic and waited him out.

"You know," he finally said. "You're going to make a great sergeant someday."

"Someday."

"Don't give up." He smiled mischievously. "I have aspirations of sleeping my way to the top." He slid out of his chair before she could hit him.

"It's your lucky day. I have it on good authority that Cameron's available."

"Nah." He nodded at her notes. "Good luck finding your answers."

She glanced at the clock on the wall. It confirmed her fears. "The person I was supposed to meet is half an hour late. I might have to look for answers elsewhere."

"You'll find them." He started to weave around the chairs to the door.

"Hey, Eli," she called after him.

He turned.

"Thanks."

He touched his forehead, then his heart, and swept his hand in a small flourish. When he got to the door, he held it wide. A small, dark woman slid past him and into the shop, blowing into her bare hands to warm them while she surveyed the room.

Dickinson made eye contact with Jo and held four fingers in front of his chest—a signal to make sure she was okay. Jo nodded and he left.

Quinn picked her way through the crowd. Unlike yesterday, she was wearing a proper coat. Patagonia. A style that Jo had looked at earlier in the season and decided she couldn't afford.

"You're late," Jo said.

43

Quinn drew her bag over her head and flopped into Dickinson's vacant chair. "I can leave."

"Or you can grab yourself a cup of coffee and we can talk."

"You buying?"

Jo sipped her tepid tea. "Nope."

Quinn rummaged in the bag and dragged out a file. "Here." She tossed it in front of Jo. A stack of printed emails fanned across the table. "You might as well start reading."

9

Quinn stood in line for coffee and sneaked a peek at the detective. Wyatt thumbed through the file, turning pages as she read. Her expression never changed, but around the fourth email she started to take notes.

Lots of people crowded the Bean today. Every time someone opened the door, the pounding sound of rain followed them in, but no one looked up. No one cared—exactly the reason Quinn had chosen this place over the diner. Here there were no ranchers camped out in their booths like they fucking owned them, giving her stink-eye when she walked in.

The woman in front of Quinn ordered one of those froufrou eighteen-syllable skim-soy-triple-something bullshit drinks, and then eyed the pastry display. For someone who knew exactly what she wanted in a drink, she couldn't figure out what to stuff in her pie hole to save her life.

"Try the peanut butter chocolate protein balls," Quinn suggested.

Indecision clouded the woman's face. "Are they good?"

Quinn had no idea, but with any luck, the woman had a nut allergy. "Fabulous."

The woman dithered some more.

"Jesus Christ, lady. Pick something."

That ruffled the woman's feathers, but before she could reply with something phenomenally stupid, the door opened and the woman's eyes widened.

"Just the coffee," she said to the barista. "To go."

The drone of the shop crowd quieted, then picked up with increased ferocity. Cold clung to the person who fell in line behind Quinn. She glanced over her shoulder. No wonder everyone had shut up. Even in the

45

Bean, this guy stood out. Everything about him was massive, especially his don't-fuck-with-me aura. The tat climbing up his neck was a bonus. "Hey."

He chucked his chin. Didn't smile. "You're up." His voice rumbled.

"Double-shot espresso." Quinn leaned sideways against the counter while she paid and boldly checked him out. Typical biker type: scraggly beard, scarred hands from too many bar brawls, layers of long sleeves that probably covered blue-ink prison tattoos. She'd bet her espresso he was holding—he didn't have the teeth for meth; maybe heroin. Although frankly, his corded neck suggested a physique too muscular for him to be sampling much of his own product.

The clerk handed Quinn her change, and she moved down to the other end of the counter to wait for her drink.

Most of the people in the Bean were trying to hide their curiosity in a don't-make-eye-contact-with-the-wild-animal type of way that didn't change the fact that they were all keeping Scary Dude in their periphery. Then there was Wyatt. She'd pushed her chair away from the table, her feet planted flat. Ready. It gave her away. Scary Dude marked her as a cop immediately. He dropped his right elbow against his waist. So he was armed. This could get interesting.

The gal behind the counter asked him what he wanted.

He towered over the counter, his voice low and quiet. "Mocha, please."

Aw, Scary Dude had a sweet side. And manners. His mother would be proud. Or not.

A chain tethered his tooled leather wallet to his belt. Even from several feet away, Quinn saw the wad of bills inside when he paid. Left a tip, too. Business must be good.

The barista slid Quinn's espresso across the counter.

Now what? The place was still packed, despite a couple of tourists grabbing their stuff and getting out. Were they cowardly or smart? Probably wouldn't know until the dust settled. She started toward Wyatt. The officer held up a couple of fingers, a subtle hint that Quinn chose to ignore.

"I don't know what you're planning, but he's made you," Quinn said when she arrived at the table.

Wyatt scowled. "I'm not trying to hide."

"Good thing." Quinn scraped the chair across the tiles and sat with her back to Scary Dude. She'd never had a bodyguard before; damn if she wasn't going to take advantage of it. If nothing else, she'd have a front-row seat to the action.

"So." The detective adjusted her position slightly to improve her view over Quinn's shoulder. "Tell me about the laptop."

"You're kidding, right?"

"You asked us to retrieve a laptop computer from Mr. Horton."

"Isn't Godzilla over there a bit more pressing?"

"Last I checked, ordering coffee didn't land a person on the ten-most-wanted list."

"Did you see his tats?"

"And?"

"Shouldn't you harass him or something? He's got a gun."

A grim expression settled on Wyatt's face. "So do I." She stood.

Quinn's head toggled between the mountain approaching them and the detective. The front-row seat no longer seemed like such a great idea.

Wyatt held her ground.

Quinn stood, too. It gave her a head start to the door if she needed to retreat.

Scary Dude placed his cup on the table, and then with unanticipated quickness, he lunged at the detective.

Wyatt giggled.

Giggled. A cop. What the hell?

Wyatt pushed against the man's chest, unable to break the bear hug. "Put me down before I shoot you."

"Again?" He lowered her to the ground, but kept an arm around her shoulder.

"Geez, let it go. Statute of limitations ran out on that a long time ago."

"You look great, Jo-elle."

Quinn would have sworn the cop blushed.

"How long you in town?" she asked.

"Oh, you know. Till it's time."

Up close, Quinn saw that the tattoo on his neck was some sort of coat of arms or something.

Wyatt handed him his mocha. "You staying at the ranch?"

Scary Dude smiled. It completely killed his don't-fuck-with-me aura. "Tonight, anyway. I'll swing by the house later."

Something flashed across Wyatt's face too fast for Quinn to catch, but it obviously left the detective uncomfortable. "I've moved." She removed a business card from her portfolio. "Here's my cell."

He flipped the card over. "Looks like we have some catching up to do." He tipped his cup to Wyatt, then to Quinn. "Sorry to interrupt."

"No worries." Still standing, Quinn admired his ass as he left. One thing she loved about Echo Valley was the Wranglers—the jeans, not necessarily the cowboy in them. The detective seemed to like them too. At least this particular pair. "You shot him?"

The girl who'd giggled disappeared. "He pissed me off." Wyatt settled into her chair, pen poised over her notebook. "I believe you were going to tell me about a laptop."

"I already told you that." Quinn dragged her espresso in front of her and removed the lid to let it cool. "I'm pretty sure we were going to talk about threats."

Detective Wyatt remained silent. Probably practicing her Jedi mind trick or something.

"You think I wanted to steal it," Quinn said finally.

Wyatt raised her eyebrows. "Guilty conscience?"

"Let's set some ground rules. You don't insult me, and I'll answer your stupid questions."

The corners of the detective's mouth twitched just enough to give her away. "Deal."

It was a small victory, but Quinn suspected it was the best she'd get from Wyatt. "It had our capstone project on it. A video game we designed."

"Talk to me about the one Professor Lucas tried to steal from Tye."

"Not much to say. Tye designed it over a year ago. Lucas tried to bogart it."

"Why didn't Tye sell it?"

"The response from one of the beta testers made him rethink the game." Quinn lowered the zipper on her jacket. "He abandoned the project."

"Who were the beta testers?"

"I was one of them. I met Tye in a class we shared on storytelling for digital design. We hit it off."

"So you played the game?"

"Kind of hard to give feedback without playing."

"Touché." Wyatt raised her cup in a toast. "What did you think about it?"

In the light, Quinn noticed the dent around Wyatt's left ring finger. Maybe she didn't wear her wedding ring on duty. Or maybe she annoyed some poor sap as much as she annoyed Quinn. "A bit lacking in story but technically challenging. Appropriate gameplay level lengths. Responsive. World-building needed some fleshing out."

"Overall that sounds like a decent assessment."

Quinn shrugged. "It was a solid game."

The detective returned to taking notes. "Who else reviewed it?"

"As far as I know, there were only three of us. Ronny, me, and Derek."

"You have last names?"

Quinn worried the cuticle around her thumb, but caught herself and shoved her hands in her jacket pockets. "Ronny's last name is Buck. He's the third guy in our capstone project."

Wyatt paused ever so slightly before writing *Buck* on her page, and Quinn knew she recognized the name. Probably was wondering if he had an active warrant or something.

"What about Derek?" she asked.

"You'd have to ask Ronny. He was the one who introduced him to Tye. I never met him in person."

"Did they like the game?"

"Everyone liked it."

Wyatt looked up, her pen still on the paper. "I don't understand the problem, then."

"Welcome to the club."

The detective flipped through her pages, searching for something. "Did Tye have a cat?" she finally asked.

"What? No."

"Are you certain?"

"You asked me a question, I answered. Yes, Detective, I'm positive. He was allergic. Some kid brought a service dog or something into the computer lab one day, and I thought I was going to have to rush Tye to the ER. He couldn't even stay in the same room."

"Any idea why he had a cat dish at his house?"

"How the hell should I know?" Quinn snapped the lid back onto her cup. "Can we get back to the threats?"

Wyatt tapped her pen against the notebook. "Indulge me. I've only got a few more questions."

"I'm beginning to doubt you understand the definition of few."

"Did Tye own any video games?"

Quinn snorted and leaned forward, curling over the table. "He designed games. He had a shitload of them."

That shut the detective up. Even the tapping stopped. Quinn could practically see the gears turning in her head.

"Did you enjoy the football game Sunday night?"

The detective had seriously lost her mind. "What are you talking about? I didn't go to any football game."

"You said you went to the game but Tye didn't show up."

Quinn laughed, started to answer, but got caught up in the ridiculousness of it and laughed even harder. "Do I look like the football type?"

"Is there a type?"

"There is. It ain't me. The game was *Dogs of War*."

"Okay." It was obvious Wyatt had no idea what the hell Quinn was talking about, and Quinn had no intention of bailing her out. "Where was it held?" the detective finally asked.

Quinn tilted her head back and rubbed her eyes. "Have you *ever* played a video game?"

"What's that one with the little plumber guy that jumps around?"

"How old *are* you?" She hadn't intended to say it out loud.

Wyatt scowled. "What's that got to do with my question?"

"*Dogs of War* is a multiplayer game." She paused for a spark of recognition. "*Fortnite*?" Nothing. "We meet online."

"So, Tye might never have left his house Sunday night?"

"He plays from the comfort of his gaming chair." Damn, she still hadn't gotten used to past tense. "Played."

"Is that why there are speakers?"

"Audio is a huge component of gaming. Tye had a pretty sweet setup. The chair's a couple months old, but he always had the latest console."

"Is that the joystick?"

"It's a lot more than a joystick. But yeah. It's how you control your game, your character, all that."

"Did he have a lot of those?"

"I'm pretty sure he kept every one he ever owned. He was a game designer. Knowing what came before is always a good thing."

"Did he have a storage locker someplace?"

"Don't you think he'd have stashed all that shit?" Then it hit her. "They weren't there, were they? The consoles, the computer. That's why the fifty questions."

"It's too early in the investigation to draw conclusions."

"Conclusions? The shit's either there or it's not."

"I can't comment on an ongoing—"

"You never planned to help me, did you?" Quinn reached across the table and snatched the folder containing her emails. "I should have known."

"It's a crime to harass someone in the State of Colorado either in person or by any electronic means. For me to make my case, I have to prove that someone intended to alarm you."

Quinn jammed the folder into her bookbag. "This should be a slam dunk, then."

Wyatt leaned back. "Why did you send yourself threatening emails?"

Quinn's mouth dropped. Was Wyatt really that stupid?

"I read the email headers," the detective continued. "The most egregious threats were from your own account."

"You don't believe me."

The detective's face softened and she lowered her voice. "You just lost a friend. Your capstone project is missing. Life is rough right now." She scrawled a telephone number on the back of her business card. "Call them. They're good people. They can help."

Quinn read the words above the number. "You think I need a counselor?"

"Talking to a professional is never a bad idea."

"I thought I was."

The display on Wyatt's phone lit up. "I'm sorry, I've got to take this. I'll only be a moment."

Coffee and anger boiled in Quinn's stomach. She lurched from the table, leaving her half-empty espresso cup behind.

The police detective remained impassive as she answered her phone.

Quinn was on her own, and suddenly everyone in the coffee shop looked dangerous.

10

Jo moved the phone to her other ear as if that would buffer the din of the coffee shop. "The district attorney does what now?"

"Owns the house Horton killed himself in. Well, he and his wife, Alice," Squint said. "It's one of several properties they own—in addition to the ranch they have out on East Mesa."

"Wonderful." Jo pinched the bridge of her nose. "Considering they live in one of the Victorians on Broadmoor, any idea who actually lives on Fifth?"

"Someone who likes chintz."

"Don't forget the gun case." She flipped her notes closed and slid the legal pad into her portfolio. "How'd the autopsy go?"

"Nothing unexpected. We'll know more when the tox screen comes back from the lab. Doc Ingersleben confirmed the identification with a family member. It's definitely Tye Horton."

"Doc offer any conjecture?"

"Does he ever?" Papers rustled on Squint's side of the connection. "Do you know a John Dryden?"

Jo mentally reviewed her caseload. "Name doesn't ring a bell. Should it?"

"He's a poet."

"Ingersleben quoted a poet?" She'd have to expand her reading list if this was a new trend. "My meeting with Quinn just ended. I'll pick you up in five and we can drop in on the DA."

* * *

"Beware the fury of a patient man." Squint reached for the stately door leading to the district attorney's office.

Jo entered the lobby and wiped her feet on the rectangular mat. "I'd be more concerned about the impatience of a furious woman."

"John Dryden." Squint slapped his hat against his thigh to dislodge any errant snowflakes and followed Jo into the building. "You now possess the means to impress Ingersleben."

The district attorney's office occupied space in a two-story building still known as the Old Post Office by the locals despite the fact that attorneys had been discussing cases in the building for more than forty years. The first time Jo saw inside, she'd been awed. She was eight years old and her father had parked her in a wooden chair in the lobby while he conferred with a deputy district attorney about a case. From her vantage, she enjoyed watching the bustle of people going in and out. Even today, the twentieth-century marble floors and gleaming brass banisters impressed Jo. It seemed fitting that the building reflected the gravitas of the few employees in Echo Valley who routinely wore business suits.

Jo approached the reception counter and greeted a woman behind thick glass. "Hi, Martha. Is Mr. Walsenberg available?"

"He just got back from court. Let me check." She phoned his office, spoke briefly, and hung up. "Go on up. He has to step out for a moment, but he'll be right back. Make yourself comfortable." She pressed a button, and the electronic lock on the security door popped open.

Jo opened the door for Squint and signaled him through with a grand flourish. "After you."

He reached around her with his long arms and grabbed the door. "You know I hate when you do that."

"Let it not be said that I don't know how to act like a gentleman."

"I don't believe that's ever been a concern," Squint said.

The area behind closed doors wasn't nearly as stately as the lobby. Beyond the receptionist's station, meeting rooms opened off the main space, which served quintuple duty as conference area, law library, storage repository, to-be-filed zone, and lunchroom. Jo preceded Squint through the room and up the rear staircase to the second floor, where Walsenberg and two of the four deputy district attorneys had their offices.

The door to the district attorney's office was open, and they stepped inside.

A large desk dominated the room, but unlike the chaos downstairs, here nothing was out of place.

Frost glazed the edges of the large window opposite the door. Plaques and diplomas hung in uniform rows on either side of the glass. For all the times Jo had been in the building, she'd never been close enough to check out the collection. Harvard Law. Assorted awards. Recognition by service clubs. A photo with Xavier Buck, another with the governor, a final one of the DA midcast while fly-fishing in the middle of a river.

No doubt about it. Zachary Emerson Walsenberg appeared to be as successful as a man with a nine-syllable name should be.

Artfully arranged personal photographs decorated the credenza under the window. His wife barrel-racing, her head held high, eyes already looking for the next challenge while her chestnut mare tucked tight around the fifty-five-gallon drum. Another of Alice, this time wearing a daring magenta gown and dancing with her husband at some gala.

In the center of the credenza was a family portrait in an elaborate crystal frame. The photo had been taken by the river, and the district attorney and his wife sat on a large boulder. They leaned into each other and smiled into the camera as if daring anyone to find fault with their life. Their daughter sat cross-legged in front, not touching her parents, her gaze focused on something low and left of the photographer. Jo picked up a black-and-white close-up of the teenage girl peeking at the camera through a veil of dark hair, noting that it had been grouped with two other photos of the same girl. She must be their daughter, but Jo couldn't remember her name.

She scanned the array of photos again. None were of Walsenberg's son.

"That's my daughter, Olivia." The DA entered the room with his hand outstretched.

"She's beautiful." Jo replaced the photo and grasped the DA's hand. Warm, with a firm handshake. A welcome relief from men who either felt it necessary to crush her hand in conquest or barely squeezed as if she were a delicate flower, easily bruised.

"Obviously, she takes after her mother." He turned to Squint and shook hands, then motioned for them to sit. "To what do I owe the pleasure, Detectives?"

"We're investigating an incident that occurred on Fifth Street." Squint held his hat on his lap. "Records show the property belongs to you, and we are hoping you can provide some information about your tenants."

Out of habit, Jo watched the DA closely. She and Squint had interviewed enough people together that they had a routine. One of them took the lead during the interview. The other watched the person being questioned. But talking to the DA was like chatting with another police officer. They were all on the same side.

Walsenberg took his own seat behind the desk. "I don't remember seeing a report about anything on Fifth. Nothing serious, I hope."

"Can you tell us the name of your tenants?" Squint pressed.

So far, neither man had answered the other's question. Jo bit back a sigh. Typical interview.

"An older lady. Eva something?" Walsenberg tilted his head back, and his eyes went left while he tried to remember. "I'm afraid I don't know. Alice manages our rental properties."

"We're more interested in the man renting the converted garage."

"There shouldn't be anyone there. The prior owners never pulled permits when they renovated it. It's not up to code."

"Does your lease allow a tenant to sublease?"

The DA leaned forward. "What happened?"

Squint hesitated, and Jo knew he was deciding how much to disclose. "It appears a man shot himself while living in the garage."

"That's horrible. Let me call my wife. If she's home, she'll be able to pull the file on the tenants." He picked up the receiver and punched three buttons.

"Have you ever met Tye Horton?" Squint asked.

The DA's fingers hit two buttons at once, and he clicked down the handset before starting over. "Not that I recall. Is that the young man who shot himself?"

"Yes."

"A shame. Perhaps Alice will know more."

The three sat in silence while Walsenberg completed dialing, then hit a final button and placed the call on speaker. After four rings, a recorded voice mail message clicked on, and he disconnected the call.

"I'm sorry, I forgot she's spearheading a new project and she's throwing a stakeholders' meeting at the house. I'll speak to her tonight and get the information for you. Will tomorrow be okay, or should I call one of you this evening?"

"Tomorrow would be just fine, sir," Squint said, and stood.

Jo followed his lead.

"Glad to help." He retrieved a folder from his briefcase and opened it in front of him as the detectives took their leave.

Jo paused in the doorway. "How did you know Mr. Horton was young?"

Walsenberg glanced up from the paper in front of him. "Excuse me?"

"Detective MacAllister never mentioned anything about Mr. Horton's age. How did you know to call him a young man?"

The DA leaned back in his chair and rested his elbows on the armrests in an attitude of openness. "Well, I guess I assumed that someone living in a tiny garage was just starting out in life. Was I wrong?"

He wore his prosecutorial face; she'd seen it in the courtroom. Charismatic and charming in the opening arguments, ruthless on cross-examination.

"No," she replied. "He was twenty-two."

He steepled his fingers. "All right, then."

"Thank you, sir."

Jo waited until they were outside before saying, "Why do I think the DA isn't being completely honest?"

They stood on the edge of the sidewalk, and Squint settled his hat on his head. "What makes you think that?"

Fat flakes fell at a steady pace. She ran her hand across the hood of the car and created a small pile. It was good snowball snow. Not too wet, not too dry. "Women's intuition."

"Last I checked, we worked under the probable-cause doctrine."

"I don't know. The *young* thing bothered me." She scooped up a handful of the snow. Squint watched her progress, but she couldn't tell whether he was concerned about becoming a target or merely thinking about what she'd said.

He shrugged. "It was a reasonable assumption."

She tossed the snowball back and forth between her hands before tossing it into the gutter. "Yeah. I know."

11

The centerpiece was off. Alice Ambrose Walsenberg crouched eye level with the top of the walnut buffet and slid the evergreens and white roses to the left until the vase sat evenly between the tiered finger sandwich tower and the antique silver coffee urn. Nestled among the evergreens, the roses gave off an elegant air. She stood back. The footed dishes and china platters coordinated nicely and added depth to the serving station.

"Do you have a minute, Mom?" Olivia spoke from behind her.

A holly sprig drooped at an awkward angle, and Alice bolstered it with one of the delicate snow-white buds. "Can it wait? The guests will be here in half an hour, and I haven't even dressed yet."

"No one's going to notice if every leaf isn't exactly perfect."

"I will." Satisfied, she turned to her daughter. Olivia wore jeans and a bulky sweater that hid her slenderness. "You're going to change, aren't you?"

Olivia's familiar exaggerated sigh drove Alice nuts. "What's wrong with what I'm wearing?"

"Mrs. Baxter is coming."

Olivia widened her eyes in mock surprise. Another one of her recent annoying affectations. "Not Mrs. Baxter! Let me get my opera gloves!"

Alice couldn't help but smile. Mrs. Edith May Baxter was legendary in Echo Valley—and owned the only larger Victorian on the Avenue. To this day the Ambroses and the Baxters maintained the uneasy alliance that had begun in the late 1800s when both families settled in the Valley. The Baxters had made their fortune in mining, first in silver and then in natural gas. The Ambroses had gambled on land, quietly buying up enormous swaths of acreage that held all the resources the Baxters sought. The relationship was at times downright fractious, but always profitable.

"Why don't you pull your hair back?" She brushed a strand off Olivia's forehead. "What's the point of a beautiful face if no one can see it?"

Her daughter drew back. "I'm going to the library. No one cares."

A flicker of guilt accompanied Alice's relief. Edith Baxter was a dowager of considerable influence. Her support of this project fairly guaranteed that the other women would fall into line with open checkbooks. Plus, her connections at the state legislature could certainly help.

"The party should be finished by seven."

"Don't forget I've got rehearsal tonight."

She had forgotten. The preparations for the meeting had overshadowed everything. "Before you know it, you'll be thanking the Academy."

"I'm the Ghost of Christmas Yet to Come. I don't say a word."

Alice should have known that. "Then why do you need to rehearse?" She tried to make light to cover her blunder.

"Avoiding Mrs. Baxter seems like a pretty good reason. Can I borrow the car?"

"No, you may not. You only have a permit."

"I've been driving for years."

Olivia's pout added a sultriness to her face that Alice hadn't noticed before. This last year had passed in a haze, and her daughter had grown up while Alice's head was turned. "On the ranch."

"Which is a lot tougher than town streets."

"I don't have time for this conversation. The answer is no." Alice's voice was sharper than she'd intended.

Olivia dipped her head, and her hair cascaded past her cheek. "You always let Derek."

"What was that?" Alice asked, even though she'd heard every word.

Her daughter's head popped up. "Nothing. You better get dressed. Mrs. Baxter will be here any minute, and your hair's a mess." She grabbed a pastel-pink French macaron from a gold-rimmed plate and left the room. A moment later, the front door closed.

Alice rearranged the remaining confections. Shoot. She'd forgotten to ask Olivia when she'd be back. Maybe that had been her daughter's plan all along. Distract and evade. As far as tactics went, it was effective.

Regardless, it was too late to worry about that now. Just enough time remained. She walked down the hall and put her back against the front door. Closed her eyes. Drew a deep breath. Lemon oil, aromas from the kitchen, evergreens, and roses. Comforting. Warm. Perfect. She opened her eyes. The twelve-foot Douglas fir dominated the foyer, clear white lights flickering among crystal ornaments. The original parquet floors gleamed. Old and new. Mother and daughter.

Her fingers wandered across the door molding behind her, searching for the initials she'd carved into the wood when she was a little girl despite knowing they'd been sanded away. At least Olivia had never taken a pocketknife to the walnut panels. Were all mothers and daughters cursed to be at loggerheads?

An Ambrose had lived in the house since it was built in 1861 by the widow of a wealthy banker who had scandalized Bostonian society by having the audacity to leave Beantown behind. That she established herself in the Wild West with her first husband's money and her second husband's love made it all the more prurient. But no one had done more to ennoble the house than Alice's mother, and her spirit practically infused the home. She'd gutted the interior, renovated the rooms, and updated all the wiring and pipes hiding within the walls. Thanks to her, they now enjoyed heated floors and en suite bathrooms. Thanks to Mother, every bedroom had those monstrous walk-in closets.

Alice pushed away from the door. Time ticked, and she had to dress. One last look at the buffet. A harder look at the bar. Plenty of wines at the ready for those desiring something more fortifying than tea. If it weren't for Edith Baxter, Alice wouldn't be offering tea at all, but some branch on Edith's family oak hailed from an obscure hamlet in North Cornwall and she acted as if she were descended from Arthur himself. And heaven forbid if Alice didn't steep the leaves—always loose; bags were for heathens—long enough. She ducked behind the bar. Maybe another wine. She rooted through the choices and selected her favorite Condrieu Viognier. Edith could keep her tea.

The caterers had placed a copper tub of ice out for the whites, and she added the bottle to the collection already chilling. Few things loosened purse strings more effectively than a silky Viognier paired with cheese. She'd learned that from her mother.

Three caterers from the Table, a farm-to-fork downtown restaurant, clattered in the kitchen, putting the finishing touches on the selection of hors d'oeuvres. It smelled wonderful. Her stomach growled. When was the last time she'd eaten?

The grandfather clock chimed the quarter hour.

"Jiminy Christmas." She hurried up the stairs, unbuttoning her shirt as she went. Zach's bedroom door stood open, and she hesitated only a moment before drawing it shut.

By habit she looked right as she entered her room, refusing to even glance at the barricaded closet.

Neatly arranged shoes and handbags crowded the floor at the foot of the bed. She flicked through the hangers on the garment rack next to the window. Flannel, tweed, black. She spied the cream slacks tucked in with the recent dry cleaning hanging at the end of the rack and exchanged her jeans for the soft wool. The snow outside dictated something warmer than the rainbow-hued blouses suspended from the second rack, and she chose a claret cowl neck. Hopefully it would add some color to her face. The cashmere sweater slid like a waterfall over her head. That was another thing her mother had taught her: dress simply, but buy quality.

Alice sat at her makeup table. Sometime during the last year she'd learned to focus only on her face. It was like studying an old photograph of herself, where everything behind her had faded away. She applied a dusting of blush, a swipe of mascara, a touch of gloss. Subtle.

Olivia was right. Her hair was a fright. She rubbed a dab of pomade between her palms and smoothed the dull gray bob. Olivia had once said her mother's hair framed her face like a storm cloud. It hadn't turned gray overnight, like in gothic novels, but the transition had been startlingly quick. Only Olivia had been crass enough to mention it.

The diamond studs Zach had given her last Christmas winked in the dull light seeping through the window. She stabbed the posts through her lobes, screwed on the backings. The doorbell rang.

"Jesus, Mary, and Joseph."

She sprang from the tufted stool in search of her wine-hued heels and then slipped them on.

Her cell phone rang, muffled as if far away. "Please don't be Edith. Please, please, please."

It took her a moment to locate her jeans, and she shook her phone from the pocket. It bounced on the bed, and her husband grinned back from the home screen. "Sorry, honey. No time." She bent over to grab the phone. Denied the call.

Standing, she accidentally found herself reflected in the dressing table mirror. The armoire behind her filled the reflection, and it was almost as if she didn't exist. She'd bought the largest wardrobe she could find and removed the doors so she could see all the corners. No surprises. The heavy piece almost managed to hide the outline of the closet it blocked. A closet so dark and monstrous a woman could lose herself in it.

A closet her mother had built.

Alice smoothed her sweater.

Showtime.

* * *

Edith Baxter was always the last to leave. Odd, considering she always acted so put out when she arrived. Alice escorted her to the door just as Zach entered the house. Nineteen years of marriage had failed to dull his looks, and he carried himself as erect as ever. He offered Edith a dazzling smile before leaning in to kiss his wife's cheek. Alice forced herself not to flinch. Not in front of Edith Baxter. Not in front of anyone. Even herself.

"Please tell me you aren't leaving already, Mrs. Baxter," he said.

Edith looked over the wire rims of her glasses. "No need to turn on the charm, Zachary. Your wife already achieved her goal."

"Then you know how I feel. I can't deny my Alice anything." Zach offered the elder woman his arm. "May I at least walk you home?"

Edith released the death grip she had on Alice's arm and wedged her hand into the crook of Zach's elbow. "Ever the gallant." Edith had a soft spot for Zach. Most women did, Alice included. Even now. Edith patted his forearm with her gloved hand. "I still won't vote for you."

"The world would stop rotating if you did." He rebuttoned his coat. "But not to worry. I'm at the end of my term. Time to let someone else take the reins. Perhaps your grandson? Tell him to come see me. He'd make a fine district attorney."

"Tell him yourself. I'm too old to play your messenger. And you can unbutton your coat. My car is right outside, and I'm not too old to walk along a shoveled walkway." She glanced back at Alice. "Lovely as always, my dear. Although next time, try not to let the tea steep so long. It was a tad bitter."

Alice's smile held. Smiling was another lesson she'd learned from her mother, and over the years, she'd perfected it. She grabbed the door handle and resisted the urge to swing it right into the old biddy. "One of these days, I'm going to brew you the perfect cuppa."

Edith tightened her scarf and hid the crepey skin of her neck from the cold. "Let's hope."

She held the rail as she descended the stairs.

"Maybe she'll break a hip," Zach whispered.

"Zachary Emerson Walsenberg." She gave him a playful swat.

"Tell me you weren't thinking the same thing."

Not that she'd ever admit.

Edith Baxter opened the door of her Bentley Bentayga. When Alice had bought an Audi last year, Edith had clucked her inevitable disapproval. Apparently, it was okay to import from England but not from Germany.

"Sorry I missed your call earlier." Alice waved to the back of Edith's head and closed the door.

"I had two police detectives in my office." He shook out of his overcoat and hung it on the coatrack, then unwound his scarf.

She took the length of cashmere from him and looped it over an empty hook. "They finally caught you, did they?"

"They wanted to know about our rental property on Fifth." He veered into the dining room, plucked an opened bottle from the copper tub, and poured himself a glass of wine. He wagged the bottle in her direction.

She shook her head. "I spoke to Mrs. Petersen's son the other day. I knew you wouldn't mind, and I told him not to worry about the rent this month. He has enough to think about, what with his mom still in the hospital and all."

"The main house isn't the issue. The detectives wanted to know about the occupant of the garage."

"We don't rent the garage."

"That's what I told them. Mrs. Peterson must have subleased it." He carried his glass into the living room and settled into one of the club chairs, his arms cast wide across the distressed leather as if inviting her in for a hug.

She stood in the center of the room. To someone who didn't know him, he appeared as open as his arms. But she did know him.

He lifted the delicate glass to his mouth and sipped the straw-colored liquid. "So you don't know why some guy named Tye Horton blew his brains out all over our garage?"

"No." Her throat constricted. She'd have that wine after all.

12

Jo drove through the open gate into Lupine Ledge Ranch. It had been in the Teague family since Aiden's great-grandfather turned his back on South Carolina and headed to Colorado. Local lore claimed he'd tired of the toil of tobacco farming and sought the adventure and riches of mining, but soon discovered it was more profitable to outfit miners than work next to them. The successive generations had chiseled away at the wealth and size of the ranch until only fifty acres and the namesake ledge remained.

The modest house was dark and the barn was closed up, but Aiden's truck was backed up to the open doors of the enclosed arena. Jo left her car between the two buildings. Underfoot, the snow crunched. Only seven thirty and already the top layer had hardened.

It had been months since she'd seen Aiden. Weeks since she'd thought about him, at least until today. That had been a surprise. Disorienting. Still pleasant.

She entered the arena. The overhead lights lit up the inside like high noon. Three barrels marked a triangular race course. Even standing, she felt herself dig her heels low, lean forward. Imagined loping the figure eight between the two side barrels. Coming out of the pocket, the burst to the final barrel. The balls-to-the-wall hundred-and-five-foot sprint to the finish line.

Her heartbeat picked up; her breath quickened. So many memories in this arena. Not all involving horses.

She turned her back on the arena and sidled through the open door of the utility room. "Wow, that didn't take long."

Aiden nodded a greeting as he shook out a length of rope over a deer carcass on the floor. "Old man Lyster's place is overrun. Thought I'd help him out with my private property tag. You want to pull or scrape?"

He'd changed out of his earlier clothes. Now he wore a pair of Carhartts and a faded green Henley with a hole along the seam of his right cuff. Both were speckled with blood. His hunter-orange vest hung from one of ten pegs that lined the wall. Most of the others held neatly wrapped halters and bridles. A sawhorse, an old refrigerator, and a canted desk and equally rickety chair rounded out the furnishings pushed against the walls.

"Pull."

He looped a rope under the deer's chin at the base of the neck. Even under the Henley, Jo saw his muscles jump as he hoisted the doe so it hung suspended from the rafters. He looked good. Fit.

She hung her jacket on the only other empty peg, pushed up the sleeves of her sweater, and cuffed her Oxford shirt. "I nicked the hide once helping my dad. I've never lived it down."

"I remember. My barn jacket's there if you want. Gloves are on the shelf."

The canvas jacket hung to her thighs and protected her work clothes. She knew from experience that the gloves he bought fit his oversized paws. She drew two latex gloves out of the back pocket of her slacks and held them up. "Have gloves, will travel." One of the perks of being a cop. At least until the gloves went through the wash. The dryer was worse.

He cut around the deer's elbows and then slid the knife under the skin and sliced toward the chest. The doe was a decent size. He'd already field-dressed it, and the cavity yawned empty.

Echo Valley kids knew where their meat came from. She'd grown up eating elk and venison her dad had brought back from his hunting trips. Over the years, two supermarkets had sprouted in the valley to feed those who didn't live as close to the land. One was a chain market, and the other catered to those who wanted to eat organic but didn't want to go to the trouble of raising or hunting it themselves. Even now, the police department training officer had to schedule qualifications and courses around hunting season or no one would show up.

Aiden sliced the hide around the neck and made a single incision from the neck to the belly. Jo reached in and tugged the cut corner of the hide, holding it taut. He covered her hand with his while he sliced through the first few inches of exposed membrane, careful not to cut the hair. Then he moved on.

The carcass started to swivel, and Jo steadied it. White hair lined the doe's ears. Impossibly long eyelashes framed clouded brown eyes that stared into nothingness.

Her throat tightened. She still tugged the hide taut, but she studied her boots. She'd seen too much death the last two days.

They worked in silence until the hide was almost completely stripped from the doe.

"Want to talk about it?"

For a second she thought he meant the deer.

"You and Cameron," he prompted. "What happened?"

She shrugged. "He wasn't you."

Aiden nudged her aside, then took the hide in both his hands and drew it off the final few inches. "Seems to me you knew that when you married him."

"He made me feel beautiful."

"Since when did you need a man for that?"

"Funny thing about men. They can't always convince you you're beautiful, but they have a knack for making you believe you're ugly."

"You're looking tired."

She started to push her hair off her face, saw her gloves, and stripped them off. "Probably not the best time to tell me that."

He peeled off his own gloves and lobbed them into the trash can. He crossed over to the mini fridge and tossed her a beer.

She caught it and raised the can in a toast. "I'm staying with Dad until I get things sorted out."

"You can always bunk here. Key's in the same spot it's always been."

The can opened with a gush, and she sipped away the foam before it overflowed. "You really should find a better hiding spot. Besides, what if I get drunk one night and try to have my way with you?"

"I'll get more beer."

Jo stuck her tongue out at him. "Dad's place is temporary. Just until I figure out how things are going to shake out. How long you in town for?"

"Might be seeing a lot more of me soon."

She'd heard that before too. "Not sure how much of you I can handle. You're looking pretty scruffy these days."

"One of the benefits of the job." He ran his free hand over his beard. "It drove me crazy over the summer, but it feels pretty good now."

"You keeping yourself safe?"

He dug his fingernail under the beer tab. "As much as possible."

Which probably wasn't nearly enough, considering the company he kept. "Well, for what it's worth, I'm looking forward to the day you shave."

"You and me both." He opened his beer. "Sorry I interrupted you today. Interview?"

"Working a dead body."

"What do you have?"

She jerked her head toward the arena and exchanged his canvas coat for her warmer one. "A single male with a catastrophic gunshot wound to the head. Shotgun inside, expelled shell where you'd expect it, and a near-empty bottle of liquid courage on the table next to him. No obvious signs of forced entry, but the door was unlocked, so no help there."

"Did you find a note?" he asked.

"Nope. The woman I was talking to at the Bean—she was the one who called it in. College classmate of the guy."

"She go inside?"

Jo shrugged. "I asked, she said no."

"But?"

Hunches had no standing in a courtroom, but they thrived in police work. "Something wasn't right."

"Grief makes people react in unexpected ways. What's your gut tell you?"

That I need to file for divorce. "Something's off."

He considered her words. "Do you know what?"

They stopped at the open doors, and Aiden killed most of the arena lights. Jo leaned her forearms against the tailgate of his truck. "I got back to the station last night, and Quinn—that's her name—was waiting for me. Wanted to report she was being threatened. That's what we were talking about when you entered the Bean. She brought copies of the emails."

"Legit?"

"It occurred to me that the two incidents could be linked. One guy shows up dead and now his friend is receiving threats? But the only current thing I could find linking them is a video game they're designing together as their capstone project." She tipped her beer can in little circles on the corner of the bed. "Oh, and get this, Ronny Buck is the other person they're collaborating with."

"There's a name I haven't thought about in a while."

"I'm dropping in on him tomorrow."

He leaned his back against the truck and propped his boot against the tire. "Squint going with you?"

"Ah, look at you," she teased. "You're worried about me."

He took a leisurely pull on his beer. "More concerned for Ronny."

"As long as his daddy isn't around, shouldn't be a problem. Besides, the threats were bogus."

"How do you know that?"

The arena lights were stingy with their glow, but even so, she suddenly felt exposed. "The only emails that contained actual threats where ones she'd sent to herself."

"Why would she do that?"

"Why does anyone make a false report? Attention, sympathy, anger, revenge? I wish I had a better read on her."

The stillness of the night wrapped around Jo. She always seemed to end up at the ranch whenever she needed answers. The day her mother died, Jo had pedaled her rickety bicycle down the county roads leading to the Ledge, choking on dust and grief. Aiden had come across her abandoned bike by the barn and figured where she'd be. He hiked up to the rocky out-look, his knapsack filled with cream cheese–and–jelly sandwiches, warm Cokes, and a bag of Oreos. After night fell, they lay side by side, staring at the inky sky until tears blurred Jo's vision. He never spoke, just moved his hand close enough that it brushed the side of hers. That was the summer their skin started to tingle when they touched.

"Could have been spoofed," Aiden said quietly.

Jo shook the last of the memory out of her head. "Spoofed?"

"Made to look like they came from one email address when they actually originated at another."

She straightened. "People can do that? I mean, I know a person can set up a false email account, but you mean someone can make it look like it's coming from your own account?"

"Anything's possible on the internet."

"How?"

"All you need is an SMTP server and some software, although really, if you know what you're doing, the software is optional. If you have access to someone's router or hack the encryption password, you can use the person's actual accounts. That takes a bit more finesse, but it opens up more options."

"Oh God." She dipped her head into the crook of her elbow, the chilled lip of the tailgate branding her forehead.

"Didn't you have cyber training?"

"In the academy. It pretty much consisted of 'Don't sign up for MySpace. Send everything else to the feds.'"

"A lot's changed in twelve years."

"Not in Echo Valley." But that wasn't true.

"The web doesn't have boundaries," he said.

"I've got to go." Jo crushed the beer can. "I screwed up."

13

Jo stood to the side of Quinn's apartment door and knocked again.

Shadows and shapes played against the inside of the curtain as if there was a television flickering, but Jo didn't hear anything. It was eerily similar to when she'd responded to Tye Horton's place. She hitched her jacket up and tucked it behind her holster.

The temperature had descended with the sun, and it had only grown colder with each passing hour. She dug her small flashlight from her pocket and rapped the metal sharply against the door. A woman two apartments down opened her door and peeked out, then went back inside.

A shadow behind the curtain solidified. The peephole blackened. Something scraped behind the door, the sound followed by the clank of a chain, and then the dead bolt being drawn back. The door swung open.

"What are you doing here?" Headphones formed a choker around Quinn's neck. She wore puffy green dragon slippers, and the wings made her sweat pants bunch at the ankle.

"I thought we could chat." Jo covered her holster. "May I come inside?"

"No."

She should have expected that. "I'm here to apologize. I obviously misunderstood the messages you showed me."

"You think?"

"I consulted with a colleague." Although describing Aiden as a colleague was stretching the definition a bit. "You came to me for help. I drew a conclusion by only assessing what was in front of me, and I should have dug deeper."

"You thought I sent threats to myself."

"I did. I'm sorry. I'm here now, and I'd like to help."

Quinn looked at her slack-jawed. "Jesus. I'm gonna get colon cancer from the smoke you're blowing up my ass."

The longer Jo stayed, the more she regretted her decision. "You're making it really difficult to apologize."

"I don't want to make this easy on you. You fucked up."

This was a mistake. "And I'm here to make it better."

"Well aren't I the lucky one."

Jo prided herself on her patience, but this was not a blue-ribbon day. "Ever wonder why you don't have any friends?" Based on the narrowing of Quinn's eyes, she should have regretted her words. But she didn't.

"That's low, even from you."

A gust picked up the snow that had accumulated on the railing and swirled it around Jo. "You don't know anything about me." It was too cold for this nonsense.

"I bet I can rattle off five things about you right now."

The prospect of Quinn calling her bluff kept Jo at the door. "I seriously doubt that."

"This is going to be fun." Quinn raised a finger. "One, you hate being wrong."

"Everybody hates being wrong."

"Yeah, but not everyone has a vagina in a workplace full of dicks. Two." Quinn's eyes dipped to Jo's left hand, and Jo fought the impulse to hide it. "Based on the indentation around your finger, you recently left your marriage. And it wasn't to the guy you loved enough to shoot, so you've got a temper. Three." Quinn flicked up a third finger.

"Four," Jo interrupted. "My temper was three."

Quinn curled all but her middle finger. "You don't like me. And if there was any way your conscience would let you walk away, you'd already be halfway home. But for whatever reason, you take your job seriously. Probably more than any of those fucksticks you work with who are flying past you on the ol' promotion ladder. But you won't say shit, because you don't want to rock the boat. Ruin your chances that maybe someday they'll pull their heads out of their asses and see you for the fucking shiny star that you are."

"That's seven."

"Bonus insight. You hate your name because every day it reminds you that your father really wanted a boy. And no matter how hard you try, you just can't fix that one."

Where the hell had that come from? "I don't love him."

"Your dad or the guy you shot?"

"The guy I shot." Now wasn't the time to mention that they'd been kids, and it had been with a BB gun.

"Out of everything I said, that's the part you want to argue?" Quinn shook her head. The chain clanked against the back of the door. "You are seriously whacked."

"I'm not the one getting death threats."

"Give it time."

They mad-dogged each other across the threshold, and Jo refused to look away. No doubt about it, Quinn's assessment was dead-on. It both impressed and annoyed her.

"Why didn't you tell me emails could be manipulated?" Jo asked.

"Spoofed," Quinn corrected.

"Why didn't you speak up?"

"It doesn't exactly inspire confidence when the person you go to for help doesn't know jack-shit about computers."

Had to give her that one. "You ever shoot a gun?"

"No."

"Take a self-defense course?"

"What are you getting at?" Quinn asked.

"Yes or no?" Jo pressed.

"No."

"I have. Handgun, shotgun, rifle. I have to qualify every quarter. Every year, I have over forty hours of defensive tactics and arrest control."

"So you're a badass."

"Who knows very little about computers."

"Great pep talk."

"Point is, even with all those skills, I still get scared. Fear is good. It keeps you alive." Jo turtled the cuff of her jacket over her fingers. "I don't blame you for being scared."

Quinn pushed the door, but Jo wedged her foot toe-to-toe with Quinn's puffy dragon. Even through the narrow crack, Jo saw Quinn's jaw clench and her hands fist.

"I'm not going to let some anonymous asshole intimidate me," Quinn said.

Jo lowered her voice as if she were speaking to a skittish horse. "He already has, or you wouldn't have come see me. We got off to a bad start. I said my piece about that. And if you don't want my help, I'm going to walk away from here with a clear conscience. But the internet is a big place. This creep could be anyone. He could be anywhere. And it's not going to get better on its own."

"He's here." Quinn exhaled, and her entire body appeared to collapse on itself. "He's in Echo Valley. I got a new email." She pulled open the door and stepped aside so Jo could enter. "He saw us at the Bean."

Part Two
RONNY

14

The road to Peregrines Roost Ski Resort wound its way out of the valley and climbed into the sheriff's jurisdiction. The drive usually took forty-five minutes, but a tiny herd of elk at the north end of the valley blocked the road as the stragglers migrated to a lower elevation for the winter. The resulting two-minute traffic jam consisted of one pickup truck and Jo's unmarked police car.

"I swear they know when hunting season's about to end." Jo tapped her fingers impatiently against the steering wheel.

Squint shifted in his seat. "Heard Aiden Teague's back in town."

Three cows leapt the ditch that ran alongside the road. A fourth cow hesitated.

Two roads diverged in a wood, and I—

"Just watch your back," he added.

I took the one less traveled by . . . She leaned sideways to bump her shoulder into his. "There's no reason to worry."

"You're my partner."

A bull elk nudged the reluctant cow onto the roadway.

"And that has made all the difference," Jo said.

In the winter, the elk congregated in large herds at the mouth of the valley, posing a danger to passing motorists. Hit a deer? Chances were good the driver would walk away with a dented fender or a crumpled front end. Smack an elk? The added height meant it would roll across the hood, smash through the windshield, and end up on the driver's lap—and seven hundred pounds of pissed-off bull elk trapped in a car rarely ended well for anyone.

Squint was like a bull elk in some respects. He was a protector of the herd, but get him riled, and best stand back.

"You ever connect with Agent Raubenheimer?" Squint asked.

"Not yet. He was called out to Pagosa to investigate a bank robbery. I'm not holding my breath that the FBI is going to be much help." The last of the elk cleared the road, and Jo put the Impala in gear. "I went to their main website. They deal mostly with big-picture data intrusion and cyber-terrorism. In their book, Quinn's small potatoes."

"What you need is a savvy fifteen-year-old."

"If only it were that easy. I got an earful from Quinn last night. Turns out spoofing is easy. It's unmasking who's behind it that's going to be tricky. Especially if the suspect is using Tor—which in a nutshell is a net-work that strips out all the identifying sender data and then pings the mes-sage through multiple browsers across the world." Jo swerved to avoid several crows picking at a dead animal in the roadway. "She was scared, Squint. She had a stack of emails, but the message she received last night was the first one to suggest someone had eyes on her."

"And you."

"I'm not worried about me."

"You want me to see if the Bean has surveillance footage from yesterday?"

"That'd be great. I already drafted subpoena requests for Quinn's inter-net and email providers. Fingers crossed for a quick response."

She slowed for a switchback. Jo loved this road. During the warmer months, she cycled the thirty-odd miles to the resort. Going out was a slog. Coming back was much faster, but infinitely more dangerous. It wasn't so much the narrow, curvy road but the steep drop-offs beyond the pavement. Definitely not a ride for the inattentive. In winter, the snow and ice upped the hazard level for drivers even further.

Elevation changed the landscape. Snow-flocked piñons and junipers gave way to ponderosa pines and Douglas firs as they climbed. Jo admired the pockets of aspens most, even without their autumn colors.

Houses and then condos sprouted among the trees with increasing fre-quency as the two detectives neared the resort. Finally they drove under the massive carved wooden sign that announced that they'd arrived. The private roadway took them beyond several levels of parking on the way to the main ski complex. A collection of lodges, lifts, restaurants, and shops spoked off the main plaza at the foot of the mountain. The resort bustled, even on a Wednesday.

Jo veered right and passed through the hotel's elaborate wrought-iron gate. Peregrines Roost Lodge claimed the edge of one mountain and offered views of another. The pitched red roof, river-rock walls, and wood framing seemed at once part of the landscape and yet distinct. The building had always struck her as somewhat haughty—as if aware of its status as the only hotel in the area to claim a five-star rating.

A valet raced to Jo's door, but she stepped from the car before he could extend his hand. She discreetly flashed the badge at her belt. "We'll only be a few minutes."

Another bellman held the door, and Squint stood aside until Jo preceded him. The two detectives wove their way through people in ski gear and UGG boots until they reached the reception desk. Jo introduced herself and Squint to a smiling clerk. "We're here to speak to Ronny Buck, please."

A little line developed between the young woman's brows. "Was he expecting you?"

"It's a surprise," Jo said.

"I see." The furrow deepened. "You're not going to arrest him, are you?"

Squint set his hat on the counter. "Not unless there's something you want to tell us."

The receptionist blushed. "No. I mean, it's . . . well. We're shorthanded." Another toothy smile. "Let me call him for you. He should be patrolling the parking lots." She disappeared behind a golden-oak partition.

Jo and Squint ambled over to the fireplace. A Christmas tree decorated the corner beside the hearth, and an elk head with a massive rack hung above the mantel. Alpine cozy. The faded chintz print on the stuffed, oversized chairs completed the illusion.

Within minutes, Ronny Buck entered the lobby like he owned the place. Which in a manner of speaking, he did. Buck & Sage, Inc., his father's company, owned the controlling share of the resort.

He strode toward them wearing a dark jacket with the resort logo on the chest. The confidence was new. The last time Jo saw him, he'd been jumping a fence to get away from her. It was always petty stuff, and when he was cornered, he always fessed up to whatever he'd done. Every officer had a Ronny Buck story, but Jo couldn't help herself—she liked Ronny.

His dad was another story.

"Hey there, Detective Jo." He shook her hand. "Detective Squint."

Squint nodded. "Good to see you, Ronny. Staying out of trouble?"

"I thought so until I saw you two."

"Not to worry," Jo said. "We're hoping you can help us."

Ronny's eyes brightened. "Maybe earn some karma points?"

"You know there's no such thing as a get-out-of-jail-free card, right?" Jo said.

"It never hurts to ask."

It wasn't just his confidence level. Something else had changed, but she couldn't quite finger what. She brought it back around to business, but kept her voice casual. "How long have you been working security for the lodge?"

"Mid-October? Definitely before Halloween." Ronny glanced around the lobby and lowered his voice. "Look, can we talk some other time? Cops in the lobby make guests nervous."

"Not to mention your bosses," Jo added.

"Yeah, there's that. Plus, I'll get written up if I don't sign in at the parking lot checkpoints. It's all computerized now."

"No problem. We'll help with your rounds."

"Great," Ronny said, although his voice lacked its earlier enthusiasm. "What's all of this about?"

Jo headed for the door. "Tye Horton."

"Oh man. I heard. That's messed up."

Outside, Jo flipped up her coat collar. The skies had cleared, but up on the mountain temperatures were always a good ten degrees colder because of the elevation. Add in the wind, and she should have brought her scarf. "Was he having problems with anyone? Classmates, significant other?"

"Didn't have one. He was pretty much a loner."

"Do you know any reason he'd want to end his life?"

"No." Ronny dug keys from his pocket. "In fact, he had some side gig going that he said was going to pay off big-time." He pointed his keys toward a cart marked *Security* parked in the red zone.

Jo studied the vehicle. If a military BearCat and a golf cart ever procreated, this is what it would look like. Utility lights on the top, roll bars, oversized snow tires, and room for four. The vinyl window panels were rolled up. Hopefully it had a beefy heater.

She slid to the center of the back seat and leaned into the divide between the front seats. "What kind of gig?"

Ronny jammed the key into the ignition, and the cart roared to life with an electric click. It was terribly anticlimactic.

"Some company wanted to buy one of his games. Set him up as a designer, or consultant, or something." He activated the turn signal and carefully looked over his shoulder.

That was new information, but the bigger surprise was Ronny using his turn signal. Ronny Buck had been pulled over so frequently that every officer knew his truck plate by heart. "Are you talking about the game you tested for him last year?"

He locked eyes with her in the rearview mirror. "How'd you know about that one?"

"Who else was testing it?"

"Me, Derek, and Quinn."

"Derek have a last name?"

Ronny pulled away from the curb. "Walsenberg."

"The district attorney's son?" Squint asked.

"One and the same."

Jo chewed on that for a moment. The DA might not know Tye, but his son sure had.

She returned to the question Ronny hadn't answered. "The game the company was interested in buying, was it the game you beta tested for Tye?" Professor Lucas had tried to steal the game once. That was bad enough, but for him to try to use Tye's death to get out of a speeding ticket made Jo realize exactly how much she'd enjoy slapping cuffs around those lily-white wrists of his.

"No."

"You sound pretty sure."

"Tye never wanted to play that game again. He'd moved on to something else." Ronny bumped across a runoff ditch at the entrance of the upper parking lot. "I asked him about the new project. He wouldn't even tell me what he'd named it. Said he'd signed something that said he wasn't supposed to talk about it."

He swerved around a pothole, and Jo clutched the roll bar to keep her balance. "A nondisclosure agreement?"

"Yeah, that's it. The only thing he said about it was he was going to cash in big."

"Could he have been trying to cash in on your capstone project?"

They drove through the lot, joining a conga line of vehicles looking for a space. "Tye wasn't like that. This was something else."

"What's going to happen with your capstone game?"

"I don't even want to think about that. I'm on academic probation as it is. I thought majoring in video gaming would be a kick. Hell was I wrong." Another glance in the mirror. "Pardon my French, Detective Jo."

"I've heard worse."

He turned down the last aisle. "It's a stupid degree anyway. Most coders learn by doing. Look at Tye. He didn't even have his degree yet, and already gaming companies were throwing money at him."

A gray utility box anchored the rear corner of the lot, and Ronny pulled up beside it.

"Why not change majors?" Jo asked.

"Dad threatened to cut me off if I don't graduate. The only thing I have left is the capstone project." He slid out of the driver's seat and unlocked the box, then tapped a code onto an electronic keypad. The cart lurched as he climbed back inside.

"That sucks," Jo said.

"Tell me about it." Ronny steered toward the exit. "Tye had it good. It was amazing what he could do on a computer."

"What about you?" He was driving faster now, and the cold air brought tears to Jo's eyes. "Were you holding up your part of the project?"

"Of course." He craned around in his seat. "Why would you even ask that?"

"You said you were on probation."

Ronny faced forward again. "Turns out the degree is more than playing games."

"What was your part of the project?"

His shoulders slumped. "I bought Tye's chair."

"The gaming chair?"

"Best money can buy." He pulled into the second lot and drove straight to the utility box.

Before he could get out, Squint asked, "Did Mr. Horton give you his laptop?"

"I wish. Then I wouldn't be sweating the project." He hopped out.

Jo followed. "So, as far as you know, Tye had no reason to suicide. Anybody mad at him?"

He tapped his code onto the keypad. "Besides Quinn?"

Jo sidestepped a slush puddle. Maybe there was more to Ms. Kirkwood's story after all. "What was Quinn's beef with Tye?"

"I don't know the details. Only know they had a falling out."

"What about you? Anybody upset with you at the moment?"

"Like I said, I'm staying out of trouble."

A black Escalade with the resort logo bounced into the lot.

A new thought. "What did you get Quinn?"

"What?" He didn't meet her eyes, and for the first time since she'd known him, she could have sworn he was holding something back.

"You got Tye a gaming chair. Quinn was part of the team. So what'd you get her to make her go along with carrying you on the project?"

He snorted. "I wouldn't give that bitch a damn thing."

Squint unfolded from the front seat and stood next to the cart, his eyes marking the progress of the Escalade as it charged toward them.

Jo knew exactly who was driving. "Ronny, what—"

The driver braked seconds before he would have rammed the security cart. The front end of the Escalade dipped, and Xavier Buck stepped out of the passenger side before the springs returned to neutral. "*Maiku*, Detective Wyatt." His expression belied the friendly Ute greeting. He held out his hand to Squint. "Detective MacAllister, I believe?"

"Mr. Buck."

"How can I help you two today?"

Jo answered. "I'm just having a friendly conversation with your son."

He brushed a bit of dirt from his shearling jacket. "I'm sure you understand he's working."

"I do. We're helping so he doesn't get behind. I heard the management here is pretty unforgiving."

The corners of Xavier's mouth turned up, but it fell short of a smile. "That's very true."

"If you'll excuse us," Jo said. "My partner and I only have a few more questions."

"Oh, you're done now. Feel free to address any additional inquiries to my attorney."

"Are you suggesting your son needs a lawyer?"

"Of course he does. He's speaking with you." He turned to his son. "Ronald, you don't have anything else for the detectives, do you?"

Ronny shook his head but didn't meet Jo's eyes. "I'm good."

15

Jo slammed the telephone receiver back into its cradle. "Still no answer." Squint leaned back in his office chair. "If you want me to add something to this conversation, you're going to have to give me a bit more to go on."

"Eva Petersen." When Squint still didn't respond, she added, "The chintz-loving gun collector from the Walsenbergs' Fifth Street rental?"

"Ah." He leaned forward and resumed typing on his computer.

"Tye's dead," she said.

Squint's chair squeaked as he once again leaned back. "Is this going to be one of your scintillating nonlinear conversations where the only reason you include me is so you aren't talking to yourself? Because if it is, I need to finish the follow-up on the Ruffini burglary and get it over to the DA's office."

Jo stripped the hair tie from her ponytail and raked her fingers across her scalp. "Derek suicided. Quinn's getting death threats."

"The cat is still missing."

Jo shot the elastic across the desks at Squint. It flew wide. "Where's that leave Ronny?"

Squint steepled his fingers. "On academic probation with no chance of graduating."

"And Daddy threatening to cut him off financially."

"Which probably positions Ronny as the least likely person to want Tye dead."

"Yeah, there's that." She drew another hair tie from the stash in her desk drawer. Most of them ended up on Squint's side of the room by the end of the day. "What I can't figure out is how Quinn's emails figure into all of this."

"Could be unrelated."

"I even considered that maybe Tye had sent them. That made sense in light of the squabble Ronny mentioned, but unless he's emailing from the great beyond, there's no way he could have sent a message saying he'd seen her in the Bean."

"Any luck with our friends at the Bureau?"

"Still waiting to hear back from Raubenheimer. I reached out to the Denver office. The agent there suggested contracting a forensic specialist to conduct a search of Quinn's computer and router to see if someone's piggybacking on her system. Something about capturing data packets. He's sending me some info, so I'll know more after I have a chance to wade through it all. But Quinn's a student. She's less than enthusiastic about giving up her laptop. Anything on the Bean surveillance?"

"They don't have any."

"Of course not." The words hung in the air until Jo finally broke the silence. "I'm starving." The institutional clock on the detective bureau wall claimed it was two thirty. Her computer put it at quarter to three. "Plus, I haven't exercised in three days." She buried her face in her hands and rubbed her eyes. "Unless you want to count running into brick walls, swimming upstream, and chasing my own tail."

"I'm exhausted just listening to you." He lifted his Southwest Regional Drug Task Force coffee mug and took a leisurely sip.

"I've left messages with Mrs. Petersen, Professor Lucas, and Quinn—I need to find out more about the kerfuffle with Tye that Ronny mentioned. No one wants to talk to me. I've officially entered the hurry-up-and-wait phase of both investigations."

"Considering your blood sugar level and my will to live, I'm going to suggest you walk downtown and get yourself something to eat."

Stacks of paperwork had taken over her desk, and the clutter set her on edge. "I should make sure Jimmy Hoffa isn't hiding in there somewhere." She pulled a manila envelope from the bottom of the stack and shoved it in her desk drawer. She'd give the documents to Cameron later. Hopefully he'd sign them without a fuss.

"My treat," Squint said.

Jo rose from her seat. "What do you want?"

"Lady's choice. I'm only doing this in the interest of self-preservation."

"I'm thinking Prospectors." She shoved her arms into her coat. "I've got a hankering for a burger."

Squint tossed some bills on her desk. "I would greatly appreciate it if you declined onions and green chili this time."

"And miss out on a meal I can taste the rest of the day?" She tossed the bills back. "I don't think so."

* * *

Jo slid on a slab of invisible ice that had formed in the shadow of the police station, then crossed to the sunny side of the street. Five blocks to Prospectors, five blocks back, five minutes to wolf it down at her desk. Once she stabilized her blood sugar, maybe she'd be able to figure out what to do next.

She cut through the recently rechristened Derek Walsenberg Memorial Garden, preferring its gravel paths to icy sidewalks. Use of the land had been gifted to the city by the Ambrose family years ago, and it stretched across two acres of prime real estate next to the courthouse. The wooded gardens radiated peace.

Her pace slowed. Pine scented the crisp air, and the sun played hide-and-seek with the clouds. The trees parted, and the stately columns framing the courthouse came into view. Her life's story was held in that building. Birth records, marriage certificate, court testimony, property records. Soon her divorce papers would add another chapter.

She rounded a holly bush, its red berries bright against the snowy backdrop, and stumbled into a woman crouched at the base of the shrub.

"I'm so sorry! Are you all right?" Jo leaned over and offered the woman support while she regained her footing.

"Completely my fault. I didn't hear you coming." She brushed ice shards from her knees. A bronze plaque peeked through the snow at her feet.

Jo recognized her immediately. Alice Walsenberg.

"I'm so sorry," Jo repeated. "I didn't mean to intrude."

"Don't be silly, dear. You're not intruding at all. I'm glad to see someone else enjoying the gardens in this weather." She knelt and dusted the remaining snow from the plaque and read the inscription aloud. "'The most effective kind of education is that a child should play amongst lovely things.' Time has changed so little since Plato spoke those words."

"He would be proud, Mrs. Walsenberg. The garden is lovely."

"Plato or my son?" She stared off into the distance, then seemed to rouse. "It's Jo, right? My husband mentioned he had spoken with you recently about a case."

"Yes." She held out her hand. "Jo Wyatt."

Alice shook Jo's gloved hand with the strength of a ranch girl, even if there was a manicure under her glove. "It is my pleasure, Ms. Wyatt. I knew your mother. A wonderful woman. And your father, of course."

"Of course."

Mrs. Walsenberg returned her attention to the memorial plaque. "No amount of time dulls the loss of a child. Do you have any of your own, Ms. Wyatt?"

"No." She and Cameron had talked about having children. Several times. He'd been all for it. She'd wanted to wait a bit, not realizing that *someday* didn't always come around. Would a child have saved her marriage?

"It's already been a year." Alice didn't have to mention since what. "Yet I still expect to see Derek come through the door. He was going through a stage where he never used a glass. He'd drive me to distraction by drinking straight from the carton. Milk, juice, soda—it didn't matter." She brushed her hand across a holly sprig, and the sharp edge snagged her woolen glove. "What I wouldn't give to feel that aggravation again."

"It's strange the things we miss," Jo said. "I miss my mother's biscuits. She couldn't bake a batch without burning the bottom of every last one of them. It was the oddest thing, because she was a great cook."

She spoke of her mother but thought of Cameron. She missed the press of his body when he spooned her as they slept, how his hand always found the dip between her hip and rib cage. His soft breaths by her ear. She'd never appreciated how much of her life he'd filled just by being present.

Alice freed her glove of the snag. "Those are the kind of memories that keep our loved ones alive."

"Yes." Jo cleared her throat. "Mrs. Walsenberg, maybe you can help me. I've been trying to get in touch with Mrs. Petersen."

"The poor dear. She's suffered some health issues recently and has been in and out of the hospital. I stopped by on Sunday. I make a point of checking on her when she's home. She's got an independent streak, but it's a big house for an older woman."

"I'm sure she appreciates it. When you've visited, did you ever notice anyone in the garage?"

"No. I park in front. I was stunned to learn it was Tye."

"You knew him?" Jo tried to hide her interest. "Tye's name didn't ring a bell with your husband."

"Oh, I'm not a bit surprised. Zachary makes a point of knowing the names and addresses of every boy who's ever shown a speck of interest in our daughter, but Derek was always a bit of a mama's boy. I only knew Tye's name because of my son."

Tye and Derek. Both dead. Coincidence? "Were they close?"

"Not at all. Derek's best friend, Ronny Buck, introduced them. If memory serves, Tye was a game designer. Derek and Ronny tested something for him."

"Do you know what he thought of the game?"

Alice smiled. "He was a teenager. He loved anything that distracted him from his homework."

"Thank you, Mrs. Walsenberg. Again, I'm sorry to have disturbed you."

"Ms. Wyatt." She brushed Jo's forearm. A butterfly-soft touch. "Jo."

The slightest hitch crept into Alice's voice. Desperate? No. Desolate. It was at complete odds with the carefully curated persona of control she always exuded. Even following the death of her son, she had appeared poised—grief-stricken, sure, but still somehow regal.

"The suicide awareness program I've been developing . . . I understand the incident at our rental property was a suicide."

"I can't—"

"Rest easy, Ms. Wyatt. I'm not asking for any details. But I understand a young woman reported it. A friend of Tye's, I presume." Mrs. Walsenberg pulled a business card from her jacket pocket. "Would you please give this to her, let her know she's not alone?"

Jo took the card. "Of course."

"I was ashamed my son committed suicide. I'd wondered where I went wrong, what I could have done differently. I was so very angry. I've since learned that what I felt was normal, but at the time, I thought I was a monster. The grief that accompanies suicide is full of unexpected struggles. She should know that nothing is the same in its wake."

* * *

Jo nudged the detective bureau door open with her hip.

Squint rose out of his seat to help her. "I was about to send out a search party."

"I ran into Alice Walsenberg when I cut through the gardens. Interesting conversation."

He took the cardboard drink holder from her grasp. "Anything useful?"

"She knew her son was testing a game for Tye."

"The DA said he'd never heard of Tye."

"He might not have, but I thought it an interesting twist." Jo placed the bag of burgers on her desk and started doling out ketchup packets and cutlery. "She was also at the rental house on Sunday, but she didn't see anyone other than Mrs. Petersen."

"Too bad." Squint cleared a space on his desk. "Ingersleben called while you were out."

Jo paused. "And?"

"The preliminary determination is that the Tye Horton case is a suicide."

Jo lowered the napkins onto her desk. "So Cameron was right all along."

"No, Officer Finch stepped all over the crime scene like a rookie just out of the academy. You were right to treat it as a homicide until the investigation ruled otherwise."

"Sergeant Finch." She flopped into her chair, no longer hungry. "I don't get it. Tye had stellar grades. Friends. He was on the verge of success. So why would someone who had it all decide to suicide?"

"Why did Derek Walsenberg hang himself in his bedroom closet?"

"That's another thing. Don't you think it's odd that Derek and Tye knew each other and now they're both dead?"

"Statistically, they both possessed risk factors. Tye was diabetic. Both were white, male, and young."

Derek Walsenberg's death had been Squint's case. Jo and Cameron had been in Glenwood Springs on their last vacation together when the death occurred.

After they returned, Jo had read the reports. Olivia had found her brother. Zachery had called the police. Alice had sat in the window seat in the solarium, staring out at the falling snow. If she hadn't known better, Jo would have thought Alice and Zachary had been interviewed at the same time. No, their son wasn't having any problems. No he wasn't depressed. No, he wasn't in a relationship. No warning. No explanation.

"No note." Jo pushed the takeout container with her burger to the side of her desk. "Derek didn't leave a note either."

16

Tye's name didn't ring a bell with your husband.

The detective's voice buzzed in Alice's ear. What did she mean? Of course he knew Tye's name.

Dozens of questions kept her company on her walk home, but only one answer was certain.

Zachary lied.

A ray of sun struck the leaded-glass panes beside the front door and shattered into a thousand colors across the porch. Maybe he'd just forgotten the name. Didn't make the connection. As district attorney, he encountered countless names every day. It was possible.

It took two tries before she was able to unlock the door.

Inside, the scent of the Christmas tree assaulted her. Without stopping to remove her jacket, she strode forward, drawn by the star that no one else knew about, and parted the boughs. Behind yards of antique lace and sparkling crystal icicles hung an ornament Derek had made in kindergarten. It was hideous. Crafted of plaster and paints, the star's points were unbalanced and he'd chosen a confusing array of colors to surround a sticker of a Tyrannosaurus rex, but his eyes had shone when he'd presented it to her. She'd displayed it for a few years and then quietly set it aside, thinking it too juvenile to mingle with Waterford.

She withdrew her hand, and the boughs fell back into place. Last year they'd ignored Christmas. This year she'd overcome her family's protestations and insisted on the tree. Some normalcy.

It mocked her with every pine-scented breath she drew.

Her keys clattered into the silver dish on the sideboard, and she peeled off her jacket.

Some mornings, while sipping coffee, she imagined Olivia's chilling scream. Even as a memory, the anguish in that cry was almost unbearable. She hadn't needed to read the clock. She had known it was 7:52.

She'd never much thought about the dynamics involved in hanging one-self before that day. Derek didn't dangle. The fronts of his bare feet rested on the floorboards of the closet. He could have stood if he'd wanted. Even as life slipped away from him, he chose to die rather than rejoin his family.

And in that moment of realization, she'd hated her son.

It was natural to suffer a setback on anniversaries, especially ones best forgotten. Following Derek's death, visiting the gardens had become her daily ritual. Anything to avoid the suffocation of the house. It didn't matter how many good memories she had of her son. Only one played out in her mind. Since the anniversary of her son's death on Sunday, she'd reverted to old habits, haunting the gardens, trying to find peace under the pine.

Tye's name didn't ring a bell with your husband.

There had to be a reason to justify this untruth. Her husband was an honorable man. She'd been at his side when he was sworn into office. His voice had rung true when he vowed to uphold the public trust. In all their years of marriage, she'd never once doubted his word. They shared everything.

No. Pain shortened her breath. They'd once shared everything. Their intimacy had changed one year and three days ago. Now they no longer shared a bedroom, let alone a bed.

On the threshold of his home office, she pretended this hadn't been her destination all along. That the detective's words hadn't propelled her to this spot from the moment she'd heard them.

Her husband had been retreating to his sanctuary more frequently since Derek's death. Only one other time had she entered his study unin-vited. That day, four months after Derek's death, she'd torn through the house, searching every room, every drawer, every last crevice and closet, desperate for answers. Answers she never expected to find.

Certainly not in her husband's file cabinet.

Her heartbeat pulsed in her ears. *He lied, he lied, he lied.*

Zachary kept both keys to the cabinet in his desk drawer on the same cheap ring they'd hung from when she bought the furniture for him. Today, they clattered against each other as her hand shook.

What else had he lied about?

She unlocked the drawer.

When she'd chanced upon the phone bill that first horrific morning, she hadn't initially realized the magnitude of what she'd found. Her son's cell number jumped out, highlighted in bright yellow. Her husband's handwritten notes marked the margins. Then there were the names. Relationships.

Today the drawer squeaked open, overloud in the empty house.

The files were still there. The same place where she'd carefully replaced them after reading them the first time.

Zachary was careful with his work. He rarely brought it home. He always tried to protect Olivia and her from the rigors and depravity of his job. The malevolence in the world. He would slay dragons for them. Even still. She clutched the proof in her hands.

In a move reminiscent of that day, she sat on the carpet and spread the files. Surrounded by paper, she reread the timeline her husband had created of Derek's death. He'd added a police report sometime in the ensuing months, but everything else was still there. Addresses, licenses, criminal histories—all the secrets law enforcement databases kept. Complete dossiers that included credit reports, social media accounts, school transcripts, schedules, and email addresses.

Tye's name didn't ring a bell with your husband.

But there they were. Three files. One each for Tye Horton, Ronny Buck, and Quinn Kirkwood.

17

The knock on Quinn's door broke through the sanctuary provided by her headphones. She stripped them from her head and paused the game. Listening.

DEFCON level 3. Doors locked. Cell phone within reach.

Few people knew where she lived. Fewer cared. And at 10:37 at night, not a single person should be at her front door. She padded into the kitchen and picked up the knife she kept on the edge of the counter. Maybe if she weren't from the People's Republic of California, she'd own a fucking gun.

Another knock. "Quinn. Open up, it's me."

Who the hell is me? She edged toward the door.

"Come on, Quinn. Hurry up. It's freezing out here."

The whiny voice sounded familiar. Stu/Stan? No. Standing on her tiptoes, she peered through the peephole. DEFCON 2.

Her hand hovered over the chain lock before she finally slid the little nub to the left, unlocked the remaining locks, and slid the chair jammed under the knob out of the way. She stashed the knife under a textbook, drew a breath, and opened the door.

Professor Lucas posed like a forties pinup girl in the doorway: one arm stretched high on the threshold, half smile, hooded eyes.

Quinn snorted.

He lowered his arm. "I was beginning to think you weren't going to let me in."

"Technically, you're still outside."

"I thought you might like this." He extended a bottle of champagne with his other hand.

It had a duck on the label. Quality stuff. "I don't drink."

"Recovery, eh?"

He smelled as if he'd bathed at a brewery and forgotten to towel off.

"Something you may want to try," she said.

"Well, I'm thirsty." He leered at her and nearly toppled over. "What do you say? Let me in?"

"Why are you here?"

He sighed. "All right. I'll play." He cleared his throat and adopted an overly stern expression. "It's high time we discussed your grade, Ms. Kirkwood."

Shit. A cold lump settled into her stomach. Her grade. Not all of her community college credits from California had transferred. Unlike Tye and Ronny, she still had another semester before graduating. She needed this grade. Wished she'd never made that goddamn promise.

Her dragon slippers clawed the floor. She invited him inside.

"You show great potential, Ms. Kirkwood. But I'm concerned I haven't given you every opportunity to demonstrate your enthusiasm for the program."

"Drop the formality," she said.

Without asking, he waltzed into her tiny galley kitchen and attacked the foil at the top of the champagne bottle. "Where are your glasses?"

"Mugs are right above you."

He raised his eyebrows.

"It's that or nothing."

The cabinet creaked, and he selected the front mug. Great. Her favorite. She'd throw it in the trash tomorrow.

He sloshed the bubbly into the oversized *Firefly* mug and slurped it when it threatened to spill over. He waited a moment, then topped it off.

Leaning his back against the counter, he drank, staring at her over the lip of the cup. Even wearing a sweat shirt, she felt exposed. Itchy.

"I have to say. I expected you to make a bit more of an effort."

Her inner optimist wanted to believe her professor was truly concerned about her grade and wanted to discuss her options now that there was no hope of finding Tye's laptop. Her inner realist dispelled that notion with the realization that she was well and truly screwed. "Your visit was unexpected."

His eyebrows furrowed, like when someone asked him a question in class that he had no idea how to answer. "What would you do for an A, Ms. Kirkwood?"

Slice you in little bits and feed you to the squirrels. "What did you have in mind?"

"You're the creative one." He raised the arm holding the mug, and champagne splashed on his hand. "Wow me."

A buzzing started in her head, and she silenced it with images of her mother. The hospital room. The parade of police officers. Shooting up in the corner after they'd gone. Her sister's look of disgust.

I promised.

She slapped on a smile. "I can tell you about the project we were working on. It's worthy of an A."

He stepped closer, and she fought the instinct to knee him in the balls. "Forget the computer. I'm talking about you. About us."

There was no *us*. No her. Only him. She could play along or not.

He traced his finger down the side of her face. "Surely this isn't the best you can do?"

She'd heard the question before, even though it had been phrased in slightly different terms—and asked without the disturbing cheek grope. *What are you going to do with your life? How are you going to make a living? What are you going to do when I'm gone?* Quinn's answer had always been the same mumbled *I'll survive.* The last time they'd spoken, her mother had reached up from the hospital bed and grabbed Quinn's hand. "Like me?" The woman had eyes that knew too much. Saw everything. Even her daughter. "Quit the smack. Go to school," she'd said. "You owe me. *Promise me.*"

Quinn had promised. Anything to shut the woman up.

She'd watched the coverage of her mother's funeral on a jumpy television in a hotel that even cockroaches avoided. She had to hand it to San Francisco PD, though—they took care of their own. Fuckers knew how to throw a funeral.

The cops never caught the drug dealer who'd shot her mom. Quinn had refused to rat him out. Seemed noble at the time. By the time she'd gotten clean, the bastard was already dead.

The only thing that remained was the promise she'd made her mom.

Quinn stripped off her sweat shirt. "Prepare to be wowed."

* * *

She'd have to go to the Laundromat. Sheets. Pillows. She'd burn her panties.

He rolled off her, gasping like he'd just summited one of the state's fourteeners the diehard hikers always raved about.

Quinn pulled the sheet over her nakedness. "Grades are due next week. I expect an A."

Sweat glistened on his chest. "That was a good solid B. Make me hard again. Then we'll talk."

Light from the living room sliced across the bed. She clenched and unclenched the fist at her side, digging her nails into her palms. The top of the mattress was only inches from the floor. She'd made sure nothing could hide under the bed, but she hadn't prepared for monsters that lurked between sheets.

She dropped her voice to a purr. "I so want an A." She stood and stretched her arms above her head. Provocative.

"That's more like it." He propped himself up on his elbow, gawking at her like he was mustering the nerve to ask her to go steady. "You got a beer? I've worked up quite the thirst."

He'd get nothing else from her. She'd already given him more than she'd wanted, but it was worth it. A promise kept. "I don't give a rat's ass about your thirst." Her voice still purred. "You're going to give me an A."

"And if I don't?"

The bands squeezing her lungs broke. "You worthless piece of shit. You come to my house drunk and dangle my grade in front of me, acting like it's something I haven't already earned. You've seen the game. You've signed off on it every step of the way."

He sat up and dragged the sheet over his flaccid penis. "What are you suggesting, Quinn?"

"That's Ms. Kirkwood to you, asswipe." The room was freezing, but she refused to cover herself. Refused to let him think he'd made her ashamed of herself.

"I've seen the tattoo on your inner thigh. I think I'll continue calling you Quinn."

Blood rushed to her face. "Let me make myself perfectly clear. You'll submit my grade. In exchange, I won't go to the police or the school administration and tell them what transpired tonight."

"And what, pray tell, do you plan to share with them?"

A warning siren alerted in her mind. Loud and chilling. "Pressuring a student for sex is still rape."

Professor Lucas laughed, the hearty laugh of someone who knew something she didn't. It froze her in place.

"Go ahead, sweetheart. Call the cops. I'm sure they'll love reading all the dirty details of what you had planned for me. You've got quite the potty mouth. Lucky for you, I'm into that stuff."

DEFCON 1. Maximum readiness. Already too little, too late.

"What are you talking about?" But she knew. She'd been played.

"You can't cry rape when you issued the invitation." He folded his arms behind his head and relaxed. "And I've got the email to prove it."

18

Jo heard the vacuum as she climbed the stairs to the detective bureau. Cody had his stocky back to her as she entered. He was hard of hearing, and she flicked the lights a couple of times so she wouldn't startle him. Without breaking stride, he raised his free arm in greeting.

She set two breakfast burritos on the desk next to the hairbands Cody had neatly piled on the corner. She knew from experience he wouldn't stop vacuuming until the job was done.

The detective bureau had a tiny offshoot break room. She plugged in the ancient coffeepot and willed it to heat up while she scrubbed the dried coffee rings from the bottom of the carafe. She placed her mug on the burner, too impatient to wait for the pot to fill. Once the coffee reached an acceptable level, she prepared for the exchange. Pot in one hand, mug in the other, she waited for a sputter and swapped spots. Only a slight sizzle of spilled coffee. It was going to be a great day.

Caffeine in hand, she returned to her desk.

Cody finished and unplugged the cord. "G-g-good morning, Mrs. Wyatt." He enunciated carefully. "You're here early."

She waggled one of the burritos. "We haven't had breakfast in a while."

"G-g-green chili?"

"Of course. And I got extra sour cream too."

His almond-shaped eyes closed in delight behind his thick glasses. "Thank you."

Cody was only a little younger than Jo and had been working at the police department nearly as long. He'd never once called her by her first name, and rather than addressing people by rank, he always used either *Mr.* or *Mrs.*

"Sit with me?" she asked.

"I can't. I have to finish before everyone gets here." He lifted the bag of trash from Jo's wastebasket and fitted it with a new liner. "Why are you here so early?"

"I have to learn more about computers."

"I can help. Do you know why the computer was cold?"

Jo shook her head.

"C-cuz it left its Windows open!"

Jo groaned. "Oh, that was bad."

"I know. But now you know something about computers." He dropped the burrito into one of the cavernous pockets of his cargo pants and collected the other trash bags. "Thanks for breakfast, Mrs. Wyatt."

"Thanks for rescuing my hair ties. I never seem to find them all."

"Maybe you need glasses."

"Maybe I do." She definitely needed something to see what was going on.

The computer took its sweet time booting up, and she stared out the window and sipped her coffee. One of the perks of being on the upper floor of the police building was the view. The elevation change between Main Street and Second Avenue wasn't much, but add in the extra story of the PD and she had an unobstructed view of Peregrines Peak from her desk. This early, she hoped to watch its face materialize as the sun rose, but even as the sky lightened, the cloud cover obscured the crag.

She turned to her email. The Denver agent had sent her a series of messages containing several links and numerous PDFs. The sheer number of attachments meant one thing: she needed more coffee.

Armed with a fresh cup, she scanned the document names: "Best Practices for Seizing Electronic Evidence," "Online Acronyms Used by Sexual Predators," "Stand-Alone Versus Networked Computers." There were files for specific devices: PDAs, cell phones, digital cameras, and storage media. When to seize. Authority to seize. What to do with it after you seized it all—which at a glance looked to be pretty simple: Don't touch anything. Get an expert.

She clicked on a document titled "Crimes and Digital Evidence" and navigated to a section describing potential evidence that could be recovered from various types of electronic devices. She found a catchall section for email threats, harassment, and stalking investigations.

Bingo. She unwrapped her burrito and began reading.

* * *

By the time Squint arrived, the only remnant of Jo's breakfast burrito was a dab of salsa on the wrapper.

He hung his hat on the coatrack and shrugged out of his jacket. "You're here early."

"TCOB," she said, without looking up.

"Excuse me?"

"Taking care of business."

He leaned over her shoulder and looked at the new stacks of paperwork covering her desk. "What is all this?"

"FMTYEWTK."

"I haven't had coffee yet."

"Far more than you ever wanted to know." She riffled through the closest pile and pulled out a paper-clipped document and shook it. "And there's a *lot* more where that came from. I mean, I knew LOL and some of the basics, but you wouldn't believe the stuff that gets abbreviated. And more than half of it isn't safe for work—which, by the way, is NSFW."

"You obviously have me confused with someone who appreciates your attempt to expand my vocabulary."

"I only looked at this"—she held up the printout—"to take a break from all this." She waved her hand over the piles.

"Which is?"

"Everything you ever wanted to know about computer forensics and were stupid enough to ask for."

"Anything interesting?"

"Tons. Sadly, I only comprehend about a pound of it." She leaned back in her chair and kicked her feet up on the corner of her desk. "The gist? Electronic stalking is the same as any other stalking case. It's the background information a suspect gathers that's going to make the case. Maps, emails, letters, photos, internet activity logs, phone records. Essentially anything that links the guy to Quinn is fair game. Unfortunately, most of the evidence we need is on the suspect's computer, not the victim's."

"Most, but not all."

"Not all, but backtracking is time-consuming and requires more knowledge than I have at the moment."

They both fell silent as someone clumped up the stairs to their office. Chief Grimes entered the bay, holding a cream-colored envelope.

Jo slid her boots off the desk. The chief rarely wandered into the detective bureau unless there was a major case, and even then the detectives usually went to his office to give him the scoop.

She crumpled the burrito wrapper, swept it into the trash can, and glanced down to make sure she wasn't wearing any salsa. "Chief."

"Morning, Jo. Squint." A large nose dominated the chief's expressive face, but it was balanced by a wide mouth and deep-set brown eyes that never seemed to focus on any one thing.

"Help you with something, Chief?" Squint asked.

He held up the envelope. "Actually, I'm here to see Jo."

This couldn't be good. She cleared the overflow files off the chair beside her desk so he could sit. He remained towering over her, and she swiveled in her chair and waited him out.

"You may have heard about the Echo Valley Alliance for Life."

"Sorry, it isn't ringing any bells."

"It's the suicide awareness program the district attorney's wife is spearheading."

"Alice." Sheesh, the woman had a name.

"She's organizing the group's debut fund raiser. For a group like hers to succeed, she needs stakeholders at the table, and she's requested a department representative. I'd planned on attending, but something cropped up yesterday and I won't be able to make it." His eyes flitted around the room. "Your soft touch is exactly what a group like this needs."

Funny, when he'd told her he was promoting Cameron, he'd mentioned that one of the hurdles she'd face as a sergeant was her bluntness. "Using that criterion, Squint is definitely the better choice."

If her partner was annoyed by being thrown under the bus, Squint didn't show it. One of the many reasons she never played poker with the man.

"Alice asked for you specifically."

So much for it being a good day. "When is it?"

"Tomorrow night." He set the invitation on her desk. "If you can adjust your schedule tomorrow, I'd rather avoid the overtime."

"Let me check the calendar."

"I'll need you to clear it."

A command performance, then. "Of course."

"It's at the resort, so . . ."

"Suit and tie?" She slid the heavy invitation from the envelope and read the details. Cocktail attire. Wonderful. Wearing heels in the snow was always fun. Only one thing could make this evening worse. "You weren't making a speech, were you?"

"The sheriff is. All you need to do is show up and look pretty."

Squint maintained his poker face. "I'm definitely the better choice then, Chief."

*   *   *

"If I ever needed proof the chief hates me, this is it." She tossed the engraved invitation onto her keyboard and kicked her feet back onto the desk.

"Sounds like you impressed Mrs. Walsenberg when you met her yesterday."

"Yay me."

"Who are you going to take as your plus one?"

Jo grabbed the invite. There it was on the front of the envelope. *Mr. and Mrs. Grimes*. Two people. Damn. "What are you doing tomorrow night?"

"Not going to the fund raiser."

"Was it because I outed you as the kinder, gentler one of the two of us? Because, obviously, that was a joke."

Squint dug a file out of his drawer. "BIDWT."

"What?"

"Because I don't want to."

"I always forget how smart you are."

"It's good to be underestimated."

"At least you're not just a pretty face."

Squint snapped the file closed, folded his arms, and leaned forward on his desk. "The chief is an ass if that's all he thinks you are."

Her mouth fell open. In all the years she'd worked with Squint, she'd never heard him swear. The compliment was a bonus.

"And while I'm on it. You've got a good head on your shoulders. You would have made a damn fine sergeant—and don't let anyone make you think any different."

A warm fuzziness infused her entire body. "Aw. You're gonna make me cry."

"I've said my piece." He sat back. "So what's the plan for today?"

"Try to identify the whackadoodle messing with Quinn." Jo excavated the case file from the stacks of paperwork on her desk. "The email mentioning the Burnt Bean concerns me. To date, it's the only one that suggests a local angle." She removed an enlarged map printout and slid it to Squint. "Quinn lives in the apartments next to the main campus gate. The parking lot fronts the place. Her car and apartment doorway are visible from the street. The complex itself backs up to the hillside. It'd be easy enough for someone to hike in, conceal himself in the trees, and use the slope to look straight into her second-story window. I drove by last night to check it out in the dark."

"And?"

"You'll never guess who I saw knocking on her door holding a bottle of champagne."

"Ronny Buck."

"Close. Fred Lucas."

"How is that even close?"

"I'm being generous." Still talking, she collected their coffee mugs and went into the break room to refill them. "Quinn didn't look particularly thrilled to see Lucas, though. But I think she has a thing for making people freeze on her doorstep." She returned with steaming cups. "With so many threads connecting Quinn, Tye, Ronny, and now the good professor—I don't know. The whole thing's not passing the sniff test."

Squint took his mug. "The autopsy ruling is only a preliminary. Doc Ing could be wrong."

"Have you ever known him to be?"

"That's beside the point. What's got you worried?"

Jo worked her pencil end over end across her knuckles as if it were a poker chip. "I haven't dug deep enough yet."

"So grab your shovel."

"Sergeant Begay nabbed me on the way in. Graveyards got hit with a string of car burglaries last night on the west side."

"Unless you need backup, I got it. Go find your answers."

19

"No way. Nothing you can say will make me believe Tye took his own life." Leila Horton's hands rested in her lap, fluttering weakly as she spoke to Jo, glancing over her shoulder at her husband, who stood behind her. She looked like a woman walking along the edge of a cliff, and he like a man about to push her off.

"Tye had problems—everyone does—but my brother-in-law was a good man," she added quietly.

Her husband twisted his mouth as if he were looking for a place to spit. "A good man."

In-person interviews always yielded more than phone conversations, and Jo had decided to drive the forty minutes to talk to Tye's relatives. The small cattle ranch consisted of a forlorn home that sagged steps from the road as if shielding the rest of the property from judgment. When she turned into the gravel driveway, a blue Australian cattle dog with an atti-tude and a man with a shotgun had come out from behind one of the two broken-down outbuildings. She'd been more worried about the dog.

"Turner," Leila chided. "He was your brother."

"Was."

Maybe Jo had been too hasty about the dog.

In contrast to the grounds, the interior of the home was spotless. Jo sat on a wooden desk chair brought into the small living room just for her. She balanced her notebook on her right thigh while holding a cup of coffee in her left hand. "When was the last time you saw your brother, Mr. Horton?"

"At my father's funeral."

Leila studied her toes. "He was Tye's father too."

Jo raised the mug toward her nose, but the smell of the coffee convinced her it was more for decoration than consumption. Mr. Horton watched her closely. She took a sip, keeping her face neutral. "And when was that?"

"Four years ago. August fifth. Four o'clock in the afternoon."

"That's very precise."

"It was my father's funeral."

"Is that when Tye moved into town?"

"That's when he left the ranch. What he did with himself after that wasn't my concern."

Leila leaned forward, her hands momentarily stilled. "Ranching's hard work, Miss Wyatt. Everyone pitches in. They have to. The chores still had to be done even after Daddy passed. But Tye, well, he wasn't the ranching type."

Jo looked for a place to set the mug, but the table was too far to reach. "I don't understand. He grew up here, didn't he?"

"He wanted to sell—"

"That's enough, Leila. Family laundry don't need to be aired in public."

Jo focused on Turner. "Did you have a falling-out?"

"I wouldn't call it a falling-out," he said.

"What would you call it?"

"Wouldn't call it anything."

Selling the ranch might not have resulted in an influx of cash, but it might have been enough to finance a game. "Did Tye ever ask you for money?"

"Oh no." Leila's hands took flight. "He was making quite a name for himself with those electronic video games."

Turner crossed his arms. "Games."

Jo placed the mug by her feet on the pretense of thumbing through her notebook. "You don't approve?"

"Not my place to judge. He never paid me no nevermind anyway."

"So he never asked you for money. Did you ever ask him?"

He narrowed his eyes. "My money ain't no concern of yours."

"I don't mean to be disrespectful, but your brother was found dead. It's my job to determine how that happened."

"Sheriff here said he killed himself with a shotgun. Seems to me it happened when he pulled the trigger."

"According to your wife, that's out of character for him."

Turner's fingers dug into the back of the chair by his wife's shoulder, leaving dents in the upholstery. "We don't know what's out of character, now do we. Fact is, we don't know my brother at all."

He spoke to Jo, but his words were clearly for his wife.

"How long since either of you spoke with Tye?"

"It's been about a year," Leila said.

"Please forgive my next question, but why do you suppose Tye listed you, Mrs. Horton, rather than his brother as next of kin?"

Leila flushed.

"Yes, Leila, why is that?"

"I'm sure I don't know."

Jo was certain she did—and that her husband knew the reason too.

"Did Tye retain his share in the ranch?"

"Don't much matter now, does it?" Turner remained planted behind his wife. "There's work needs to be done, and I'm sure you'll be wanting to head back before the storm hits."

Jo retrieved her cup. "Thank you for the coffee. Again, I'm very sorry for your loss."

Leila sprang from her chair and grabbed the mug from Jo. Together they walked to the door. "It's strange to see a woman detective. Don't you get scared?" She glanced over her shoulder at her husband and lowered her voice. "Does Tye's partner know anything?"

Jo spoke quietly as well. "Partner?"

"Boyfriend. Surely you've talked to him?"

"I don't know anything about a boyfriend."

Turner's voice cut across the room. "In or out, but I'm not paying to heat the entire neighborhood."

Leila pushed Jo out of the house. "I think his name is Dennis. Daniel? Something like that."

Jo spun. "Derek?"

Leila shrugged her shoulders. "Maybe."

The door closed.

20

Alice drove to the college to find Quinn.

From behind, the boy she followed from the campus parking lot could have been Derek. He walked with the same loose-jointed amble of young men not yet accustomed to the length of their limbs. Dark hair peeked from under his knit cap and curled at his neck. She ached to touch it. Touch Derek. Tell him she was sorry.

The Digital Arts Building was her destination, but she continued past it just to revel in the moment. Intellectually, she knew there were no more minutes to share with her son. But emotionally, the shock of finding a piece of him in the real world tore open the cavity in her chest and reminded her how empty it had become.

The man turned toward the Student Union Building. In the vestibule, he stepped sideways and held the door for her.

"After you."

The voice was too deep. This man's face held none of her son's features. She drew a breath. Frigid air spread through her body until even her fingers went numb, freezing her in place while she stammered something about being lost.

He pointed toward the Digital Arts Building and then disappeared inside. She straddled the threshold, a foot in two worlds.

Another student pushed past her. She drew a second breath, inured to the cold. The past released its hold reluctantly. Cursing herself for wasting valuable time, she crossed the quad.

The hallways inside the Digital Arts Building were nearly deserted. Wet with snow, her rubber-soled boots squeaked against the tile.

The last time she'd been on the college campus was for the rededication of Ambrose Hall after its renovation. Derek was accepted into the digital arts program shortly thereafter. She'd never known for certain if that most recent endowment had anything to do with the decision. Considering the downward spiral of his senior year grades, she had her suspicions. Regardless, it should have been him, not her, wandering the school corridors.

Alice entered the stairwell, and the fire door shut behind her with a thunderous clap. She climbed the stairs to the third floor. Here, more students milled around the halls.

But not Quinn.

A narrow window allowed Alice to peer through the door into the computer lab. According to Quinn's schedule, she should be inside. Students took up every station. Most had earbuds or headphones on; some still wore caps. They all had their backs to the door, and Alice studied each one, determined not to overlook Quinn. It didn't matter. She wasn't there.

Maybe this was God's way of letting her know that meeting Quinn was a bad idea.

Retracing her steps, she had to pass through the elevator lobby to reach the stairs. A petite woman stood inside the elevator as the doors closed. She had the kind of thousand-mile stare that suggested approaching her would be as much fun as dragging a badger from its burrow.

Quinn.

Alice rushed to the end of the hallway and descended the wet tile stairs as fast as she dared. At ground level, she hurried to the elevator and mashed the call button. Almost immediately, the doors opened. No one was inside.

With a stifled oath, Alice dashed through the front door of the building and out onto the quad. Quinn was heading toward the parking lot. Lengthening her stride, Alice lessened the space between them and willed her heart to slow.

"Ms. Kirkwood?"

Even though the woman kept walking, she hesitated ever so slightly. It was enough.

"Ms. Kirkwood, please."

The woman veered off the salted pathway and stomped across the unbroken expanse of snow. Alice followed in her footsteps. "Quinn."

Quinn spun, closing the distance between them, and Alice stumbled backward, her hands raised.

Quinn stopped inches from Alice's chin. "How do you know my name?"

The file copy of the woman's driver's license hadn't prepared Alice for the girl's diminutive stature. Even wearing a down jacket, Quinn gave the impression of being dainty—which in her case certainly didn't equate with demure.

"I read it in the police report."

Her eyes narrowed. "Which police report?"

Good God, how many police reports did the woman have? "You found Tye Horton. I'm Alice Walsenberg." She extended her hand but withheld her smile. Quinn wasn't the type to be disarmed by a twitch of the lips. "My husband and I own the property where Tye lived."

Quinn ignored Alice's hand. "I don't know you."

"No." Wind-whipped snow stung Alice's face, and she lowered her hand. "But you knew my son, Derek."

"How did you know where to find me?" Quinn pressed.

Alice had expected the question but couldn't very well disclose that her husband had an entire dossier on the young woman's comings and goings. A different truth would have to suffice. "I serve on the executive board for the college foundation."

"That still doesn't explain how you knew where to find me."

"I've obviously stepped off on the wrong foot. I merely want to speak to you for a few minutes. May I buy you lunch?"

Quinn crossed her arms. "Why would you want to do that?"

Tye. Ronny. Quinn.

Of the three people Alice's husband had linked to Derek, Quinn was the wild card. Her file was full of contradictions, and beyond those snippets of information, Alice knew nothing of the woman.

Ronny Buck was different. The Buck and Walsenberg families shared the same social strata and had been close for years. Every summer the boys had run wild at the Ambroses' high-country ranch or the Bucks' cabin on the lake. Despite a three-year age gap, the boys were inseparable. Initially, Ronny's influence over her son worried her, but Derek had either never joined Ronny on his criminal escapades or he'd had the good fortune of never getting caught.

Then there was Tye. The dossier had given Alice the impression that Tye was the sun around which everyone else orbited. But he was gone now. That file was closed.

After rereading the files, Alice had convinced herself that she needed to talk with this woman. Quinn had shared in her son's last passion. Perhaps she could explain why that had become more important to him than life itself.

Finally, she smiled. "If I feed you, I'm hoping you won't be as grumpy when I offer you a job."

*   *   *

The coffee bar in the Student Union Building served an assortment of pastries, soups, and paninis to pair with their bigger selection of coffees, teas, smoothies, chais, and espresso drinks that college kids needed to sustain their energy.

Alice picked at her salad. It was Quinn who interested her, not the food, and at the moment, the object of her curiosity was indelicately cramming the corner of a grilled cheese sandwich into her mouth. The woman's manners were every bit as delightful as her demeanor.

"If you knew my son, you know he killed himself."

"I didn't know he was your son until today." She slurped her tomato soup.

Alice's fork clanked against her plate. No condolences. None of the usual niceties reserved for someone who'd just announced they'd lost a loved one. "Perhaps this is a mis—"

"My mother was shot and killed by a drug dealer." The declaration was delivered without emotion.

Alice sat back in her chair. "I'm sor—"

"Don't be. You know nothing about my mother."

"I know she was shot and killed by a drug dealer. Isn't that enough?"

"For what?"

"To want to offer comfort to a grieving daughter."

Quinn cocked her head. "That assumes I'm grieving."

"Yes, it does."

"What if I told you my mother was a hype and she tried to double-cross her dealer?"

Was Quinn testing her? "Who she was doesn't change who you are." It was a meaningless platitude. Then again, truths often were.

"That's where you're wrong."

For the first time, Quinn smiled. It transformed her face. Gone was the wariness. Gone, too, was some of the tenseness that had practically turned her shoulders into earmuffs. Alice wanted to reassure her, but Quinn had made it abundantly clear that she was a woman who didn't want to be perceived as weak.

"Why are you going to school in Echo Valley?" Alice asked. "Why here?"

"Scholarship."

"You're a smart woman, then."

"Poor."

"You forget, I serve on the foundation. I know the criteria that must be met to be awarded one of our scholarships."

"Then you know nothing beats a good hard-luck story."

"So what's your story?"

"Told you." Quinn spoke around a smaller, yet still impressive, bite of sandwich.

"No, actually, you didn't."

She swallowed. "I'm the daughter of a police officer killed in the line of duty. That sad fact, plus my financial situation and grades, resulted in an all-expense-paid ride to the middle of nowhere. Here I am."

"So your father—"

"Mother," Quinn corrected.

Nothing in Zach's files had mentioned that Quinn's mother was a police officer—or that the woman had been murdered. Quinn's face remained impassive, and it was impossible to tell what, if anything, she said was true.

"Your mother wasn't a drug addict."

"Obviously."

"But she was killed by a drug dealer."

"You mentioned a job."

The abrupt change in the conversation threw Alice, but for whatever reason, it lent Quinn credibility. Her defensiveness certainly made more sense. She was wounded. Angry. In a way, they were kindred spirits, although she'd probably not appreciate the comparison. But they'd both had someone they loved torn from them.

It cemented Alice's belief that Quinn would be perfect for the position. Now it was just a matter of letting her come to the same conclusion. "I did, but after our conversation, I'm no longer certain it's a good fit for you."

"I guess we're through here, then." Quinn crushed more saltines into her soup and pressed them under the surface with the back of her spoon.

Alice had been privy to Quinn's bank account, and the minuscule balance was inversely proportional to the woman's current nonchalance. Time to call her bluff.

Alice pulled money from her wallet for a tip the waitress would probably never see. "Thank you for your time."

"Wait." Quinn dabbed the corner of her mouth with her napkin—a flash of decorum that vanished when she crumpled the brown bit of paper and dropped it into her soup bowl. She stretched out her legs and crossed her hands over her belly. "You never said what the job was."

"I've formed the Echo Valley Alliance for Life, a suicide awareness program. I'm looking for a student advocate to act as my liaison with the campus social groups."

"Why me?"

"You've been touched by death. You've seen things." Alice decided to lay everything on the table. "I recently learned that Tye belonged to the LGBTQ group on campus. Members of that community are at greater risk for suicide than any other population—on or off campus. Echo Valley is a small city, and tolerance isn't the first word that comes to mind when I think about the people from around here. Don't get me wrong. The vast majority are God-fearing."

"That's part of the problem."

"Perhaps." Alice gathered her purse. "You knew Tye. You'd have credibility. No one wants to listen to me—I sound too much like their mothers. You're one of them."

"How much does it pay?"

Alice wanted her to accept the position, and she added a bit more than she'd originally intended to offer. Her motives were less than pure. She wanted Quinn close. Wanted to learn who this woman had been to her son and to hold on to what little bits of Derek she remembered. She might have been telling the truth about her mother, but Alice felt certain Quinn knew more than she was letting on about Derek. After all, there were three files. "Twenty dollars an hour."

"In exchange for what?"

"Carrying the Alliance's message to the campus groups and assisting me. I understand you're a student. Coursework comes first. We can work around your schedule, and all told, I figure it's about fifteen hours a week."

"I thought I wasn't a good fit." Her words were a challenge.

"How about this. The executive board meets tomorrow morning at the resort, and then I'll be spending the afternoon putting the final touches on the fund raiser we're hosting tomorrow night. Help me set up. Commit to the evening. See what we're all about. I'll arrange a room for you. If nothing else, enjoy the banquet. They've got fabulous food, and the resort is amazing."

"And if I decide it's not for me?"

"I'll cut you a check for your time. We go our separate ways."

Quinn worried the cuticle on her thumb. "I'm not a touchy-feely kind of person."

The candor surprised Alice. "Maybe not, but you're a survivor."

21

Jo entered the police department lobby through the double glass doors in the front. Three bullet holes marred the wall, courtesy of a disgruntled customer. The cavities had been patched, but the impressions remained. Even a police building wasn't always safe.

Small and utilitarian, the lobby contained a single pew, discreetly bolted to the floor. The few people who wandered in for assistance faced a counter where, depending on the day, they spoke to either Young Sarah or Simply Sarah, the mother-daughter team who had been doling out records and generally riding roughshod over Echo Valley's finest since water first flowed down the Animas.

"Cutting it close, aren't you?" Simply Sarah remarked from the window.

Jo stomped the snow off her boots on the doormat. "Plenty of time."

"One-Point-Five is looking for you." She pressed the buzzer to unlock the door to the inner sanctum. "She predicted you'd be a no-show."

Jo caught herself before she made an unladylike snort. The chief's radio designation was Echo One. Harriet Landeau was the chief's administrative assistant. She didn't have a call sign, but that didn't stop the officers from making one up—and using it out of earshot. There wasn't a single thing that occurred in the station that Harriet didn't somehow orchestrate. Chiefs came and went, but she held the real power.

"Wouldn't miss it." Although Jo had been ready to jump on any call that went out over the radio to have a valid excuse not to be here.

"That's what I told her."

Jo double-timed it through the empty hallways. Maybe she was later than she'd thought. She rounded the corner and slid into the back of the crowded briefing room. The clock showed exactly 1630 hours.

116

Cop shows on television always had spiffy briefing rooms. Maybe it was because they usually called it a squad room. It elevated the purpose.

Magnetic whiteboards hung on three walls in the EVPD briefing room. The one on the back wall always displayed the shift rosters so the sergeant could read it from the front of the room. The board behind the sergeant's table contained current issues plaguing the city and usually had Ronny Buck's name on it somewhere.

The last one was affectionately dubbed the bullshit board, a six-by-four receptacle of off-color jokes, photoshopped pictures, red-pen-edited newspapers articles correcting factual inaccuracies, and transcripts of things officers shouldn't say on the radio—even at 03:30. Harriet removed the offending items at least once a day, but no matter how many memos came out about workplace propriety, it always held the most interesting info.

Cameron stood by the lectern at the front of the room and winked at Jo as she leaned against the back wall. Officers and admin folks vied for chairs and collected in clusters. Her father and some of the other retirees sat up front. The overlap between swing-shift officers reporting on duty and the day-shift officers calling off guaranteed an audience. Squint stood next to the award case. She wanted to sidle over to him to update him on the latest about Tye's relationship status, but Chief Grimes arrived and wove his way toward the front.

Dakota slid in next to Jo and whispered, "You doing okay?"

She refused to look at her best friend. "Aren't you supposed to be dispatching?"

A reporter from the *Valley Courier* craned around in his chair, using his pen to conduct a head count. He nodded at Jo.

Chief Grimes cleared his throat, and the chatter subsided. "Today we're gathered to honor one of our own with a new badge, a new title, and most importantly new responsibilities."

"What, is this a wedding?" Dakota's hushed southern drawl almost made it sound like a legitimate question.

Jo tried to keep a straight face.

"Cameron Finch," Chief Grimes intoned. "Please step forward."

Cameron moved closer to the chief. He wore his Class A uniform. It looked odd without a badge.

"Officer Finch joined us six years ago. It's said that every story has a woman." He picked Jo out of the room and smiled. "And we have Detective Wyatt to thank for enticing Cameron to our community."

Heat traveled up Jo's neck. She adjusted her scarf to hide the blush.

"In the short time that Cameron has been here," the chief continued, "he's forged strong relationships with his peers."

Dakota elbowed Jo and whispered, "Brownnosed his superiors."

"Established bonds with the community."

"And broke those with his wife," she continued.

"And earned a well-justified reputation with the district attorney's office."

"Not good, just well justified," she clarified.

"It is my honor to promote Officer Cameron Finch to sergeant. Sergeant Finch, is there someone you would like to help you with your badge?"

Cameron locked eyes with Jo.

She gave the slightest nod.

Cameron faced the chief. "Yes, sir. My wife."

His wife. No name, just a title. She'd think about that later.

The crowd parted. Jo hadn't told anyone other than Squint and Dakota that she and Cameron had split, but it was hard to keep secrets from people who investigated crimes for a living, and the murmurs and dipped heads told her that most people in the room knew. She concentrated on placing one foot in front of the other and walked the gauntlet of curious faces that included her father's. One more thing she'd survive.

Chief Grimes handed her the oval shield. Badges were symbols of the office, a representation of the public trust bestowed on the wearer. Every element of the design was imbued with meaning. This badge was the same weight as her own, but the word *Sergeant* engraved on the blue banner under her city's name gave this badge more heft. Gravitas. She unclasped the catch and extended the long, thick pin.

"Hey, Finch, you wearing your vest?"

Laughter filled the room. Leave it to Estes.

Jo drew a steadying breath. Once before she and Cameron had faced each other with a symbol of trust between them. She hoped this one remained unbroken. "Ready?"

He looked deep into her eyes. "Are you?" he asked softly.

She slid her hand under the vee of his uniform shirt and stabbed the pin through the reinforced badge tab, pricking her finger. She pressed the pin into the groove. Twisted the catch. Done. She smoothed his shirt.

Cameron grabbed her hand. "Thank you."

"Congratulations, Sergeant," she said. And she meant it. She'd been honored yesterday when he asked her if she would pin his badge. Try as she might, she couldn't help but read into the request, but what it meant eluded her.

He leaned over and kissed her cheek. Whispered in her ear. "When did it become a competition?"

"It never was," she said.

"Ladies and gentlemen," the chief said. "May I present Sergeant Finch."

The room erupted into applause. From this point forward, Cameron's word meant more than hers. Perhaps it had always been that way.

The chief shook Cameron's hand, and the crowd surged forward to congratulate him. She was trapped. Awash in a wave of adulation meant for someone else, she could only wait it out.

Dakota materialized at her side and pulled her toward the door. "I need a drink."

*　*　*

The cold air hit them as soon as they walked outside.

"Elks Club or somewhere else?" Jo asked.

Dakota stopped in the middle of the sidewalk. Her blonde hair framed her face in a demented halo of static electricity, and she whipped the hood of her pink parka up. "Seriously? Haven't you had enough of the good ol' boys for one day?"

Jo shoved her hands deeper into her jacket pockets. "Finnegan's it is."

Tourists on a quest for good food and drink rarely wandered beyond Main Street. Locals ventured a little farther afield. Three bars catered to the disparate personalities of the Valley, and none of them were on the main drag. Cowboys drank Coors at the Hitching Post. Bikers raised their tankards in Valhalla. Cops relaxed at Finnegan's Irish Pub. Full of cozy nooks, good whiskey, and Guinness imported from Dublin, it had the added benefit of being two blocks from the station.

They walked quickly and remained silent until they reached the dark doors of the pub.

The place was empty except for Merlyn, the only cowboy in the county who hated Coors. The Australian cattle dog under the table lifted his head but decided the ladies didn't need herding and went back to sleep. Merlyn tipped his pint glass in greeting and went back to his careful study of the foam.

Sully pulled a Guinness behind the bar. He was a bear of a man, but whether that was a grizzly or a teddy bear depended on how a person held his liquor.

"Well, now if the two of you aren't a sight for sore eyes." He set the pint glass aside to settle and wiped his hands on a bar rag. "A Smitty's for you today, Jo?"

"Please."

Dakota perused the bottles of spirits behind him. "I don't suppose you can make a cosmo?"

The crinkles around Sully's Wedgwood-blue eyes deepened. "I can, but it's going to taste a good deal like Jameson."

"I'll stick to a Strongbow."

"A fine choice."

Jo pointed to a table by the fireplace. "Anyone have dibs?"

"All yours," Sully replied. "Go thaw yourselves out. I'll bring your drinks around in a moment."

Jo peeled her jacket off as she walked toward the inviting corner. "Since when do you drink cosmos?" she asked Dakota.

"I just binge-watched two seasons of *Sex and the City*. I'd be wearing four-inch Manolo Blahniks if it weren't for the snow."

"I'd settle for a new pair of Vasque hiking boots." Jo sat with her back to the wall.

Sully followed a minute later and set the Irish ale in front of Jo and the cider in front of Dakota. "You ladies interested in food or just solving the world's problems tonight?"

Jo reached for her pint. "It's a troubled world, Sully."

"I'll keep 'em coming, then."

She lifted the glass in a toast. "You're a good man."

Dakota tapped a text on her phone, then slid it back in her pocket. She waited until Sully was beyond hearing before she pounced. "I can't believe Cameron sprang the badge pinning on you like that."

"He didn't."

Dakota missed her coaster, and the glass thunked against the table. "What?"

"Can we talk about something else?"

"Let me get this straight. You *agreed* to pin the badge that should have been yours onto someone else?"

Jo sighed. She should have just wrapped up for the day and gone home. "Yup."

"You are seriously cracked."

Jo took a long pull on her ale. "You've mentioned that before."

The pub filled with the five o'clock crowd as most of the downtown businesses shuttered for the night. Merlyn and his dog left as the reporter from the *Courier* entered.

Great. "What's-his-face just arrived."

Dakota twisted. "Everett Cloud?"

Everett propped his foot on the brass rail that ran the length of the bar. He glanced toward their table and then leaned toward Sully.

The relationship between cops and reporters was complicated. In kinder moments, Jo acknowledged that the media and law enforcement both wanted to uncover the truth, but how they went about it often played the two entities against each other.

Sully approached their table with two more pints. "Courtesy of the gent at the bar."

"Not finished with this one," Jo said.

"That's so nice!" Dakota rose out of her chair and waved him over.

"What are you doing?" Jo grabbed Dakota's arm, but it was too late.

Everett Cloud approached the table and directed his words to Jo. "May I join you?"

"Of course," Dakota said, before Jo could object.

He sat next to Jo, blocking the heat from the fireplace. "I saw you at the badge ceremony. That was very gracious of you."

Gracious. She sipped her beer, alert. "Shouldn't you be interviewing Sergeant Finch?"

He pulled his messenger bag strap over his head and flipped the flap back. Jo straightened in her chair. He noticed and very slowly pulled out a piece of paper and slid it in front of her.

Dakota didn't even glance at the Echo Valley PD memorandum. Jo had seen the memo before. Had her own damn copy and had memorized every word.

Congratulations to Officer Cameron Finch, who has been selected to fill the vacant sergeant position. His promotion will be effective Sunday, December 9th. An eligibility list of successful sergeant candidates will remain in effect through the end of the year in the event of an additional opening.

"Twenty-two days. Aren't promotional eligibility lists usually good for a year?" he asked.

"Where did you get this?" Jo demanded.

"Did you know there's never been a woman promoted above the rank of officer in the entire history of the Echo Valley Police Department?"

"It's a numbers game, Mr. Cloud. You have to have women test before they can promote."

"I'm curious," he said. "How many women work in your agency?"

"I suspect you already know the answer to that question."

"Currently there are three. A school resource officer who has twenty-one years on the job, and a patrol officer in training."

"Don't forget me."

"A detective who has been recognized for her service by several community groups and been awarded a medal of valor."

"For a traffic stop." As her father was quick to remind her.

"For apprehending a murder suspect from Albuquerque who had his next victim tied up in his trunk."

"Is there a point to all this?"

"Is there anyone on the eligibility list other than you?"

Jo slammed down her pint. "We're done here, Mr. Cloud."

"Nearly a dozen women have tested for sergeant over the years."

Jo pushed out of her chair. The heat from the fire blazed against her face.

"I only have one question." He stood and looped his messenger bag strap over his head. "Was Officer Finch really the best candidate?"

Sully appeared at the table with a hint of grizzly in his posture. "Looks to me like you've worn out your welcome with the ladies."

"Story of my life." Everett dug a business card out of his pocket and tossed it in front of Jo. It slid to a stop in a condensation puddle. "Thank you for your time."

Jo marked the reporter's progress through the door and then settled back into her chair.

Sully gathered the two untouched drinks. "Let me get rid of these and bring you something fresh."

"Thanks, but I'm going to pass," Jo said. "The world's going to have to solve its own problems tonight."

"Let me know if you change your mind."

When they were alone, Jo stared into the fire. "Want to tell me where he got the memo?"

"I suppose it could have been anywhere. It's on all the city announcement boards. Public records?"

A log split, and sparks spiraled upward.

"Why, Dakota?"

She took her time answering. "You scored fourteen points higher than Cameron on the written."

"Doesn't mean I did better in the interview."

"Don't kid yourself," Dakota argued. "You might not have scored higher, but I'd bet my life you did better."

"Never bet your life on anything."

Fatigue infused Jo's very bones. She wanted to go home. A place with all her stuff. A bathtub. Candles. Her fluffy robe and slippers. All the things residing in a house she still held in joint title with her husband.

A pop from the fire startled her.

"He didn't cheat on me," Jo said. "Cameron. He didn't cheat."

Dakota traced designs on the side of her glass. "That's not what's going around."

"I don't care what the gossip is. I know my husband."

"You don't owe him anything, Jo."

"I don't know what you hoped to accomplish tonight, but I'm not having any of it. I love my job. I need it—now more than ever. I'm not going to be that girl—"

"Woman."

Jo glared at her. "The girl who complains because she was picked last in dodgeball."

"We're not on the playground anymore."

"No." Jo drained her glass. She could knock it over, smash it into pieces, and nothing would spill out. She had nothing left. "If you ever do an end-around on me like this again, it will be the end of our friendship."

Dakota reached for Jo, but then slowly withdrew her hand and nodded. "What did Cameron ask you? After you pinned his badge. He whispered something to you."

When did it become a competition?

"He wanted to thank me."

It never was.

But that wasn't the truth. It had become a competition the day her father told her she didn't have what it took to be a sergeant.

22

It took Quinn forever to get to the resort. Maybe she should have insisted on a gas allowance—the driveway alone burned another gallon. She finally stopped under a giant wreath in front of the hotel, and after a brief argument with the valet, she parked in the side lot.

Growing up in San Francisco, she'd seen plenty of over-the-top Christmas displays—Macy's in Union Square led the pack—but they didn't come close to the Peregrines Roost lobby. A pianist sat behind a baby grand and pounded out carols. There was a cider station. Add in the snow outside, and she found herself smack-dab in the middle of a winter wonderland from hell.

Quinn dropped her backpack in front of the reception desk and slapped down her identification.

The man behind the counter wore an alpine-inspired sweater more at home on the slopes than inside. He launched into the standard spiel about check-in time and then stopped. "I see Mrs. Walsenberg made special arrangements for your room, Ms. Kirkwood. It's ready for you now. Would you like one or two keys?"

"One." She leaned closer. "If I get lucky later, I'll come back for the second one."

He blinked several times. "Of course. Would you like assistance with your luggage?"

She pocketed her license and slung her backpack across her shoulder. "I can manage."

"Enjoy your stay." He handed her the electronic key card. "The elevators are to the right of the gingerbread village."

"Thanks."

The village was more like a small metropolis. Cordoned off with green and red silken ropes suspended from candy cane posts, it was large enough to shelter the Claus family, their elven empire, and an entire stable of reindeer, plus an assortment of shepherds, babies, and wise men. If she got hungry later, she knew exactly where to go.

The resort had five levels, and Quinn rode the elevator to the top floor. The plush hallway carpet silenced her footsteps. She pushed open the door to her room and gaped. A four-poster canopied bed dominated the room, while a fireplace and flat-screen television graced the opposite wall. French doors opened onto a balcony with a view of the mountain. The seating area consisted of two overstuffed chairs with a round marble table between them. Quinn tossed her backpack onto the duvet. The room even smelled expensive.

A card with her name on it leaned against a vase of flowers. She tore open the envelope. The script consisted of bold strokes. *Thank you for coming! I hope you find the room to your liking. I'll meet you in the lobby at three o'clock. Alice Walsenberg.* Got to give the lady credit. She knew how to make an impression.

Quinn left her room at three and found Alice by the giant fireplace, talking with a man who had just enough gray in his black hair to be considered experienced but not old. Alice saw her enter and enthusiastically waved her over.

"Quinn. I'd like to introduce you to a dear friend of mine. We've known each other now, what?" She tilted her head in that way beautiful women did when they wanted to look stupid. "Forty years?"

He covered her hand with his. "That's impossible. You aren't that old."

They both laughed.

Blech. If this was what the night held in store, she was screwed. "You forgot to tell me his name."

They laughed again. He bowed. An honest-to-God bend-from-the-waist bow. Who the fuck did that?

"Xavier Buck."

Ronny's dad, that's who. She kept her hands jammed in her pockets. "Quinn Kirkwood."

"Please forgive me, ladies, but duty calls." A head nod this time; Quinn almost felt cheated. "Ms. Kirkwood, the pleasure is mine."

Several responses came to mind, but she merely matched his head bob. No sense getting fired before she'd at least earned enough to make the trip worthwhile.

As soon as he left, Alice turned the full wattage of her smile on Quinn. "How is your room?"

Earlier, after she'd thoroughly checked out the contents of the minibar and nabbed an overpriced package of M&Ms, Quinn had stood out on her balcony. Some type of fast-flying bird had swooped past her, and Quinn had wanted to follow it back to the valley. This place reeked of a lifestyle she'd never known. It made her uncomfortable. What did Alice do? Quinn's mother had worked like a dog her entire life. She'd never come close to being able to afford such luxury—and she'd deserved it far more than her screw-up of a daughter.

"I can see why you like this place."

Alice beamed. "Well, you are welcome. First order of business is to give you the lay of the land and show you the ballroom." She strode toward a timber-vaulted corridor. She had the best posture of anyone Quinn had ever seen. She was rocking a simple blue sweater, dark jeans, and heeled boots. If it hadn't been for her gray hair, Quinn would have pegged her for midthirties. Tops. But Derek had been seventeen when he died, and that was over a year ago. Women of her class didn't squirt out a kid at sixteen, so she had to be in her forties.

Quinn's curiosity got the better of her. "Have you really known the Bucks for forty years?"

"Gosh, yes. He knew me when I was an Ambrose. We went to the same elementary school—actually, it was the only elementary school at the time. We've been friends since first grade."

That put her at forty-five or forty-six. Impressive.

The next hour and a half consisted of rearranging floral centerpieces to get them all perfectly balanced, polishing already sparkling wine goblets, ensuring that the chairback ties hit exactly an inch above the floor, and straightening tableware. Quinn had once seen a BBC documentary about royal state dinners that showed butlers with rulers measuring the distance between table settings. The royal family had nothing on Alice Walsenberg. She had resort staff practically standing at attention awaiting orders, and she did it all with a smile.

One thing was certain: the Echo Valley Alliance for Life was going to be a tremendous success—Alice Ambrose Walsenberg would stand for nothing less.

It was approaching five o'clock when Alice stepped back from the final table, put her hands on her hips, and pronounced, "There." Quinn didn't see that their efforts had made much of a difference, but Alice surveyed the room and gave a crisp nod. "The only thing left is collecting the auction paddles and swag bags."

Finally, a task Quinn felt qualified to do. "Where are they? I'll get them."

"They should be arriving any moment. I was so excited to get here, I forgot the boxes at home. Xavier's son picked them up on his way to work."

"Ronny."

Alice either didn't catch the snark in Quinn's voice or chose to ignore it. "That's right. He works security here."

"Ronny?" Quinn repeated, and bit the inside of her cheek to keep from busting out laughing at the absurdity of Ronny Buck as a security guard.

"I forgot you two know each other. You're in the same program at school."

"Unfortunately."

"You don't like him?"

"I wouldn't cross the street to save his life. But the feeling's mutual."

"He was my son's best friend." She'd aged in the time it took to talk about Ronny. "Did you feel that way about my son too?"

An unfamiliar emotion clogged Quinn's chest. The woman's pain was palpable. Visceral. Four years hadn't been nearly enough time for Quinn to get over the guilt of her mother's death. How could a mother get over the loss of her son in just a year? "I was telling you the truth earlier. I only knew *of* your son. But others cared for him very much."

Alice's perfect posture slowly returned. "Thank you." She removed her phone from her rear pocket. A text banner ran across the screen, and she clicked it. "Ronny's arrived." She slid the cell back into her jeans. "I can do this last bit by myself if you'd rather go get ready."

Quinn was already wearing her party clothes—a black sweater, black jeans, and Doc Martens boots. Against a backdrop of holiday red, green, and gold decorations, she stuck out like a gargoyle. "I can play nice."

Uncertainty crossed Alice's face, but then she cheered up again. "Splendid. Shall we?" Without waiting for an answer, she swept off toward the lobby. When they reached the door, the bellman held it open for them. Neither of them had their jacket, but the cold didn't appear to bother Alice.

"We should only be outside about ten minutes, "Alice said. "Are you going to be warm enough? If not, you can stay in the lobby."

The cold bit through Quinn's sweater, but damn if she was going to be outdone by a forty-five-year-old woman. "I'm fine."

Ronny Buck rounded the corner holding a cup of coffee that hadn't done anything to brighten his bleary eyes.

"There's my savior now." Alice rushed forward and gave Ronny a quick kiss on the cheek. "I still can't believe I left the house without everything. Thank goodness you were scheduled to work tonight."

"No problem, Mrs. Walsenberg. Olivia was home, and they were right where you said they'd be."

Ronny noticed Quinn and stiffened. "Quinn."

"Ronny."

Alice stepped between them as if afraid they were going to throw down right there under the portico. "Quinn has been helping me put the finishing touches on the ballroom. The boxes are the last of the tasks. Where are you parked?"

"I'll get the security cart. I'm in the employee lot. It's a bit of a yomp."

He stowed his coffee in the valet vestibule and grabbed the keys to the cart. Quinn slid in the back behind Alice.

The employee lot was behind the resort in an extension of the main lot and butted up against the tree line. There was nothing to distinguish it as employees-only. Of course, with only Quinn and the valets parking cars, it probably didn't need the separate designation.

Ronny stopped the cart at his Dodge and hopped out. He lowered the tailgate and yanked off the tarp that covered six boxes in the back of the truck. They each grabbed a box and carried it to the cart.

"Why don't we just pile them on the back seat?" Alice suggested. "When we're finished loading, Quinn, you can sit up front with Ronny. I'll walk back. The air will do me good."

"That's okay," Quinn said. "I'll walk back with you." Ronny Buck could fend for himself.

23

The Alliance for Life event was in full swing by the time Jo arrived. She gave her coat to the cloakroom attendant and tucked the claim receipt in the outside pocket of her purse. The shoulder bag was a necessary evil, but carrying a gun in a thigh holster only worked in the movies—and those women certainly weren't carrying Glock 22s with full magazines of .40 caliber jacketed hollow-points. Fortunately, people in cocktail attire usually remained well behaved.

Massive double doors stood open and allowed Echo Valley's glitterati to flow in and out of the Aspen ballroom. A large fireplace graced the far wall. Garlands and myriad white lights imparted a festive atmosphere, and based on the din, the alcohol flowed freely.

Jo took up position in the corner. The valley's two judges had their heads close together. Mrs. Baxter held court by the fireplace. Xavier Buck and the district attorney entertained a gaggle of downtown business owners. The governor's local representative held a folio that probably hid a proclamation—which likely meant the mayor would respond with a proclamation of his own. No wonder the chief had made other plans.

Alice Walsenberg breezed toward Jo with her hand outstretched. "Detective Wyatt, I'm so glad you could make it. You look lovely."

A polite lie. Jo tugged at the wraparound neckline that ended in an overblown silk bow. Online, the dress had appeared chic, a deep hunter-green velvet that came with a price tag Jo could afford. The reality was a scratchy velveteen fabric that hung awkwardly from her frame and imparted a jaundiced glow to her skin. "Thank you. And thank you for the invitation. I wouldn't miss it." Another polite prevarication.

"After the sheriff speaks, I'll turn the microphone over to you."

Jo's mouth went dry. "I'm sorry, what?"

"The lectern will be up front. Be sure to adjust the microphone so it's the right height. Oh, listen to me ramble. You know what you're doing."

"The chief neglected to mention that he was going to address the audience." The bastard.

"Speak from the heart." She dipped her head close to Jo. "And remember, the best speeches are short." She twirled back to the other guests, leaving behind only a whiff of perfume and a sense of impending doom.

Quinn stepped into the space Alice had vacated. "You look like you're about to puke."

"Always a pleasure, Ms. Kirkwood. What brings you here?"

"Just hanging with my peeps."

"You're avoiding my calls."

Quinn pulled her cell phone from the rear pocket of her pants. "Oh, look at that. Voice mail."

The woman's casual disregard pushed Jo dangerously close to an edge she hadn't known she'd been skirting. "I can't help you if you won't talk to me." She swallowed her frustration. The last thing she wanted to do was alienate Quinn. The conversation with Leila Horton demanded answers—and Quinn was the most logical source. "Were Tye and Derek Walsenberg dating?"

Quinn tapped her screen and dismissed Jo's voice mail notification. "So much for small talk."

"Yes or no?" Jo pressed.

"It's my understanding that the whole reason for this shindig is because Derek Walsenberg is dead." She slid the phone back into her pocket. "Kind of hard to date someone like that."

"What about you and the professor? What's your relationship?"

Quinn exploded like a bronc released from a bucking chute. Back arched, nostrils flared, fire in her eyes, she spun toward the exit. Jo figured she had the requisite eight seconds before Quinn left her in the dust.

She grabbed Quinn's arm to slow her down. "What aren't you telling me?"

Quinn's narrowed eyes sliced across Jo's body. "You really should burn that dress."

*　*　*

Jo drew a few steadying breaths before she followed Quinn out the front door of the hotel. The valet hopped to attention, but Quinn flashed her pack of cigarettes, and he settled back into his vestibule. Overhead heaters in the portico kept patrons warm while they waited for their cars. Quinn chose the one farthest from the door to settle under.

Jo invaded Quinn's personal space. "Mind telling me why a question about your professor has you so riled?"

"None of your business."

"Okay, then let's start with something easier. What's up between you and Ronny Buck?"

Quinn tapped a cigarette from the pack and placed it between her lips while she dug a lighter out of her jeans. "We don't see eye to eye on much."

"Well, that little nugget told me a lot." Every encounter with Quinn turned into a sparring match. Cops dealt with uncooperative people all the time, but Quinn took it to a new level. It ended now. Jo didn't need Quinn's permission to investigate a crime, nor did she need her cooperation. With or without her help, Jo would find the truth. "Look. It's my job to ask about relationships and uncover all the nonsense people hide to make themselves look better. It's how I reconstruct events. Maybe you don't care if someone murdered your friend. That's on you. But maybe—just maybe—you want to consider the link between the two of you." Most people ran their words together when they got excited. Jo slowed hers and delivered each word hard as a punch. "Let's play out the possible scenario, shall we? Derek's dead. Tye's dead. You're getting death threats. So by all means, play the odds. Continue blocking me whenever I try to chase down a lead. Just remember, when I go home tonight, I won't be shoving a chair under my doorknob."

Quinn took a step back and cocked her head, appraising Jo. "I think I'm starting to like you."

"I doubt it."

She grinned. "Yeah, the moment's passed."

"I'm going to ask again, and if you decide not to answer, I'm going back inside before I freeze out here in this god-awful dress."

"It really is hideous."

Jo pressed her lips together. She didn't know how many questions Quinn would deign to answer, so she started with the one she most wanted to know. "Was Tye seeing Derek before he died?"

Quinn flicked the lighter and touched the flame to the end of the cigarette. "Yes."

"Did Derek's parents know?"

Quinn blew smoke out of the corner of her mouth. "I don't know." Jo's expression must have conveyed her annoyance, because Quinn hastened to add, "Seriously. I don't know. Tye told me he'd found someone really special, but he was conflicted."

"Why?"

Quinn countered, "You're a cop, you tell me."

Jo thought a moment, trying to suss out the intentions of a man she'd never met. "Derek was underage."

"Bingo." Quinn tapped a bit of ash onto the pavement.

But there was more. Jo read it on Quinn's face. Indecision tightened the lines around her mouth, skittered behind her gray eyes.

Finally Quinn sighed. "I already told you that Tye wanted feedback on a game he'd designed. He hit up Ronny and me, and then Ronny suggested adding Derek. Tye didn't want to give his game to just anyone, and he insisted on meeting him first. Tye told me later it was love at first sight. But here's the thing. Derek was still in high school. He hadn't come out as gay. At first it was strictly about the game. Tye didn't want to pressure him into anything. Derek was the one to make the first move." She dropped the cigarette and ground it under her Doc Martens boot. "Then it was too late."

"Derek suicided."

"Tye was devastated."

Close-set headlights sped up the driveway, and the security cart careened around the corner. A green interior light from the dash area cast a ghoulish glow on Ronny Buck's face. Without his police escort on board, he drove the cart like he drove his truck. Under the portico, he slammed the brakes and slid into the curb. He waved to the valet. Halfway out of the cart, he noticed the two women and reversed course. He cranked the steering wheel hard and stomped on the accelerator. The electric engine whined in protest and the rear tires sent a spray of slush onto the sidewalk.

"What an asshole," Quinn muttered after he'd passed.

"Why does Ronny dislike you?" Jo had met the woman only five days ago and she already had a list of reasons, but what had she done to Ronny?

"I told Tye he was batshit crazy for even thinking about starting a relationship with a confused high school kid."

She'd sidestepped the question, but her answer piqued Jo's curiosity. "Did Tye break it off? Is that the reason Derek killed himself?"

"Yeah, but I don't know if that's why Derek offed himself. Could be. After it happened, Tye took back his games and refused to talk about Derek."

"That still doesn't explain Ronny."

"He thinks I killed his best friend."

24

Quinn would donate an ovary if it meant she could sleep.

The party had ended hours ago. She pummeled her pillow into a new level of fluff and rolled over. Ten seconds later, she rolled again.

It was too quiet. The resort walls were thicker than the toilet-paper-and-spit walls of her apartment, and Stu/Stan's latest musical addiction wasn't wafting up to her apartment on a cloud of premium-grade sinsemilla. She flopped on her back, her tank top a twisted mass around her waist.

What the hell was she doing here?

All night she'd been surrounded by a bunch of rich assholes, and Alice had made it her mission to introduce Quinn to every last one of them. The only time she'd had any relief was when Alice went off to corner some poor staff member and demand they do something trivial to keep the fund raiser humming at a level of unattainable perfection. People had reacted to Quinn in one of two ways. They'd either pegged her as waitstaff and ignored her, or they'd fawned over her because Alice Ambrose-fucking-Walsenberg had returned to the ballroom and was within earshot.

Other than Detective Wyatt, Ronny Buck had been the only person she knew. Neither had particularly brightened her evening, although the cop was starting to grow on her. Quinn liked anyone who was having less fun than she was, and Detective Wyatt hadn't been able to get out of there fast enough when it was all over.

She gave a good speech, though.

The muffled snick of a key card sliding into the security slot of her hotel door thundered across the room. The little electronic sensor whirred, and the person in the hallway pushed down on the door handle.

Quinn slid from the bed.

A man's voice mumbled a curse.

By the soft glow of the bathroom night-light, she pulled on her jeans, then searched for a weapon. Pillow, ice bucket, alarm clock. She unplugged the banker's desk lamp and wrapped her fingers around the brass neck. It would do.

The person in the hallway swiped the key card a second time. The lock held. Another curse, followed by a gentle tap.

She'd thrown the interior security latch. Hell, she'd even hung the do-not-disturb sign on the door. But she missed having a chair to jam under the knob and a kitchen knife close at hand. This was a five-star resort. She hadn't planned on needing such preparations.

Another tap. Slightly louder this time.

She tiptoed to the door, the marble base of the desk lamp held high, and peered through the peephole straight into an eyeball trying to peer inside. She hammered her free fist against the door. A man stumbled backward, and amber liquid sloshed out of the tumbler he held.

Alice's husband.

He regained his balance but wobbled as he approached the door. "My key doesn't work. Let me in," he whispered.

Not a chance.

"Come on, sweetheart." He tapped again. "This isn't funny."

"You've got the wrong room," Quinn said.

He straightened to his full height and tugged the bottom of his suit coat. "This room was rented by my wife." He abandoned his whisper. "Who are you?"

"Not your wife. Go away or I'll call security."

She imagined the confrontation between Ronny Buck and Alice's husband. Her fingers itched to make the call.

"Quinn."

It wasn't a question. Goose bumps rose on her naked arms.

"I'm calling security."

"Wait. You were one of Derek's friends. I just want to ask you a few questions about my son."

"Hello, yes. I need to talk to security." She pretended to speak to the receptionist, never looking away from the peephole.

"Please, Quinn. Let me in."

She raised her voice to make sure he heard her through the door. "I've got some creepy old guy trying to get into my room. Yes. Room five-oh-three. Thank you."

He squeezed the tumbler until his knuckles whitened and she thought the glass would break, but then his shoulders slumped, and he shuffled toward the elevators.

She stared through the peephole for several minutes, waiting. Nothing moved in the hallway, but that didn't mean he wasn't camped out around the corner.

This was bullshit.

The entire Walsenberg clan was seriously whacked. Alice could keep her money. Quinn rummaged in her backpack for her hoodie and pulled it over her tank top, not bothering with her bra. She finished dressing and then swept the toiletries from the bathroom into her opened bag. The free shampoo was the only thing that even came close to making this place worthwhile.

Packed, she crept to the door. Another peek. No one. She eased the door open. Rather than heading toward the elevator, she took the stairs.

The lobby was deserted. Even the bellhop had abandoned his post, although based on the giggles coming from behind the reception area, she suspected she knew where he was and exactly what he was doing.

Soft lights illuminated the covered valet area in front of the hotel. Sometime during the night, the landscape had morphed into one of those overblown Victorian Christmas cards. Old-fashioned streetlamps bordered the driveway and highlighted fat flakes of falling snow.

The driveway circled the resort and led to the darker parking lots. It had to be heated. Already five or six inches of snow covered the cars, but the driveway was merely wet. Maybe that was how they earned that fifth star. It certainly wasn't for the quality of their security.

The valets had the last laugh. She found her Mini Cooper sandwiched between a white SUV on one side and a Hummer parked so close it blocked her driver door. One more thing to add to a royally screwed up night.

Snow stuck to her eyelashes, and she blinked away the moisture. Fuck if she'd cry.

She opened the passenger door, threw her bag on the floorboard, and retrieved the ice scraper from her glove box. She swept the snow near the top of the windshield off with her sleeve so it wouldn't come sliding down the first time she used the brakes. That had been a fun lesson. She scraped the windshield and made sure the blades weren't frozen in place. By the time she was through, her fingers were numb.

She crawled across the console, contorting her body and managing not only to snag her jacket pocket on the emergency brake but to bump her head against the steering wheel before flopping into the driver's seat. She stashed her cell phone in the cup holder.

The snow continued to fall outside the car. San Francisco in December was beautiful. Brisk enough to wear sweaters, not so cold as to need eighteen layers of clothing. Quinn growled and hit the steering wheel three times with the palm of her hand.

"I hate this fucking valley!"

She jammed the car in reverse and plowed backward, unable to see over either car. Clear, she started down the mountain.

The road beyond the resort had recently been plowed, and Quinn eased the Mini Cooper faster. The craggy walls of the mountain kept her from straying too far to the right. No one else was on the curvy road at this ungodly hour, and she edged into the center to avoid any deer harboring a death wish.

Her headlights flashed against the falling snow, and the slap of the windshield wipers lulled her. She turned on the radio. Static. She climbed up and down the dial, searching for a station with reception.

The road curved right.

"Shit!" She yanked the wheel. The tires lost traction. Wide awake now, she jammed the brakes. The car spun. Time slowed while a sickening slide show of images unfolded in her headlights: the jagged mountainside, the road she'd just traveled, the abyss beyond the edge. Rocks, road, darkness. She squeezed her eyes shut. Her hands clenched around the steering wheel.

The Mini lurched to the side, and Quinn's head struck the window. Metal scraped rock with a screech she felt in her fillings. The car rolled backward. Finally stopped.

Adrenaline pumped through her body, and she sucked in huge, gulping breaths. When she finally screwed up the courage to open her eyes, she saw that one headlight shone higher than the other. It took a moment before she realized both left tires had slid into the drainage ditch that ran parallel to the mountain side of the road.

With a shaky hand she touched her temple. Nothing warm and sticky. Good. She unlatched the door and pushed. Pebbles and snow tumbled in through the tiny crack she'd created. She battered the door with her shoulder, but it refused to open wider. The car was too close to the rocks.

But it sure as hell beat the alternative.

She had to get off the mountain.

Her cell phone was no longer in the cup holder. Wonderful. She groped under the seat and found a pen, a couple of crumpled receipts, and a bent cigarette before her fingertips brushed against the phone.

Ugly yellow light flooded the passenger compartment. She popped up and was blinded by oncoming headlights. Quinn sat frozen in her seat, unable to breathe. The lights drew closer, bearing down on her. A pickup. It slapped the passenger side mirror. So close she saw Ronny's terrified face.

It scraped past.

And then Ronny Buck and his truck slid right off the mountain.

25

The phone rang.

The light from the home screen illuminated the wall beside Jo's nightstand like a lopsided Bat-Signal.

Jo cleared the sleep from her voice. "Hey." She rolled onto her back but refused to sit up until she knew there was a reason to get out of bed.

"Are you awake?" Dakota's drawl sounded more pronounced.

"It's two forty-seven in the morning. Do I have to be?"

"Up to you, but I just fielded a call in dispatch. It was Quinn."

Jo sat up. "Is she okay?"

"She is, but Ronny Buck probably isn't."

Jo threw back the covers. "Details."

"Quinn crashed into the side of the mountain about two miles south of Peregrines. She said she was fumbling for her phone to call nine-one-one when Ronny's truck nearly sideswiped her and then slid off the edge."

"The edge of the road?"

"The edge of the mountain. Deputies are on their way."

Jo pressed the phone between her neck and shoulder. "Who's primary?" Her foot caught in the leg of her jeans, and she hopped to regain her balance.

"Garibaldi."

She reached for a wool turtleneck. "Put me en route."

"What about Squint?"

"I'll call him when I know more."

* * *

She spied the lights before she saw the scene. Splashes of red and blue bounced off the snowy mountainside, only to be swallowed by the inky sky.

A deputy blocked the roadway south of the curve. She killed her headlights and pulled alongside the car, rolling down her window. Up close, she recognized one of the recent academy graduates. "Morning, Corbett. Is this Garibaldi's mess?"

"Yeah. Stieger's up there too."

"Thanks." Jo switched her patrol radio to the sheriff's office comm channel and raised him on the air. Once she was given the all clear, she entered the scene, keeping to the left of the roadway as directed. As soon as she rounded the curve, she encountered the usual cluster of patrol cars, fire engines, and medical equipment that accompanied any major accident. Another patrol car blocked southbound traffic farther up the road. That left maybe one more deputy and a sergeant to protect the rest of the county. The joys of rural policing.

The ambulance straddled the middle of the road. The doors were shut against the cold, but in the lit interior, Jo recognized the two medics tending Quinn, who held an ice pack on her forehead.

The Mini Cooper was a bright-yellow mess pressed tight against the mountain. Deputy Tony Garibaldi prowled the edge of the roadway, his flashlight sweeping back and forth. A break in the berm left by the earlier snowplow revealed where the pickup truck had gone over. The other deputy was photographing the ghost depressions left by the truck's tires before the snow completely obliterated them. She saw the deeper depressions of footprints. Frickin' firefighters. The ultimate evidence-destruction team.

Jo approached Garibaldi. The man was impervious to cold. She'd never once seen him wear a cap over his bald head. "Morning."

"Hey, Jo. Slumming?"

"Working a case that happens to involve the woman in the back of the bus and possibly the guy in the truck. Have you confirmed it's Ronny?"

He jerked his head toward the ambulance. "We only have her word at this time. She watched him hit a patch of ice and go off the road." He stepped over an undamaged portion of the snow berm. Beyond that stretched a paltry five or six feet of snow before the point of no return. "All

I've got at this time is a red truck about sixty feet down. The fire department sent a rookie over the edge to get some rappelling experience. He confirmed the driver's dead, but didn't recognize him. He forgot to get the plate. Didn't notice if there were black stripes the size of his fucking fire truck along the side either."

"That's why he drags hose for a living."

"RP says she saw Buck working at the resort tonight. I called. He got off at zero two thirty. The timing's definitely right."

"I was at an event there last night and saw him early in the evening." Jo toed the berm with the tip of her boot and stepped over to the other side. Even with a cap pulled down around her ears, double layers, and her winter patrol coat, the cold air made her nose run. "There's no love lost between Kirkland and Buck. Any chance this was a road rage incident gone bad?"

He shrugged. "There's red paint transfer on the Mini Cooper, but she said he scraped past her and tore off her side mirror. And riddle me this, who the hell drives a Mini Cooper in Colorado?"

"The same person who spun it into the side of a mountain." She held out her hand. "Anchor me?"

Garibaldi dug his heels down, and they grabbed each other's forearms while Jo peeked over the side. A sharp drop ended in a clump of trees. The truck had landed nose down, although in the beam of her Streamlight, the crumpled roof indicated it had gone end over end at least once. Branches hid the rear plate. With the growls from the fire engine and ambulance behind her, it was impossible to tell if the engine still ran, but a single wan headlight burned through the pines.

"The tow trucks are en route. We'll know a lot more after the sun comes up and the truck's winched back onto the roadway."

The sun wouldn't rise for over two hours. Jo stepped back from the edge. "Who gets the lucky job of rappelling the tow hook down?"

"Pretty sure the same rookie's going back for forgetting the plate. 'Course, they live for this kind of shit."

"Do you mind if I talk to Kirkwood?"

"She's all yours."

She might have imagined the relief on his face. "Thanks. Oh, and when you get the truck to the yard, do you mind if Squint and I come take a gander?"

"As long as you don't mind cutting a supplemental. I'll get Doc Ing rolling when they start winching the truck up, but I'm figuring we'll be here a couple more hours. I'll give you a shout when we're en route."

"Awesome. What's your case number?"

He rattled it off, and she jotted it on her notepad and jammed it back in her pocket. A supplemental report was a small price to pay to be able to have Squint take a look at the truck. The man rebuilt antique tractors for fun, scouring the country for vintage John Deeres. He had a Quonset hut on his property full of tractors in various stages of restoration. Jo knew enough about cars to change a tire, check her oil, and call Squint when a case required an expert.

The first of the tow trucks arrived while Jo walked toward the ambulance. Quinn had ditched the ice pack, but even from a distance the goose egg on her temple was visible. She sat on the bench with her legs drawn to her chest and her eyes closed. Tom must have drawn the short straw. He sat between Quinn and the door. His partner was probably reclining in the cab counting her blessings.

Jo rapped on the door twice and entered the heated ambulance, quickly closing the door behind her.

"Hey, Tom, mind if I interrupt?"

Tom leaned across the stretcher and stashed a blood pressure cuff into one of the cubbies. "Not interrupting a thing. Ms. Kirkwood just declined our offer of a first-class ride to St. Francis."

Quinn opened one eye. "I can Uber it for a fraction of the cost."

"What's an Uber?" Tom asked.

Quinn closed her eye and rested her forehead on her knees. "Now you're just screwing with me."

Tom picked up his clipboard and opened the back door. "I'll leave you ladies to your gabbing, but if a call comes up, we're back in service."

"Thanks, Tom."

He slammed the door, and a few seconds later the ambulance dipped to the side as he climbed into the cab.

Jo sat. "You doing okay?"

"Not even close."

"Anything hurt beside the lump on your forehead?"

Quinn raised her head. "What? You a medic now?"

143

"Nope." It was too early in the morning to deal with attitude on an investigation that wasn't hers. Jo slid off the bench and opened the rear door.

"Wait. I'm sorry. It's been a long night."

Jo pulled the door closed but didn't latch it. "I'm not the enemy, Quinn."

"I know." She raised one hand and rubbed her eyes. "Zachary Walsenberg came to my room tonight."

"What?"

"I heard him try to open the door, like it was his room. Maybe he really thought it was. I mean, his wife rented it for me. So it's possible, I guess."

"You don't sound convinced."

"When I didn't let him in, he called me by my name. Said he knew I was a friend of Derek's and he wanted to ask me a couple questions about his son. Morbid curiosity, I guess."

"Did you let him in?"

Her face twisted. "No." She pulled a pack of cigarettes from her jacket.

The medic's voice floated through the pass-through window from the front seat. "Unless you want to blow us up, put the cancer sticks away."

"There's oxygen on board," Jo clarified.

Quinn stared at the pack with a yearning that suggested it was a risk she was prepared to take before finally returning the cigarettes to her pocket. "I pretended to call security. He was shit-faced. He staggered away."

Jo had spoken with the DA last night around ten o'clock as she was preparing to leave. Nothing had suggested he was intoxicated. In fact, he'd apologized for not recalling that Tye and his son had known each other. When Jo mentioned she was investigating a cyberstalking case, he'd suggested stepping it down to the Colorado Bureau of Investigation rather than using the Feds. He hadn't slurred his words. His eyes were clear. Of course, that had been hours before he contacted Quinn.

The emergency radio crackled, and Jo listened to Dakota's voice dispatch a PD unit to a prowler call at an address belonging to an elderly woman with a well-documented raccoon problem. She waited for the transmission to end. "Is that why you left the resort?"

"Looks like I should have stayed," Quinn answered.

"What happened out here?"

"Hit some ice. Hit the mountain. Hit my head."

"And Ronny?"

"I honestly don't know."

Warning flags. *Honestly* was a word seldom used by someone telling the truth. They simply told it. "You called nine-one-one."

"He came hauling ass down the mountain. I thought he was going to hit me head-on. Then he headed straight toward the curve. Didn't look like he even tried to turn. He blasted through the berm. Fucking snow everywhere, and then he was gone. Poof."

"Did you see brake lights?'

"Maybe. I don't remember. I'd just had my ass kicked by a mountain." She tilted her head back and rested it against the ambulance wall, eyes closed. "I climbed out the passenger door. Ran to the side of the road. I yelled his name, but nothing. Any chance he's still alive?"

"No. I'm sorry. He's not."

"I didn't like him, but I wish I wasn't the last person to see him alive."

Tye. Ronny. Both of them were dead. "You know what this means," Jo said softly.

"Yeah." Quinn pulled her legs tighter against her chest. "I'm the only one left."

Part Three
QUINN

26

With a couple of hours to kill before meeting up with Garibaldi, Jo returned to the PD. Her wet socks were in a heap on the floor, and she rummaged in the back of her desk drawer until she found her last pair of emergency socks. She really needed to get a new pair of boots—or at the very least, do laundry. She drew on the dry socks and went to work.

The Horton case binder lived on the rickety shelf next to her desk. Quinn's case file was on the shelf below it, and despite their different locations, in her mind the two investigations had melded. Therein lay the rub. She had to figure out how to move from believing the cases were linked to being able to convince others of that certainty.

She opened the folders and set them side by side on her desk. She'd already created independent timelines for both cases. On the surface, Tye's suicide and Quinn's threats were unrelated events. But Ronny's accident and Derek's death made that more unlikely. Jo had nothing concrete to link her cases, just an itch that there was more to the story than she'd been able to unravel.

As early as the academy, officers were taught the principle of Occam's razor: the simpler the solution, the more likely it was to be correct. A suspected suicide was usually an actual suicide. The freak accident wasn't anything more nefarious than an unfortunate event. If it quacked like a duck? It was a duck. The more complicated the crime, the more things could go wrong. It didn't mean people didn't plan complicated heists, but they usually screwed them up.

All she needed was to find one mistake. Inevitably, that error would lead to a second one. And then yet another until all the loosened threads could be rewoven into a coherent pattern.

She leaned back in her chair and closed her eyes. Her thoughts flirted with possibilities as she searched for commonalities between the cases. She disregarded the manner of death—considered only that three individuals were dead. Factored in Derek's newly revealed relationship with Tye. The tension between Quinn and Ronny. Her death threats. His accident. The video game that had brought them all together.

Jo grabbed a legal pad, turned it sideways, and drew a line. She made three tick marks and labeled them from left to right with the three deaths. Under Tye's and Ronny's names, she added the date of occurrence.

Logic dictated that Tye had handed out the game before Derek suicided. She added that to the timeline.

She referred to her incident report in Quinn's file. The first threatening email had been sent on March fifteenth, and she entered the event between Derek's and Tye's deaths.

March fifteenth. The Ides of March. Symbolic, or simply another in a long list of coincidences?

"*Et tu, Brute?*"

There was no answer forthcoming, and she turned her thoughts to the phone-call-dodging Professor Lucas. The most obvious issue was his attempt to steal Tye's game.

She tore a page from the pad and wrote Tye's name in the middle, then ringed the page with names. She drew a line between the professor and Tye and then connected Ronny and Quinn to Lucas as well. She tagged those lines *school*. That left out Derek. She added relationship lines in red ink. Tye to Derek. Quinn to Lucas? He'd showed up on Quinn's doorstep with champagne, which certainly indicated a cozier relationship than either had alluded to in person. Then there was the frosty relationship between Quinn and Ronny.

Did Quinn have something to do with Ronny's death? For that matter, had Ronny run Quinn off the road and lost control of his own truck? The way he drove, anything was possible.

Lines overlapped across the page. Hell, they'd all known each other—they lived in Echo Valley, for Chrissakes. She wadded up the relationship chart and returned to the case files. She spent the next hour culling snippets of information from the pages to add to her master timeline.

The empty space below Derek's name threw off the timeline's symmetry. She'd been collecting firsthand intel on Ronny Buck for years. Tye's printout was in his binder. Quinn was from San Francisco, and prior to requesting a welfare check on Tye, she hadn't racked up any contacts with the police. Jo made a note to contact SFPD.

That triggered another thought. Maybe an agency further afield had requested info on one of her players. Jo sent a quick email to the elder Sarah in records and requested a search of the state and national databases to see if anyone had queried Tye, Ronny, or Quinn. Even if it didn't end up in a report, sometimes a simple contact was enough to be significant.

The timeline still lacked Derek's info, and she tapped his name into the PD system. Within seconds, the records management program had searched all the reports, citations, contacts, parking violations, pawns, and miscellaneous entries generated by both the PD and sheriff's office. Two hits. Evidently being the district attorney's son hadn't been enough to dissuade a deputy from writing him a speeding ticket. She clicked on the death investigation.

Her desk phone rang. She didn't recognize the number. "Wyatt."

"Hey, it's Garibaldi. I'm following the tow truck to the yard. We're about twenty minutes out. You still interested?"

"If you don't mind."

"Misery loves company."

"Ronny?" She wrote the date of Derek's report on the timeline.

"Yeah, it was him. The sergeant just notified his father."

Her heart went out to Xavier. She didn't like the man, but no one should have to bury their child. She lowered her pen. "I'm going to miss Ronny."

Garibaldi cleared his throat. "The first time I picked him up, he was only eight years old—barely tall enough to look over the steering wheel. He'd been driving that very same pickup out on County Road 122. 'Course, at the time, it was still his granddad's. You'd think with all his high-speed practice since then, he'd know enough not to push it coming down the mountain."

"You'd think." Jo read the date she'd just written. "I owe you one."

"See you at the yards."

Squint entered the office as she placed the receiver in the cradle. "Sonofabitch."

"A little early for name-calling isn't it? You haven't even shot me with one of your hair thingies yet."

Jo pointed her pen toward the computer. "Tye died on the anniversary of Derek's death." She toed the carpet and swiveled her chair. "Which certainly supports a suicide determination. Despondent lover. Nothing left to live for. Guilt."

"Something to consider."

She held up her pad. "Already on the list. Anyway, that was Garibaldi. He confirmed it was Ronny. The tow's about to pull into the yards. I'd still like to take a look at it with you if you're game."

"Waiting on you."

*　*　*

The county's fleet maintenance yard occupied half a block on the road out of town. A boxy tan building, it squatted in the shadow of the county jail. Four bays marked the front, and all four doors were down. During the week the place buzzed with activity, but on a Saturday the yard was empty except for Garibaldi's patrol car and the flatbed with Ronny's wrecked truck strapped on the back. The tow truck driver, Owen, stood outside the cab holding an A&W can and talking with Garibaldi.

Jo pulled into the lot and killed the engine. For a moment she merely stared at the crushed cab of the pickup. Ronny's truck had started life as a dingy blue 1970 Dodge ranch truck that belonged to his grandfather. From the time he could hold a wrench, Ronny had helped with the maintenance. When his grandfather passed, the truck became his. By the time he turned sixteen, he'd rebuilt the engine, restored the interior, and painted it cherry red with wide black stripes down each side. The V-8 sucked gas, but the truck hauled ass. Just ask any of the cops who'd chased him over the years.

That truck no longer existed. Pry marks revealed where the fire department had used the Jaws of Life to cut away the driver door, exposing the interior. A McDonald's bag hung trapped between metal and the seat.

"I hope it was quick." She flung open her door and approached the standing men.

"Don't know what you're expecting to find." Garibaldi nodded to Jo and shook hands with Squint. "But as soon as you're done poking around, Owen's going to take it to their yard to store until Xavier sees fit to claim it or scrap it."

"Thanks for holding on to it for us," Jo said. "Hey, Owen."

He touched the soda can to his lower lip and spit tobacco juice into it. "Hey."

Squint reached up to the grab bar on the protective screen and swung himself onto the flatbed as easily as if he were mounting a horse. His Carhartt jacket looked as if it had scraped more than one garage floor. He took a pair of leather work gloves out of his pocket and slipped them on.

"What are you looking for?" Garibaldi asked.

Squint ran his hand over the battered side of the cab. "Won't know till I find it."

From the ground, Jo watched him work. She followed his path as he skirted the outside of the truck, examining the dents and scrapes that told the story of its trajectory down the mountain. Both sides showed damage, but it was the crushing slant of the roof that made her wince. To Jo's reckoning, the driver's front tire had gone off first and rolled a complete revolution. Squint would know. He read collision damage as easily as a road map. Which, in a way, she supposed it was.

Squint muscled the hood open, and it gave way with a tortured creak. He leaned into the cavernous maw of the truck. A moment later, he backed out.

Jo recognized the look on his face. "What did you find?"

"Something, maybe nothing."

Garibaldi moved closer. "You better not be making more paperwork for me."

Jo headed off the deputy so Squint could work unimpeded. "Quinn say anything more after I left?"

"Not a word."

"How did she get off the hill?"

"We pulled her car out of the ditch, changed a tire, and she drove it down. Driver side looks like hell, but it ran."

Ronny's pickup almost completely filled the flatbed from side to side and had about three feet of clearance in front of the hood and an equal amount behind the bed. The front left wheel had collapsed, but Squint was able to crawl under the passenger side and check the back side of the right front wheel.

He shimmied out. The creases in his face had deepened.

Garibaldi groaned. "I'm not going to like this, am I?"

Squint worked his way under the rear wheel. When he reemerged, his face was grim. "Not even a little." He slid off the flatbed. "The bleeder valve on the front right brake drum was loosened about a quarter turn. Same on the right rear. I figured you'd want to call in forensics before you check the other two, but I'm betting they're loose too."

"Maybe he had his brakes serviced recently."

But Jo knew the answer to that. It was written across Squint's face. And it changed everything.

"The boy knew his truck—and he knew how to drive it," Squint said. "No way he would have made it up the mountain without figuring something was wrong."

Garibaldi ran his hand over his bald head. "Master cylinder?"

"Empty," Squint confirmed. "I'd be willing to bet someone siphoned most of the brake fluid out of the master cylinder, then loosened the bleeder valves just enough so they didn't leave a puddle at the resort. Every time Ronny pushed the brakes, he would've been forcing fluid out and sucking air back in. I figure he had five or six curves before he lost his brakes completely. Couple that with a slippery road, and his emergency brake wouldn't do a damn thing. He never stood a chance."

"Well, shit." The enormity of the situation crept up on the deputy, and it launched him into action. He spoke to the tow driver. "Let me open the bay door. I'm going to need you to drop the truck inside. It just became a crime scene." He pulled out his cell phone. "The sarge is going to love this."

"I owe you one," Jo said. PD officers were cross-deputized by the sheriff in the event that their work took them into county jurisdiction. "We can head back to the resort if you want. Figure out where Ronny parked last night. At least secure the area until you can scramble your investigators."

"That'd be great." He punched some numbers on his cell phone. "I would have sworn it was an accident." Garibaldi mouthed *thank you* to the detectives and then spoke into the phone. "Hey, Sarge."

The rest of his conversation was lost in the clatter of the metal bay door heading skyward.

Jo wanted to get on the road before Garibaldi or his sergeant had a chance to call them off. She signaled Squint, and they returned to the car.

Ronny's death wasn't an accident.

She imagined the timeline she'd created earlier. Pieces of the puzzle swirled and fell into new positions, only to move again. Everything had to be reframed. The suicide, the threats, the accident.

So much for simple.

27

Quinn sat in front of the television and watched a Saturday afternoon *Road Runner* marathon. The cartoon had been her go-to program whenever she got wasted. Wile E. Coyote always made her laugh, but now she knew exactly how he felt. A huge boulder was headed her way, and all she had to stop it was a fucking parasol.

She tipped her cereal bowl to her lips and drank the last of the Cheerio-flavored milk. Her hands still shook a little. The funny thing about nearly being a wet spot on a mountainside was the overwhelming desire it inspired to live—so thick it choked her throat and set her blood on fire. It had hit her after her mother died. She'd felt it again last night.

Now this.

At first the threats had pissed her off. But they were shots in the dark. Sticks-and-stones kind of creepy. Sure, they were meant to scare her, but when someone threatens to kill a dog you don't have, well, it's kind of hard to take that shit seriously. But then they started getting worse. Misogynistic bullshit turned into rape threats. Rape threats graduated to murder threats. She took precautions. Looked over her shoulder a lot more. She'd like to wire her apartment with cameras. Get an honest-to-God alarm. But that took money.

The email about seeing her in the Bean had rattled her. That particular shot in the dark had landed a lot closer. Lucky guess, or did someone really have insider information about her life?

After the email to Lucas, she no longer wondered. Whoever had sent that email knew about at least one portion of her life. How they'd gotten the information remained a mystery. Her social media footprint was minimal. She had an Instagram account where she posted her concept art for games. That was it. Growing up, her mom had laid out a series of ironclad rules about what she and her sister could post. No birthdays, no cars. Nothing about where they were going, only places they'd already been. Nothing that would give some loony tune a way to contact her. Find her. And Quinn had listened to her mother for most of her life. At least before the heroin.

To this day, she didn't know why she had tried the drug. Maybe she was tired of being the good daughter. Maybe she thought bringing home good grades meant she was smart enough to use the shit only once. Hell, maybe getting wasted was a ploy to get her mother's attention. After she tried it, she no longer cared about the why, only how she was going to score the next ride. The real reason she'd used heroin remained a mystery that ached like a rotten tooth. She'd poked at it a couple of times, but it only hurt when she messed with it and she'd decided the reason didn't really matter.

The first time she shot up, she'd been too scared to inject herself. Her boyfriend-of-the-moment did the honors. The heroin entered her arm in a tingling rush, followed by an explosion of pure pleasure that sent shock waves pulsing through every cell in her body. She puked only that one time. Even that felt good. Try explaining that to anyone who'd never experienced it. They looked at her like she was fucking nuts.

Maybe she was. Nearly four years clean and she still missed smack. Even now she itched to shoot up. There was something calming about the ritual that lasted long after the high faded.

The worst part of getting clean had been the day she realized her mother's love for her daughter was what had gotten her killed.

Quinn tried to rewrite the story. A revisionist tale where she'd quit the smack right away. In reality, days, maybe weeks, after the funeral, her sister had found her strung out in some shithole motel and dragged her out by the hair. "Mom can't save you anymore." Her sister's face had twitched between rage and scorn. "You're going to die." There was a lot more, but those were the parts Quinn remembered.

And just like that, she had wanted to live.

It was almost funny. She'd finally gotten her act together, and now someone wanted to kill her. Karma. A yawn split her face. She needed more sleep. And coffee. Not to mention a new car. All that could wait. She had business to take care of.

First Professor Lucas.

It was fucked-up logic, but her grade was more important than her life. Maybe it was because everything she wanted from life depended on her grade. She had to suck it up and come clean with Lucas about the bogus email invitation. He could think what he wanted. It wasn't like it was the first time her reputation had taken a hit.

All the professors kept office hours the last week of term while they prepared grades. She had backups of everything but the final product. If nothing else, she'd beg for an extension. It was the one thing in her life she had to do right. She owed it to her mother. And with any luck, she could knock that out Monday.

It was also time to come clean with Wyatt.

She hadn't believed the detective when she'd floated the idea that there could be a connection between Tye's death and her threats. She had chalked Tye's suicide up to losing Derek. After all, losing a person you loved was a powerful motivator. Throw in guilt, and there was no telling what a person was capable of. She'd given up smack. She'd figured Tye had given up life.

But now Ronny. She'd watched him literally go off the edge and been helpless to stop him. No one had pushed him. It looked like an accident. Maybe it really was, but she didn't think so. Not now.

Wyatt wouldn't either.

She slid her cereal bowl out of the way and readjusted the laptop screen to read the email again. Five words changed the whole goddamn game.

. . . and then there was one.

She slammed the laptop shut. Fuck that noise.

Someone had forgotten an important detail. She might be the only one left—but it also meant she was still standing.

And that's how it was going to stay.

28

Jo unspooled bright-yellow crime scene tape and cordoned off the employee parking lot. It was always better to start big than to find evidence beyond the initial perimeter. Four rows. Ten spaces each row. It was a standard parking lot with one exception. Lighting.

Dark-sky initiatives had swept Colorado in an effort to reduce light pollution and protect the nighttime environment. The resort used lighting fixtures with fully shielded bulbs. The lights that decorated the front drive were styled after Victorian gas lamps, but the walkway bollards that lined the paths and surrounded the parking lots were low, and they disappeared altogether at the employee lot.

Contrary to popular belief, bright light didn't deter crime, but it made it a whole lot easier for surveillance cameras to record it. Despite the number of cameras inside the resort, Jo detected only one camera overlooking the parking lot.

Several parking spaces were empty, but until Squint finished reviewing the security tape, she wouldn't know which spot Ronny had chosen yesterday. Normally they'd talk to the guy working security at the time of the incident. But that had been Ronny himself.

She tied the end of the bright-yellow tape off to a snow gauge at the rear corner of the lot and studied the drift at the base of the pines. If someone had tromped through the trees, last night's storm had obliterated the trail. It didn't mean there wasn't any evidence under the snow; it just meant they wouldn't find it before spring.

Movement caught Jo's attention. Alice Walsenberg had her head down and was walking toward the lot, her dark coat flapping over an equally dark sweater and jeans. She raised her head, and the two women made eye contact. She stutter-stepped as she tracked the crime scene tape and then increased her pace toward Jo.

"So it's true. It was Ronny who went off the roadway. Xavier told me what happened a few hours ago, but I can't bring myself to believe it." Her eyes glistened with unshed tears.

"I'm sorry."

"Oh dear. I saw him just last night."

"While he was working?" Jo asked.

"Well, yes, but also before. I'd forgotten the swag bags and auction paddles at home, and he was kind enough to stop by the house and bring them here."

"Where did he park?"

"It was one of the spaces along the back aisle. I'm sorry, I don't remember exactly which one." Alice crossed her arms. "You've strung crime scene tape. Xavier said it was an accident." Her voice held a question.

"I'm assisting the sheriff's department. It would be improper for me to comment on their investigation."

"So it is suspicious." She was silent for a long beat. "That makes his death even worse." She walked a handful of steps and then returned, clearly uncomfortable.

Jo waited her out.

She sighed. "I hope I'm not speaking out of line, but have you spoken to Ms. Kirkwood?"

"About?"

She rubbed her biceps as if to keep warm. "She was my guest last night—an employee, actually. We spoke about a lot of things." She stopped rubbing. "Please don't think of me as a gossip."

"Did Ms. Kirkwood say something about Ronny?"

Alice straightened her shoulders. "She said she wouldn't cross the road to save his life." Her expression hardened. "If that girl had anything to do with Ronny's death . . ." The second half of the statement remained unspoken.

"Were you with Ms. Kirkwood the entire night?"

"It was such a busy night, I'm not sure I was with myself every minute. But no, there were some fairly long stretches when she disappeared. And then, of course, we went our separate ways when the fund raiser ended. I'd reserved a room for her, but I was told she left in the middle of the night." Tears spilled down her cheeks. "Poor Xavier. We've both lost our sons." She pulled a delicate handkerchief from her pocket. "Is there anything else I can help you with, Detective? If not, I should . . ." She waved her hand in the direction of the resort.

"No. Thank you, Mrs. Walsenberg. Again, I'm sorry for your loss."

She dashed away the tears. "I'm a silly old woman."

No one would mistake Alice Walsenberg for either silly or old, but she had seen her share of heartbreak, and her shoulders slumped as she returned to the resort.

Cold seeped under Jo's clothes and sidled up next to her skin. She'd just decided to sit in the car and blast the heater when the employees-only service door opened on the back side of the resort and Squint exited. Most people never noticed, but he walked with a slight limp—a hitch in his gid-dyup, as he called it. It became more pronounced in the cold, but if it slowed him down, his long legs made up for it, and not many people got away from Squint when he gave chase.

She waited until he got closer, and they ducked under the tape together. "I spoke with Alice Walsenberg while you were inside. It may be an unfor-tunate choice of words, but Quinn told Alice she wouldn't cross the road to save Ronny's life. Any chance you saw a small dark-haired woman tamper-ing with the truck on the surveillance video?"

"That'd be too easy." He turned down the back aisle. "The empty slot on the end, next to the Subaru. According to the tape, he pulled nose in at sixteen fifty-eight, an hour before his shift."

"He transported a bunch of swag and auction stuff for Mrs. Walsen-berg. Otherwise, in all this snow, I'd imagine he'd have backed in."

"That matches the tape. The three of them transferred several boxes out of the truck bed into the cart. Ronny drove it back to the resort. The two ladies walked."

"Did you see anything else on the tape?"

"The valets were busy—especially around twenty-two hundred. Your car was parked right over there." He nodded his chin toward the main lot. "Quinn left a little after two. She didn't appear too keen to find her driver door blocked by a Hummer."

"I'm betting she was more upset the DA tried to pay her a visit last night. Supposedly that's why she bugged out when she did."

"What did he want?" Squint asked.

"According to her? Info on his son."

"At two o'clock in the morning?"

"Yeah. Before we leave, I want to take a quick gander at that footage." Quinn was so evasive, it would be nice to have a statement Jo could actually corroborate—or not. Either would provide good intel. "Anyway, I meant, did the tape show anything else with Ronny's truck?"

"Too dark to distinguish much. Around twenty-one hundred, the hood went up."

"How could you tell?"

"The tape shows a flash. He had a chrome bulldog hood ornament. When the suspect popped the hood to get to the master cylinder, it caught the light. There's actually three flashes."

"Up, down, and what?"

They both turned toward the trees at the same time. New officers rarely looked up, yet a surprising number of crooks climbed trees in an effort to outwit the cops. They also threw things into the branches that they wanted to retrieve later but didn't want to get caught holding.

The detectives skirted the Subaru and peered into the branches.

Jo saw the glint first, but it was going to take better eyes than hers to figure out what it was. "One o'clock." She pointed. "Any idea what that is?"

"Something I'm betting the sheriff's department will be happy you found for them. From this angle, it looks like a tin cup. Maybe even small enough to dip into a master cylinder."

"Bet they'd be even happier if we got it down for them," Jo said.

Squint nodded in solemn agreement. "The goal of securing a crime scene is to ensure the integrity of any evidence contained therein."

"What if a squirrel decided to use it as a storage container?"

"It's our duty to make sure that doesn't happen. But for the report, I'd suggest you use the deteriorating weather for your justification."

"You always did know best."

Jo jogged back to her car and retrieved her camera case from the trunk. She was poaching, but she wouldn't cut any corners. It also meant she'd be on the subpoena list if the case ever went to court. If her suspicion about this being one interconnected case was correct, she'd be at the top of the list anyway.

When she was through taking ground photographs, she held the camera out to Squint. "You're taller."

"I've also got seniority."

Jo blinked first. "Fine." She slung the camera strap around her neck and tucked a paper evidence bag under her jacket. Scrutinizing the snow and the tree, she chose her path. "I'm going to need a boost."

Squint followed in her footsteps, then squatted with his back against the pine. "Watch the hat."

Jo grabbed his shoulder, stepped on his thigh, and then wrapped her hand around the lowest branch. The camera swung forward and narrowly missed his face. "For the record, that wouldn't have happened if you'd been climbing." Stepping onto his shoulder for stability, she readjusted her grip, then walked her feet up the trunk until she could hook her leg over the branch. From there, it was a matter of reach and pull until she was on the proper branch.

"This used to be a lot easier," she called down.

"I can call the fire department if you'd like. Get a ladder."

She brushed a dusting of snow from the needles over her partner. "I'd rather fall, thank you."

Belly first, she inched along the branch, weaving through the snow-laden clusters of smaller branches all around her and brushing springy needles out of her face. Closer, she saw the metal wasn't a tin cup but rather a measuring cup—the type a baker used when working with dry ingredients. A couple of shutter snaps later and she tucked the camera back under her arm. Balancing herself, she pulled on a pair of gloves. She pinched the silver cup by the bottom and rim, careful not to smudge the most likely areas for prints, and plucked it from its perch. The narrow handle was engraved with *1/3 C* near the end.

Her thighs clamped tight against the branch, she sat up. Wet snow seeped through the denim and numbed her legs as she caterpillared backward until her butt hit the trunk.

"It smells fishy," she said.

"That's brake fluid."

"Good to know this wasn't just an opportunity to demonstrate my tree-climbing prowess."

Squint slapped his hat against his thigh to knock off the snowflakes Jo had dislodged. "I'm not convinced you've demonstrated that."

Braced, she shook out the evidence bag and deposited the cup inside. She'd label and seal it later. For now, she pressed it against her chest and zipped her jacket over the bag. It took twice as long to get down as it had to climb up the pine.

Finally, she landed next to Squint. "My caseload just got a whole lot more complicated."

29

El Tecolote sold the best homemade tamales north of the border, and every year at Christmas, Jo bought a few dozen to throw in her freezer. She was lucky if they lasted until New Year's. The only remaining evidence of the two she'd brought back to the station was the corn husk wrappers and a bit of string.

Squint pushed aside his enchiladas and lowered his fork.

"You going to finish that?" she asked.

"I'm pacing myself."

She eyed the grease-spotted bag beside his plate. "What about your sopapilla?"

He tossed her the bag. She split the fried pastry in half, opened the condiment packet of honey with her teeth, and slathered the golden goo inside the two halves. A couple of indelicate bites later, she leaned back in her chair with a contented sigh.

Squint watched her eat with bemusement. "I swear you have a reticulated jaw."

Jo licked the last of the honey from her fingers. "I can think now."

They'd left the resort as the sunlight dimmed and the temperature plunged. She'd always felt more confident with a plan, and the ride back from the resort had given her time to think.

Ask anyone how long a cop had to solve a murder, and the common answer was forty-eight hours. But the clock didn't stop. It never stopped. It just meant investigators transitioned from a lengthy list of in-progress tasks to a more measured review of what they'd already done. From there they devised a new game plan.

Meanwhile, life went on. New cases piled up; old cases didn't go away. Priorities shifted.

Crime hadn't stopped in Echo Valley during the past week. Normally, new cases were split between the two detectives, but Squint had been shouldering the majority of the incoming cases while she worked her current cluster.

Ronny's death restarted the clock.

"Someone went to a great deal of trouble to make Ronny's death look like an accident," she said.

"Quinn?"

Most people lived their whole life without calling the police to report a dead person. Quinn had reported two deaths in the last week. "Maybe. She was at the resort. She didn't like Ronny. He didn't like her. She'd even popped off about him to Alice Walsenberg."

"Not normally the thing you'd do if you were plotting to kill the guy." He polished off the last of his enchiladas and pulled another sopapilla from the to-go bag.

"You were holding out on me."

"Not my first rodeo." The honey package looked tiny in his oversized paws. "How do you think it ties in with Horton?"

"I think the game is somehow the epicenter. Think about it. First Derek Walsenberg kills himself. Then a year to the day later, Tye does the same thing. Quinn is getting death threats, and someone tampers with Ronny's brakes."

"Did they mean to kill him or scare him?"

She shook her head. "Who knows. The point is, the game's been trouble from the get-go. Professor Lucas stole a copy and tried to profit from it without Tye's knowledge. There's big money in gaming. Maybe Lucas wants another run at selling it and thinks he's got to knock off anyone who knows who really designed it."

"You think I missed something on the Walsenberg suicide?"

Squint was the most conscientious officer she knew. "No." She cradled her head in her hands and looked out through her fingers. "I don't know. Maybe?"

He placed his plate in the trash can and wiped his hands with a napkin. "There was no sign of forced entry. Nothing suspicious."

"Why'd he kill himself?"

"The stress of not being able to live up to the Walsenberg name? His grades had dropped. His mother worried he'd spent too much time playing video games and not enough time studying until she found out he'd decided to pursue the digital arts program up on the hill. Then she considered it research."

"Quinn said Derek was in love with Tye."

He crumpled the napkin. "Did his parents know?"

"Quinn wasn't sure, but she said Tye broke it off."

"Maybe that's why he suicided."

God, she was tired. Every time she thought she had something, it circled back to supporting the suicide theory. "I'm going to call it a night. I can't think straight anymore." She stared at the window. The light in the office bounced against the night, and all she saw was a washed-out reflection of herself.

Squint shut down his computer. "It was a good call on Ronny's truck."

"Do you ever wonder if it would be easier to look the other way? I mean, it's bad enough that the Bucks lost their son. Would it have been kinder to let them think it really was an accident instead of turning it into a murder investigation?"

He slung his coat over his arm. "You've got good instincts, Jo."

"Sounds like there's a but coming my way."

"Get some sleep."

She lifted the phone receiver. "I'm just going to make a quick call."

He gathered his hat. "If you find yourself needing more sustenance, there's one more sopapilla in the bag."

She smiled. "I know where your licorice stash is too."

He left and she replaced the phone. Only the whir of her computer tower and the sound of the wind buffeting the building intruded on the silence. She continued to stare at her reflection. Occasionally a gust would hit the window and make the reflection shiver. Squint was right. She really should get some sleep. Her day had started too early and she'd been working ever since.

A ping on her computer alerted her to an email, and she opened it. The resort had sent her the surveillance footage of Walsenberg in front of Quinn's room. She hit play. From the moment he entered the hallway, the encounter lasted a whopping minute and forty-seven seconds.

In the beginning, it looked as if the DA had second thoughts about trying his key card, but then he moved forward. Ran the card. Once. Twice. A quick knock. He tried peeking through the peephole, then stumbled back as if startled. He said something at the door. A complete sentence. Another string of words. Then he mouthed what looked like Quinn's name. More words. A final slump of defeat, and he left in the direction of the elevators.

Jo played it again. Whispered the name *Quinn* in time with the DA. Her lips pursed and relaxed exactly like his. She scribbled some notes she could barely read.

She should go home.

Instead she picked up the phone and dialed the number she'd jotted onto a sticky note earlier. "Records, please."

*   *   *

The San Francisco Police Department was a twenty-four-hour department. Echo Valley had police available around the clock, but an agency the size of San Francisco had twenty-four-hour clerical support as well. John Q. Citizen might not be able to walk into one of their ten stations on a Saturday night and get a police report, but an officer from another jurisdiction could call in and talk to a night-shift records clerk.

But that didn't mean it would be easy.

"No such record exists."

Code for a juvenile record that's either sealed or expunged.

Jo decided to press her luck. "And if such a record did exist?"

"Theoretically speaking, maybe a drug arrest or four. Maybe heroin." The three states between them failed to blunt the surliness in the woman's voice. "Are you looking at her as a suspect?"

"Victim."

"Well, that's too bad."

Which wasn't at all the response Jo had expected. "You seem to have some personal knowledge of Quinn Kirkwood."

"Her mother was a sergeant with us. Killed in the line of duty."

A fuzzy news report snapped into focus. "Isabella Kirkwood was Quinn's mother?" Maybe it was because there weren't as many women in law enforcement, or maybe it was because she shared the same gender as the fallen officer, but when a female officer was killed in the line of duty, Jo remembered—even from four or five years back.

"Was." Background noise on the other end of the line made it sound as if Jo were talking to someone in a call center. "Quinn's dealer shot Izzy when she tried to drag her daughter out of his flophouse. Even knowing her mom was on her deathbed, the ingrate wouldn't give up the bastard. We all figured she'd be dead by now."

"No, but someone's threatening her."

"I'm shocked."

"Did Sergeant Kirkwood have any other children?"

"A daughter, Celia. She's an officer assigned to the Tenderloin Station. Doing a good job filling her mom's boots too."

Jo wasn't sure what surprised her most: that Quinn's sister was an officer, or that there was a station called Tenderloin.

"Do you have the phone number for the station?"

The records clerk rattled off a string of numbers. "Don't think it's going to do you any good. Last I heard, she'd washed her hands of her baby sister."

Jo asked for the woman's name and ID number.

"Remember what I told you," she said.

"No such records exist," Jo replied.

"That's right, Detective. You stay safe out there, hear?"

"Yes, ma'am. Thank you."

Jo reached for Squint's sopapilla. No sense letting it go to waste. It would be stale by the time he returned to the office. She sighed. If only it weren't so easy to rationalize everything.

She picked up the phone and punched the speed dial.

"Hey, want some company?"

30

The gaming console felt like an extension of Quinn's hands. It translated her every thought. Powerful. Nimble. She made her character dance. Fly. Do all the things she couldn't do herself. A new landscape. Barren this time. Arid. Thank God it wasn't snowy. She paused at the edge of the screen. She'd never entered this level before. There was no place to hide. Her woodland glamour did nothing to camouflage her against the dusty yellows and sun-bleached browns.

Fuck it. "Ready or not, here I come."

Her cell phone buzzed. She glanced at the call screen. Unknown number. Local.

"I'm busy."

A slavering beast bounded toward her on all fours. Teeth suggested predator. But looks could be deceiving. Attack or greet?

The phone rang again. A different number. Another unknown.

"Still busy."

She held out her hand in greeting but readied her staff. A gal could never be too safe. An ebony raven croaked from the uppermost branch of a lone skeletal tree, and a disturbance by the trunk shimmered like heat waves, growing in intensity. A portal? She'd need a port-key. Could it be the hellhound bearing down on her, or was the creature the portal guardian sent to prevent her from crossing through?

Lightning sparked with its every footfall. Magic sparked from the portal. Her laptop throbbed with color. Excitement.

An email notification banner slid across the top corner of her laptop and then disappeared. Someone knocked on her door.

"Oh, for fuck's sake."

The gaming console hit the worn couch cushion with enough force that it bounced. Ignoring caution, she kicked the dinette chair from under the knob and yanked open the door.

Stu/Stan had his hand up as if to knock again. He took a half step back. "Whoa."

"What do you want?"

He held up his open laptop. "I knew if I waited long enough, you'd go out with me. I just didn't figure I'd have to pay. Well, I mean, I knew I'd have to buy beers or something. Anyway, here I am."

"You have five seconds to tell me what the hell you're talking about."

He turned the screen toward her.

A lingerie-clad Quinn stared back at her. She snatched the laptop from his hands. "Where did you find this?"

"Colorado Party Girls."

She scrolled through the photo gallery. A picture of her rocking a Catholic schoolgirl outfit. Her in a thong and stockings biting her lip. One wearing only a fur cap, snow boots, and a smile. The profile details listed her name, phone, address, and school. "What the hell is Colorado Party Girls?"

"What do you mean? It's a hookup site." He laughed, an ugly sound that fell somewhere between *don't be stupid* and *I've seen you naked.* "Oh, damn. Don't tell me this is revenge porn. Who'd you piss off? Oh wait. That could be anybody."

"It's not revenge porn. These photos aren't me."

His eyes traveled down her body, stopping at her crotch as if he could already picture himself between her legs. "Keep scrolling. I especially like the one with you and the redhead. She's almost as hot as you."

Since being in Echo Valley, she'd done her best to keep a low profile, but it might be worth getting arrested just to smack the smug look off his face. "They're photoshopped." Although it bothered her that she didn't recognize what photos had been used as the source of her face.

"The rape fantasy surprised me."

Her eyes flicked to the section titled *Fetishes & Fantasies.*

"I had you pegged as more the dominatrix type," he continued. "All bitchy and hot. I gotta tell you, the thought of you in a Catwoman suit with a whip makes for an instant boner." He glanced down. "See?"

The outline of his erection strained his pants.

"Go away."

"So how about it?" He pulled a fabric wad from his pocket and let it unspool like a yo-yo until the necktie dangled from his hands. "Honest-to-God silk. Or at least high-quality polyester."

"Why are you still here?"

He dipped his head at her hands. "Dude, you have my laptop."

She had an overwhelming urge to sling the laptop over the railing. Watch it go end over end until it hit the parking lot pavement and smash into a thousand pieces. But she risked the chance it would land in a snow-drift. Then she'd have to chuck him over the rail to make up for it.

"By the way, the link is cross-posted on the college student forum, so I'd expect company if I were you."

"How did it get cross-posted?"

He bumped his shoulders. "Maybe you shouldn't park people's cars in the gimp spot."

She shoved the laptop into his belly. "You're such a dick."

He clutched the laptop across his chest as if using it as a shield. "Be nice to me and I'll delete the post."

She slammed the door and leaned her forehead against the peeling paint. His laughter trailed behind him as he clomped down the stairs. The karma gods seriously needed to put some ice in his path.

His words sunk in. Oh God. The student forum. The air in the room evaporated. She opened her mouth, unable to draw a breath. She placed her hands on either side of her face and pushed away from the door.

Conduct unbecoming. Her scholarship. This was grounds for expulsion.

The edges of her world darkened. What else was out there? She stum-bled to the couch. Her laptop sat on the low coffee table. On-screen, the raven picked at her carcass while the hellhound howled, though in victory or despair, she didn't know. What she wouldn't give to enter the portal. Magically transport to a new realm.

It had been a mistake to think she could start over. Atone for the shit she'd pulled. Karma wouldn't find Stu. It was too busy fucking with her.

She shut down the game. Opened a browser.

Quinn wasn't the first female gamer to have become the target of online trolls. Whole campaigns had been waged against women in the industry, or those who tried to defend them. Any disenfranchised idiot with a keyboard and a grudge could anonymously slander or threaten their target. Some took it to the next level and doxed their targets—posting addresses, phone numbers, social security numbers. That led to assholes landing on their target's doorsteps or harassing them at work. SWATting ratcheted up the danger even more. Armed with the doxed information, any assclown could initiate a fake emergency that required a SWAT response. Adrenaline-jacked officers expecting an armed confrontation weren't exactly known for their restraint. Bad things happened.

This was just the beginning. She drew a ragged breath.

Then she girded herself. Someone had sent an email to her professor. Someone had set her up with a dating profile with her contact information. There was going to be more. More sites. More damage. More danger.

She reminded herself to breathe and typed her name in the search bar.

Within a nanosecond, the returns poured in.

It was so much worse than she'd thought.

31

Curled up on the couch, Jo sipped her wine and stared into the flames. Aiden's legs stretched toward the fire, the heels of his feet lost in the sheepskin rug that warmed the plank flooring between the couch and raised brick hearth. The embers beneath the hardwood glowed and pulsed with a life that would eventually become charred and cold.

The Teague living room had only subtly changed since his mother passed away four years ago. The doilies were gone, but the same oak bookcases flanked the fireplace, and the knockoff Remingtons still decorated the walls with their portrayal of cowboy life. The biggest difference was the smell. Mrs. Teague had baked fresh bread every day, and the scent of yeast had permeated the house. Now the room had a more masculine aroma, equal parts sweat and saddle soap. Each scent held its own appeal.

Jo's entire life was entwined with this ranch, this family. Aiden.

Every year on the anniversary of her mother's death, Jo hiked up to the ledge above the Teagues' ranch. No matter how long she stayed up there overlooking the precipice, Aiden always waited for her until she came down, first next to her bike, and later leaning against her truck. He never hugged her, as if he knew she'd shatter into pieces too jagged to ever put back together. The year he left for college was the first time he hadn't been there for her. She'd walked behind the barn where Mrs. Teague couldn't see her through the kitchen screen door and sank against the wall, the splintered wood catching the thin cotton of her shirt. She'd sat in the dust, narrowly missing a rosette of Scotch thistle. Aiden's German shepherd, Bjørn, had flopped next to her and nosed his graying muzzle against her hand until she stopped crying.

174

Tonight, Aiden said little. They'd spent so much time together over the years that they'd developed a sixth sense of when to push and when to let the other wrestle their thoughts alone. Early in her career, she'd learned to compartmentalize her emotions. But her ability to coordinate her thoughts with her actions had fallen out of step lately. The compartments she worked so hard to keep separate were collapsing into each other, leaving behind a mess that drove her crazy.

The last log broke apart, sending sparks spiraling upward.

He reached for her hand. "I heard the news."

The past released its hold grudgingly, and she roused as if from a long sleep. "News?"

"The promotion."

"Ah." She took another sip. The heavy Malbec settled on her tongue, and the term *sour grapes* flitted through her mind.

"It should have been you," he added.

"Yes." She'd lie to anyone else, but not Aiden. "But it's not."

"Who's next up for retirement?"

"Rumor mill puts Larson out in about three years."

"A lot can happen in three years. Ever think about the Feds?"

"And grow a beard like yours?" She gave it a gentle tweak. "No thank you."

"You've already got the start of a moustache."

"You're such an asshole." But her voice was warm with affection.

"So choose something other than DEA. Although if they ever partnered us, we'd make a hell of an undercover team."

His thumb absently stroked her knuckles, igniting little sparks that made her shiver.

She pulled away. "Maybe." She'd never considered leaving the PD. Should she? Compartments opened and slammed. Broke down and rebuilt.

"You were so earnest the day you graduated from the academy. All spit-shined and chomping at the bit to hit the streets and save the world."

She tipped her wineglass toward him. "Not true. Most of the world was out of my jurisdiction."

"I was scared the job would change you. But all these years later, you're still that idealistic cadet."

"With no stripes to show for it. What am I doing wrong, Aiden?"

Her phone rang, saving him from answering her question—not that she'd expected one. She'd been trying to figure out that little gem ever since the promotion memo came out. Everett Cloud's insinuations had further muddled the situation with possibilities she didn't want to consider. She set her wineglass on the side table. Her backpack sat by the door, and by the time she dug out her phone, she'd missed the call. Quinn. She waited for the voice mail, but it never came.

"Work?"

"Can't be too important. It wasn't worth a message." She slid the phone back in the front pocket of the bag. It was after ten o'clock, and she'd been up since when? Two thirty? A fresh wave of exhaustion washed over her.

The fire had burned down, and the night sky knocked against the living room's picture window. The slivered moon offered little light, and vibrant stars speckled the sky in familiar patterns.

She leaned over the couch and draped her arms over Aiden's shoulders and rested her hands on his chest. Through his soft wool Henley, his heart beat steady and true. She closed her eyes. His cologne had a base of sandalwood and something exotic she couldn't identify. She breathed deeply. It was warmer, and far subtler than the English Leather, Old Spice, and Pinaud Clubman that typically scented Echo Valley.

Aiden covered her hand with his and pressed it closer to his heart.

She should go. Instead Jo asked the question she'd wanted to pose since calling him from her office. "Can I stay with you tonight?"

In answer, he leaned forward and moved the throw pillow from her side of the couch and placed it next to the one beside him. "Ready for another log?"

"Not yet. I'd rather look at the stars for a bit."

He stretched sideways and made room for her.

A twinge of indecision kept her upright. "Are you sure?"

"You're blocking my view."

Dragging the crocheted blanket from the back of the couch, Jo lowered herself in front of him. His hand cupped her hip, his chin resting at the top of her head. The steady rise and fall of his chest soothed her, and soon her own breaths rose slower than his.

The fire smoldered, a soft glow that threw more heat than light. Beyond the glass, the stars shone like beacons. "Cassiopeia," she whispered.

He lowered his voice to match hers. "Too easy. There, the five bright stars forming the W." He paused. "Andromeda."

"Talk about easy. There, below Triangulum."

"You can't even see Triangulum through the window."

She burrowed her face into the throw pillow. "No, but it's still there."

He chuckled softly. "Are your eyes even open, or are you doing this by memory?"

"We can go outside if you'd like."

"No need," he said. "I'd rather stay here where it's warm."

"That was the right answer." Stretched out, she was too tired to move, let alone slog through the snow. Perhaps the recent turmoil in her life had colored her perception of this season. She'd never been one to lament winter's arrival and wish for spring. Echo Valley sparkled in the winter. A piping of snow collected along its red-rock ridges and frosted the pines, creating a vista that stole her breath no matter how many times she viewed it.

This season bore the smudge of something darker. Clouds smothered the sun and shadowed the ridges, isolating the valley and leaving it bereft of anything but a biting and relentless cold.

"Winter has just begun, and already I can't wait for it to end."

"You're just tired." He tucked the blanket around her shoulder.

Mrs. Teague had crocheted the blanket that covered them, the wool yarn softened by the years. Jo relaxed against him.

The heat from the fire warmed her face, and she slipped into that half sleep where she could hear her own snores but was too tired to care.

He gathered her close, and winter slipped further away.

32

The street parking around the church would already be taken, and Jo left her car at the station. She'd overslept, and for the first time since landing the Horton case, she felt rested. The cold air made her eyes water and she adjusted her scarf to cover her lower face, but it was the kind of winter day she loved: crystal-clear skies and ridges that looked close enough to touch. The walk—brief though it was—would do her good. Maybe she could retrieve her bike trainer on Tuesday. Next week's docket listed Cameron's name. She could swing by the house and pick up a couple of things while he was at court.

She rounded the corner and the church came into view. Two elm trees and a ragged hedge of blackbrush framed the facade and drew attention to the ornate west window centered above the portico.

All Saints in the Valley Episcopal Church had guarded the souls of Echo Valley with varying success since 1853. The original church had been a clapboard eyesore and met its demise in a fire of suspicious origin. The Broadmoor Avenue elite of the day, in their freshly constructed Victorians, had banded together and determined that the new All Saints should have the trappings of an English country church—resulting in a creamy sandstone exterior, sparkling stained glasswork, and a gated contemplation garden, complete with a labyrinth.

As a child, Jo had walked the labyrinth with her mother every Sunday the weather allowed. Her mother had explained how walking the path often helped make sense of life. Sometimes Jo would lead; other times she'd follow. The last time her mother navigated the labyrinth, she'd been in a wheelchair Jo pushed. The sun had been relentless. The wheels crunched the gravel, carving ruts in the path that would have to be raked out. Each turn became an ordeal that grew harder and harder the closer to the center they drew. They didn't speak. When they arrived at the end, her mother reached over her shoulder and patted Jo's hand. She died a week later.

It wasn't until Jo worked graveyard shift that she had visited the gardens again. Before deciding to marry Cameron, she'd walked the path several times. She'd trod the path only once when she decided to leave him. If it weren't for the two feet of snow obscuring the labyrinth today, she'd travel the path for Tye and Ronny and Quinn.

This morning, a few stalwart folks milled outside with their heads close together, and Jo recognized her high school history teacher at the center of one group of women. As she neared, she heard someone mention the newspaper. The teacher responded, "Smart as a whip, but she's always been a bit full of herself, even as a student." One of the other women saw Jo and touched the teacher's arm. They all stopped talking and nodded at Jo but quickly broke eye contact and tightened ranks. Not wanting to intrude, Jo veered around them and climbed the sandstone steps. The normally bubbly greeter stoically pressed a program into Jo's hand.

Inside the nave, piano music and chatter roosted in the wooden trusses that spanned the vaulted ceilings. A center aisle divided two rows of polished wooden pews. The Walsenbergs had already claimed their seats in the front pew. There were no reserved seats, of course, yet Jo had spent most of her Sunday mornings in this church—at first wedged between her mother and father, then beside her father, and finally by herself—and at no point had anyone dared encroach upon that pew. Mrs. Baxter sat ramrod straight in her equally exclusive pew across the aisle. The thought of having an entire congregation stare at her back week after week made Jo twitch. She slid into the rear pew, and the heavy weight of the gun in her purse clunked loudly against the wood. Several people craned around and nudged their neighbors. Conversations quieted, then resumed with whispered ferocity until Reverend Morris entered and everyone opened their hymnal.

The pianist struck a new chord. The congregation rose, and with a collective inhale launched into the first hymn. The constant shift between kneeling and standing, with an occasional perch on the pew, kept Jo's thoughts from wandering during the service. It was like tai chi with a Book of Common Prayer.

Her phone vibrated against her waist with an incoming text during the Eucharist. With her head still bowed, she peeked around the nave. Two rows to go before it was her turn to step forward and receive communion. It wouldn't be the first time she'd been paged out of church to respond to a call, but she hoped it wasn't so urgent that she couldn't finish the service. She held her phone low and tapped the message from Dakota.

I'm so sorry. I didn't think he was going to run it.

The row ahead of her stood and moved toward the aisle. The message was too cryptic. Jo responded with a question mark.

It took an eternity for Dakota to respond.

Everett Cloud—the reporter.

"Oh God." A prickly feeling started at the top of her head and spread across her face, down to her chest. Dakota wasn't in dispatch. It was her day off. They had planned to go snowshoeing before Jo's caseload had exploded.

The man next to her stood for communion, and Jo staggered to her feet, her head still bowed.

What the hell?

* * *

The moment the service ended, Jo bolted from the church and rushed home. The smell of burnt coffee greeted her when she arrived, and she found the newspaper on the counter where her father had abandoned it next to the coffeemaker. She pulled the pot off the burner and reached for the paper.

The lead photo depicted a stunning Alice Walsenberg in deep conversation with Mrs. Baxter at the Alliance for Life shindig. She scanned the article. Nothing.

"Keep reading."

Jo jumped.

Her father used his coffee cup to point at the paper. "Below the fold."

She flipped over the paper and stared at an image of herself holding a sergeant's badge above two columns of text. The photographer had cropped out Cameron, but it was obvious she was pinning the badge on someone else. The byline belonged to Everett Cloud. He used a lot of words, but the story boiled down to a systemic problem in the police department that discriminated against women. It was nothing like the fluff story that had announced Cameron's promotion the day before.

The story continued on A5, and she ripped the page in her impatience to continue reading.

Cloud had done his homework and unearthed historical data from the Echo Valley Historical Museum to substantiate information he'd gleaned from the *Courier*'s own archives.

"Oh no." Reading her name left her gasping like the time she'd jumped into a springtime river. The frigid water had rushed over her head, filled her ears, and snatched her breath. The cold wrung every bit of warmth from her body, leaving behind a numbness so complete it took hours for feeling to return.

She hurled the paper into the recycling bin.

"Trashing it doesn't make it go away. What were you thinking, girl?"

"I had nothing to do with this."

His face twisted as if he'd eaten a lemon, rind and all. "Don't lie to me. You were seen talking to that reporter at Finnegan's." He pulled the paper out of the bin and smoothed it on the counter. "Dragging down the entire department because you got your feelings hurt. The department I dedicated my life to. I'm ashamed to call you my daughter."

Jo stood rigid. Afraid to move. Afraid if she did, she'd unleash something she wouldn't be able to control. "I don't deserve that."

"Where were you last night?"

Ignoring his question, she grabbed the pot and plunged it under the faucet. "You can't tell me you think Cameron is more qualified than I am."

"Dammit, girl." He slammed his mug against the counter. "Policing's a man's job."

"You can't be serious." She turned off the water. "All you've ever wanted was someone to follow in your footsteps."

"I didn't plan on it being my daughter."

"Maybe you should have thought about that before naming me Jo."

He pointed his finger at her. "Don't pull that sass on me. I never wanted you to be a cop."

"Funny, that's not how I remember it."

"I couldn't very well tell you not to. You'd be hell-bent just to spite me." He scrubbed his hand over his face, and she saw herself in the habit. "I never thought you'd make it through the academy. Hoped you'd wash out in field training, but Squint said from the beginning you had guts. I could have told him that." He scraped a kitchen chair away from the dinette and sat down heavily. He suddenly looked old. "You know the worst night of my career?"

She didn't even need to think twice. "The night you blew out your knee and had to retire."

"The night of the Fowler shooting at the college. I was on scene when you found the shooter's car. I watched your emergency lights cut clear across the valley as you chased him. He cranked off a round. You got on the radio just as calm as you please and called out shots fired. It was one of those summer nights that sound travels forever, and I'm stuck on that god-damn ridge listening to some asshole take three more shots, wondering if one of his bullets had your name on it."

All the bluster left Jo. She came up behind him and laid her hands on his shoulders and kneaded his ropy muscles. "I'm good at what I do, Dad."

"You're not just good. You're better. That's the problem." He brushed aside her hands. "None of them boys want to be shown up by a girl. They'd rather fuck you than follow you. You out catting around at night is only going to make that worse. Now this." Before she could respond, he whirled out of the chair and picked up the newspaper, shaking it in her face. "I can tell you exactly how this is going to unfold. Guys are going to be slow to back you up. Maybe not show up at all. Chief isn't going to be none too happy either. No sir. Not when he has his sit-down with the mayor and tries to explain why he's got an upstart causing trouble and tattling to the goddamn newspaper."

"I didn't have anything to do with this article," Jo said. Her father opened his mouth, but she cut him off. "Not a damn thing. The reporter stopped by my table at Finnegan's. He already had a copy of the promotion memo, and I sent him packing. You think I'm stupid?"

"No one's going to believe that."

"I don't care." She stormed toward her room.

Her father dogged her heels. "You better well should. Because life as you know it just ended."

She spun, and her father ran into her. The rush she felt when she was about to go toe-to-toe with a suspect pulsed through her body. "I've never once complained. Not when someone hung a tampon from the rearview mirror of my patrol car. Not when I was denied the out-of-town training I'd requested because the department didn't want to pay for two hotel rooms, so instead they selected a second guy who didn't even want to go." Her speech slowed. "No. I learned to roll with the punches. Be one of the guys. The third time Estes called me 'squaw,' I told him to fuck off. He laughed and never called me that again. In defensive tactics, I always went up against Bull."

"He kicked your ass."

"Yes, he did. But no one can accuse me of trying to take the easy route. I never expected the job to be a cakewalk, but I expected to be treated fair."

"You didn't grow up brawling. I had to make sure you were tough enough to go home at night."

"Oh, you toughened me up all right."

"This is different, Jo. These aren't the mopes on the street. These are the guys you work with. They're not going to take kindly to this article. And it worries me I'm not there to protect you."

She suppressed the urge to laugh. "Don't kid yourself, Dad. You never were."

33

Jo ran.

The trail wended through a collection of maples, elms, and oaks, their bare limbs jutting skyward in tortured twists. She should have warmed up, started slow. Instead she pushed harder, ignoring the hitch in her side. Her winter trail shoes bit into the snow as she chewed up the miles. A small incline rose before her and she leaned into a sprint. Her lungs burned, but she had to keep moving or she'd explode.

By the third mile, she was willing to concede that her father was right. It wouldn't matter that she'd had nothing to do with the article. She wasn't the only female officer mentioned in the article, but her story claimed the most column inches. Her life was going to be hell moving forward until it all blew over.

She spent the next mile blaming Dakota. Why had she spoken to Everett Cloud? Had he contacted her for the story, or had she approached him? It took Jo another half mile to realize it didn't matter. The article was out there. There was no way to unring that particular bell.

Without breaking stride, she peeled off her outer jacket and tied it around her waist.

From the moment she'd raised her hand and taken the oath, Jo had known she'd have to prove herself. Every rookie did, but women had to do it over and over. Every scuffle, every chase, every damn investigation. Even the Tye Horton case illustrated how quick people were to second-guess her. And now she was back to ground zero. Her credibility shot—for something she hadn't even orchestrated.

The thing that chafed the most was that the department trusted her enough to train its rookies and investigate major crimes, but not enough to wear stripes.

She'd tested once before, more for the experience of going through the test than because she thought she was ready. She'd done well, but it hadn't surprised her when someone else was selected.

This time around was different. Only two people had put in, and they both resided in the same household. The department made it clear that neither would be able to directly supervise the other. Not a big deal if Cameron promoted. Patrol and investigations were different divisions. More of a problem if she promoted. But as a newbie sergeant, she'd be assigned to graveyards. That meant Cameron could choose either day shift or swings. Again, nothing insurmountable.

They'd studied for the test. Or more honestly she'd busted her ass and Cameron had occasionally cracked the book and scanned her notes. At first she didn't mind. They'd told each other it wasn't a competition, that regardless of who was selected, there would be a sergeant in their family. It sounded good, but the reality couldn't compete with their intentions.

It was her fault, really. The harder she studied, the more she wanted the position.

Cameron didn't care. She was the one who convinced him of the value of a dry run. *What's the worst that could happen?* they joked.

The day of the test, she entered the room with confidence, and by the end of the day she'd tested highest on the written and aced the scenario-based questions. She thought she'd nailed the oral board, but the expressions of the four men across the table from her had made it hard to tell. It wasn't until the chief's interview that she learned the panel had unanimously endorsed Cameron for sergeant.

The more she considered her performance in light of what she knew her husband to be capable of, the less she was able to rationalize his selection. Was she delusional or just blind to her own shortcomings? She had the experience, the tenure, and the personnel file of a future sergeant. Cameron had less time on the job and had never held a specialty position. Plus, he'd had more than one closed-door conversation with a supervisor that ended up documented in his personnel file. She tried to placate herself with the reminder that she was a detective. Yet an assignment wasn't the same as a promotion. And the truth was, she wanted to be the department's first woman sergeant. Make her father proud.

Fat lot of good that had done. But it was only a half-truth anyway. The full truth was more complicated.

The trail cut through a shaded area, and she adjusted her neck gaiter to ward off the sudden chill.

The more she contemplated her motivations, the clearer it became that she was lying to herself. Making sergeant was less about earning her father's respect and more about outdoing him. He'd made sergeant in under ten years. She'd missed that deadline, but she was playing the long game, and her sights were set on outranking him. The problem was, without sergeant's stripes, she'd never be able to earn her lieutenant's bars.

The hills were suddenly too steep, the snow too deep, and her muscles ached with more than fatigue. She should call in sick tomorrow. Avoid the drama. Let the hullabaloo die a natural death without her. But even as she considered it, she knew she wouldn't. She'd man up. Just like always.

The trees thinned as she descended toward the river basin. Poplars lined the water, looking as if someone had stuffed giant peregrine falcon feathers quill-first into the snow. She picked up her pace, and her feet pounded across the plank bridge that spanned the Animas River. The Spaniards had dubbed it the *Rio de las Animas Perdidas*—the River of Lost Souls. How annoyingly apropos. A cross-country skier poled toward her, and she edged closer to the rails to avoid his narrow skis.

A man in waders stood in the river, fly-fishing with graceful casts. She was almost upon him before she recognized the district attorney. He acknowledged her on the backstroke of his cast. She fluttered her fingers and kept running. The trail climbed. A hundred yards later, she slowed. At the top she stopped, bent over with her hands on her thighs, her breath frosting the air in steam engine puffs. The chance to talk to the DA outside the office was too good to pass up, and she clasped her hands behind her head and retraced her steps.

There were people, mostly in the temperate zones of the United States, who thought running in the snow was a couple of degrees south of crazy. Clad in a beanie, several thin layers of tops, leggings, Gore-Tex shoes, and merino wool socks, she was toasty. The person who had lost his senses was the man in the frigid waters of the river wearing a cap, jacket, and waders that Jo fervently hoped kept the water at bay. His hands were bare, the knuckles a bright shade of chap.

The burble of the river masked the crunch of her steps as she left the trail and picked her way toward the rocks that lined the riverbed. She wanted to ask him about Quinn. Still, a pang of guilt stopped her midstep. The DA and Xavier Buck were close. His friend had just lost his son—a boy who had also been his own son's best friend. Perhaps Walsenberg needed to fly-fish as much as she'd needed to run.

"Something on your mind, Detective?" With his thumb on top of the rod, he smoothly accelerated through the back cast, watching the line unspool. After the slightest pause, he snapped the rod forward and stopped, casting his fly into the center of the river.

Jo raised her voice only enough to be heard over the wash of water. "Nothing that can't wait. I didn't mean to disturb you."

"The fish are sluggish today. I'm just practicing my cast."

She chose her route carefully and moved closer so she could lower her voice. "I'm really sorry about Ronny. I know your families are close."

Sadness settled on the DA's face. "The boy always drove like the laws of physics didn't apply to him."

He made it sound as if it was Ronny's fault. Hadn't the sheriff's office briefed him? Or Xavier. She'd figured that the moment he was informed someone else might have contributed to his son's death, he'd be on the phone pressing for answers. If not Xavier, certainly Alice. She'd seen the crime tape. She knew it wasn't an accident. She'd even offered up Quinn as a possible suspect.

"There might be more to it, sir. Deputy Garibaldi is handling the investigation."

"Another suicide that isn't?"

If his smile was meant to soften the dig, it missed the mark. Her guilt about disturbing him on a Sunday dissipated. "Did you have a chance to talk to Quinn on Friday night?"

He reeled in his line in preparation for another cast. "I spoke to a lot of people that night. Can you describe him for me?"

"Quinn is a woman. She was assisting your wife."

"Ah. No, sorry. I'm afraid I never had the chance to actually meet her. Alice was so busy, I just tried to stay out of her way. Still, the event was a rousing success, don't you think?"

"You knocked on Quinn's hotel room door early Saturday morning."

"That's quite possible." He lowered the rod. "I'm afraid I celebrated Alice's success a little too much. I tried to open the door to the wrong room. When my key didn't work, I knocked. No one answered. I didn't realize I'd disturbed someone."

He initiated another back cast, then flicked it forward. The movement reminded Jo of the tail of an angry cat.

"By the way," he said. "I saw the newspaper."

Her face flamed, and she imagined the snow around her melting from the heat. So this was what it was going to feel like. Uncomfortable, but she'd survive.

"About time someone rocked the boat." He laughed. "You remind me of Alice. You both appear to be so *nice*." He popped the tip of his reel against the surface. "But heaven help the person who underestimates either of you."

She refused to be sidetracked. "Quinn said you called her by name. Wanted to ask her something about Derek."

"Derek?" He blinked. Unlike Jo, Walsenberg wasn't wearing sunglasses, and the action appeared exaggerated. "He's been dead a year, Detective." His words had turned as deliberate as his blink. "I don't know what this Quinn Kirkwood is playing at, but I most certainly was not wandering around the resort asking strangers for information regarding my son. What is this really about?"

"Tye Horton."

"That case is closed."

"Not quite."

"My son died over a year ago. I fail to see how he is germane to the discussion."

The next question was indelicate, but he'd already lied once and it was time to push. "Did you know your son was gay?"

He swung the rod around and pointed it at her. "You overstep, Detective. My boy is none of your concern, and I'll thank you to honor that."

She stood her ground. "Do you still have Tye's belongings?"

"His family is picking up his effects tomorrow. I suggest you contact them." He turned his back to her. "If you need anything else, make an appointment. Good day, Detective." The rod swished the air, and the fly nearly landed on the other bank.

"Again, my apologies, sir."

Jo traversed the rocks back to the trail and reined herself in to a demure jog. Once out of the DA's sight, she picked up her pace, eager to finish the loop back to her car. She had work to do, and topping the list was finding out why the district attorney was lying.

He had said Quinn's last name unprompted. He might have remembered the name as the reporting party on Tye Horton's police report, but Jo'd seen the resort's surveillance tape. Seen Zachary Walsenberg standing in front of Quinn's door with a drink in his hand, talking to the person in the room. He'd clearly mouthed the name *Quinn*.

34

Quinn glanced in her rearview mirror. Was that truck following her?

The Mini Cooper clanked as she accelerated to a fast crawl, the front quarter panel held on with duct tape and a prayer. Circling a city the size of Echo Valley didn't take long. Every time she considered stopping somewhere, she'd slow down like she was casing the place to rob. Then she'd see someone and wonder if he was the moron making her life miserable and she'd keep going. At least behind the wheel, she controlled something— even if it was only which direction to turn as she put more miles between her and the Stu/Stans of the world.

She was already on her fourth lap. Only this time, she had company.

Her phone lit up in the cup holder. Another unknown number. "Jesus H. Christ!" She flipped it so she couldn't see the screen and almost overshot the curve. The Mini Cooper hobbled up the hill. The truck closed the distance between them until it rode her bumper. Filled her mirror with grille. Quinn mashed the accelerator, and the Mini Cooper wheezed. "Come on, baby."

The road straightened. The truck revved his engine, a deep diesel growl louder than her clacking fender. Outrunning the beast was impossible. The best option she had was to choose a driveway with lots of cars in the hope that someone would help her out if she needed it, but the ranches in this part of town were sprawling. Not a damn driveway in sight.

The truck crossed into the other lane behind her, tucked back in. Taunting?

Another curve. Another straightaway. This time the truck surged forward. Drew next to her. Quinn braked and the truck shot past, the driver not even glancing her way.

She raked her fingers through her hair. She was seriously losing her shit.

Her stomach rumbled as she neared the college. She'd kill for some dim sum and green tea from the little place on Jackson Street in Chinatown where she and her sister used to eat as teenagers. Might as well add that to the list of *things that ain't gonna happen*. It was a long list. Her apartment complex was a block away and she inventoried her culinary options. Not many, but cheap. She slowed down to casing speed. Since yesterday, an alarming number of strangers had landed on her doorstep thinking she was open for business. No one was at her door at the moment, but a strange blue Explorer was parked ass-first in the space next to hers.

Time to make a run for the border.

Out of her periphery, she saw the Explorer pull out of the parking space.

Her hunger dissipated. The fender flapped in the breeze as she sped downhill. Maybe she could pull around the back side of the strip center at the bottom of the hill without being seen. Her car was distinctive in the best of times. A hangnail fender only made it more memorable. Two curves later and the SUV was on her.

Just like the truck. Her paranoia had spiked to the point that every car on the roadway was a threat. She really needed to get a grip. Get some food. She was the epitome of hangry.

The headlights on the Explorer flashed a friendly *Hey pull over* pattern.

Not a chance.

Glare on the windshield prevented Quinn from seeing the driver. Her frustration surged. The lights flashed again, accompanied by a quick horn toot. She'd had enough. This was going to end now. She fumbled with her cell phone and turned on the camera.

The light at the bottom of the hill turned green as she hit the intersection, and she barely slowed before whipping into the gas station. The Explorer pulled in behind her, boxing her in by the pumps. The driver door opened.

Quinn burst out of her car and charged toward the Explorer. Phone high. Recorder on. "What the fuck do you want?"

She barreled into the door, trying to pin the driver, but the driver sprang aside and the door slammed against empty air. Unable to check her momentum, Quinn slid the length of the Explorer and landed on the ground. Her cell phone skittered under the SUV. She rolled and came up in a crouch, slush dripping off the back of her jacket.

"Are you okay?" The driver, a woman decked out in running gear, approached cautiously.

A scratchy female voice came over the speaker at the pump. "You two behave yourselves. I'm calling nine-one-one."

The runner raised her sunglasses onto the top of her beanie and waved at the camera. Quinn recognized Wyatt. She looked tired.

"I'm Detective Wyatt," she spoke toward the speaker. "Everything is fine."

"Jo, that you? Hey girl, it's Tina. We shared senior home room together."

"Hey, Tina. Sorry for the disturbance. You can cancel the police."

"No worries, girl. I was just trying to scare you guys away. Hey, I saw the paper today. Too bad about sergeant. Cool about Cameron, though. You must be proud, him being your husband and all."

"Thanks, Tina. You take care." Wyatt rolled her eyes at Quinn. "My God," she whispered. "I should have let you squish me."

"For the record, I thought you were someone else," Quinn said.

"Good to know." The detective offered her hand and leaned back for balance as Quinn stood.

"That dickwad I met at Tye's is your husband?"

"Long story that's absolutely none of your business. Do you ever answer your phone? I've been trying to get in touch with you for the last hour."

"Another long story." Quinn brushed the sleet from her sleeves. "Why were you at my apartment?"

"I wanted to ask you if you'd be willing to walk through Tye's place before it gets packed up. See if anything strikes you as odd."

"Like what?"

"I don't know. What I saw and what you see could mean different things. But I also know he was your friend, so if it is going to make you uncomfortable, it's okay to say no."

"But you think it might help, or you wouldn't ask."

The detective lowered her sunglasses, as if to hide her thoughts. It was Quinn's decision.

"You going like that?" Quinn asked.

Wyatt glanced down at her tights. "It's a very small window of opportunity."

"Let me find someplace to park my car."

35

A thin strip of yellow crime scene tape remained caught in the hinge of Tye's door. Jo knocked.

"Seriously?" Quinn danced from foot to foot in an effort to keep warm.

"Come in," a voice yelled from inside.

Jo turned the knob. "The property belongs to the Walsenbergs. I can't just walk in. It's not an active crime scene any longer." She pushed the door open and motioned for Quinn to follow her inside. A pile of boxes and a roll of packing tape stood at the ready inside the door.

At a glance, the focal point of the room had changed. Tye's chair had been pushed against the wall, and a barren square marked where the bloody carpet had been cut away. A brochure for a cleaning company specializing in biohazard remediation was on the seat. Jo's gaze climbed to the ceiling. It had been scrubbed, but the scent of death still lingered—an unsettling combination of coppery staleness and chemicals.

Alice knelt beside the mini refrigerator. She dropped a bottle of ketchup into a large black trash bag and used the top of the fridge to pull herself upright. "Detective Wyatt, always a pleasure."

"Thank you for allowing me to stop by on such short notice, Mrs. Walsenberg. Please excuse my attire." Jo indicated Quinn. "You already know Ms. Kirkwood."

"Of course." Alice's face pinched with worry. "I didn't expect anyone else to accompany you. Is that legal?" She took a half step toward Quinn. "I'm sorry dear, I don't mean anything personally, but I have an obligation to safeguard Mr. Horton's possessions until his family collects them. I'd hate for them to think I didn't take my responsibility seriously."

"Yeah. I'm sure that's it." Quinn turned a small circle as she took in the room, stopping with her back to Mrs. Walsenberg.

"You have nothing to worry about," Jo said. "I spoke to Mrs. Horton."

"Thank you. It was quite a shock to discover someone was living here. It's not permitted for habitation, you know. My husband . . . Well, it certainly wouldn't do for someone in his position to appear to be circumventing the law."

"Because that's really the sad part of this whole story." Quinn reached her fingers toward the corner of Tye's chair but withdrew them without touching the stained upholstery.

"I'm sorry. That was insensitive of me." Alice wiped her hands against her thighs.

Death had brought the three women together by circuitous routes. And yet, here they all stood.

"So, how do we proceed?" Alice said.

Obviously, things had been moved, cleaned—and Jo was glad Quinn was spared the worst of the carnage—but it meant Quinn wasn't seeing Tye's place so much as his things. The context was gone. "Has anything been thrown away or picked up yet?"

"I didn't want Mrs. Horton to have to deal with . . . well, I thought it best to have things cleaned up a bit and have Tye's items packed. My husband dropped off the boxes earlier, but the only things removed are what you collected for your investigation." She indicated the trash bag. "And the things in the refrigerator."

"I'd like to walk Ms. Kirkwood through everything. Give her a chance to note anything that might have a bearing on the case," Jo explained.

"I didn't realize there was still a case to have a bearing on. My husband said the coroner had ruled the incident a suicide."

"That's the tentative ruling, yes. I'm just tying up loose ends before we close the case," Jo said. "It would be best if we did this in private," she added.

"Private. Yes, of course. I'll . . . Well, I've got some errands to run." She gathered the top of the trash bag together and lifted it. "I'll finish up later."

Jo held out her hand to stop her from leaving with the bag. "If you don't mind."

She hesitated only slightly. "Whatever you need. Call me when you're done." She tied the bag and slid it against the mini fridge.

Rogue snowflakes blown from the trees entered the apartment when Alice left. They twirled like drunken butterflies and then fell to the ground, spent.

Quinn faced the center of the room once more. "Well, that was awkward. Do you suppose she knows her husband tried to pay me a booty call?"

"I don't know I'd characterize it as a booty call."

"And what would you call it?"

A valid question, for which Jo had no reasonable answer. She snapped into tour mode. "As you can see, things have been moved around a bit. We collected a few things and booked them at the police department. The recliner was centered on the television, and that small round table was next to the recliner."

Jo didn't say anything else. She wanted to hear what Quinn had to say. See what she'd key in on. Some of the changes were obvious. The mattress had been flipped on edge and leaned against the wall, but the matted carpet showed where it had been. Tottering piles of clothes littered the floor.

Quinn stopped in front of a makeshift cinder block–and–plank bookshelf next to the television. "That's where he piled his game consoles and stuff. He had a collection of old movies. Musicals, mostly." She tapped the CD player on top of the television. "He kept his favorite here. He even had a display stand for it. I don't remember the title, but it starred Gene Kelly— you know, the dude who danced? It's the one where he's some sailor or something and jumps around with that cartoon mouse."

"Tom?"

"Or Jerry. One of them. He'd play that stupid movie on a loop while he was coding. It put him in his happy place." She ran her hand slowly across the empty shelf. "Why would someone take a bunch of old gaming consoles? You couldn't even use them anymore."

"We checked the pawn shops in the county. Nothing."

Quinn wandered into the bathroom. Jo followed her and stood in the doorway. A box had been placed over the toilet seat and Quinn peeled down one of the flaps, revealing soap-scum-spotted shampoo bottles and toiletries from the shower. She thrust her hand into the box, and when she withdrew it, she held the orange cap of a syringe. A strange expression twisted her face. Longing? Maybe, but something more, too. Something Jo suspected didn't surface too often.

"Once upon a time, I had a problem with heroin," Quinn said. "One night while I was in rehab, I snuck out of the facility. It didn't take any time at all to score a needle. Even less time to boost a bottle of saline from the drugstore." She peeled the flap back further and rummaged through the box. "I couldn't wait. I sat on one of those cement parking curbs behind the store. Had to use my shoelace to tie off. Thought I was never going to find a vein."

She rested her hand on the lip of the box and went somewhere Jo couldn't follow. The perpetual wariness fell from Quinn's face but was replaced by pain so raw, Jo felt she should look away even as she continued to stare.

"The prick was exquisite." The timbre of Quinn's voice changed. "I teased myself, pulling back the plunger just a bit until the slightest trace of blood swirled into the barrel like crimson smoke." She blinked several times, and then her eyes met Jo's in the mirror. "When I was through, I snuck back to the facility." The familiar Quinn returned. "Idiots never noticed I'd left."

"What was the saline for?"

"I couldn't very well shoot heroin, now, could I?" She folded the flaps to secure the box. "Kind of defeats the purpose of rehab."

"You injected yourself with saline? What did it do?"

"Nothing. Well, other than saving me an air embolism. But it wasn't the high I was chasing. I just wanted my body to believe everything was going to be okay."

"Did it work?"

She pushed the plastic cap through the gap on the top of the box. "Long enough."

They retraced their steps to the main room. There was precious little to mark the passing of Tye Horton. Dirty clothes. Spoiling food. Scum-crusted toiletries.

"Other than the missing consoles and movies, is there anything else you can remember Tye owning that you don't see?"

"The laptop—unless Ronny had it. It's hard to miss. It has a sticker of Marvin the Martian holding a flag stuck over the Apple emblem."

Jo talked from the back of her throat. "I claim this planet for Mars."

Quinn snorted through her nose. "That was scary good. There's hope for you yet."

"Now if I only had my Illudium Q-36 Explosive Space Modulator." She slid the trash bag aside and opened the refrigerator. Alice had completely cleaned it out. "I asked Ronny about the laptop. He said he didn't have it. Anything else?" She toed aside the boxes and the stack fell over. The space against the wall was empty.

"It's hard to tell. I was only here a couple of times."

Jo stared at the empty baseboard. "The cat's bowl is missing."

"He didn't have a cat."

"Which doesn't negate the fact that he did, however, own a bowl meant for a cat."

"How do you know it was a cat dish?"

Jo opened and closed the two doors that served as a cupboard. Paper plates, five Comic-Con coffee mugs, no cat dish. "It was on the floor and had *meow* scrawled across it in a ridiculous font."

"Sound like the stupid Easter egg Tye planted in his game."

"How is an Easter egg remotely like a cat dish?"

"Sorry, the Marvin voice threw me. I keep forgetting you're a pop culture disaster. An Easter egg is something game designers sometimes hide in their programs. It could open a new portal, give the player something unexpected, or just be an inside joke. Tye created this cat character. Only it was the fucking Jar Jar Binks of video games. Not a fan favorite."

"Jar Jar Binks?"

"*The Phantom Menace*? Star Wars? Seriously. What kind of heathen are you?"

"How did Tye hide an entire character?"

"The cat wasn't the egg. Its bowl was. The cat followed players as they trekked through the game. It was kind of a two-prong test. First they had to notice the damn thing. Then they had to care enough to show the cat some kindness. If they stopped to fill the bowl it carried—poof. The font rearranged itself into runes and the player gained a pretty beefy protection spell plus a cush place to relax for a bit."

"Because they fed the cat."

"Actually, because they shared their water with it. Water was the most valuable commodity in his game world."

A prickle of excitement fluttered in Jo's belly, and she struggled to hide it. She could be wrong about it being missing. The dish was one of the few breakable knickknacks in the apartment. Maybe Alice had slipped the bowl between Tye's shirts to protect it from breaking. Jo riffled through the clothes. Nothing. She put her hands on her hips. "Of all the things to go missing, why that?"

"If it was anything like the bowl in the game, it was one step above—"

"Trash," Jo whispered to herself.

Jo worked the knot of the garbage bag free and loosened the draw-string. She hesitated only a moment before upending the half-filled bag over the carpet. Condiment bottles, deli meat containers, something unidentifiable, and one ugly cat dish.

"Mystery solved," Quinn said.

But it wasn't. At a glance, the bowl was the only item in the trash bag that wasn't rotting or about to become a science experiment. Why was it there, and had Alice been the one to toss it?

"You mentioned runes and a protection spell." Jo sat back on her heels, thinking. "That sounds a lot like *The Lord of the Rings*."

"You saw *Lord of the Rings*?"

"I'm the kind of heathen who read the books."

"Should have guessed. Yeah, it was a bit derivative."

Quinn reached for the bowl, but Jo stopped her. "Hold on a second. The place where the players got to relax. Describe it for me."

"You read the *Rings*, so you know the hobbits were all about hearth and home and shit. Right? Well, this was kind of like that. Fill the bowl, and suddenly players found themselves in front of a roaring fire, with a pipe in their hand, ale in their cup, and a loved one by their side. Plus, when the player reentered the game, they carried a protection charm."

"Tye didn't drink, did he?"

"Alcohol messed with his sugar levels too much. He always had one of those supersized cups of McDonald's iced tea. The man was seriously addicted."

"Did he smoke?" Jo asked.

"Hated the smell."

"So if I told you I found Tye sitting in front of a television set that had a mood CD of a crackling fireplace set on a loop with a bottle of Jameson's and a long-stemmed pipe on the table next to him, what would you think?"

Quinn bumped her shoulders. "If there was water in the bowl, I'd say he was trying to recreate his happy space."

"Surrounded by alcohol he couldn't consume, a pipe he wouldn't smoke, and without the man he loved? Sounds more like hell to me."

The door swung open, and Zachary Walsenberg's shadow divided the room. "What are you doing here?" He still wore his fleece jacket but had ditched his fishing vest. "Where is my wife?"

"I'm reviewing Mr. Horton's possessions before his sister picks them up."

"I told you to contact her if you wanted to see them."

"I did. She told me she hadn't made arrangements to pick them up yet. I called Mrs. Walsenberg and obtained permission to take a final peek." She removed her fleece and used it to pick up the cat dish. "I'm also collecting one more piece of evidence."

"You're not taking anything out of here."

Quinn brazenly stepped between them and shoved out her hand. "Hey. I'm Quinn. What exactly did you want to know about your son that you think I could tell you?"

"I don't know what you're talking about."

Quinn leaned her shoulder against the wall and crossed her legs at the ankle. "Oh, I'm throwing the bullshit flag on that. Are district attorneys allowed to lie? It seems to me that would be bad for business."

The DA pressed his lips together and towered over Jo. "I certainly don't mind helping out with an investigation, but I have no intention of allowing you to continue to insult me on my own property. It's time for you to leave."

36

The run for the border took a whopping ten minutes after they left the rental property.

Jo squirted fire sauce on her crispy taco. "Talk to me about games."

"What do you want to know?" Quinn sat sideways on the plastic booth bench with her back pressed against the wall, her jacket balled up like a pillow.

"You're getting a degree in digital arts. You tell me what's important."

The teen at the counter spoke into a small microphone. "Number thirty-seven, order up." An entirely useless announcement, since they were the only two people currently in Taco Bell.

"Hang on, that's me."

A moment later, Quinn returned with a tray laden with what looked like one of everything off the menu. The whole meal cost seven dollars and change, which made it the best eight bucks Jo had ever spent.

Quinn organized the items on her tray by size. "Games are an important educational component of society. They're puzzles. They teach us how to recognize patterns, spatial relationships, how to complete tasks, reason, explore."

"Blow things up."

Quinn lowered the burrito in her hand and scowled. "I can dumb things down for you if you want, but I didn't peg you for that kind of person."

"Point taken. My apologies."

"A lot of people think that shooter and war games are all about power. For some, yeah, sure. But these games teach players about reaction times. Tactics. Planning. How to make the most of your opponent's weaknesses.

Critics overlook that the real lesson in these games is teamwork. You can't go in by yourself and save the day. You have to trust your partners or you're all doomed." She took a massive bite of burrito.

"Why is there such a backlash against women in gaming?"

She swallowed. "Because there's a vocal minority who are scared to death we're going to do away with the games they like and make everything more touchy-feely."

"No offense, but you don't strike me as touchy-feely," Jo said.

"Funny, that's exactly what Alice Walsenberg said." The straw squealed against the lid as she drank her Mountain Dew. "There's room for both. Traditionally, game designers were guys—just like cops. They designed games centering around shit they liked to do. Lots of war games. First-person shooter stuff, martial arts. Here's the kicker. Half the gamer community is women, but it's still perceived as a male pastime. Take that little kid who just walked in with his dad." She pointed with her cup. "Check out his shirt."

"Superman?"

"A comic book character, but it will still prove my point. Pretty buff, right? When women characters were first incorporated into comics and games, they all had huge boobs, tiny waists, itsy-bitsy costumes, and squat in the way of survival skills—always needing to be rescued." She popped the lid off her nacho cheese container and dipped a chip. "Then the industry wonders why women don't feel included." She rolled her eyes dramatically.

"But you like gaming."

"Yeah. I do. Did from the moment I first played. That's the problem with generalities. There's always exceptions to the rules. There's a lot of women who love first-person shooter games. Some of them probably became cops." She nudged Jo with her foot under the table. "But what happened was a group of gamers—mostly men—got it in their craw that they ruled the industry. Any woman trying to change the status quo was viewed as a threat—one that needed to be destroyed. Or at least stopped."

"Gamergate."

"You know about Gamergate?"

"I've been trying to wrap my head around what's going on with your case."

"Yeah, well, Gamergate was the tipping point that brought the issue into the mainstream. Here's the thing. It wasn't the start of the problems in the industry. It really wasn't even representative of it. But it showed how social media could be weaponized. Doxing, trolling, SWATting. They're all ways to try to control and frighten people."

"I never thought I'd be glad you've only been spoofed."

"Yeah. About that."

"Number thirty-eight. Your order is up. Number thir-tee-eight." Talking into the microphone appeared to be the highlight of the teen's shift. The father didn't even have to step forward to collect the two bags. They walked out, leaving the restaurant empty of everyone but Jo, Quinn, and the two workers. Clearly, Taco Bell was the happening place to be on a Sunday night.

Quinn wiped her hands on her napkin and dug out her phone. "I called you last night." She hit a couple of buttons and handed the phone to Jo. "I need to update my report."

"You might consider leav—" Jo abandoned the rest of her sentence, ambushed by a photo of Quinn in a lingerie ensemble with a come-hither look on her face. She tried to reconcile the woman on the screen with the one devouring a double-shelled taco on the other side of the booth. She failed. The gallery contained seven photos in all, each one more provocative than the last.

She clicked on the profile and read Quinn's phone number and address. "Is this why you weren't home?"

"The main one."

"But not the only one?" The home page suggested a dating site, but the photos and bios clearly suggested escort services and more. "How did you find out about this?"

"My neighbor's a freak who's been trying to get into my pants since I moved in. He found the site and was kind enough to cross-post it to the college forum. I guess I should be flattered. I've gotten so many calls, I had to turn the ringer off."

"Which explains why you didn't pick up when I called you today to let you know I was at your apartment."

"I didn't see a call from the PD."

"I called from my personal phone. Don't make me regret trusting you with it."

"Aw. I feel so special."

"Where did the photos of your face come from?"

"How do you know it's only my face?"

"I'm a detective." She handed the phone back to Quinn. "A, you're showing me the site, and B, none of the women in the photos have an infinity tattoo on their wrist."

Quinn twisted her wrist, the small symbol clearly visible below her pushed-up sleeves. "Yeah, they don't have anything on their thighs either."

"Anything in the photos you recognize?"

"The sunglasses. I got them at the beginning of summer and lost them a month or two later, which means whoever this weirdo is, he's been watching me for months."

"What about your neighbor? He's got the hots for you. Kind of convenient he found the website."

"Maybe."

"Any chance you think it's Professor Lucas?" Jo posed the question casually, as curious about Quinn's thoughts on the matter as she was on whether the woman would disclose the relationship. The last time she'd mentioned the professor's name, she'd gone ballistic.

Quinn piled her empty wrappers one atop the other until she had a neat stack to hide behind.

"He came over to my apartment one night. To talk about my grade." Her voice had turned flat. "Made it clear I could influence the outcome, if you know what I mean."

After twelve years of police work, Jo knew exactly what Quinn meant. Quinn's features twisted as she described the encounter, but her body remained perfectly still, her eyes never leaving Jo's face as if daring her to disbelieve her.

"And then I kicked the bastard out," she said. "After everything I'd done, I still managed to blow my grade." She drank deeply of her soda and then rattled the ice. "No pun intended."

Jo balled her fist under the table. "We can pursue charges." A small consolation that would turn into a he-said/she-said slugfest with Quinn the ultimate loser.

"Right. All he has to do is show the email and I become a woman who cried rape after changing her mind. No thank you."

She couldn't argue. Quinn was right. There wasn't a DA anywhere that would touch a case where consent was so neatly implied.

Jo slumped against the plastic bench. Every day, the bastard taunting Quinn remained hidden behind an impenetrable curtain. It pained her to admit, but she was no closer to identifying him now than when she'd taken Quinn's initial report.

"Do you think Lucas is telling the truth about receiving an email, or do you think he's the mastermind behind everything?" She was so tired. Tired of death. Tired of threats. Tired of falling short.

"He doesn't have the balls to mastermind anything. I should know." She pressed her thumb and index finger close together and held them up in front of her eye. "I've seen them." She dropped her hand. "There's more. I found two escort services, five social media sites, a couple discussion boards that all have my name attached to them. But that's not the worst of it."

Jo waited. She'd learned as a rookie not to ask what could possibly be worse. In police work, there was always something.

"I got another email. Well, actually, I got several, but one sticks out."

"Sticks out how?"

"All it says is 'And then there was one.'"

The implication hit Jo immediately. She'd been right. The cases were linked. Even if Tye Horton had suicided, something bound all the deaths together. But in Jo's mind, there was no longer any doubt. Tye had been murdered. She'd overlooked something, and she was going to figure out what it was.

In the wake of Quinn's pain, Jo tried to ignore her growing excitement, but it took root in her gut and grew. Whoever was harassing Quinn had stumbled. Given her a clue. Several really. Social media sites could be tracked. Discussion boards could be infiltrated. She'd need a new round of subpoenas for records. Go back over the items collected at the Horton scene. Hunt down Lucas. With any luck, she'd be too busy to think about the article.

Quinn broke in on Jo's thoughts. "There seem to be two themes to the bogus profiles—I'm either a whore for hire, or a game designer who is going to single-handedly topple the industry with my social-justice-warrior shit."

"Social justice warrior? That sounds like a good thing."

"Not in these circles. It's a slur against anyone considered too politically correct. You know, those nefarious people who think equal rights and inclusiveness are the devil's work. Heaven forbid we gamers push back against the kidnapped-princess trope. The world isn't going to stop if a woman turns out to be capable of saving her own ass."

A new thought struck Jo. "Are you?"

"What?" Quinn asked.

"Capable of saving your own ass. I mean, other than in video games. You charged my car today. What if I'd had a gun? Your cell phone isn't a magic shield." She crumpled up her wrappers and dropped them on the tray, suddenly eager to leave. "You ever get that feeling on the back of your neck that says you shouldn't do something?"

"Only when I'm with you."

Quinn talked a good game, and she looked fierce with her spiky hair and edgy clothes, but she was up against an unknown. Were these new developments ramping up to a finale? The email stated that Quinn was the only one left—which meant she now had the stalker's undivided attention. A smart mouth wasn't going to save her.

"Fear is a gift," Jo said. "It's an early-warning system. Based on your earlier actions, it's something you need to start paying more attention to. It's not enough to flee danger. You have to run toward safety."

"I suppose you're going to teach me everything I need to know about personal safety in ten easy lessons?"

People were amazingly intuitive about danger, but too often they allowed themselves to rationalize the threat. She'd taken countless police reports that began with the victim telling her they'd had a funny feeling about someone, or that they knew something wasn't right. Maybe, just maybe, she could teach Quinn something about situational awareness. And she knew the perfect way to do it.

"Even better," she responded. "Grab your jacket."

37

Wyatt had been all hush-hush about where they were going, and even when they arrived, Quinn didn't have a clue where they were. The cinder block building on the edge of an open field had all the warm fuzzies of an apocalyptic outpost.

"Is this the part of the movie where you confess to being a serial killer? Because you should know, I can't be a victim. My underwear doesn't match."

"This is our gun range."

"If that was meant to be comforting, your delivery needs some work."

"It's also where we have our training simulator." She tapped a code onto a keypad and opened the door. "After you."

"Great. Should we agree on a safe word?"

Wyatt flicked on the lights. "Where's your sense of adventure?"

A table inside the door had a computer with its own tower and other electronic equipment that Quinn didn't recognize. A giant three-piece screen was set up flat against the back wall with massive wings that jutted into the room at oblique angles. A rack to her left displayed a selection of guns.

"Platypus," Quinn whispered.

"What?"

"My safe word." She was equal parts awed and spooked. "What is all this?"

"Pretty much anything you want it to be." Wyatt booted up the computer. "Critical incidents, active shooters, hostage scenarios, in-progress crimes, traffic stops. You name it. The system is comprised of one hundred and eighty degrees of laser-reactive screens, high-definition projectors, surround sound, and the computer system to run it all." She typed in a password. "You supply the adrenaline."

Quinn glanced to her right. "What's the treadmill for?"

"It makes things a bit more realistic if your heart rate is elevated before you start the scenario."

"You know how to run all this?"

"I'm one of the use-of-force trainers. We got the system through a grant when I was a training officer. I still operate it when we qualify."

"Shmup."

A line formed between Wyatt's eyebrows. "What?"

"Shoot 'em up. You want to play games, you gotta speak the lingo."

"Copy that." Using a remote, Wyatt went around and powered up the projectors suspended from the ceiling. "Once a year we have a citizens police academy and we run them through it."

"Do any of them survive?"

"Depends on the scenario, but they all have a better appreciation for how quickly decisions need to be made."

The screen flickered to life and displayed the simulator's corporate logo.

Wyatt strapped a duty belt around her waist, adjusted it to a smaller size, and selected a handgun for the holster. "The guns we use are real, so the weight and feel is accurate, but they've been modified with a laser, so if you squeeze the trigger, you'll register the hits on the screen. If you miss, that's registered too."

She added a radio and clipped the shoulder mic to the collar of her fleece. "Normally we use our own equipment and are dressed a little differently. Drawing from a belt that isn't actually anchored to my pants is going to be a hoot."

"The perils of tights."

"On the outdoor range, we practice with our off-duty guns too. I carry mine in a backpack. Occasionally a purse. Imagine how much slower it is to dig it out, aim, and fire. But that's another point. You have to work with what you've got." She gestured toward the computer. "I'm going to set it on autoplay so you can watch me go through one of the scenarios. The whole point of this type of training is to expose officers to different situations in a controlled environment. Stress makes people do stupid things, but it can be managed. Cops who say they never get scared are liars."

"I'm not a cop."

"No, but there are plenty of takeaways."

Wyatt hit a button, and the front of a police car entered an alley. She walked into the area in the center of the frozen screens and pointed at the back door of a business. "Just because you're focused on one threat doesn't mean you can ignore the rest of your environment." She turned and pointed to a parked car, a dumpster, and a guy smoking a cigarette two businesses away. "Always look at a person's hands. Are they holding a gun or a cell phone? Can it be used as a weapon? Sometimes the best thing you can do is return to your car and throw it in reverse. Create a safe distance until you have backup."

"Run away."

"We prefer to call it a tactical retreat." She stepped back. "Ready?"

"Whenever you are."

Wyatt hit the remote.

The radio crackled to life with three short tones. "Unit to clear for a possible robbery in progress. Twelve-sixteen Main Street. One-two-one-six Main Street. Conflicting reports of a man with a gun inside the business. White male, black hoodie and jeans. Nothing further."

Even standing behind Wyatt, Quinn felt as if she'd landed in the middle of a video game.

"Echo, David-three." Wyatt spoke into the microphone on her collar. "I'm on scene in the alley behind the store with a visual—"

The door flew open so hard it banged against the wall. Quinn jumped. A man wearing a black hoodie backed out while shouting at someone inside.

Wyatt drew her gun, the whole belt rising as she freed it from her holster. "Police. Stop. Show me your hands!"

The man continued to yell inside the building, but he started to shuffle backward away from the door. A woman followed him into the alley from the business. She yelled at him, flailing one arm like a crazy Italian, the other hand down at her side holding something.

Wyatt transformed. "Gun!"

Gone was the runner with a messy ponytail peeking out through a hole in her beanie. She moved like a fucking superhero ballerina, barking orders. Her eyes seemed to glance everywhere and yet never leave the two people, even as they broke apart.

The woman swung the weapon toward Wyatt. Wyatt squeezed the trigger twice, then aimed slightly higher and fired again. The woman dropped to the ground.

The guy in the hoodie bolted.

Wyatt talked into her radio again. Telling other officers the guy was running, his direction of travel, details Quinn hadn't noticed. Then she moved toward the screen, her gun pointed at the woman on the ground, giving her more orders, even though she wasn't moving.

Quinn wasn't even between the screens, and her pulse hammered in her neck. She wiped her hands on her pants.

Finally, Wyatt holstered. She clicked the remote, freezing the program. "Quick. What do you do?"

"You dropped one, you can't let the other get away."

"It's hardwired into a cop's DNA to chase anyone who runs from them." She spoke to Quinn while walking back to the computer. "It's not always the right choice."

She tapped several commands onto the keyboard. The scenario backed up slightly, the scenery changing as if an officer was chasing hoodie guy. Within seconds, the woman on the ground reared up and shot.

Wyatt stopped the program. "You're dead. Why? Because you thought neutralizing one threat meant there weren't any others. Close your eyes."

Quinn was too overwhelmed to argue.

"Describe the woman."

All she remembered was the gun. It was huge. "She was white, I guess."

"What else?"

"She had a gun."

"What about age, hair color, clothing?"

"I got nothing."

"Not unusual. What about things in the alley?"

"Just the normal collection of dumpsters. I suppose you could have used one of them to hide behind."

"Good catch. Officers still need to engage, which means we're sticking our noggin out, but you may need to hide. If you have a choice, hunker down behind something that will stop a bullet, not merely hide you from view. The garden wall is a lot better than a fern."

"You let one of the bad guys go."

"Did I? Maybe. Dispatch never has all the answers. Even if he was part of the problem, as you can see, I couldn't go past the woman on the ground until she'd been secured. She still had a gun and wasn't out of play."

"You make it sound like a game."

"It's got similarities, but what happens on the street isn't a game."

Wyatt stripped the gun belt from her waist and held it out to Quinn.

"Nope. I'm good."

"You sure?"

As the daughter of a cop, Quinn had learned how to shoot and all the gun safety shit that went along with it. But a gun hadn't done diddly to save her mother. It had still been in her holster when she was shot. Too busy dealing with her stoned daughter to hear the real danger approaching.

Quinn plunged her hands into her pockets to keep from reaching out for the gun belt. "Platypus."

Wyatt gave her a funny look, but didn't press. "Tell me about your capstone project."

The change of subject was a relief. Maybe that was the point of the question, because the detective had a softer look in her eyes than normal. Quinn didn't know whether to be grateful or pissed.

"The whole idea of a team project was to prepare us for the real world of game design. We had to create a game prototype. Picture all the people it takes to make a movie. Same concept, smaller scale. But there's a whole crew of creatives, coders, and coffee fetchers contributing to the final product. I designed the story and world-building. Tye did most of the heavy lifting when it came to coding. Ronny played it, which was about all he was good for."

She hadn't wanted him on the team, but Tye and Ronny had worked out an agreement. He'd stayed away from her, so it really hadn't mattered.

His death mattered. She kept seeing his face. The explosion of snow when his car hit the berm. The darkness after he left the road.

"Sounds complicated," Wyatt said. "But Tye knew how to do it all, right? I mean, he'd created a video game before."

"True. None of us was worried about acing the project." At least not originally.

"What was it about Tye's first game that made it so special?"

It still caught her by surprise that she was the only one of their group still alive. "Some of the lessons games teach aren't all that useful anymore. A lot of games don't reward players for breaking the rules, instead inspiring a type of blind obedience. War games in particular use force to overcome obstacles in order to advance. Enemies are offed without ever getting to tell their side of the story."

"The terrorist versus freedom-fighter argument."

"Exactly. How one is viewed in one country can be way different in another. It's called othering. The more different a character is perceived to be from the player, the more dangerous it becomes in our mind."

"Where did Tye's game fall in all that?"

"He made the mistake of designing a game that addressed social responsibility. He managed to erase the othering component. It was brilliant, really."

Wyatt returned the gun and belt to the rack. "How'd he do that?"

"The characters were gender-fluid. Alliances were based on mutual good, not personal gain. Winning could only happen when the survival of the group was obtained even if it came at the expense of the individual. It focused on cooperation, not control."

"Sounds like the kind of game the trolls were worried about."

"Yeah. It checked all the boxes."

"What was the challenge?"

"It was an explorer game. You traveled through scenarios. Unlock enough secrets or complete enough tasks, and you leveled up to an entirely different gamescape. It drew on memory of established patterns and then threw in new patterns or shortened allowable time to keep things fresh."

"Would something like that have been profitable? I mean, it strikes me as an indie film, when I'd have thought all the gaming companies would be eager for a blockbuster."

"Not everyone likes chocolate. Why else would Baskin-Robbins have fifty-two flavors?"

The detective zipped her jacket up to her throat. "Any guess why Tye shelved the project?"

She didn't have to guess. "Tye had created an email group for the game's beta testers and sent us all a kind of evaluation sheet. Derek returned his to me by accident."

She strode into the center of the screens, stood where Wyatt had stood. The woman on the screen pointed the gun straight at Quinn's chest. It wasn't a game in this room. Officers confronted their monsters on these screens. Some figured out how to slay them. But like Wyatt had pointed out, sometimes the lesson was how to let the monsters go.

"I read the email before I forwarded it to Tye. Derek didn't know anything about jump times or other technical aspects of the game, but the game touched him in a different way. Something way more significant." Quinn recalled the email. The goofy enthusiasm. The hope she'd read between the lines. "Tye's game gave Derek the courage to come out."

Wyatt pointed the remote toward each projector, and one by one the screens darkened. "Do you know if he told his folks?"

"No clue. Two days later he was dead."

Part Four

JO

38

Jo entered the police building at zero six thirty. Day shift was in briefing, and the likelihood of bumping into someone in the hallway was remote. Cowardly, maybe. She'd have to face the guys at some point, but for now, she charged up the stairs, eager to start working all the new angles that had cropped up over the weekend.

The detective bureau door at the top of the stairs stood open, but the office was dark. Detectives had keys; otherwise one had to be a sergeant or higher to access the investigative office. Squint must have come in early and gone downstairs to the patrol briefing. She flipped on the light.

Vacuum tracks lined the carpet, and a collection of her hair ties was stacked on the corner of her desk. A magazine leaned against her computer, left open to a photograph of a naked woman on her hands and knees giving a blow job to one man while a second man entered her from behind. Angry red ink crawled across the top of the page.

She knows her place.

Jo dropped her backpack. For a moment all she could see was the image, but that wasn't the point. The message was. Her jaw clenched so tight, she heard her teeth grind. Then she heard another sound. A vacuum.

She found Cody in the chief's office.

As soon as he saw Jo, he ducked his head and increased the speed of his vacuuming to a furious pace, banging into the base of the knickknack-filled bookcase that lined one wall of the office.

She stepped in front of the vacuum, forcing him to stop, and he turned it off.

"You sh-shouldn't be in here, Mrs. Wyatt. No one is allowed in the chief's office when he isn't here."

"Cody, did you let someone in the detective office?"

"I'm not allowed to do that. I go in. I clean. That's it. Otherwise I'd be breaking the rules. Like now. Please, Mrs. Wyatt. You need to go so I don't get in trouble."

"Cody, you're not in trouble, but someone put something on my desk that isn't mine. Did you see the magazine on my desk?"

A bright red flush climbed his neck, and he blinked several times behind his thick glasses. He pressed the switch, and the industrial vacuum whirred back to life. "I have to finish, Mrs. Wyatt."

She yanked the plug from the wall socket. "I don't care if you looked at it. Do you know who put it there?"

He studied his toes and shook his head. "Please, don't be mad at me, Mrs. Wyatt." His chin quivered.

There was no way Cody was responsible for the magazine, and his distress tore at her heart. Jo wiped her face of the rage growing inside her—not at him, but the person who'd placed him in the cross fire. She touched his forearm. "We're friends, Cody. I have no reason to be mad at you."

"I took the trash downstairs. I was only gone a few minutes." He worked his thumb against the cord as if it were a rosary. "When I came back, the dirty magazine was on your desk."

"Did you see who left it there? I'd like to give it back to him." More to the point, she'd like to shove it up his ass.

He shook his head again. "I understand if you have to report me. I should have shut the door behind me."

"I'm not going to report you, Cody. Please don't worry about that."

"Why would someone give you a magazine full of dirty pictures?"

"That's what I want to find out."

"I heard a new joke, Mrs. Wyatt."

She forced herself to smile. "It's not another computer joke, is it?"

"Even better," he said with his normal enthusiasm. "Why can't you trust the king of the jungle?"

"I don't know, why?"

"'Cause he's always lion." He laughed. "Get it?"

"That was pretty corny."

"I know. I have to finish now, Mrs. Wyatt. I'm sorry I left your door open."

He bent over and plugged the vacuum into the wall.

The roar followed her down the hall, and she was almost to the property room before she realized the roar was in her ears, seething with each beat of her heart. One of her brothers in blue—a person she'd give her life for—held her in such low esteem that he thought it was okay to drop a filthy magazine on her desk. All because he didn't have the balls to talk to her face-to-face. The only thing she knew for certain was that she'd be damned if Cody took the fall when someone else deserved the blame. She'd hold on to the magazine. Fingerprint it at some later time. Today she had too much on her plate to get sidetracked over some officer's puerile idea of a joke. She trudged toward the property room.

"Anybody home?" She peered through the welded steel mesh that partitioned the secured portion of the police department property room like a cage. Row upon row of deep floor-to-ceiling bookshelves held evidence from past murders, current cases, found property, and all manner of minutiae awaiting forensic processing or court requests. Behind the shelving, refrigerators held perishable items. One entire section held nothing but firearms.

Officially, the property tech started at seven, but Reginald was old school. Anything less than ten minutes early was late.

"Hello?" she called into the abyss again, half expecting to hear an echo.

Reginald bustled toward the front as fast as a seventy-two-year-old with a bad hip could bustle. He wasn't swift, but he was precise. Exactly what liability-concerned administrators and attorneys wanted in a property room technician.

"Detective Wyatt. What can I do you for?"

Jo wove her fingers through the mesh. "I need to review the Tye Horton evidence."

Reginald sat down at his desk and nudged the glasses on his head over his eyes like a warrior closing his helm. "Case number?"

She rattled off the number, and his fingers methodically tapped his keyboard.

"Let's see. Seven boxes, multiple items. Do you want anything specific or the whole kit and caboodle?"

"The full monty, please." Which, in light of the recent reading material placed on her desk, was a poor choice of words. "But one box at a time. I'll swap for a new one when I bring the first one back."

"Give me a minute."

A minute stretched into nine while Reginald plumbed the depths of the locker. Finally, he emerged from the bowels of the storage room holding a banker's box. He set it down on his desk and slid open the pass-through window and had Jo sign the custody log.

"Thanks, Reggie."

The heft of the box felt deceptively light, considering the gravitas of its contents. But it would take only one piece of evidence to lend credence to her theory that Tye Horton had been murdered. It was in there, she knew it. All she had to do was recognize it.

The scent of fresh coffee greeted her as she returned to the office, and Squint sat behind his desk.

"Need a hand?" he asked.

She steered toward the break room and parked the box on the table. "I got it. You doing anything this morning? I've got a ton of new info I'd like to run by you." Of all the people in the department, Squint's opinion meant the most to her. She returned to her desk but remained standing. "First, though, the article."

Squint rocked back in his chair. "I don't much picture you talking with Cloud, so who was the source?"

A relief so profound it almost hurt washed through her, and she gripped the back of her desk chair. "It doesn't matter."

"Not everyone is going to think that way."

"Oh, someone's already made that abundantly clear." She glanced down, then looked in the trash can. "Did you take the magazine off my desk?"

"I'm not in the habit of stealing other people's ammo."

"Not a gun magazine. Paper. Porn, to be exact. Someone left it on my desk, thoughtfully opened to their favorite page."

"Only sergeants have keys to this office."

"And Cody." Even saying his name made her miserable, but Squint was her partner. He deserved to know the truth. If her father was correct, the department's wrath against her could have repercussions for him too. "I spoke to him already. He took the trash down. When he came back, he noticed the magazine, but not who left it."

"Other than timing, what makes you believe it was a response to the article?"

"It was personalized. The photo showed a woman servicing two guys at the same time. Someone titled it 'She knows her place.'"

He set his mug down so hard that coffee splashed onto his blotter. "This is not okay."

"Not even remotely, but let it go—at least for now. Quinn's threats just ramped up, and that's a helluva lot more important than me getting an unwanted skin magazine. Besides, it's gone."

"But not forgotten."

"That would take a better person than me." She pointed to his cup. "You want a refill? This is going to take a bit." Without waiting for an answer, she grabbed the cup and disappeared into the break room.

When she returned, she set his coffee down and perched on the corner of his desk. There was so much to relay, she didn't know where to start. Finally she settled on the obvious. "I'm convinced Tye was murdered and that Tye, Ronny, and Derek Walsenberg's deaths are linked."

"Why?" Squint asked.

Hitting the high notes required a half-hour briefing. By the time she'd finished recapping her Sunday, her coffee had cooled. "The DA surprised me the most. He flat out lied about knowing who Quinn was."

"Could he have been telling the truth? The room was rented by his wife."

"True, except I have Quinn's statement and the surveillance tape that backs her up. By the way, did you ever notice the DA blinks funny when he lies?"

"I've never known him to lie." A deep furrow formed on his forehead. "This is a serious accusation. One that will have definite repercussions."

"I'm not accusing him of murder, but it doesn't change the fact that he lied to me. Twice." Her butt cheek was going to sleep, and she started pacing. "I think Tye's original game is ground zero in this cluster."

"And it's been percolating for a whole year?"

"We already knew that Derek, Ronny, and Quinn were all linked to the game as beta testers. Derek was either so impressed by the game or by its

221

designer that he had decided to come out as gay." She held up her hand. "And before you ask, no, I don't know if he actually did. The DA shut me down hard on that. But according to Quinn, he suicided a mere two days after announcing his intentions. Let's say he didn't get around to it. We know he'd found someone he cared about. He'd proclaimed in his email he was secure enough to acknowledge his orientation."

"Do we have the email?"

"Not yet. Quinn promised to send me all the latest missives and links this morning."

"So we only have Miss Kirkwood's word for it."

"Funny thing about Quinn. She's starting to grow on me. After you left Saturday, I called San Francisco PD to see if they had any background info on her. Her mom was Isabella Kirkwood."

He drew his brows together. "Should I know that name?"

"She was the female sergeant killed in the line of duty a couple years back." Jo paused. "Isabella was shot while trying to extract her daughter from a dealer's house."

"That doesn't add to Miss Kirkwood's credibility."

"No." Jo walked into the break room and grabbed a knife from the drawer. "But I no longer doubt the threats Quinn's getting are real. SFPD hates her guts. I suspect she thought long and hard before asking a cop for help."

For the first time, it struck Jo that she and Quinn were both the daughters of police officers, but the similarities seemed to end there. Jo had set her sights on being a cop from the first time her father plunked his police hat on her head. She'd never looked back. No one aspired to be a heroin addict.

"But back to Derek." Jo slit the tape holding the box closed and folded back the flaps. "What if he *had* come out? Who would he tell first? Tye and Quinn knew. Ronny was his best friend. You'd think he'd know. Who's left?"

"Family."

"I bet he'd tell his sister before Mom and Dad." Bag by bag, Jo placed the contents of the box on top of the table, then shifted the empty carton onto a dinette chair.

Squint entered and rinsed his mug, then leaned his back to the counter. "No one mentioned it during his death investigation."

"Maybe his folks didn't approve." The evidence collected on the table was a mishmash of shapes and sizes. Plastic bags for dry items. Paper bags for anything that might have had blood rain down on it. All sealed with red evidence tape, initialed, and tagged with a litany of information to identify its provenance and the chain of custody. "Walsenberg went ballistic when I asked him if he knew Derek was gay."

"He might have thought you were disparaging his son."

"There's no shame in being gay. It's like being left-handed. You either are or not."

"Remind me of the last time you arrested someone for perpetrating a hate crime against a southpaw." Squint leaned forward and studied the unused syringes in their poke-proof tubes. "There's plenty of people out there who don't approve."

"Yeah, well, they need to get over themselves." She lifted the bag with the long-stemmed pipe and admired the craftsmanship. "So why stage Tye's place to replicate the game? The fireplace, booze, pipe, and cat dish were all part of the gamescape."

"Crime scenes are usually staged to confound investigators. Frame someone else for the crime. Send a message."

"I'm leaning toward the message, but to whom?"

"The cat?"

"Funny man." She indicated the syringes. "Quinn told me an interesting story. When she was in recovery, she once shot up." Her voice trailed off.

"Nothing unusual about that, people often relapse in recovery," he observed.

"What? No. She didn't relapse." She snatched the tube. Could it really be so simple? Could this be the one piece of information she'd been looking for? "Quinn used saline. It gave her the comfort of shooting up. Said it tricked her body into thinking everything was going to be okay." She shook the syringe. "It always bugged me that Tye used a gun to kill himself when he had a needle." Her mind raced. "Ingersleben hasn't gotten the tox screen back yet, has he?"

"Not that he's shared."

"So we don't know Tye's alcohol or sugar levels."

"If he consumed the amount of alcohol we think he did, wouldn't his sugars be off the chart?"

"I would imagine so," she murmured.

Even though Jo had collected and recorded all of Tye's medications and supplements, Doc Ingersleben had taken possession of them at the scene. They helped create a medical profile during the autopsy.

"With such an obvious manner of death and without something to initially indicate foul play, would Doc Ing have initiated testing on the vials of insulin?" She had no doubt that if the toxicology report came back with something of interest, there'd be further tests, but forensic testing was expensive, and nothing was sent to the lab before it had to be. "What if the vials had been altered? Tye could have fallen into a diabetic stupor. Kind of hard to manipulate a shotgun when you're unconscious. What if the blast was a cover-up to hide the true manner of death?"

"That's a lot of what-ifs." He pushed away from the counter. "Let me call the good doctor. As much as I love to speculate, he can give us actual answers."

The evidence on the table blurred as Jo focused on the tube in her hand. If she was right, the murderer must have had some sort of ongoing relationship with Tye; how else could someone have gotten close enough to him to swap his medication?

Behind her, Squint rang Ingersleben's office, but his voice couldn't compete with all the questions running amok in her head. The interviews she'd conducted had all reinforced the impression that Tye had a small circle of friends—two of whom were now dead.

But not Quinn.

Jo recoiled from the thought. Her gut said Quinn was a complicated woman, but not a murderer. Still, she forced herself to examine the possibility. Quinn knew how to wield a needle. She was in Tye's circle. She and Ronny didn't get along. But what was her motive?

Squint hung up. "Ingersleben has back-to-back appointments until late afternoon."

"That's disappointing."

"It'll take you that long to go through all the evidence."

"Now that we know the scene was staged, I'll need to print a bunch of things. Not to mention write up a new round of subpoenas. The major social media sites have online instructions and templates, but some of the other sites are pretty obscure and don't offer much. Good news is they'll all accept faxed requests and promise quick responses on homicide cases."

"Faxes?"

"Ironic, right? In a digital age, faxes are still more secure than scans."

"I'll start drafting the requests," he said. "You can fill in the blanks after you get the info from Ms. Kirkwood."

Quinn. Everything always came back to Quinn.

39

For the second time in as many hours, Jo found herself in the chief's office. The day was definitely not off to an auspicious start.

Chief Grimes sat at his desk, the phone pressed to his ear. He motioned her in. Harriet, her lips flattened into a slash of disapproval, discreetly shut the door.

A large conference table dominated the corner office. Windows on both exterior walls allowed in plenty of light when the blinds were open, but they had yet to be drawn, and harsh fluorescent lighting painted everything in the room with an unhealthy patina.

The chief's computer sat atop a plain banquet table that ran perpendicular to his desk and displayed the status of the on-duty officers and every call in real time. Her call sign indicated that she was clear. If only.

"I'll most definitely speak to her about it." The chief tightened his grip on the receiver, his knuckles momentarily white before he relaxed enough for the blood to flow back into his fingers. "Yes, of course, sir. Thank you."

Sir. City manager or mayor? Neither one boded well for her.

"Please extend my personal regards to your wife." He hung up the phone and leaned back in his chair. "Sit."

Normally, she appreciated brevity. Today, not so much. Two chairs crowded the space in front of the chief's desk, and she selected the one closest to the door.

"That was the district attorney." He steepled his fingers in front of his chin. "He's under the impression you feel it's appropriate to harass him on his day off."

He hadn't asked a question, but his silence implied that he expected an answer. "I wouldn't say the word harass is correct. I merely asked him a few questions."

The vein in Chief Grime's forehead started to pulse. "And was one of those questions if his son was gay?"

"No, sir. His son was gay. I asked him if he knew it."

The tempo increased. "The boy has been dead a year. It's none of your business."

"Under normal circumstances, I'd agree, but the information could be relevant to a case. You already know a man died at a property owned by the district attorney and his wife. Are you asking me to compromise an investigation because of who is involved?"

"Tread carefully, Detective." He dropped his fingers. "Are you happy here?"

The question took her aback. "Very."

"Then please, enlighten me. Why did I have to field telephone calls yesterday from reporters from as far away as Denver wanting to follow up on an article that I knew absolutely nothing about until it hit the newsstands? And to add to that, if you're so damn happy here, why is the district attorney calling me before I've even had my morning cup of coffee to complain about your behavior? It seems to me, Detective Wyatt, that you may actually be happier somewhere else. Would that be closer to the truth?"

"No, sir. I was as surprised as you by the article."

"Really."

"Probably even more so. I've worked hard to gain the respect of everyone on this department."

"Before I ask this question, let me remind you that lying is a fireable offense. Did you speak to Everett Cloud?"

The very assumption that she'd lie felt like a slap. "Yes." The word had a bit of a hiss at the end, and she steadied herself. "He came up to my table at Finnegan's the night of the badge ceremony. He had a copy of the memo and wanted to ask me questions. I shut him down."

"Was that before or after you complained to him about not being promoted?"

"I wouldn't do anything to jeopardize my job. The day I took my oath of office was the proudest day of my life. I told you I'm not the one who instigated the story, and I've never given you any reason to question my integrity." She leaned closer to the desk. "Do I need my union rep?"

He assumed a disappointed air, but the vein in his forehead still pulsed. "I certainly expected better of Joseph Wyatt's girl. We're done here, Detective."

If his earlier salvo had been a slap, this was a broadside. She opened her mouth to respond, but the chief's expression stopped her. She rose so abruptly, the chair nearly tipped over, and the short walk to the door stretched on forever. When she finally placed her hand on the knob and opened the door, she paused. Her father might not have always been the best role model, but he'd damn well taught her to never run from a fight.

"With all due respect, sir, I may have given you the wrong impression. I'm not responsible for what's in the article, but that doesn't mean I don't agree with it."

She shut the door behind her.

40

The browser was taking forever to load. What had Derek taught her? When things slowed down, it was usually a sign the cache needed cleaning out? Or something. This kind of stuff had been second nature to him. Olivia too. Alice would have to check the instructions she'd written in her notebook. She'd come a long way in the past year and didn't have to reference her notes nearly as often, but she'd never be able to navigate the digital world as easily as her children. The sheer volume of information on the internet never ceased to amaze her. No wonder there were so many data breaches. Everyone lived their lives online. It made people vulnerable.

"Are you even listening to me?"

Alice jumped. "Holy smokes!" She slammed shut the laptop. How on earth had Olivia arrived home from school without her hearing her walk through to the sun-room? "What did you need, sweetie?"

An oversized drab pea coat hung off her daughter's narrow shoulders and practically hid her from view. She was going through a phase where everything she wore appeared too big for her. Alice couldn't wait for her to abandon it.

"I asked if you remembered to pick up my costume from the dry cleaners."

Crap. In her rush to beat the detective to the rental property yesterday, she'd forgotten all about the cleaners. Packing up the belongings had been on her to-do list since the police finished their investigation. But every day, something else had popped up to delay the task. Then Zachary's call had completely derailed her. He'd been so annoyed. In hindsight, she couldn't blame him. She should have known not to allow anyone onto the rental property without making sure he was available to supervise. But the possibility of a civil suit had never crossed her mind. One more thing to worry about.

Olivia was still waiting for an answer.

"I'm sorry, it was closed when I went by yesterday." A white lie seemed less hurtful than the fact that she'd forgotten her daughter's costume.

"I told you we have dress rehearsal tonight."

Accusation dripped from her voice. Another phase Alice hoped her daughter would outgrow quickly. "Tell Mr. Foster I didn't have time to pick it up. I'm sure he'll understand."

"He won't. He was very specific. Everyone had to have everything with them tonight."

Her daughter had morphed into four-year-old Olivia, and Alice almost expected her to stomp her foot. "I'm sorry, Olivia, but what's he going to do? Fire you?"

"I posted a reminder on the refrigerator." She whipped out her phone, her fingers flying. "The dry cleaner's open until six. We still have time."

"Except I'm working." She braced herself for Olivia's outburst. It seemed to be their lot lately. "Setting up a nonprofit takes a lot of work."

Olivia's demeanor changed from accusatory to sad with just the slumping of her shoulders.

If her intention had been to make Alice feel guilty, it worked. Although she'd read somewhere that guilt was a self-imposed emotion. "It's only seven blocks away. Let me give you some money."

"Have you even looked outside lately?"

Alice craned around in the love seat. Framed by the picture windows, the backyard shivered under a new layer of dreariness.

"Fine. Let me get my keys."

"You know what. Don't bother. I'll tell Mr. Foster you've been under a lot of stress lately. Freaking out over launching the foundation and haven't had time for your family. I'm sure he'll understand."

That's what Alice hated about teenage girls. Give them what they wanted and two seconds later they'd changed their mind—all while making it patently obvious that you were single-handedly responsible for ruining their lives. This time it wasn't going to work. "Your choice."

Olivia rolled her eyes and let loose an Oscar-worthy sigh. She was going to make a heck of a Ghost of Christmas Yet to Come.

"If I'd been Derek, you never would've forgotten." She whirled around, and her coat knocked the dainty side table next to the settee. The small vase of winter-white peonies tottered.

"Whoa! Where did that come from?" Alice called after her, but Olivia was already stomping up the stairs, her displeasure echoing through the house. Alice counted down the seconds, and as if on cue, her daughter's bedroom door slammed.

The therapist had warned her that they'd all have bad days. That each of them needed an outlet—for the anger and the unexpected wallop of sadness that would catch them unawares.

It was a cruel twist of fate that something that had meant so little when Derek was alive could reduce her to tears after his death—Olivia eating the last of Derek's favorite granola and then crumpling the empty cereal box into the trash, or the time she'd found Derek's sock clinging to the inside of her favorite sweat shirt.

She supposed it was impossible not to favor one child over the other. She used to tell herself she loved them both equally. It was more honest to admit that she loved them fiercely, but in different ways. Alice had a wonderful husband, a beautiful house, respect in the community. But Derek. He was her lodestar. The first time his tiny mouth latched on to her breast, she experienced a love so profound it hurt.

Derek was always the sensitive one. His relationship with his father was more guarded, and he always turned to her for comfort. At least in the early years.

Olivia was born with an independent streak and became the avenger of the family. There was no injustice too petty for her to champion, no grievance that didn't wound her personally—and no rest for the remaining family until she'd remedied the insult to her satisfaction.

Her daughter had never needed her like Derek had.

But she needed her now. Over the last year, Alice had withdrawn. Maybe Olivia was right. Alice had abdicated her role as mother, too consumed with her own grief to notice the struggles of her daughter. Things with Derek needed to be put to rest. Through the Alliance, his name would endure. Now it was time to focus on Olivia.

Gathering the laptop, she tiptoed upstairs. At Derek's room, she stopped. On the other side of the door, she imagined him doing his homework. Perhaps getting ready for a date with the girl of his dreams or rereading his acceptance letter to college.

Living.

Alice continued to her own room, keeping her eyes averted from tracing the ghostly outline of the closet, and she stashed the laptop until her return. She still had more work to do, but it could wait.

Once again downstairs, she donned her coat. It was a little act of service—picking up a costume from the dry cleaners. A fifteen-minute errand to ensure that Olivia had what she needed, and Mr. Foster wouldn't need to know anything about the forgotten errand. She could hold things together for another day.

Family first.

Always.

41

The cell phone on the break room table buzzed with a call. Her father. Again. He hadn't once left a voice mail, and Jo let it ring through. She was still smarting from yesterday's lambasting. That the very thing he'd warned her about had come to fruition a mere twenty-four hours later only reduced her desire to talk to him. She couldn't avoid him forever, but she could while she was at work.

Butcher paper covered the break room table, its curling corner weighted down by the tackle box containing her print kit. She gently twirled the dusting brush until the filaments flared and deposited a faint layer of fingerprint powder on the crystal tumbler. She brought the glass closer to her face and inspected it. No ridges, no smudges. Nothing.

The glass had nothing. The bottle had nothing. The remote had nothing. The pipe, nada. A pattern had emerged, but sadly it wasn't of a fingerprint. She slipped the glass back into its evidence bag and resealed it with a new strip of evidence tape.

Footsteps on the staircase announced Squint's return to the office, his distinctive gait giving him away.

He rounded the corner. "Still fighting the good fight?"

"Down, but not out." She slid the fingerprint brush into its tube and stowed it in the case. "Everything I've thrown powder on had already been wiped."

"On the bright side, that supports it was staged by someone other than Mr. Horton."

"A print would have been nice. But whoever staged the scene had a working knowledge of the game."

"Ms. Kirkwood?"

"I can't rule her out. Although to play devil's advocate, if it was her, why would she share the details of the game?"

"Guilty conscience?" He hung his hat on the rack and shucked his coat. "You want the good news or the bad news first?"

"Go ahead with the good news. I need the lift." She placed the evidence bag holding the glass with the other evidence.

"Ingersleben's appointment ran late, but according to his assistant, the toxicology report hasn't come back yet."

"If that's the good news, I can hardly wait to hear what's next." The plastic gloves made her hands sweat. She stripped them off and lobbed them into the trash, reveling in the touch of the chilly office air on her damp skin.

"He also hadn't had any reason to send off the vials of insulin."

"So we got nothing." She closed the flaps on the storage box. The tape gun screeched as she ran a line along the seam.

"Not true. The Doc and I are playing phone tag. He left me a message and said he'd taken a closer look at the vial at lunch. He doesn't know if it's saline, but he's certain it isn't insulin."

Jo dropped the tape gun on the counter. "How does he know that?"

"He smelled it."

"He did what, now?" she sputtered. "What if it's toxic?"

Squint held his hands up in the air. "I know. But apparently, insulin has a distinct aroma of Band-Aids."

"You mean like what you put on a skinned knee?"

"Precisely."

As a kid, she'd loved that smell. Weird, considering she encountered it only when she was hurt. "I know he's not much for speculation, but did he offer anything else?"

"Not on the phone, but he'll be here in about ten minutes with the vials so we can print them."

"That'll give me time to run the evidence down to Reginald before he closes up shop for the day." She hefted the box. "Be right back."

Minutes later, she handed the evidence off to Reginald.

"Do you need me to pull anything else?" he asked.

"No, that does it for today. Have a good night."

In the hallway outside the property room, she encountered the chief's secretary. Harriet's upper lip curled, and she veered into records without saying a word. The snub wasn't unexpected, but it still stung.

Jo ducked into the women's locker room.

It was well known in the department that to determine the chief's stance on a matter, one needed only to look to Harriet for the clue. Her curled lip made it abundantly clear that Jo was still at the top of the chief's shit-list.

Jo splashed water on her face.

The subpoenas had been sent, the evidence reviewed and printed, but the only new thing she'd learned was that insulin smelled like adhesive bandages.

She raised her head and studied the face in the mirror. Taken in parts, she had too square a chin, a slightly crooked nose, high cheekbones, and curious eyes. When mixed together, she'd always considered it a strong face. Not too pretty. Pleasing enough. She'd never much cared what others thought of her looks. Her mother had taught Jo from an early age that looks gave no indication of a person's character. Only actions could do that.

And what had her actions in the chief's office said about her? She'd popped off to her boss—the man who stood between her and the promotion she desperately sought. Her mother would have been appalled at Jo's lack of diplomacy. From a political standpoint, it was nothing short of rash. Maybe the chief was right— she was Joseph Wyatt's little girl after all.

But she'd told the truth.

Grabbing a paper towel, she blotted her face. Ingersleben would be here any minute. She tossed the towel in the bin and turned away from her reflection.

Just as Jo reached the door, it opened inward and Simply Sarah charged through. The elder records clerk squeaked when she saw Jo in her path.

"Gosh, Jo. If I didn't have to go to the bathroom before, I do now." She chuckled and slid past. "I emailed you the information you requested last Friday." She disappeared into one of the two stalls.

"Thanks." Jo racked her brain, then remembered the email she'd sent Sarah asking if anyone from another agency had queried Tye, Ronny, or Quinn in the national databases. "Anything turn up?"

"The DA ran all three names back in February."

"Can you tell me exactly who from the DA's office ran which person?"

The toilet flushed, and a decidedly less harried woman emerged and moved to the sink. "Not the office. The DA," she said. "Zachary Walsenberg."

"Walsenberg himself?"

"Child, you aren't questioning my ability to run a query, now, are you?" She reached for a paper towel.

Jo collapsed on the narrow bench that ran between the two rows of lockers. Why in the world would the DA run all three of them? Hell, why would he have cause to run any one of them? Of course he'd known who Tye was the day she and Squint spoke to him. He'd known exactly how old he was too—he'd slipped when he called Tye a young man. So what had compelled the DA to lie? "Have you told anyone else?"

Confusion crossed Sarah's weathered face. "Why would I do that? Are you feeling okay? You look pale."

Jo's mind raced with implications—and repercussions. The info might be meaningless. Or explosive. Which would it be? "I need you to keep this confidential."

Sarah touched Jo's forehead. "You're clammy. So, I'm going to give you a pass on doubting my discretion. Chalk it up to whatever's possessing you at the moment."

Jo grabbed Sarah's hand and squeezed. "You can't even share this with Young Sarah."

"Don't you worry none." Sarah sat on the bench next to Jo. "I've been doing this job a long time. And if I've learned anything, it's that just when you think you've got it all figured out, something new comes along to spin it on its head."

Something in Sarah's eyes reminded Jo of her mother, and with surprise, she realized it was pride.

"You go figure out what it all means." Sarah patted Jo's leg and then stood, drawing Jo up with her. "Show this whole damn valley what you're capable of."

* * *

Doc Ingersleben had already arrived by the time Jo returned to her desk, her mind buzzing with the implications of Sarah's bombshell. Distracted, she'd hoped she'd missed his quote quiz and was disappointed when he cleared his throat.

"A man should never be ashamed to own that he is wrong, which is but saying in other words that he is wiser today than he was yesterday." Before either she or Squint could hazard their guess, he continued, "Alexander Pope first spoke the words, but I find myself needing them now. It appears I may have jumped the gun with my preliminary assessment—if you'll pardon the expression."

"That's why it's called a preliminary," Jo said. "And it still might prove to be correct."

"You are kind to try to soften the truth, but I would imagine that if you questioned the vials, there may be more to the story than we first assumed, no?"

"We're still not ready to name a murderer—just the possibility that there may be one," Jo admitted. That the suspect was a person with access to all the reports, she left unsaid. "What are your thoughts now?"

"I'll definitely know more when I receive the toxicology. I've contacted the lab and asked them to prioritize the screening, so perhaps we'll see it sooner rather than later. As for thoughts, let me start at the beginning. As I'm sure you are aware, sugar is an energy source that fuels the body's cells." He slid the brim of his driving cap back and forth between his fingers. "Problems arise when the sugars can't permeate the cell walls. Insulin helps sugars break into cells."

Jo extracted a notebook from her desk. "So insulin is the burglar of the pharmaceutical world."

"You do have a way with words, my dear. The human body is remarkably adaptive—a work of art, really. When it can't produce enough insulin, the body looks for an alternate energy source. That source is fat, and in order to break fat down, the body releases hormones."

"And no one's capitalized on this as a diet measure?"

"It's not without complications. The process produces an acid byproduct called ketones. If left untreated, it would lead to ketoacidosis—also known as diabetic acidosis or DKA."

"DKA it is," she said, adding the acronym to her notes. "Would that have killed Tye?"

"That all depends."

Her pen stilled. "On what?"

"One must consider the variables involved. Each of the many types of insulin has its own pharmacokinetics. Onset of action, peak effect, duration of action. Patients typically use a daily basal insulin, then a short-acting bolus to account for the carbohydrate content of their food."

There were many reasons why Jo hadn't pursued being a doctor. Words like *pharmacokinetics* topped the list. "Can you explain it in a Diabetes-for-Dummies kind of way?"

"Ah, layman's terms. Yes. Based on the medications that accompanied Mr. Horton, his insulin regimen included an injection of long-acting insulin that he took morning and night. He supplemented that with short-acting injections to account for the sugars and carbohydrates in his meals and to correct for any spikes or dips of blood sugars outside the normal range."

"Hypothetically speaking, is there a set of variables where saline would either incapacitate or prove fatal?"

"Saline itself, no. However, *substituting* saline for both the long-acting and the short-acting insulins could be devastating to a patient in need of insulin therapy. Say Mr. Horton unsuspectingly injected saline instead of his long-acting insulin in the morning. It wouldn't take long before he felt a bit off. In all likelihood, he'd check his blood sugar level, and then use a short-acting injection to remedy the variance. If that was also saline, and he then consumed a hypothetical slice of cake—"

"Or a shot of whiskey?"

"Or a wee dram. Mr. Horton very easily could have gone into a diabetic stupor."

"He was alive when he was shot."

"Most definitely, but it's impossible to tell if he was conscious."

"Then it's possible he could have been positioned and someone else could have pulled the trigger?"

"If we're still talking hypotheticals, it's possible. There was no sign of a cadaveric spasm."

It had been four years since her homicide investigations class. She recalled the term but not its definition. "I'm sorry, can you refresh my memory on what that means?"

"No need to be sorry, my dear. Instantaneous rigor. It's a phenomenon that is most often evident if the victim is gripping something at the instant of death. Unlike regular rigor mortis, it doesn't leave the body—well, at least not until putrefaction—and it can't be broken without force."

"You said sometimes. So even if a person was clutching a weapon, it might not be present. That means its presence is more of an investigative clue than its absence."

"Precisely. If the cadaveric spasm was present in Mr. Horton, I would stand by my preliminary finding that Mr. Horton met his demise with a self-inflicted gunshot wound. Without its presence, I can't help you determine who pulled the trigger. It still could have been Mr. Horton, or it could have been someone else."

In light of Sarah's information, the next question was delicate.

Before she could figure out how to ask it, Squint spoke. "Does this mean you will be amending your finding?"

"I intend to do so when I get to the office."

"Is that something that must be done immediately?" Jo asked.

Squint's eyebrow shot up, and Dr. Ingersleben's brows scrunched. Funny how one piece of the anatomy could go in two different directions and still convey the same WTF expression. She added, "I'm not at liberty to discuss the specifics, but it could be beneficial to the investigation if news of the status change wasn't known yet."

Dr. Ingersleben thought about it. "I can certainly wait until I receive the toxicology, but if that shows what I think it will, then suicide is no longer a foregone conclusion."

"I would appreciate whatever time you can give me."

"Of course." He stood and retrieved his tweed coat from the rack. "I very much look forward to learning what nefarious plot you've uncovered."

As would she.

They said their good-byes, and Doc Ingersleben clomped down the stairs.

Jo waited until he'd hit the bottom tread and then turned to Squint. "Remember when I said I wasn't accusing the DA of murder? I've changed my mind."

42

Jo knew better than to enter the chief's office for the third time in one day without reinforcements, and although she again selected the seat closest to the door, this time Squint sat next to her. She was grateful for his reassuring presence.

Chief Grimes capped his pen. "You've got two minutes."

Two minutes wasn't nearly long enough, so she chose the one sentence that would buy her more time. "I think Zachary Walsenberg is involved in the murders of Tye Horton and Ronny Buck."

On the desk a clock ticked, filling the silence until the chief finally spoke. "You what, now?" He locked eyes with Squint. "Please tell me she's joking."

"I can't do that, sir."

"And what do you think, Detective MacAllister?"

"I think she has a compelling case that you should hear."

The chief swiveled his gaze back to her. Based on the staccato rate of the pulse in his temple, the man needed to have his blood pressure checked.

"Let me hit the highlights." She drew a deep breath. On the heels of this morning, she needed to reestablish her credibility. "The DA's son, Derek, suicided last year after he, Ronny, and Quinn Kirkwood were involved in testing a video game designed by Tye Horton. In February, the DA ran all three of their names in the national and statewide databases. College records indicate Horton moved into the property owned by the DA in March. Coincidently, that's the same month Quinn started receiving insulting and threatening emails related to gaming. Many showed that she'd sent them to herself."

"How is that the DA's fault?"

"It's called spoofing. Think of it as the email equivalent of a carjacking. A suspect shoves the driver into the passenger seat. The owner is still along for the ride, but no one knows who's actually behind the wheel."

"Go on."

"Squint and I interviewed the DA after Tye's apparent suicide. He denied knowing Tye Horton, but during the conversation called him a young man. We know based on the records check that he had run the name. That's lie number one."

"I don't know that I agree with the characterization of that being a lie. He ran the name nearly a year ago."

"When the DA called you this morning to complain about me, did he mention he'd lied to me yesterday about Quinn as well?"

"Stick to the facts, Detective. Your time is running out."

"During the fund raiser on Friday, I spoke to the DA about a case involving internet threats. That night, someone tampered with Ronny Buck's truck. Around zero two thirty hours, Zach Walsenberg knocked on Quinn's hotel room door. He addressed her by name and said he wanted to ask her about Derek. She threatened to call security and he walked away. She packed up her stuff and left the resort. During the drive home, she rounded a curve, hit some ice, and skidded into the mountain. A couple of minutes later, Ronny Buck hit the same curve, the same ice, and with no brakes, went off the side of the mountain."

She broke off to gather her thoughts. "Yesterday, I saw the DA fishing. I asked him if he'd spoken to Quinn on Friday night. He pretended not to know who I was talking about. When I reminded him about knocking on her door, he agreed it was possible but said the room had been rented by his wife and he'd made an honest mistake. I have the surveillance photo showing him call Quinn by name. If that wasn't enough, after I asked if he still had Tye's belongings, he told me that the family was picking them up the next day—which would have been this morning. I called them. They hadn't heard the property had been released. That covers lies two and three."

"It's my understanding that the coroner ruled the Horton case a suicide."

"That was his preliminary assessment. He's going to amend that."

"To an undetermined manner of death or a homicide?"

Squint answered. "That depends on the continuing investigation."

"There's still more, Chief," Jo added.

He rubbed his temple and then picked up his telephone and jabbed a speed dial. "Hi honey, I'm going to be a few minutes late." He paused. "No, it shouldn't be longer than a half hour. I'll see you soon." The receiver banged into the cradle.

Without waiting, Jo continued her argument. "That brings the death toll to two—three if you count Derek. Tye's home had been staged to mirror a section of the game he had designed. His laptop and all his games and gaming consoles were missing, presumably stolen. Tye is an insulin-dependent diabetic. We don't have his toxicology back yet, but at least one of his vials contained something other than insulin. My working hypothesis is that the murderer withheld Horton's insulin until he fell into a diabetic stupor and then killed him with the shotgun, staging it to look like a suicide. Meanwhile—"

"My God, there's more? This seems a rather elaborate conspiracy."

"Meanwhile, the threats against Quinn have escalated. We also have the first clue that links them all together—an email that said simply, 'And then there was one.' This one came right after she'd received an email from someone claiming to have seen her inside the Burnt Bean—coincidently right after she'd been in the Burnt Bean with yours truly."

"So you think the threat is from a local source."

"I do. Saturday, Quinn found several internet sites in her name. Mostly social media, a couple of escort services. We faxed subpoenas requesting account information to all of the providers. The escort service already responded. The account was set up four days ago by Tye Horton, and the IP address comes back to Echo Valley. This is problematic, considering Tye Horton is dead, and as an aside, his laptop is still missing."

"What are you proposing?"

"Chief," Jo said. "I recognize this is a political hot potato."

"Do you? This is the goddamned district attorney we're talking about. But you still haven't described any sort of motive. Why on earth would Zachary Walsenberg risk everything he's built in this valley to commit the type of crimes he's dedicated his entire life to combating?"

"Because of a game that gave his son the courage to declare himself gay after he fell in love with its designer."

The chief shot out of his chair. "Jesus Christ, Jo."

"Our next step is procuring a search warrant."

Chief Grimes paced between the door and his desk. "There's not a judge out there who is going to sign off on that."

"I've gotten warrants with less."

The chief stopped and wagged his finger at her. "Not for a district attorney, you haven't."

"I'll admit, this is uncharted territory. But if I'm correct—"

"If." He turned to her partner. "And what about you, Squint? You've been awful quiet while she laid all this out. One would think you disagree."

"One would be wrong. She's speaking because she's the one who kept gnawing on this case after everyone else—myself included—was willing to chalk up Mr. Horton's death as a suicide. For a reasonable person to believe a crime—"

"I know the definition of probable cause, Detective. But what's going to happen if you're wrong? The media would have a heyday. We'd be the laughingstock of the state. Not to mention that any goodwill between our department and the DA's office would be irreparably damaged."

Jo's ire rose. "Not to mention the conversation you'd have to have with the city manager."

"You're dangerously close to being insubordinate, Detective Wyatt."

"Tye Horton deserves justice," she shot back.

"Then find me more than circumstantial evidence and innuendo. Once you have that, CBI can take over. Until then, don't even think of pursuing a warrant." He pushed in his desk chair. "Time's up."

* * *

Jo was so angry she couldn't speak, and they climbed the stairs in silence.

Squint closed the office door behind them. "Well, that was fun."

"I've had fun before. I'm pretty sure that wasn't it."

The courthouse, with its looming bell tower, sat a block away. How many people had shivered in its shadow, waiting upon justice? How many had walked away from that place disappointed, disillusioned, disheartened? Jo had lost her faith in a lot of things over the years: the Tooth Fairy, Santa Claus, her father. On occasion, even herself. But she'd never lost faith in justice.

243

"He told us we couldn't get a warrant," Jo said. "He didn't say anything about talking to the DA."

Squint wasn't a man who laughed easily, but he laughed now, and his amusement held a warm timbre. She enjoyed the sound more when it wasn't directed at her.

He pulled out his chair and sat. "Are you going to clean your desk out before or after the conversation?"

She was too riled to sit, and she paced beside the desks. "Neither."

"So what's our game plan?"

"Not ours, mine. You're the acting sergeant of this unit." She paused next to his desk. "I distinctly heard you tell me to listen to the chief and stand down."

"I don't recall saying that."

"Well, maybe you didn't actually say it, but you should have." She resumed pacing.

The levity left his face. "I'll be damned if I'm going to allow you to pay a visit to a murderer by yourself. So unless you want me to tail you for the next few days and miss my much-needed beauty rest, let's not pretend you're going anywhere without me. And as I see it, Walsenberg isn't going to be inclined to speak to you after yesterday. Add me to the picture and he's more likely to think it's a legit consultation. At least enough to get us through the door."

Squint was right. But then again, it was the rare day he screwed something up. The department would lose him in a couple of years. She wanted to imagine him on a beach somewhere, sipping an umbrella drink, enjoying retirement. But that wasn't his style. He'd paint his barn, regrout the tub, restore another tractor. Something responsible, something no one else had time to finish. But that was the very fabric of his being. Dependable.

And there was no sense trying to sidestep him. "I'm going to visit him tomorrow morning before he goes to work and ask him about the queries." Jo placed her backpack on her desk and transferred the holster from her belt to the bag. "It will be an unexpected broadside—I'm hoping to rattle him into saying something stupid."

"Why at the house and not the office?"

"I want to invade his space. We're like vampires at the moment. Without a warrant, he has to invite us in. Who knows, maybe we'll get lucky and see something in plain view."

"He's too smart for that."

"He thinks he is. But we're also dealing with a man who used databases that log every query. I'm telling you. Watch for the blink." She shut down her computer and slung her backpack over her shoulder. "Meet me here at seven. We'll knock on his door at seven thirty. Until then, I'm going to go pick up my bike trainer from the house and then do my best to pedal away my frustrations."

43

The deed still listed Jo as half owner, but the house she'd shared with her husband no longer felt like home. Cameron had packed up some of her things, and a stack of boxes lined the foyer wall. Block letters identified the contents. Her heart lurched when she saw a box labeled *Jo's China*. She pulled it off the top of the stack and opened it, expecting to find her mother's vintage Limoges china in shards. Instead, each piece was in a sleeve and tucked neatly on edge in the sturdy dish barrel.

The end of their marriage had been a year in the making. In truth, they'd both dragged their feet. Now, standing at ground zero of the wreckage, she couldn't blame him for wanting to pack up her things. Erase her. The only things she encountered on a daily basis were the items she'd taken with her last month. Cameron was surrounded by the debris of their marriage. Every room held memories, and Jo's mark was still very much in evidence. She wandered among rooms until she stopped in the bedroom. It was at once familiar and yet so devastatingly foreign.

Drawer by drawer, she reminded herself of what still remained. She collected the last of her lingerie, a few sweaters, some outdoor gear, and piled it all on the chair in the corner. She was still in the bedroom when the garage door opened. Guilt coursed through her and she felt like a thief in her own home.

The inner door opened, his footsteps echoing through the kitchen. *His* kitchen.

"Jo?"

"I'm upstairs, just grabbing a few things."

"Yours, right?" He bounded up the stairs.

Exactly the kind of crack she'd been trying to avoid. "Very funny. I'm sorry. I didn't expect you to be home."

"I've got court tomorrow. I traded shifts." His eyes fell on her lavender silk nightgown, and she wished she'd left it in the dresser drawer. "The first time I ever saw you, you were wearing a dress that color."

"I was a bridesmaid," she reminded him. "There were three of us in that color."

"Yeah, but you were the only one I asked to dance." He smiled, but it was weighted with sadness and disappeared quickly. "I heard you'd hooked up with Aiden since he's been back."

She was too tired to parse words. "If by hook up, you mean visited, yes."

"Sorry. That came out wrong." He picked up the nightgown, then quickly released it as if the fabric sparked something in his brain that said he couldn't—shouldn't—touch such things anymore. "It's just . . . I've been doing a lot of thinking. About you. Us."

The nightgown slid off the chair, landing in a messy heap on the carpet.

"Don't," Jo whispered.

He ran his hand along the back of his neck. "Of all the people in your life, Aiden's the only one who ever made me jealous. From the first time you introduced me to him. There was . . . I don't know. It's like you two shared a secret language or something. I never understood it. I could never break in."

"We grew up together."

"It's more than that. Why?"

"Why what?"

"Why didn't you marry him?" He made a feeble attempt at a chuckle. "I'm sorry. It really doesn't matter."

She struggled to find the right words. "Aiden is my friend. I married you."

"And in a few months, he'll still be your friend." He tried to mask his pain, but it thrummed just below his skin.

He deserved an answer, although she suspected the real question was not why she hadn't married Aiden, but rather why the man she had married hadn't been enough.

"We're too much alike, Aiden and I. Someday one of us would've gotten the call that required a choice between the relationship or the job. The job would always come first."

"It's just a job, Jo."

"It's always meant more to me."

"You can get a job anywhere. What's hard is finding someone who's seen you at your worst and still loves you." Cameron removed his watch and laid it on the dresser. When he turned, he looked her in the eyes. "I found a couple of the guys gawking at a magazine in the locker room yesterday. One of them said he'd left it on your desk as a joke. He realized after seeing you charge down the hallway with your hair on fire that you probably hadn't found it nearly as funny. He hightailed it back to your office and grabbed it. It's a disciplinary action, so I can't go into detail. But it's taken care of. You won't have anything like that happen again."

A joke. Her money was on Estes. "Not even a week with stripes and you've had to deal with a personnel issue. That's brutal."

"I'm trying, Jo."

"Thanks."

"You could have told me."

"It wouldn't have served any purpose."

"You could have told me," he repeated.

Jo hugged her husband, and that was her undoing. He rarely wore cologne, but he was today. The same cologne he'd worn on their first date. The first time they'd slept together. Their wedding day.

Her desire surprised her. Blindsided her as effectively as a sucker punch.

Cold still clung to the hair at the nape of his neck, and she twined her fingers through it. Any longer and he'd be breaking department policy.

She tilted her head back and brushed her lips against his—the man she'd promised to leave behind after vowing to love him forever.

"Look at me, Jo-elle."

Reluctantly, she opened her eyes. This close, the flecks of green in his irises seemed to separate from their blue background. When had this whole person ceased to be everything to her? Was it too late? Truly?

"I've never kissed a woman against her will. I'm not about to start with the woman I loved enough to marry."

Had he tried to take something from her, she'd have resisted. Hidden behind her outrage. His reticence only made her want him more.

Heart pounding, she unbuttoned the top button on his shirt. It caught on a thread. His hand rose, and she thought he was going to stop her; instead he snapped the thin strand.

She wanted his weight against her. Needed the release of too many emotions all tied up in a bow of indecision. She wanted her husband back. A return to the life they had shared before it all went sideways. She placed her hand against his stomach. Traced the trail of dark hair to the top of his jeans.

"Jo-elle."

His voice had a throaty note of hesitancy she didn't recognize. It thrilled her. She brushed her fingers against the front of his jeans. Felt his desire for her.

She peeled off her clothes until she stood clad only in her underwear. Deliberately she removed her bra.

"Are you sure this is what you want?" he asked.

Jo backed up until the bed hit the back of her knees and drew her husband down on top of her.

He fumbled with her panties, pushing them aside. Her skin tingled where his fingers brushed.

This. This was the man she'd married. They'd pledged themselves to each other once. She knew how his chest hair felt against her breast, the heat of his breath against her thigh. She craved the taste of his sweaty skin and the weight of him pinning her to the bed. Spent.

His thrusts were fierce, urgent, and she clasped him tight. She needed him to make her forget. Forget their broken marriage. Forget the gut-wrenching disappointment of not getting the promotion. Forget the horrible things people did to each other in the name of love.

He buried his face in her hair, groaned, and it was over.

Jo needed more.

Cameron's weight eased as he propped himself up on his elbow and looked down into her face. He traced the outline of her breast. Smiled that crooked little grin that made her melt. "I'm glad I traded shifts."

"Me too."

He rolled off the bed and headed toward the bathroom. "You saved me a trip."

She stretched, enjoying the expanse of the bed. Their bed. "A trip?" Oils from his face and hair had stained the pillowcase over time. Couldn't he remember to wash his sheets?

The sound of the shower turning on nearly muffled his reply. "I went to the courthouse today and filed the final papers. Your copy's on the table."

The shower door clanged behind him as he washed away the last trace of his wife.

Jo gathered her clothes and dressed.

The bike trainer would be in the garage. She draped the outdoor gear from the chair over her arm. The nightgown she left on the floor.

44

The Walsenbergs' front door was flanked by two massive urns filled with spruces and bedecked with tartan ribbon that struck a holiday note. While Squint knocked, Jo kept a lookout down the street and tried not to yawn.

District attorney Zachary Walsenberg approached, his figure indistinct and wavy through the antique glass panels on either side of the portal. He unlocked the door and greeted Squint. "Good morning, Detective. You're off to an early start."

"Yes, sir, I'm sorry to disturb you at home, but I was hoping to discuss an unfolding case with you."

"Of course, come in."

Squint stepped forward, and for the first time the DA saw Jo. His lips flattened into a grim line, but he held the door until she entered. Inside, a crystal-covered Douglas fir towered in the center of the foyer. Even this early in the morning, tiny white lights blinked within the boughs. The DA brushed past her and led them both into his office.

Unlike the spartan tidiness of his work office, a more relaxed feel pervaded his home office. He still favored dark-wood furniture, but this was as much a retreat as a working space, with sports memorabilia on one wall, two leather club chairs angled around a small table, and a floor-to-ceiling bookcase behind them.

"Won't you sit down?" Walsenberg offered.

"No thank you, sir," Squint answered. "This isn't a social call."

"I didn't believe it was, Detective MacAllister. Friends usually wait until a more civilized hour."

Jo wandered over to the bookcase and perused the titles. Plenty of law books for gravitas. Biographies took up an entire shelf—mostly political personages. Julius Caesar. Machiavelli. Churchill. Powell. More sports. A collection of thrillers—again leaning toward the political. The history of Echo Valley. Scrapbooks and photo albums.

"Sir," Jo said, taking over now that Squint had gotten them through the door. "Is there anything you can share with us about Tye Horton?"

The DA stood with his back to the wall. "I've already told you I didn't know the man beyond that he was an acquaintance of my son's."

"Yes, that's true, but originally you hadn't even remembered that. I was hoping you might have remembered something else. Anything could be helpful."

"I'm afraid I don't."

"You ran his name through NCIC and other databases last February. Does that remind you of anything?"

He blinked. "February. That's ten months ago. I don't recall why I'd have the occasion to run his name."

"I'm perplexed about it as well, because as far as I can tell, he wasn't involved in any sort of investigation. You're certain you don't recall the reason?" She considered mentioning the other two names but decided to hold that back.

She caught a movement out of the corner of her eye. Alice Walsenberg stood with her hand raised as if caught midknock. How much had she heard? Jo inclined her head. "Mrs. Walsenberg."

Alice's gaze fell first on Jo but quickly skittered between Squint and her husband. "Zachary?"

The DA smiled at his wife. "There's been a misunderstanding, Alice. It'll be sorted out in no time."

That seemed to satisfy her.

"Would anyone like coffee? I was about to make a pot."

"That's kind of you, sweetheart, but we're almost wrapped up here. They won't be staying."

Alice took a step toward the door.

"Ma'am," Jo said. "Is anything in this room yours?"

Alice laughed, but her eyes flicked toward a short file cabinet next to the DA's desk. "We've been married for nineteen years, Detective. Last time I checked, Colorado was a community property state."

"Your business is with me, Detective. This is my office."

"So everything in here belongs to you, Mr. Walsenberg?"

"Asked and answered. Get to your point."

"May we search your office, sir?" Jo asked.

Another slow blink.

"Surely you know my answer, Detective Wyatt."

"How dare you." Alice sprang forward like a lioness intent on bringing down a threat. "My husband is the district attorney." She rounded on Squint. "Does Chief Grimes know of this?"

The outburst was not entirely unexpected, but Jo had anticipated outrage from the DA, not his wife.

Squint held his hat in his hand and motioned with it as if to direct her to a chair.

"Don't you dare tell me where to go in my own home." She swatted his hand and knocked the Stetson to the floor.

Jo took a step closer, but Squint remained unruffled and calmly retrieved his hat off the rug.

"I'll see to it that you'll both be out of jobs come tomorrow," she continued.

"Alice." The DA intervened and wrapped his arm around his ramrod-straight wife and kissed the side of her head. It had the desired effect, and Alice relaxed against him.

Jo took her cue from Squint and remained nonchalant. "We are grateful for everything your husband has done for our agency," she said. "But this is a different matter."

The gloomy morning light stripped Alice's face of vibrancy. "I heard you mention Tye—"

"Don't say another word, sweetheart. They're fishing. Why, I have no idea. Perhaps one of you detectives can enlighten me as to why you're questioning me about a man who suicided?"

Jo had no intention of appeasing his curiosity. "If there's nothing in your files regarding Mr. Horton, then you have no reason to worry. We can end this all right now."

"What's in my files is none of your business. And I resent the implication that it is. Tye Horton killed himself. That it happened on our property is unfortunate, but not criminal. Frankly, I don't know why you feel compelled to make this into something that it is not."

"I'm not at liberty to say at the moment, but I'm here as a professional courtesy. If I need to pursue a warrant, I'll be forced to discuss things that could be harmful to your reputation with the local judiciary."

Alice bristled. "My husband has nothing to hide. Do your darn search and be gone." She said it like an incantation to expel the detectives from her home.

"Sweetheart, stop—"

Jo broke in. "This is your husband's office. Permission must come from him."

"Zachary." She twisted so they faced each other. "You and I both know there's nothing in there. Let them do their job. It's time to end this charade." She raised on her tiptoes and kissed her husband's cheek. Whispered something.

He dropped his arms. "Go ahead."

"I want to confirm that you are giving me permission to search," Jo said.

"Yes."

Before he could change his mind, Jo selected the file cabinet Alice's eyes had marked earlier. She pulled on the top drawer. Locked.

"Sir, I'll need the key."

The set of the DA's jaw made it abundantly clear that he was reconsidering. Jo asked again.

Alice raised her hand. "Detective?"

"What is it?" Jo asked.

Alice pulled her husband's hand to her lips as if trying to reassure him, then spoke to Jo. "The key is in the top desk drawer."

Squint placed his hat on the edge of the desk and guided the Walsenbergs to the club chairs. Alice glared, but sat. "This will only take a few moments," he assured them.

The first key opened the cabinet, and Jo methodically searched the drawers. The DA maintained orderly records; there was enough room to view the contents without lifting the file from the drawer, and each folder was properly labeled. Even with her back to the silent room, she knew they watched her every move. Tracked each file she scrutinized. Their silence encouraged her.

She finished the first cabinet and moved to the second. Behind her, the Walsenbergs resumed speaking in hushed tones. Were they no longer worried about what she would find?

Jo's disappointment mounted with every clean file. The truth was she hadn't anticipated finding the database printouts, but based on the DA's blinks, she'd expected to find *something*. Maybe not a smoking gun, but a cat dish receipt would have been nice.

When Jo closed the final drawer, Alice rose. "I hope this puts an end to whatever misconception you harbored about my husband."

"Thank you—both of you—for your cooperation. I'm sure you understand that we want to be as thorough as possible in our investigation. Ruling things out is as valuable to an investigation as actually finding things." The DA had been right. She'd been fishing, but she had one more fly to cast. "My hope this morning was that since Derek and Tye were friends, you would have remembered something more about their relationship."

The DA took the bait. "That's a faulty assumption, Detective Wyatt. I wouldn't say my son and Mr. Horton were friends."

"No." She set the hook. "That's probably a mischaracterization of their bond. Especially since they had a sexual relationship."

Confusion fell across Alice's face. "Are you implying they were lovers? Derek and Tye? What—"

The DA flushed purple. "Out. Now."

"Thank you again." Jo signaled to Squint. "We can show ourselves out."

"The hell you will," he replied. He gave Alice a perfunctory kiss. "We'll talk tonight. I've wasted enough time this morning." He waited for the detectives to precede him from the office and then dogged their heels down the hallway, picking up his keys along the way.

In the foyer, the Walsenbergs' daughter peered at them from beside the Christmas tree. Unlike her father, the girl didn't blink.

"Merry Christmas," she said.

45

The bell above the door jingled as Jo entered the Echo Valley Tobacconist. A warm earthy scent of pipe tobacco wrapped itself around her, and she couldn't help but take several deep breaths while she took in the dark woods and leather seating areas in the store. Holiday lounge music played softly in the background. Add a fireplace and a snifter of brandy and she'd consider moving in. The place was everything she needed after a day spent waiting for the DA to file a complaint.

An elf of a man wearing an argyle sweater and the weight of the world shuffled out of the back room. "Good morning to you, Miss." His voice sounded as if it hadn't been used in a while. "If you're looking for the marijuana dispensary, it's around the corner and up three blocks."

"No, sir. I'm right where I want to be."

"Excellent. How can I help you?"

"I'm interested in a pipe."

"You truly are in the right place." He pressed his ample belly against the glass case and pushed aside a shallow velvet-lined box so he could peer into the glass display case. "We've got pipes made of briar, meerschaum, corncob, and clay. As for styles, well, we have acorns, calabash—that's the style favored by Sherlock Holmes, you know." He moved down the counter. "Then there's chimney bowls and nose warmers," he continued.

Jo dug the photograph of the pipe she'd collected from Tye's place out of her bag and laid it on the counter along with her credentials. "Actually, I was hoping you could tell me something about the pipe in this photo."

"Ah, a churchwarden." The shopkeeper's eyes practically caressed the pipe before flickering back to Jo. "May I?"

"Please."

He raised the photo to eye level, scrutinizing the details through thick eyeglasses. "Churchwardens have elongated stems, typically between nine and eighteen inches long. There are a couple of competing theories about how the shape came about. Some speculate it harkens back to when churches remained unlocked and the night watchmen needed pipes that didn't block their vision while they kept watch. Others suggested that the length of the stem allowed the smoker to rest his pipe on the pew in front of him."

"Can you tell me anything about this particular pipe?"

"Indeed I can." He placed the photograph on the counter facing Jo and pointed. "The bowl is mallee root burl—an Australian eucalyptus." He moved his finger. "The stem is beechwood, a fairly standard wood, but if you were to look inside it, you would see it's lined with acrylic. Much easier to clean."

"How can you tell from a photo that the stem is lined?"

The shopkeeper shook out a ring of keys until he found the right one, then walked to another case. "The artisan who crafted this pipe is out of Santa Fe." He unlocked the curio cabinet and removed a similar-looking pipe from the shelf. He placed it carefully on the display pad in front of Jo, next to the photo of Tye's pipe, and she discovered that the two pipes were nearly identical.

"Do you know how I can contact the artist?"

"I do. I can also give you some information on the person who bought the pipe in your picture."

Jo smiled. "That would be even better."

"She came in as I was closing one evening. It was a Friday night, and I was putting my weekly deposit together in the back room."

She. Even disguised, no one would ever mistake Zachary Walsenberg for a woman. Had Tye's sister-in-law, Leila, bought him a gift?

If the tobacconist was aware of her disappointment, he didn't show it. "She asked if I had anything elven."

"Elven," Jo repeated.

"Oh yes. The churchwarden is quite a popular style now, what with Renaissance fairs, Dungeons and Dragons, Tolkien, and the like. The churchwarden style had never completely lost its appeal, but long-stemmed pipes saw a resurgence in popularity after the Lord of the Rings films came out. The Harry Potter films clinched it. Dumbledore and all. Everyone wanted to be either a ranger, a wizard, or an elf. That, I'm happy to report, required a long-stemmed pipe."

"May I please get a copy of the receipt with the woman's name on it?"

"I can give you a copy, but it won't do you any good. She paid cash. I remember, because the more expensive pipes are almost always purchased with a credit card, but she pulled out her wallet. Seemed in a hurry."

"I see." Disappointment soured Jo's mouth, but maybe there was a way to salvage this. She'd seen the discreet red light of a surveillance camera in the upper corner of the room almost hidden in the crown molding. "It appears you have security cameras."

"You have a good eye, most people don't see them. You're welcome to review the footage. There are cameras covering the entrance, the cigar humidor, my office, and the rear door."

"That would be wonderful, thank you. I don't suppose you know the name of the woman?"

"No, I'm sorry." He returned the photo to Jo. "But her picture was in the paper on Sunday—the same day yours was. She's the woman putting together that suicide prevention group."

46

Alice had lived in the old Victorian forever. Her mother forever before her. Men might have held title for a year or two, but the house always belonged to the women in the Ambrose family. It was as if something beyond reason intuited that only the women could keep its secrets, tend to what needed to be done, appreciate its scars.

Olivia's namesake had been the mistress of the house when it was built, and she'd added two hidden niches to the design. Their whereabouts passed between generations. Alice had found one on her own after reading about hidden passages in one of the many Nancy Drew mysteries she'd voraciously consumed the summer she turned eleven. She'd pressed and probed the house for three days, despite her mother's admonition to go outside. Finally, a decorative panel had yielded to her pressure and revealed the cubbyhole in the room her husband had since claimed as his study. It was a room she'd found to be dull and oppressive as a child, and even now, as she sat in it waiting for Zachary to return home, the darkness seemed reluctant to retreat despite two burning lamps.

She'd had to wait seven more years before her mother showed her the hiding place in the pantry: a false wall that made Prohibition easier to bear and still held two bottles of illegal hooch that no one had the courage to taste.

Now the grandfather clock in the hallway struck six o'clock. Her husband was late. Not a particularly uncommon occurrence, but one that tonight smacked of avoidance. Alone with her thoughts, she felt her confidence lessen with each minute that passed until she no longer knew what she wanted to say. The half hour had already chimed by the time she heard the rumble of Zachary's car in the driveway. It seemed forever before his keys clattered into the silver tray on the hall table—the signal that he was in for the night.

Her husband made the rounds, his progress marked by clues that allowed her to track his whereabouts: his heavy tread on the stairs, the floorboards of his bedroom creaking while he rid himself of the tie he considered a work-noose, the flush of a toilet.

She waited.

At last he shadowed the doorway. If he was surprised to find her in his study, he didn't show it. "Where's Olivia?"

"Upstairs, doing homework with her headphones on."

"Can I get you anything?" he asked.

"I'm good."

He rolled his head to stretch his neck—he always held his tension in his neck and shoulders. "I'm going to pour a Chardonnay. Are you sure you don't want anything?"

She wanted plenty of things. Answers, mostly. "No."

He returned a short time later holding a sweating glass. In a western town of whiskey drinkers, her husband favored wine. It said something about him, but she wasn't sure what.

Her first salvo was planned. "What were the police hoping to find?" Zach had two choices: confess to the files, or prevaricate.

"They were fishing."

"That doesn't answer my question." Although in some ways it told her everything she needed to know.

"Whatever it was, they didn't find it. Perhaps you can tell me why not?"

Living together as many years as they'd been together, she'd learned to recognize the way he manipulated discussions. Sidestepped the question. Redirected the focus. Parried with a question of his own. Evade, feint, strike. It made him a brilliant litigator.

Over the course of their marriage, she'd adopted some of his strategies. "Did you know our son was gay?"

A silence so deep she thought she'd drown in it swamped the room.

"Did you know our son was gay?" she repeated.

"He knew." Olivia's voice startled them both.

The door concealed half her body; an Echo Valley College sweat shirt nearly hid the rest. Derek had one like it, purchased right after he'd been accepted into the digital arts program.

"Darling, your father and I are having a private discussion."

"Tell her, Dad."

He swigged the last of his wine. "Not now, Olivia."

"Tell me what, Zachary?"

Olivia remained in the doorway, poised as if to flee. "Tell her how you reacted the night Derek told you he was gay."

"I said, not now!"

But he'd said enough. He had known. "When? When did he tell you this?"

Zach rubbed his eyebrows as if he had a migraine. "One night."

Olivia was crying now. "Not just any night."

"Which night?" Alice's voice rose. "Goddammit, Zachary. What aren't you telling me?"

Her husband hung his head. Silver frosted his temples, but his gray lent him a distinguished air. In truth, this moment marked the closest she'd felt to her husband in all of the past year. He finally looked as miserable as she'd become.

Olivia sobbed—a display Alice's mother had taught her to consider undignified. Ambrose women were above such histrionics. "Leave us, Olivia."

She snuffled.

"Now."

Olivia spun out of the room, leaving Alice and her husband to their truths.

Her son was gay.

"He told you the night he killed himself, didn't he?" How much had she known? Guessed? Ignored. "Why you?" she demanded.

"What?"

"Why did he tell you and not me? We were always closer than the two of you. Why would he trust you with such news before telling me?"

"He didn't tell me." Zach sat down heavily on the edge of the desk, upending his pen holder. "I found out."

The time for evasiveness had passed. "Explain."

Zachary raised his head. His eyes were red. Anguished. "He was on some sort of video conference with Tye Horton. He didn't hear me come up behind him, but as soon as he knew I was there, he slammed his laptop shut. But it was too late."

"Quit dribbling this out in bits and pieces, Zachary. What do you mean, too late?"

"I'd heard him say 'I love you.' To Tye."

"Tye? Maybe it didn't mean what you think it did. The detectives were wrong. Just goading us." Alice was grasping, trying to make sense out of something she should have had a year to process. "There's all kinds of love. It didn't mean—"

"They'd fucked, Alice. All right?"

She jerked as if he'd punched her, although she couldn't say if it was from the vulgarity or the thought.

"You want the particulars?" he asked. "They were in a relationship that had nothing to do with that stupid game he'd been playing. He admitted it to me. Came right out and said it."

Her throat closed. Only a hoarse whisper escaped. "And what did you do?"

He blinked. That goddamned blink that meant that even after all he'd said, he hadn't yet disclosed the worst of it.

He reached for his neck as if to loosen the tie he'd already taken off. "I said no son of mine was a faggot."

"And?" Her rage built beyond the etiquette her mother had instilled in her.

"And what? That's it."

"It's not it. What did you do?" Alice lunged. "What did you do to my son?"

He raised his arms. She rained blow after blow on him until he grabbed her biceps. "Enough, Alice."

She jerked out of his grasp, heaving. "Tell me." She lunged again.

"Stop it!" Olivia stood by the door again, her eyes wide. "Both of you! He hit him. Okay?" Tears and snot streaked her face. "Dad hit Derek. There, you know. Just stop fighting."

Olivia sank to the ground. Her beautiful, sensitive daughter slumped in a mass in the center of the doorway.

Zach righted his lamp and then retreated behind the wooden monstrosity of a desk as if hiding behind a barricade. Bloody furrows marred his cheek.

Alice ran her thumb across her broken fingernails. She drew her shoulders back. Smoothed her hair. Tugged her sweater straight and walked past the outstretched hand of her daughter.

Overbright light spilled from the chandelier in Alice's bedroom, and she blinked in the sudden glare. Her legs seemed oddly disconnected as she walked with the excessively careful steps of a drunkard to her dressing table. Dumping the trinket box, she rummaged through the earrings, safety pins, and buttons until she latched on to the key.

The Victorian had a third place hidden from view. One Alice had created the day she locked up Derek's room and pocketed the only key.

She went there now. Unlocked the door. The faintest wisp of teenage boy hung in the air. A low moon threw a beam of light into the room that slashed it in half. Everything remained the same. The computer on his desk, the schoolbooks she'd never returned, the indent in his pillow. Alice stepped into the darkened room and closed the door behind her. Clicked the lock.

The door to the closet stood open, and she stared into a past that had already transpired and couldn't be fixed.

This was the only closet in the whole house she could breach. She couldn't even go into the pantry; instead she'd moved all the cans of tomatoes, the boxes of cereal, the bags of pasta, to other cabinets. Ones where the shelves stretched to the edge. Storage areas that could be used only for storage. Nothing else.

But this closet. This closet was different. She'd never tried to articulate it. Not to her therapist. Not even to herself. By all rational accounts, this should be the one closet she couldn't—shouldn't—be able to bear. And yet, this was her refuge. The one place she could unleash the emotions she hid from the world. There were no surprises here. The worst had already happened. She'd survived.

She ran her hands along her son's clothes. Soft cotton T-shirts, stiff denim jeans. The felted JV letterman jacket he'd worn only once but had to have after his father convinced him to try out for the football team when he was a gawky freshman. They all hung from the rails that surrounded her in two tiers. Her son still lived in this room.

He lived as long as she came there.

From high school on, Derek had spent untold hours in his room gaming. His grades had plummeted, and he'd withdrawn from anything that wasn't connected to a console. His whole life took place in an alternate reality, populated by people she'd never met. People she'd grown to hate with an intensity she hadn't known was possible.

After Alice found the files her husband was too cowardly to act upon, Derek's closet had become her war chamber. It was where she fueled her rage. Schemed against those who'd dragged her son into their world and swallowed him whole.

She slid down the back wall until she sat on the floor. An empty hanger hung between sweat shirts, its arm canted downward as if the item it held had been stripped off it in a hurry. Her hand shot out, patting the floor, but she knew. The sweat shirt hadn't slipped off the hanger.

Olivia.

Alice stretched her arm deeper under the clothes. The air cooled around her and an icy tingle crawled along her scalp and spread across her chest, slowing her heart. Her fingers scraped the baseboard of the rear wall, but it was gone. Her teeth chattered. It was all gone.

She scrambled to her feet, striking the clothes rod with her shoulder, and nearly fell back down.

"Olivia!"

The bedroom door refused to open and she yanked several times, rattling the door in its frame before remembering to turn the key in the old-fashioned lock. Freed, she stormed Olivia's empty room. Then she half ran, half slid down the stairs.

"Olivia!"

Her husband sauntered out of his study. "She's not here."

She hated him for his nonchalance. "Where is she?"

"She had rehearsal."

"Did she have anything with her?" she asked.

"No, she said she was going to walk over to Kim's house and catch a ride with her."

"Not anyone." Alice gritted her teeth. How could such a brilliant man be so dense? "Anything. Was she carrying any*thing*?"

"Her schoolbag, I think."

"Soft brown leather, worn across the body?"

"I guess," he said.

Her bag. Not Olivia's. *Hers.*

She ran her hands through her hair. Strands caught on her ring and then dragged like spider webs across her skin. She'd have to deal with her daughter later. It wasn't too late to fix this. She was an Ambrose.

"You should have told me." She paced the foyer. Her shoulder brushed against the Christmas tree, and the crystal ornaments clinked festively. "How can I make things right when I don't know what's truly wrong?"

"Make what right?" he asked.

Alice scooped up her keys. "It's too late to play the innocent, Zachary. The files. Why did you create the files if you weren't going to avenge our son?"

"My God, Alice. What have you done?"

After the dossiers. The lies. The horror on his face enflamed her.

"Everything you couldn't."

47

The tobacconist's small office barely had room for them both. Jo's attention remained riveted on the security footage playing on the computer screen while Jakob Anders counted the till and prepared his bank deposit.

She still couldn't wrap her head around the fact that twelve days ago—two days before Tye Horton was murdered—on a Friday evening at 1647 hours, Alice Walsenberg had entered the smoke shop and bought a churchwarden pipe. Mr. Anders had emerged from his office and greeted the woman. After a brief discussion, he unlocked the corner display case, removed the pipe, and placed it on a pipe stand in front of her. Never touching the pipe, she nodded. He boxed it and then slid it into a bag. She removed several bills from her wallet, and at the conclusion of the transaction, he handed her a receipt. She was nearly out the door when he spoke to her and she paused. He rushed over to her and gifted her with a small package of tobacco, which she accepted. She tilted her head, and the camera captured the smile that warmed her face and left no doubt as to her identity.

Alice Walsenberg.

And Jo had probably just met the only person in Echo Valley who didn't know her by name.

"Well, she was all glammed up in the newspaper photo," Anders explained. "When she came in here, she was wearing a ball cap and boots like she'd just stepped out of the stables. But I'm fairly certain it was her."

The footage from the multiple cameras played simultaneously. With each pass, Jo viewed a different quadrant of the screen. It was harder to identify Alice from the other angles, but it didn't matter. It was Alice.

Had Tye's murder been a family endeavor? Or was Alice an unwitting accomplice? Alice Walsenberg was an outdoorsy woman. A ranch girl who had never outgrown her love of horses. She could have a whole collection of caps. Olivia certainly would. Was the ball cap a convenience or an attempt at subterfuge?

Jo expected her shock to diminish, but it hadn't.

Alice and Zachary had both been at the resort the night Ronny's truck brakes were tampered with. Alice had cozied up to Quinn. The DA had tried. Neither had been very successful. Had there been two intended victims that night?

After Jo watched all the camera angles, she copied the footage onto a flash drive. Considering what she'd done to the chief's blood pressure yesterday, she'd have to put medics on standby when she briefed him tonight.

Her phone vibrated and her pulse spiked, until she saw it was Squint and not the chief. She excused herself and took the call.

He cut to the point. "Dispatch just sent officers to the DA's house for a DV. Sergeant Finch and Dickinson are on their way."

This couldn't be good. "Who called it in?"

"The daughter. I'm at the north end of town. Meet you there?"

"En route."

* * *

Jo parked a block away and used the shadows to approach the stately Victorian belonging to the Walsenbergs. After nearly three days without fresh snow, the clouds were moving in and a storm was forecasted to blanket the valley later tonight. Clouds scuttled across the moon and bleached the colors of the house to gloomy shades of gray.

Olivia sat on the front steps with her back against the spindled rail, her knees drawn to her chest. Tiny white lights tucked into the foliage in the urns by the door twinkled in a complex pattern behind her.

"It's a lot warmer inside," Jo said.

Olivia stared off into the distance. "Your friends are inside."

Jo tugged her jacket down as far as it would go and sat on the other side of the steps. Even with the extra layer, the cold bled through her slacks. "Is that why you're out here?"

Olivia responded with a slight shake of her head that could have meant anything.

"Are you okay?" Clearly she wasn't. She'd just called the cops on her parents. But Jo was afraid that if she reached out and touched Olivia, the girl would shatter. "You're not hurt, are you?"

"You were the one here earlier, weren't you?"

"Yes. With my partner, Squint." Jo pitched her voice low, soothing.

"You think my dad did something."

Teenagers were smarter than a lot of people gave them credit for, and they possessed finely calibrated BS detectors. Jo couldn't share a lot about the investigation, but she could confirm this. "I do."

"You're wrong," Olivia said. "Dad didn't do what you think he did." She traced the outline of a heart on the frosted porch. "My mother did." She reached for the leather messenger bag next to her.

Jo held out her hand. "Before you open anything up, why don't you tell me what you're getting."

The youngest Walsenberg pushed the bag toward Jo, obliterating the heart. "Proof."

"Of what?" Jo dragged the heavy bag onto her lap and unzipped the main compartment. The silvered edge of a laptop glinted in the moonlight.

"The laptop was Tye's," Olivia said, and went back to her thousand-mile stare.

The sudden reappearance of the laptop prompted an overwhelming number of questions, but Jo forced herself to start at the beginning. "How did you know Tye?"

"Derek introduced me to him." Olivia's hair fell across her cheek. "He seemed nice. Derek thought so. That was enough. At least for me." She straightened her legs, and the bottom of a sweat shirt peeked between the flaps of her pea coat. "I don't know if you knew it, but Tye designed a really cool game. Derek let me play it a couple of times."

"How did you get Tye's laptop?"

"It was hidden in Derek's room."

The laptop's chronology was going to be important. "Had Tye given it to your brother?"

Olivia shook her head again, this time more forcefully. "He couldn't have. It didn't show up in his room until last week."

"How do you know this?"

A car approached the intersection at the end of the block and rolled through the stop sign.

Olivia waited until it had sped past them. "Derek was a goof, but we loved each other. He looked out for me. The whole older-brother thing, you know?" Her eyes welled with tears. "Mom had locked up his room after he died, but I knew where she kept the key. I used to sneak into it when she wasn't home, and I'd sit there for hours trying to understand how things got so bad that Derek thought killing himself was the only answer. Wondered what I could have done different." Jo opened her mouth, but Olivia cut her off. "I know. It's not my fault."

"Knowing and believing are two different things."

"Yeah, they are." She pulled her sleeves over her hands. "The anniversary hit me hard. I just missed him so much. I went into his room." She plucked at the fabric of her top. "After Derek had gotten his acceptance letter, Tye gave him this sweat shirt. He used to wear it all the time. I found it in the closet. It even still smelled like him for a while. Every time I went into his room, I'd put it on. Pretend he was hugging me. Last week I found the laptop."

"I'm going to need to keep all this."

Olivia gave a tight nod. "Yesterday I found more stuff. A notebook. Files. Ronny's name was on one. He could be a jerk, but he didn't deserve . . . My mom . . ." Olivia buried her face in her hands and wept.

Jo moved closer and put an arm around the girl's shoulder.

Olivia leaned into Jo. "That's when I knew I couldn't leave that stuff in the closet anymore."

A small movement on the sidewalk caught Jo's attention. Squint. Jo subtly shook her head. He dissolved back into the shadows and stood watch.

After several minutes, Olivia pulled away. "What's going to happen now?"

"I won't know for sure until I read everything in the bag. Is your mom inside?"

"Dad said she's out looking for me."

"Does she know you have all this?"

"She knows. She locked herself in Derek's room after the argument. I grabbed the bag from my room and hid in the yard, trying to figure out what to do. Even out here, I heard her yell my name. Then she charged out of the house, got in her car, and left. A minute later, the two cops came. They wanted to talk to Dad."

"How come you didn't give the bag to one of them?"

"I hadn't decided for sure what I wanted to do with it."

"Your mom—"

"Don't." She inhaled a ragged breath. "Everything you need to know is in that bag. "Please. Don't make me say it."

"I'm sorry. You're shivering." Jo stood and drew Olivia up with her. "Let's go inside where it's warm." She signaled Squint.

Panic pushed people into making bad decisions. Alice might have left in search of her daughter, but at some point she'd realize her plans had gone terribly, terribly awry. And when that happened, Alice Walsenberg would do everything in her power to regain control, clean up loose threads.

And one of those threads was Quinn.

48

Quinn limped the battered Mini Cooper into its assigned parking spot by the dumpster. The meeting with Professor Lucas had gone better than she'd thought possible. She hadn't even sat down before Lucas blurted that Detective Wyatt had come by his office earlier in the day. It saved Quinn the necessity of explaining everything. Instead of eating crow, she'd presented a final version of the capstone project. It didn't have Tye's final polish or all of the upgraded graphics, but it represented the game in its entirety. She'd left with a grade she could live with, an awkward apology she'd never expected, and the knowledge that she'd never have to deal with the man again.

Score one for Wyatt.

The apartment complex parking lot was icy but empty. Most of the people who lived in the apartments were students and they'd gone home for winter break. Stu/Stan watched her as she picked her way across the slippery pavement.

"I only had to chase one guy away today," he said. "I warned him you'd doctored the photos. In real life you were hideous."

"Thanks, I think."

"I'm ordering pizza tonight," he said. "Want some? My treat."

"Why are you being nice to me?"

"The discussion board. That was a dick thing for me to do."

"Is that an apology?" Because seriously, if that was the best he could do, she was going to hit him in the throat.

He upped the ante. "I'll throw in some Mountain Dew."

"Deal. But it still doesn't make you a nice person, and your apology sucks."

He retreated into his apartment. "I'll let you know when it arrives."

This evening the stairs stretched into forever. The homecoming routine sapped her energy, but it had to be done. Check the corridor. Empty. Footprints? Hard to tell in the slush. Business card in door. Undisturbed. Breathe. Unlock door. Thread keys between fingers. Go! Living room, kitchenette, bathroom, bedroom, closet. Safe.

Breathe.

She set her messenger bag on the dinette table next to an empty canvas duffle bag. She'd expected to hear from Wyatt by now. The detective had checked in with annoying frequency over the past several days. On the one hand, it was comforting to know that Wyatt took her safety seriously. On the other hand, it was a reminder that a cop believed she had reason to be worried.

A surprising amount of safety tips were available on the web. Most of the forums agreed on one thing: after politely but firmly telling the whackjob to fuck off, don't engage. But the websites assumed that the victim knew who was doing the stalking. Quinn didn't know a phone number to block, an email address to blacklist, or the name to write on a restraining order. The best she could do were the things Wyatt had advised: carry her cell phone with her, lock her doors, and have an escape plan—which in a second-story apartment with only one door was not very complicated.

She flipped open the messenger bag and transferred some newly acquired toiletries to the duffle. In her bedroom, she riffled through her drawers. If she pretended she was going away for the weekend, it didn't seem as bad. Plus her underwear didn't need to match.

A buzz against her hip made her jump. She jammed the clothes in the duffle, then pulled her phone from her jeans pocket. Rather than Wyatt, Alice Walsenberg's name appeared on her screen.

"Nope." Quinn sent the call to voice mail and tossed the phone on the table.

Her current circumstances reminded her of a time when she was ten and her sister's cat, Ms. Snugglebunny—Snuggles for short—had cornered a mouse on their apartment balcony. Each time the mouse tried to dart past, the cat's paw whipped out and swatted it back into the corner. The standoff ended when the cat stretched, then hopped onto one of the plastic patio chairs, where it curled up. Quinn was about to go finish her homework when the mouse took a few tentative steps. The cat didn't move. One more hesitant step and then the little gray rodent made a break for it, its tiny pink feet a blur. In a flash, the cat pounced. With a pathetic squeak, the mouse disappeared under the cat's belly. After a quick skirmish, the cat batted the mouse back into the corner with such force that it somersaulted against the wall. Quinn couldn't watch any longer, and she locked Snuggles inside.

It was Wyatt's lesson with the training simulator all over again. Just when you think it's safe—*whammo!* Some new threat pops up.

She added a package of cookies to the bag.

Since Sunday, Quinn had been trying to think like a cop. It was exhausting. She played the what-if game with everyone she encountered. What if that pedestrian was armed? Welcome to Colorado. Every truck on the roadway had gun racks in its rear window. What if the waitress wanted to brain her with the coffee carafe? Somehow she didn't think ducking under the counter and returning fire with little thimbles of creamer was going to be very effective. And no matter how hard Wyatt tried to even the odds, in a game of cat and mouse, the cat had all the advantages.

Which meant Quinn had to start thinking like a cat, not a cop. Ms. Snugglebunny hadn't been the least bit stressed. She'd just waited until the time was right and attacked.

Quinn inventoried the contents of the bag. Toothbrush, toothpaste, extra underwear, a change of clothes, her wallet, every bit of extra cash she could put her hands on, car keys, and an unopened package of Oreos. All life's necessities in one bug-out bag.

Someone knocked softly on the door. The pizza delivery guy must not have stopped for his normal toke this time. She sidestepped the dinette chair shoved under the doorknob and peered through the peephole.

Alice Walsenberg. And she wasn't holding pizza. The woman already had two strikes against her, and she hadn't even spoken.

"What are you doing here?" Quinn asked through the door.

"You worked the fund raiser," she said. "I owe you a paycheck."

The promise of money was like hitting a foul ball. It gave Alice another chance before striking out. "Hold up the payment," Quinn said.

"What?" The light by the apartment door turned Alice a sickly yellow, and she shivered in the cold.

"How do I know you're telling the truth?" Quinn asked.

"Why on earth would I lie about paying you for a job I told you I'd pay you for?"

It was a good question. But it had to be asked. One, Quinn needed to satisfy herself that Alice was legit, and two, there was a tiny bit of satisfaction in making the woman as uncomfortable in the cold as her dumbass husband had made Quinn feel inside the resort.

"Show me the check and we're good."

"Jiminy Christmas, just a moment." Alice dug around in her purse and held up a check made out to Quinn Kirkwood in the amount of two hundred and thirty dollars. "We agreed on twenty dollars an hour, you worked nine hours, and I added fifty dollars as a thank-you for giving it a chance. I'm sorry it didn't work out."

Quinn wouldn't be able to cash it until tomorrow, but it was more money than she currently had in her bug-out bag.

Starting at the top of the door, she unhooked the security chain, unlocked the dead bolt, unlatched the door, and dragged the chair out of the way. She turned the knob.

The door exploded inward. Quinn's arm crumpled, and her head took the force of the blow. She stumbled backward. Landed on her ass. Tried to blink away the darkness.

"Oh dear. I forgot how much head wounds bleed." Alice's voice echoed, the words slightly out of sync.

Quinn shook her head. Almost puked. The barrel of a gun came into focus first, then a hand, and finally Alice towering above her.

Alice?

The room spun. The heel of Quinn's foot skidded through a slick of blood as she pressed her back against the wall, struggled to think. Come up with a plan.

Before Alice pounced.

49

"I don't like it," Squint said to Jo. "Not one bit."

The front door opened, and light from the Christmas tree winked in the foyer. Jo stepped aside while Sergeant Finch walked Zachary Walsenberg to his patrol car.

"Quinn still isn't answering her phone. I'm going to run by her apartment to make sure she's okay."

"At least wait until you can take one of the patrol guys with you."

"That could be hours and you know it," she said.

"Then I'll run up the hill with you before I go to the station."

"Stop." She put her hand on his arm. "I'm not going to do anything stupid. If I see Alice's car in the lot, I'll call out the cavalry. But our guys are busy, and I'd rather have the deputies out looking for Alice instead of tagging along with me. In the meantime, go sweet-talk the DA. You and I both know there's no way he's going to speak to me. So work your magic before he changes his mind about the interview."

"I still—"

"Go." She moved behind him and pushed. "And take the bag with you. I've read enough to know it's Alice we're looking for. As soon as I'm done yelling at Quinn for not answering her phone, I'll meet you back at the station."

The door opened again, and Olivia stood in the swath of holiday light. She'd tucked her hair behind her ears and appeared far more composed than when she'd been sitting on the steps. "Would you guys like some coffee or something?"

The Ambrose poise.

"No thank you," Jo answered. "We need to take care of some things. Officer Dickinson is going to hang out here for a bit. Make sure you're okay until your dad comes back."

"Aren't I a bit old to need a babysitter?"

"It's not you I was worried about. I was hoping you could keep an eye on Dickinson for me."

Olivia's eyes shone when she rolled them, but she smiled. "Sure."

"I'll check in on you tomorrow, if that's okay?" Jo asked.

"I'll make coffee." She closed the door.

Jo handed Squint the bag and descended the steps. "Be back in a flash."

*   *   *

The first signs of the impending storm had arrived with the freshening wind and intermittent snowflakes, and Jo turned her collar up against the cold. The wind had worn down the drifts around Quinn's apartment complex and was sowing the snow across the lot, filling in her tracks as quickly as she moved.

She found Quinn's car parked in the shadow of a dumpster. With the exception of a dark Dodge muscle car, the tiny parking lot was empty. Still, Jo didn't want to assume anything. After all, her own car wasn't in the lot either, but here she was skulking around in her raid jacket.

On the first floor, music with far too much bass thumped from the apartment below Quinn's. The rest of the complex was eerily quiet.

Stepping away from the building opened up her view to the second floor. An anemic exterior light cast a yellowed glow across Quinn's front door. The area behind the window was dark. Jo rounded the corner to the back of the complex and climbed the snowy hill. Light fought its way through the drawn drapes of Quinn's bedroom, but no shadows moved to indicate that anyone was inside.

Completing the loop around the building, Jo paused at the bottom of the stairs. The landing had been blown clean. But in the lee of the staircase, she found footprints overlaid with blood spots. Two distinctive treads. She trained her flashlight on the red blotches. The cold, wet surface kept the blood from darkening, and the hue struck her as too bright. Too festive.

She swept the beam upward. More spots speckled the stairs. She drew her gun and stayed to the edge of the treads. At the top of the stairs, she assessed the scene. A sugar-fine layer of undisturbed snow had blown from the railing onto the walkway in front of Quinn's apartment. The door was cracked open. More blood—too much blood—painted the threshold.

Tucking her flashlight under her arm, she keyed the mic and requested a cover unit. The dispatcher's response came through her earpiece.

"Unit to clear to assist David-three on suspicious circs, welfare check at College View Apartments."

The dispatcher paused. When no one answered, the dispatcher repeated the request. More silence.

Jo had to go now. Even if it wasn't Quinn who was hurt, someone needed medical attention.

"Echo, David-three, I'm making entry."

The bass line of the music below her reverberated through her body, but there was no noise coming from Quinn's apartment. That silence was ominous.

She rapped her flashlight against the door and announced herself. The force of the knock pushed the door open farther and she toed it the rest of the way, her gun and flashlight eye level, sweeping the front room. Light from the bedroom spilled into the living room and shimmered on a dark puddle. Jo entered and swept the dinette. Without slowing her movements, she quickly cleared the remaining two rooms. Nobody. More importantly, no body.

She holstered her gun and took a deep breath. Quinn wasn't lying in the apartment dead, but that didn't mean she was safe. Not by a long shot.

"Echo, David-three. I'm code four. The apartment is empty."

She returned to the living room and tried to reconstruct what had happened. The puddle inside the door told part of the story, but it was the smear of blood on the edge of the door at Quinn's head height that told the most important part of the tale.

The go-bag Jo had insisted Quinn pack was still on the dinette table, along with her messenger bag and cell phone. Wherever Quinn had gone, she hadn't gone voluntarily.

The apartment was a crime scene, but processing it could wait. She had to find Quinn. Fast.

Barreling down the stairs, she pounded on the apartment with the music. A lanky male opened the door, holding a bong. He saw her badge and his Adam's apple bobbed. "It's legal. I bought it at the dispensary."

"Do you know Quinn Kirkwood?"

"The chick upstairs. If you're looking for her, she went to the hospital about twenty minutes ago."

Relief flooded through Jo, and some of the tension that accompanied a solo search dissipated. Quinn might be hurt, but at least she was in a safe place. "Can you tell me what happened?"

"Her mom said she fell. I don't know. She was pretty out of it."

The relief dissolved. "Thin woman, gray hair?" Jo asked.

"I guess. I was too busy looking at the cut on Quinn's head. I'm betting at least a dozen stitches. Nasty." He shuddered. "Hey, do you like Mountain Dew?"

"Excuse me?"

"I ordered a monster cup of it for Quinn to go with tonight's pizza. It's going flat. You want it?"

"No. Did you see the woman's car?"

"Oh, yeah. I helped load Quinn up. She must have been hurt pretty bad. She actually remembered my name."

"What was it?"

"Stan."

Jesus. How much had he smoked? "The car," she said. "What kind of car was it?"

"Oh. A sweet silver Audi SUV."

Alice.

50

The blue and red strobes of Jo's detective car pulsed against the falling snow, each flake dragging the color to the pavement to be run over. Jo pressed the speed dial for Squint on her way down the hill and put the call on speaker.

"I need your help." She gave him the rundown regarding what she'd found at Quinn's apartment and her conversation with Stan. "Can you call the hospital? It's a long shot, but I need to confirm Alice didn't have a change of heart and take Quinn to the ER."

"Where are you now?"

"En route Tye's place to check for Alice's SUV," she said. "Ask the DA if any of their other rental properties are vacant. We'll have to check them all, but might as well start with the most likely places to hide. As soon as you've got the info, we can rally. I'll call dispatch and ask them to send deputies to the Walsenbergs' ranch, plus have them alert Dickinson that if Alice comes home, she might be bringing company. What am I missing?"

"I'll brief Sergeant Finch. Ask him to call in the graveyard guys early. We're going to need more people."

"Thanks. I'm on the air. Raise me when you've got info."

"Be careful," Squint said.

"Always."

A twenty-minute head start meant Alice could be anywhere. The clock on Jo's dashboard read 7:42, but on a Sunday, the sidewalks had rolled up hours ago and the streets were deserted. Three blocks from Tye's place, she shut down her lights. A block away, she turned off the headlights and coasted into a red zone and parked.

The car door closed with the slightest snick, and Jo walked the full block in search of the SUV. Nothing.

By the time she retraced her steps to the front of the rental house, the falling snow had erased her trail. The house was dark, and the front drapes were drawn. From prior visits, she knew the side yard stretched the full length of the property from street to alley. A wrought-iron gate yielded to her touch, and she crept down the path. In springtime, the landscape would be lush, but in winter the skeletal boughs and branches clawed at her jacket and snatched at her hair.

Ahead, a weak light filtered through the rear window of the converted garage, casting ghostly shadows of dead rosebushes against the snow.

Although the yard continued past the converted garage, the path made a ninety-degree turn between the two buildings and ended at the top of the driveway by the rear porch.

The lack of voices concerned her. Alice might not be in a talkative mood, but if Quinn were conscious, Jo was pretty sure she'd have something to say.

She remained on the path, the main house to her left and the solid wall of Tye's place on her right—so close she could touch it. Step by step, the driveway came into view. The hair on the back of her neck lifted, and she dropped her hand to her holster. Careful to stay behind the plane of the garage, she edged closer to the house to widen her view of the driveway.

Empty.

She retraced her steps. It was possible the light inside Tye's home had been left on, forgotten after his property was packed or removed. It was also possible, although less probable without Alice's car present, that someone was inside. Jo circled around to the back of the garage. Off the path, the snow was deeper, and she slowed her pace to maintain her stealth through the knee-high drifts. At the window, she tried to peer inside, but curtains blocked her view. Still no sound to indicate anyone else was present. Continuing to the alley, she checked for the Audi. No cars. No trucks. Not even an abandoned bicycle in the deepening snow.

She kicked the snow berm that had formed in the gutter. Where the hell had Alice gone?

Around the front, a sliver of light escaped Tye's door. Jo crept up the driveway and listened at the threshold. A faint scratching noise competed with the wind. She didn't have a warrant, but she wasn't looking for evidence; she was searching for Quinn. She drew her gun. With her other hand she turned the knob and burst into the unlocked garage.

The room was empty save for the gaming chair; even the dorm fridge was gone. Outside, the wind blew the dead rosebush branches across the window.

"Shit."

Out of habit, Jo double-checked the bathroom to make sure it was empty. She caught her reflection. Two days ago she'd stared at Quinn's face in this mirror and learned the puzzle piece that had broken the case wide open. Now that same woman was injured, in need of medical attention, and had last been seen getting into the car of a person who had murdered two other people. Jo's reflection rebuked her.

"Echo, David-three. I'm code four. No sign of suspect or her vehicle."

If Jo had to guess, moving Quinn hadn't been part of Alice's impromptu plan and Stan's pizza date had necessitated the change of venue. For a woman already unhinged, new obstacles would only ratchet up her desperation. Alice was a smart woman, but her world was imploding.

When trying to hide, most people sought a familiar place. Jo had bet that Alice would return here. For the past several months Tye's place had been intimately tied to her plans.

But Jo had been wrong. Now it was time to be more methodical.

As soon as Stan provided the information, Jo had broadcasted an alert confirming Alice's car. Dispatch had already sent teletypes to the neighboring agencies that an arrest warrant would be pending. Now she needed to rendezvous with Squint at the station. Together they'd notify the chief, set up a command post, call in reinforcements, and orchestrate the hunt.

There was no doubt Alice Walsenberg would be apprehended. But Jo needed to make sure it happened before any further harm befell Quinn. She owed her that.

In the center of the room, Jo spun one last time, hoping something in the space would indicate where to look next. Nothing.

She rested her hand on the doorknob. Outside an approaching car neared, its tires chewed through the slushed snow in the alley. She waited to leave until it passed. Instead, the vehicle slowed, and tires bumped across the gutter with a double splash as it pulled into the driveway.

There was no way to verify whether the car was Alice's Audi without opening the door. If Jo charged outside and it was Alice, all the woman would have to do was throw the car in reverse. By the time Jo ran to her own car, Alice would be gone. Any chance of saving Quinn would disappear with her.

Think.

The empty room didn't provide cover or concealment, and holing up in the bathroom would limit her maneuverability and trap her. The only other place to hide was behind the door. She could use it as a weapon and hit Alice as she walked into the room. Exploit the element of surprise. Take her down at gunpoint. Prepare for a close-quarters fight.

There was only one problem. Quinn.

Factor in a hostage, and all Jo's options sucked.

51

Using a voice barely above a whisper, Jo called for another unit. The guys would make her pay for it later if she was wrong, but pinned down in a converted garage and unable to see who was coming? Worth the risk.

A second later, Squint put himself en route to her location. His voice had never sounded so reassuring.

Outside, a car door opened.

Gun drawn, Jo plastered herself against the wall and tried to think small. Her heart threatened to jump out of her chest, and she was certain whoever was on the other side of the building could hear her.

Footsteps stomped unevenly through the snow. Closer. A voice. She strained to hear the words, but the wind snatched them away.

She drew a breath and held it for a four count. The plan: Save Quinn. She exhaled slowly. Arrest Alice. Simple.

The voice stopped. Had someone noticed her footprints?

She drew another breath. Readjusted her grip on the Glock.

The knob turned. The door swung inward.

Jo focused through the tiny strip between the door and the wall. Quinn. Bloodied. She stumbled across the threshold. Alice gripped the younger woman's left arm. Holding her up or controlling her? Unknown, but Quinn stood between her and Alice.

"This'll work," Alice muttered. "You'll have to sit in the gaming chair. I don't know any other way to do this."

Quinn staggered forward. A couple more steps and Jo would have the space to push Quinn out of the way and confront Alice.

She tensed, ready to spring.

Quinn's head lolled toward Jo. Her eyes widened and she sidestepped, crashing into Alice. "She's gotta gun!" Quinn slurred a warning.

The element of surprise evaporated.

Jo kicked the door and grabbed for Quinn, but Alice already held the injured woman and danced out of reach.

Jo trained her gun on Alice. "Drop the gun."

Alice used Quinn as a shield, stooping slightly to make herself a smaller target, and pressed the barrel of a revolver against Quinn's neck.

Blood caked the left half of Quinn's face, and one eye was swollen shut. She swayed on her feet.

"Drop the gun," Jo ordered again. Even this close, it would be a difficult shot. One Jo wouldn't take while the barrel of the revolver kissed Quinn's skin.

"Jesus, Joseph, and Mary, will nothing go right tonight?" Alice laughed.

Jo swallowed. She'd expected a calculating woman. Controlled. This Alice was something altogether different. And Jo didn't know how to appeal to her.

"Shmup," Quinn said.

Shoot 'em up. Jo shook her head slightly. This wasn't a game. If bullets started flying, no one would survive.

"My fight isn't with you, Detective," Alice said. Her voice was oddly singsong, but her gun hand shook. Not a good combination.

From a tactical standpoint, Jo was screwed. No cover. No concealment. No viable shot. "Put down the gun. We can work through this."

Statistically, the most dangerous time in a hostage scenario occurred when the suspect first realized they were cornered. But Alice wasn't cornered. Jo was. Alice had a clear shot. Jo didn't.

"Please understand this wasn't what I'd wanted," Alice said, her voice steadier. "But I promise you'll die a hero." Her eyes pinged across the room. "It'll look like a shootout, of course." It was as if she was thinking out loud. "Sadly, you'll succumb to your wounds, but not before mortally wounding the woman who single-handedly killed Tye Horton and Ronny Buck."

"It's too late for that." Jo remained still, trying to calm the fear that raced through her body like a whippet. "We know everything."

Alice's gun remained pointed toward Quinn, but that could change in a blink. "Oh, I doubt that."

"The laptop. Your notebook. The files. They're all at the police station."

"You're lying." She licked her lips. "Olivia would never betray me."

Jo changed tack. "Olivia needs you. Needs her mother. Put down the gun. Let's figure this out."

"You know nothing."

"I understand why you did it. You found your husband's files. Befriended Tye. Financed a new game. All so you could gain access to three innocent people you mistakenly thought were responsible for your son's death."

"They weren't innocent." Alice spoke through clenched teeth. "They enabled him. Gaming consumed my son. He couldn't eat. Couldn't sleep. He lost interest in anything that wasn't connected to a goddamn console."

Alice's anger pulsed through the room, and Jo steeled herself to take the shot.

Quinn's head bobbled. "Let me tell you about the Derek I knew." Her voice rasped as if she'd been choked.

Alice jabbed the gun deeper into her neck. "You never met him."

Jo's finger pressed the slack out of the trigger.

Quinn could barely keep her eyes open, but there was a freakish calm about her. "Wasn't games. Your son'd fallen in love. Yeah, he lost weight, couldn't sleep. He was in love. With Tye."

"He would have told me," she said. "He should have told me," she repeated quieter.

She lowered the gun slightly.

Jo had to keep her talking. Reinforcements would be here any second. "Gaming didn't destroy his life, it gave him hope."

"Hope doesn't come from a video game," Alice said.

Jo watched Alice's shoulder, waiting for it to telegraph the woman's next move.

"Video games tell stories." Quinn's head jerked as if she was on the verge of collapsing. "Your son found one that told his."

Tears welled in Alice's eyes, but she blinked them away. "I've heard enough, Ms. Kirkwood. Be quiet now, please."

The older woman's posture changed. Confusion or defeat? Or something else entirely?

"Mrs. Walsenberg, please, lower the gun," Jo said. "Don't make a third mistake."

"That implies I made two others." A tiny smile flitted across Alice's face and was gone. "All I ever wanted to do was protect my family."

"This isn't the way to achieve that."

"How did it get to this? I'm an Ambrose. I am an *Ambrose*," she repeated, and then flinched. "And I have failed." She lowered the gun and shoved Quinn aside.

Quinn tumbled to the floor, but rather than rolling toward Jo, she took refuge behind Tye's chair. Behind Alice.

Alice's arm hung limply at her side, and she locked eyes with Jo. "Kill me."

For the first time, Jo had a clear shot, but as long as Alice kept the gun pointed at the floor, there was hope for a peaceful resolution.

The chair was too small to cover Quinn's entire body, and she fidgeted behind it. Jo willed her to stay put, out of the line of fire.

"Mrs. Walsenberg. Alice. No one else has to get hurt. We can all walk away from here."

Quinn poked her head out, as if trying to get the lay of the land, and then crawled forward like a demented toddler.

Jo kept talking, desperate now to hold Alice's attention. To keep her from perceiving Quinn as a new threat. "You made a mistake. But what you're asking is cowardly. You are not a coward."

Alice Ambrose Walsenberg pulled her shoulders back. Her grip tightened on the revolver.

Jo inhaled and let the breath out halfway. Hands steady. Resolved.

"I am an Ambrose." Alice swept her arm to the side in an arc and leveled the gun at her temple.

52

Quinn couldn't—wouldn't—allow another cop to die while saving her sorry ass.

"Kill me," Alice had said.

What was Wyatt waiting for?

On her hands and knees, Quinn peeked around the base of the chair. Tye's chair.

Wyatt faced her. Her gun had to be heavy, but Wyatt's aim never wavered. Her hands never shook. And if she pulled that trigger, there'd be a hole in Alice's chest the size of a Mini Cooper.

All she had to do was pull the damn trigger.

Blood dripped on Quinn's knuckle. She could see out of only one eye, and every time she moved, the floor came up at unexpected angles. It was like being drunk, without the fun of being buzzed first, and her head ached as if she were coming off a three-day bender.

Alice had her back to Quinn, her attention on the detective. Maybe Quinn's words about Derek had hit the mark. Honesty had a funny way of stabbing square into the truth a person most wanted to hide. Alice still held her gun, but it was pointed down, like she'd given up.

No. That wasn't the Alice Walsenberg she'd come to know in recent days.

Quinn's ears still rang with a high-pitched squeal that only she and the neighborhood dogs could hear—a souvenir from using one's head as a doorstop. Wyatt was yapping again, but her words were garbled. Probably trying to convince Alice to put down the gun or something else from the po-po playbook that Alice had no intention of doing.

Quinn edged closer, carefully picking up each knee and hand so she didn't alert Alice. When she was close enough, she balanced on her hands and shifted her weight to her legs. A half-standing, half-something crouch.

Through her one good eye, Quinn saw Alice tense, her fingers whitening where they wrapped around the grip. The gun came up.

Oh hell no.

Quinn didn't stop to think. Didn't try to signal Jo. Wasn't sure she remembered to breathe. She just lunged. Aimed for the center of Alice's back.

Hit her shoulder.

Time stopped doing all the things Quinn had taken for granted over the years. It twisted back on itself, slowed, sped up, stopped.

Alice spinning. A noise so loud it silenced everything. Wyatt. The floor smacking Quinn's already hurt head. The tangle of arms and legs. The detective holding a gun one second, handcuffs the next. Or were the handcuffs first?

Nothing made sense.

A man she'd never seen before crashed through the door. Tall. Another gun. Friend? Must be. No one shot him.

Wyatt shook her awake. Her lips moved, but Quinn still couldn't hear shit. Or maybe the detective was fucking with her. That'd be just like her.

The tall guy held Alice by her elbow. Her wrists cuffed behind her back.

Quinn blinked. Everything changed.

Alice was gone. More cops. Different uniforms. Someone pricked a needle into her arm. Attached a line.

"No morphine," she said. Or had she only thought it?

Wyatt leaned close to the guy with the IV. Shook her head. *No morphine*, she mouthed.

Quinn blinked again, and they were outside. Red and blue Christmas lights throbbed against a dizzying white swirl that fell on her face.

She closed her eyes.

Fucking snow.

53

It was three thirty before Jo escaped the station and returned home. The wind drove icy flakes across the beams of her headlights, melting the black night and white snow into a disorienting swirl of gray.

Tiny shards of ice stung her face on the short walk to the dark porch. Inside, slush clung to her boots, and she unlaced them. Left them on the mat. She eased out of her jacket and hung it on the coatrack by the door. She ran her fingers across the cloth badge sewn on the breast. Fisted the fabric. Buried her face against the fleece lining and smelled remnants of the night—her sweat, her fear, her relief—and she cried. Standing at the coat tree, trying to be quiet in a house that wasn't hers, she cried.

"That you?" her father called out from the living room.

She jammed the heels of her palms into her eyes and wiped her nose against the sleeve of her turtleneck. "Sorry. I didn't mean to wake you."

Her father clambered out of his recliner as she entered the living room. "Didn't wake me." He handed her a tumbler containing a generous pour of bourbon. "Wanted to see for myself that you hadn't collected any new holes."

"No."

The amber liquid glowed in the firelight. She swirled it slowly, staring beneath its surface.

"All right then." He shuffled toward the kitchen.

"Join me?" she asked.

He stopped but didn't turn around.

"It's been a long night," she added.

"I imagine it has."

He took two more steps toward the kitchen and then hung his head. Turned.

His knee must be acting up. He was dragging his leg more than usual.

At the mantel, he stopped. Clicked off the scanner. Then he picked up the wrought-iron poker and jabbed at the logs until they broke apart, sending sparks and embers in different directions.

She sat heavily on the couch and tucked her feet underneath her. Her socks were damp. "The DA is going to step down tomorrow. Personal reasons."

She sipped the bourbon and held it in her mouth for a long moment before swallowing. What consequences the DA faced next was above her pay grade. The state would review her investigation, start one of their own. The only thing that looked like a slam dunk was the unauthorized use of confidential databases. He'd merely wanted to learn who his son had become, he'd told Squint. And then he'd blinked.

Her father refilled his glass and settled into his recliner. "Wasn't it his wife you were chasing all over town tonight?"

"Alice tried to goad me into shooting her."

"Never known you to let someone push you into something you didn't have a mind to do."

"Then she turned the gun on herself. That didn't work out very well for her either."

"You got everything you need for your case?"

"Everything but a signed confession. She lawyered up."

It didn't matter. Jo had spent hours poring over Alice's notebook. The woman had kept excruciatingly detailed notes on diabetes and insulin therapy and knew more about the deep web and how to exploit it than Jo did.

The journal read like a manifesto. Alice had believed the files meant her husband was going to deal with those responsible for their son's death. When he didn't, she vowed to do it herself.

She'd targeted Tye first. Ingratiated herself as a silent investor in his game, set him up in the converted garage rent-free until the project took off—all to get close to him. Gain his trust.

Access to Quinn had proved more challenging. Ironically, it was Tye who had sparked the solution by mentioning how misogynistic gaming could be and how Quinn had already suffered. Alice had pressed him for details and duly recorded the possible consequences. Trolling, doxing,

SWATting. She'd written pages about the dark web. How to access it. Search it. Step-by-step instructions on spoofing. She'd relished being able to weaponize the internet. And for a while, it was enough.

For months she'd plotted her revenge. On the anniversary of Derek's death, Alice put her plans into action. She guilted Tye into raising a toast to Derek and calmed him when he began to feel ill. Made sure he was seated before he passed out. Anger drove her to recreate the scene he'd considered the pinnacle of his game. And she took a grim pleasure in destroying Tye while he was surrounded by all the things he'd thought would bring him comfort. She smashed every game and console and joystick he owned. Belatedly, she worried that the damaged items might prompt questions, and she gathered the pieces and disposed of them in a dumpster. But she kept the laptop. It was another portal to the dark web, and she wanted it for her final plans for Quinn.

Ronny was the last to be mentioned, and Jo had the impression that Alice almost felt bad about murdering him. Maybe because he was the son of a friend, or because of his relationship with Derek. She didn't torment him, didn't want him to suffer, but in the end, she couldn't forgive him.

Jo struggled to reconcile the woman captured in the pages with the woman who had led such a charmed life before her son killed himself. The rage and desperation and sheer meanness contained in those pages would take Jo a lifetime to forget.

"What's really bothering you?" her father asked.

The journal aside, she could choose any one of a handful of options. Getting passed over for promotion. A personal best for the number of times in a single day she'd had to explain herself to the chief. The way her coworkers looked at her, as if afraid to even say hello. Her impending divorce. She stuck with the truth.

"I still don't know jack-shit about internet crimes, and someone got hurt because of it."

"You didn't know a thing about money laundering before you went up against Xavier Buck. You didn't let that stop you. Figure it out."

The fire popped and spit an ember at the screen.

"I talked to Aiden about applying to the FBI. He thought I'd be a good fit."

"You don't do anything by half measure, do you?" He scratched the stubble on his cheek. "I suppose I should have seen that coming. You were the only one at the department with the balls to take down the Walsenbergs. I don't imagine car burglaries or stolen bike reports are going to seem very exciting by comparison."

The level of appreciation she'd had for her hometown had waxed and waned over the years, but she'd never been able to break its pull. Some days Jo wondered why that was. Then she'd gaze up at the mountains, breathe the fir-scented air, and feel the relentless tug deep within her chest.

This was home.

The place she'd sworn to protect.

"I decided against it."

She had only to close her eyes, and it was as if she stood on the edge of the ridge. Red cliffs hedged the valley with still-green firs and spruces, bare-limbed cottonwoods and paper birches. Even now, next to a fire, she heard the piercing call of a bald eagle winging along the Animas River.

"The world's changing, Jo. Crimes are changing." He knocked back his shot. "What doesn't change are the people breaking the law."

He used both hands to push himself out of the chair. "What time you need to be back at the station?"

God, she didn't want to think about that yet. "Squint and I are serving a search warrant at ten." After that, the hospital. Get an update on Quinn's condition. Make sure the docs weren't still worried about a brain bleed.

He nodded. "I'll make sure the driveway's dug out."

54

Six Months Later

The June sun highlighted the scar that peeked out from under Quinn's graduation cap. Jo tracked her progress as the recent grad pressed her way through the throng toward the bleachers where Jo sat with Squint. It was the first time Jo had seen Quinn wear anything remotely resembling a dress.

"Well, that was an excruciating ceremony," Quinn said from the edge of the track as she waited for them to pick their way down. "Can I peel this thing off yet?"

"You're a graduate," Jo said. "You are free to do whatever you want—within certain statutory limitations."

Quinn waggled a scrolled and beribboned paper in Jo's face. "Blank. With all the tuition the college collects, you'd think they'd at least hand out a coupon to El Tecolote or something."

"You were here on a scholarship," Jo said. "I'm sure they'd be happy to accept repayment in exchange for a coupon."

"Always giving me shit."

Squint stepped forward. "I'm just happy you've given her another target." He handed Quinn a small bouquet of wildflowers. "Congratulations."

"Awww." Quinn briefly placed her hand on Squint's arm. "Thank you." She turned to Jo. "Take notes." Then she sobered. "I heard she finally accepted the deal."

There was no need to ask who she meant. "Yesterday. The new DA took the death penalty off the table. No small concession, considering he's a

293

Baxter and she's an Ambrose." Mrs. Baxter's grandson, Edwin, had proven himself to be an astute DA, but the two families were the Hatfields and the McCoys of Echo Valley.

"Rich people are fucking weird." Quinn removed her cap, and her short hair bristled. The addition of the scar gave her an even edgier look. "How much time will she serve?"

Jo tilted her head. "If she's convicted of first-degree murder, she'll get life. If it gets dropped to a lesser offense, it'll depend. But even the Ambrose name isn't going to shave off much time. Sentencing is scheduled for the end of July."

"You'll email me? After it's all done?"

"Sure you don't want to stick around?" Jo teased.

"Seriously?" Quinn rolled her eyes.

For the first time, Jo noted the similarity between Quinn and Olivia. It wasn't so much a look as an attitude. When Olivia performed in the church's annual play, she'd never said a word as the Ghost of Christmas Yet to Be, but she *owned* that stage. They both had a slightly haunted vibe, but wind them up and they became two very determined, strong women.

Quinn shucked the graduation gown, revealing a white tank top, slouchy shorts, and Doc Martens. A new raven tattoo took flight along her collarbone.

"When are you leaving?" Jo asked.

"The car's already packed. I start my internship Monday at the Letterman Digital Arts Center in the Presidio. It'll be good to be back in San Francisco."

"For what it's worth. I think they're lucky to have you."

"That and a dollar will buy me a cup of coffee."

"Only if you finally go to Hank's with me."

Quinn made a face. "I'd rather hit your partner up for a couple extra bucks and go to the Bean and get a real cup." She stuck her nose in the bouquet and promptly sneezed. "Will there be justice?"

Justice was merely a word—and too often, a word conflated with vengeance. An eye for an eye, a pound-of-flesh philosophy that implied an equitable restitution. But that's not how it worked. Justice was a goal. An ideal.

It couldn't bring someone back.

But it offered hope.

Jo shrugged. "Depends on how you define it."

They walked along the track, weaving among the other grads and attendees on their way to the parking lot.

Quinn pulled up short to allow a person in a wheelchair to cut in front of her. "How's Olivia?"

The youngest Walsenberg was redeeming the Ambrose name. "She's good. Getting her feet under her." Jo said. "She asks about you all the time. Said to give you her congratulations."

Quinn glanced down at her feet as if embarrassed, but a slight smile pulled at her lips and she started walking again. "I read online the department is getting a new chief."

The rank and file had known about the chief's departure for a few weeks, but the story had broken in yesterday's morning edition. Everett Cloud had written the article. Happily, he hadn't approached Jo for a quote.

"Chief Grimes is retiring next month," she said. "Health issues."

"His blood pressure, I believe." Squint cupped his hands behind his back and rocked on the heels of his boots. "But Jo would probably know more about that than me."

She flicked the brim of his Stetson. "Careful. Someday I might be your sergeant."

He tipped the hat politely and drew it back into place. "I'm counting on it, ma'am."

"Ma'am." Quinn made a flourish with her hand. "Sounds like you should put in for chief. All the publicity you're getting lately couldn't hurt."

Jo pulled a face. "One step at a time."

Promotion didn't seem like such a big deal anymore. She still planned on testing again for sergeant when Larson retired. But chief wasn't even a blip on her radar. Not that a detective could jump to that level anyway—at least not without collecting a couple of intermediary ranks first. The city manager had four applicants already. Rumor had it one of the candidates was a woman. That would certainly spin Echo Valley on its head.

"In the meantime," Jo added, "the computer forensic course I'm taking is pretty interesting. Intense." She covered her face with her hands and laughed. "Oh my God, it's complicated."

"It gets easier," Quinn said. "I promise."

But life didn't.

And that was okay too.

Since the night of Alice's arrest, Jo had redeemed herself in the eyes of the department. Guys congratulated her on her tenacity. High-fived her. Asked her for advice when they got stuck. Once she might have basked in it. Taken it as validation. But that was before.

Quinn, Alice, Jo. They'd all learned lessons that night—hard lessons. But Jo had finished what she'd set out to do. And in the end, it didn't matter who believed in her as long as she remembered to believe in herself.

At the edge of the parking lot, they stopped. The dilapidated Mini Cooper was on the end of the row. Quinn had hammered the major damage out with a ball peen, leaving it with the pockmarked rind of a giant lemon—but it ran. Squint's truck was a few aisles farther down. Her own car was on the other side of the campus close to the widening in the road that served as an overlook.

Squint shook Quinn's hand. "Safe travels."

"Thanks. Watch over your partner for me. I won't be there next time to bail her out."

When Squint was out of earshot, Jo rounded on Quinn. "Bail me out? Since when is passing out and falling against someone's back considered a tactical response?"

"It worked." Quinn handed Jo the flowers. "Watch your six."

"You too."

Once Quinn got into her car, Jo strode toward the overlook.

The cerulean-blue sky of summer stretched into forever, and for now, the closest thing to snow was the cottonwood duff that swirled in mini dust devils along the river. She inhaled the intoxicating scent of cedar and earth and obligation that was Echo Valley. Winter would come again. The snow would fall. Jo had new boots in her locker.

She was ready.

Acknowledgments

First, thank you. I believe a book isn't truly a book until it's been read. It is at once both humbling and thrilling to know that my part as the author is done and I've passed the baton to you. I'm grateful to all the readers, librarians and booksellers who have chosen this book.

Numerous people helped me create this story. I count myself lucky to be surrounded by an incredible group of friends and talented people willing to share their time and expertise and I am beyond grateful.

My thanks to Dr. Deidre Anastas for helping me understand enough about pharmacokinetics to enable me to write about it while simultaneously cementing my belief that both Jo and I made the right career decisions.

Matt Martin, thank you for checking that I wasn't trying to off my husband before teaching me how to sabotage a truck.

Few people spend more time behind the lens of a camera than Daniel L. Bender. His images of southwest Colorado inspire me daily. That we are friends and he likes chocolate as much as I do is a bonus.

Beckstrom Observatory is an amazing resource for stargazers. Thank you for the detailed star maps you created so Jo knew where to look.

A special thank you to my wonderful agent, Helen Breitweiser of Cornerstone Literary, for your professional and unwavering belief in this book. To my editor Faith Black Ross: Your dedication to craft is inspirational. My appreciation also to the entire team at Crooked Lane Books for their support.

I had the distinct honor of attending Eckard College Writers in Paradise Conference—a special debt of gratitude to Dennis Lehane, Les Standiford, Sterling Watson, Stewart O'Nan, and my WIP group. Your commitment to writing is boundless.

Acknowledgments

The value of community is not to be underestimated. I've benefited from the generosity of many authors who shared their expertise with me. Thank you Laura Disilverio; Robin Burcell; Hank Phillippi Ryan; my fellow writers at Murder Books blog; and my friends at Sisters in Crime, Mystery Writers of America and International Thriller Writers. A special shout out to Laura Oles, Elena Taylor Hartwell, Bruce Robert Coffin, and Ellen Byron for their enthusiastic support.

Then there are the people who try to brush off my thanks when I tell them how much their contributions have helped me. Thank you Carla Shuck, Autumn Blum, Norma Hansen, Lisa and Gerry Carroll, and more. You all rock.

My deepest appreciation to Mandy Mikulencak; there are truly no words that can capture the depth of my gratitude for your generosity, support, and friendship.

I am blessed to have an amazing family from which I draw strength. While I love you all, I would be remiss if I didn't thank Ricky Connor for sharing his hunting skills with me.

To my dearest David, thank you for your unwavering support and your steadfast belief that I'm doing exactly what I was meant to do. I can't wait to see where our adventures take us.